WHAT READERS ARE SAYING ABOUT
Great and Beloved Physician

A destiny with its origins in his childhood, a journey not just physical, but encompassing his very mind and soul, from Roman soldier who witnesses the healing of the Nazarene, to participating in his crucifixion, Lucius becomes the Beloved Physician, follower of the Apostle Paul, spreading the new religion to every corner of the known world. Rich Hites brings us to the end of his third book in the saga of Marcus Cornelius, Chloe of Corinthia and finally Lucius, beloved of women and the Followers, sacrificing his own happiness to bring healing in the name of the Nazarene to those in need. What a rich and exciting journey it has been in all three books. Read them all, and find joy and peace in a new awareness of these Biblical characters, and in Christ.

~Victoria Storm, Retired Elementary Teacher of Grover Beach, California

*

Author Rich Hites has again succeeded in writing a story seen through the eyes of a witness to the crucifixion, resurrection, and what followed. While the narrative is fiction, it truly describes, in stark detail, the reality of life in those times. From the beginning to the mysterious manner in which the protagonist learns the healing arts to the Healing House, following the apostles, and the return, the reader will be treated to an experience that is guaranteed to enliven the theater of the mind.

~Ray Watters, Actor

*

In any book particularly of an historical nature, two things will always draw me in. The first is deep descriptions that touch my senses such as the slapping of sandals on surfaces, the smells in a place called Healing House, and the touching of rough fabric to see if it is real and lastly the relief of rescue as in this novel. Secondly, character development and Rich introduced us to a conflicted man who loved deeply and who was loved in return but his greatest love was to follow the Nazarene, to spread His love and healing. It was not an easy path although he stayed steady until the end, whatever that end may have been.

~Leslie Avant, Dental Office Manager

*

The Great and Beloved Physician is a dream, a vision of adventure, war, love, betrayal, and salvation. You don't know what's going to happen next, but there are clues along the way. At times it is nightmarish. There is slaughter in war, crucifixion, pain in sickness in many lands, mysterious kidnappings, love so close yet so far. There are the conflicts of empires, religions, regions, and groups. All of it revolving around and citing the Gospel of Luke. Reflecting the language, customs, demography, and situations of two millennia ago, there are insights into the people and writings of long ago.

~James Aynes, Esq., Attorney at Law

*

This is a wonderfully written book about the life and experiences of the Great Physician, Lucius. Based on the book of Luke in the Gospel, the author shows the growth of knowledge for Lucius as he went from a Roman Centurion to a Follower of the Nazarene. Lucius becomes a highly respected Physician and Healer while in prison in his early years. He uses his knowledge and gift of healing for the good of all people while giving glory to "the Nazarene". The author's two previous novels intertwine and build on the characters in all three books. Fascinating reading. Biblically based, the book will educate and fascinate the reader on the life, challenges and traditions of the people during the time after the Resurrection.

~Christine Kister, Retired Hairstylist of Redlands, CA

*

In "Great and Beloved Physician," Lucius often takes the reader to the edge of wonderment. Is he a healer or a soldier? Is he a Follower or a Prosecutor? Is this experience real or is it a dream? Who is a friend and who is a traitor? Each of these questions hang in balance as first century Christians navigate the political atmosphere of the times. The storytelling and character development invite the reader to see how much of life is a puzzle and how Lucius weaves the paradoxical pieces together.

~Katherine Peters, Seeker

*

This book spoke to me of "what could have been" regarding the life of Jesus, Luke and those turbulent times. It also brought to the forefront the men themselves: Paul the mercurial follower, Luke the Centurion turned doctor turned missionary, and Jesus the man and Zealot. A very compelling book about an extremely compelling man....Luke!

~Ray Lyles, Real Estate Agent

*

Rich does a brilliant job of bringing the stories of the early Followers of Jesus (or the Nazarene) to life through the lens of the Great and Beloved Physician—Lucius. Stories are told through the lens of Lucius as he travels with companions such as St. Paul, Timothy, Chloe, Bartholomew and Priscilla and Aquila. Readers will resonate with the tension Rich highlights between political climates and Christianity, the trust and betrayal of friends and the length a mother will go to "save" her child.

~Deborah Johnson, MSW, MAR, Deacon, NC Synod of the Evangelical Lutheran Church in America

GREAT & BELOVED PHYSICIAN

GOD'S HEALER

RICH HITES

GREAT AND BELOVED PHYSICIAN

Copyright © 2020 Rich Hites
Cover Design © Deranged Doctor Designs
Interior design by Mikey Brooks

ISBN: 0-9980533-4-1
ISBN-13: 978-0-9980533-4-9

DEDICATION

Dedicated to the many healers
who have given me and so many
the gift of life and wholeness
in the spirit of the Nazarene.

Dedicated to those believers who
follow the King of Kings and
Lord of Lords
without subjugating His Empire
to any other, including ours.

A WORD FROM THE AUTHOR

The story *by* Luke, the Evangelist, is well-known throughout Christianity (and beyond) mostly because of the account of the birth of Jesus, read every Christmas. But the story *of* Luke is not. Few know that he also authored a second book of the New Testament beyond "The Gospel of Luke," an account of the early church called "The Acts of the Apostles." Most do not realize that he is named in neither of these works but only in the letters of Paul, including Colossians 4:14, II Timothy 4:11 and Philemon. Otherwise, he appears in Acts (beginning in the sixteenth chapter through the end of that book in chapter twenty-eight) because of one simple change in pronouns from "they" to "we," which means that Luke himself possibly joined up with the Apostle Paul on his second missionary journey to the eastern Roman Empire and stayed with him until the Apostle's final departure for Rome. Nothing else is recorded and any other stories are fictional or from early church writings, not the Bible.

Yet, Paul in Colossians 4:14 does give him one title and vocation, "physician." Medicine in the first century C.E. had no relation to what we experience now. It could be considered mostly magic and spiritual, not the science which we rely on to cure us today. Miracles were, therefore, as commonplace as a doctor's prescription filled by our local modern pharmacies. Most of the "cures," which ancient peoples found helpful, were either mechanical procedures like suturing wounds, or prayers and sacrifices to ancient gods like Aesculapius.

Because of this view of health, the "*caduceus*" was the wand or scepter of mystical healing power often portrayed in ancient sculptures or frescoes of Hermes (Mercury), the messenger god, or of Aesculapius, the god of healing. Even today we recognize the symbol of two snakes curling up a winged pole on our prescription bottles or the letterhead of our insurance forms. In our story about Luke (Lucius Maximus) it will have the same purpose but take another form altogether as you, the reader, will discover and I hope, enjoy.

"Snakes," winding up a *caduceus* scepter also had a different meaning for the ancients. Whereas we might think of them as evil or poisonous, they were seen as a metaphor or symbol of healing because their venom was extracted and used in medicine, much like we might use anti-venom today. Also, snakes shed their skins which was a great mystery in ancient times and was the symbol of "new life" and resurrection. This is also the meaning which my character, Lucius Maximus, would give them.

Finally, here is a bit of geography for the world of Luke (Lucius). Modern Turkey was what the Romans called "Asia" or "Asia Minor." Illyricum was the land of modern Serbia, Croatia, or the former Yugoslavia between Italy and the Greek peninsula. The Romans referred to all of Greece as "Macedonia." Parthia was away to the East and beyond the Euphrates where modern Iraq and Iran are today.

Parthia itself was another empire at the time of the Romans. The Parthians were excellent horsemen and rode on saddles with no stirrups (not invented until much later). They were also skilled bowmen, riding and shooting at the same time in a particular maneuver which is part of our story and was named by the sarcastic remark, "a Parthian shot," right into the eighteenth and nineteenth centuries. Without drones and satellites, the Romans lived in constant dread of the Parthians on their eastern frontier, especially after a disastrous defeat from them in 53 B.C. While this threat never loomed large in the time of Luke, the panic about it did. King Herod built Masada as an escape palace from the Parthians much like Americans built bomb shelters in the 1950's because of the Soviet nuclear threat. But Herod really had nothing to fear as the Parthians maintained no standing armies in their empire; and they often fought one another in continual tribal warfare as much as they fought Romans and other outsiders.

Our story of Luke (Lucius) is told by a character who, if you have read my second novel, has a connection to him. Chloe was a Corinthian Follower of the Nazarene, one Jesus of Nazareth. Because she is an educated business woman, speaking Greek, Hebrew and some Latin, the story of Lucius may feel stilted and formal at times. It should. She only descends into the street language of the poor when she is sometimes expressing their responses to her "beloved Physician."

So, enjoy the ride as Chloe shares her friend and lover, "the great and beloved Physician," with her grandchildren. And how that lady can spin a story all in one afternoon!

~Rich Hites

TABLE OF CONTENTS

PART TWO
AFTER THE APOSTLE

GREAT & BELOVED PHYSICIAN

GOD'S HEALER

"Luke, the beloved physician,
and Demas greet you."

— Colossians 4:14

PART ONE
BEFORE THE APOSTLE

(14 C.E. TO 44 C.E)

PROLOGUE

(72 C.E.—REIGN OF VESPASIANUS)

"Few knew him and no one truly understood him," I said, "nor did I until I was about to lose my very life, and not in Corinthia's arena." Three sets of young eyes blinked up at me from the floor of my atrium. The afternoon had begun to fade in the faces of my great granddaughters, my *puellae,* as the trickling water played its soft rhythm in my center room pool.

Livia broke this pinging and said, "But we do not care about Lucius. We want to hear about you."

"Yes, *avi,* tell us again how you beat the gladiators in Corinthia's Amphitheater and won everyone's freedom from the evil Governor Gallio," Miriam, her cousin, added. Her voice echoed along the atrium walls of my Ephesian Terrace House.

I brushed my graying blond hair back into my veil and smiled at my little lovelies. They did not call me Chloe as the Followers of the

Nazarene did, nor "Prophet," nor "great grandmother." To them, I was their *avi,* a Latin slang for "grandma," but, in truth, I was not their *avia,* their "grandmother," but their *prodvia*—their great grandmother—all but one of the three before me being the granddaughters of my daughter, Mara, and my adopted daughter, Eurydice.

Together, they pestered their *"avi"* for my stories, usually the same ones, again and again: Livia with her seven-year-old face, dark brown eyes and light brown hair, the very twin of her grandmother, Eurydice, at this age; Miriam, age five with ebony eyes and dark brown hair like Mara, my daughter; and the most godlike of them all, Anoys, four nearly five, with a bronze face like a polished shield of Artemis and piercing pale blue eyes as mysterious as her name.

Their play with dolls and straw-stuffed animals no longer commanded their interest as they fixed upon me, waiting for the account of my adventures some thirty years in the past. I paused, then I re-directed their request.

"Yes, my life has been more than I ever believed that it would become; but this evening I want to tell you about the one who rescued me—the one who is far braver than I ever could hope to be," I protested. "The one called 'the Physician,' Lucius Maximus."

"But you told us that he was a soldier, and a Roman," Anoys now joined the conversation of her cousins. "How could he be a doctor and still rescue anyone?" She dropped her doll into her lap, shifted from one leg to the other as she knelt and waited.

"Ah," I said, leaning my fiftyish body back into my leather chair and smelling its familiar pungent odor. "He was a soldier who was rescued himself by the one who has rescued us all. And his courage and his story contain a secret---a mystery especially about you, my darling Anoys."

The other girls were whispering to each other; but with this news, their chatter ceased like a stream suddenly dammed into silence. They fixed upon Anoys who was staring at me.

CHAPTER ONE:
THE MAKING OF A
MAN—AND A HEALER

"This child is destined for the falling and the rising of many
in Israel and to be a sign that will be opposed."
— Luke 2:34

Aurelia rose in her foggy damp night robe and blinked, straining to listen from her bed. Had she heard it? Wood clanked on wood, like a carpenter hammering a nail only with less rhythm. She slipped on her sandals to avoid the cold stone floor of her sleeping quarters and glided into the atrium of her Tuscana house.

The dwelling, while modest, boasted marble floors and a few frescoes on the walls, mostly military history of battles from the Punic Wars to "Horatio at the Bridge." "Crack, crack, crack" interrupted the vivid colors of troops and generals since Aurelia's family were not just farmers in the hills north of Rome, but more akin to what this artwork portrayed. Crack, crack, crack.

The clattering cleared the morning fog from her ears as there in the center of the atrium, with mist rolling down through its center opening and Rome's soldiers and enemies staring in from its walls, another "battle" commenced. A huge brawny man struck blow upon blow at his small spindle of an opponent—a boy of six with a tussle of brown hair flopping down into his eyes.

Crack! The well-trained muscles brought another decisive strike against the horizontal wooden sword of their little opponent. The boy ducked and made no attempt to counter the attack pounding upon him. Instead, he attempted not to be struck, which by the bruises on his face and arms, as Aurelia now noticed, had not been possible.

"Lucius Maximus!" the huge man shouted, "you cannot hold a sword at that angle and expect it to save you."

Crack! The boy's weapon collapsed into his cheek. "Ow!" he screamed. Blood spurted over his face and onto his tunic from this latest wound.

"Please stop this!" Aurelia shouted, "he's too young for this, Horatius."

Her husband looked up, hardly winded from the contest with his son. Lucius was rubbing the red liquid on his cheek and staring at the bruises on his arms as his mother's plain face contorted with pleading and anger toward her husband.

"Aurelia, keep out of this," Horatius reprimanded. "Tomorrow we go to the Temple. I will dedicate the lad to Mars. That will shape his strength and courage and grow him into a good soldier. I was a full year younger than he when my father gave me to Mars and Mithra and sealed my destiny with the Emperor's legions. Now bridle your tongue, woman!"

Aurelia spun away from Horatius and her whimpering son. The morning light caught a tear at her cheek, and though Horatius did not hear her, she whispered to herself, "I have other purposes for *my* son—and for a more glorious destiny dedicated to another."

Two slaves in flaxen tunics offered questioning looks, not from *her* words but towards Horatius as they scurried past Aurelia, then Lucius.

CHAPTER TWO:
AN UNINTENDED DESTINY

"Every firstborn male shall be designated as holy…"
— Luke 2:23

The temple priest looked up from his robe and squinted at the morning mist which swirled between the columns of the shrine to Aesculapius. Two pairs of sandals slapped the marble floor, of that he was certain even at such an early hour.

Suddenly the fog drifted left and right exposing a tall slender figure, the silhouette of a woman emerging as she held the hand of another, a child with tussled brown hair trying to keep up with her rapid determined steps. As they drew near, the priest could see the woman's face, plain with dark brown hair drawn back in a proper Roman bun. The boy at her side continued to look up at her but suddenly glanced forward, seemingly unsure of her purpose.

Once their sandals silenced; the woman, dressed in a long maroon robe, pulled the boy of six, in front of her. She pushed him toward the priest, now adjusting his curved hat and his golden robe to appear more "official." Her hands went to the boy's shoulders and she smiled.

She said, "My name is Aurelia, wife of Horatius Maximus. His name is Lucius," she said, nudging him forward a little further. Lucius rubbed his eyes as much from sleep as from the incense and wood smoke which now replaced the morning fog. He coughed from the acrid odors of sacrifices.

"Is he ill?" the priest questioned. "He seems well enough to me." He stroked his own clean-shaven face, studying the young face in front of the mother, then said, "Why have you brought him to Aesculapius for a healing?"

"He is quite well, except for the bruises from a contest with his father yesterday." Aurelia assured the priest. "I do not wish him healed even though he could use it. I wish to dedicate him before—"

"Before" broke Lucius from hearing his mother's request, separating his thoughts from the mystical golden robe of the priest and carrying him back to Aurelia's wake-up visit to his room that morning. She had tilted him up from his deep sleep and had whispered to him, "A dedication made first is a dedication made for all eternity."

Now here in the Temple of Aesculapius, Lucius was beginning to realize what that meant: she would get to him before Horatius, while her husband slept away the early morning. And though Aurelia slid Lucius' damp tunic over his bare chest without any other word, though he had said to her, "Where are we going, Mother?" and though she remained silent, grabbing up his sandals, forcing him to walk barefoot on the cold marble floor to pass in silence by his father's room, he now knew that "before" Horatius had his way, she was having hers *here* in the Temple of Aesculapius in the center of Tuscana. "Before" meant all of this as the voice of the priest returned him to his mother's mission.

"You wish to give your son to the great healer, Aesculapius, son of Apollo?" the priest said. He looked up at the smoky altar behind him with an early sacrifice for the dawn still smoldering on it then pulled his golden robe tighter around him. Once more he studied the round young face below him and said, "But why?"

"His father desires for him to be a soldier and a killer, a man of violence. I want more for him. I want him to *give* life, not take it—to be a healer," Aurelia said.

"Very well," the priest relented. "Do you have the price of the sacrifice?"

Aurelia stretched her hand from under her robe and held out a small pouch. Lucius looked beyond them both to the hazy sacrifice that continued to choke him and to burn his eyes. Through his stinging tears, he saw it, or did he? *There* at the corner of the marble facing on the altar and below the smoke, it slithered along and around the corner of the table—a black snake disappeared into the shadows.

Lucius shivered again and thought, *a dedication made first is a dedication made for all eternity.*

They met Horatius, still shrugging off his sleep, as he looked up at them coming shoe-less through the front door. The burly soldier did not notice how odd their early morning barefoot walk was, as he only demanded that Lucius depart from Aurelia's company for his own "dedication." He spun his son around in the atrium and ushered him back out the door, not even bothering to ask what he and Aurelia had been doing at such an hour.

As for this second act in Tuscana, the Temple of Mars was larger than that first visit to Aesculapius boasting white columns, twice as high. The voice of the priest boomed and echoed before the altar, "Great Mars, we dedicate this son of Rome to your service, to the service of Emperor Tiberius and to Rome's legions!" Flames shot from the altar and the carcass of a calf ignited. Burls of thick smoke swirled up through an opening in the roof.

But Lucius felt no shiver, no awe, nothing. All along the walk home, Horatius babbled on about soldiering and dedication to the Empire as Lucius' mind floated like the smoke from passing cooking fires in the market area of Tuscana and returned to what his first "dedication" had been—a priest in a golden robe, a slithering snake and a chill that made him shiver again with its memory.

"It's fine," his father said, "a chill is a sign of your dedication to Mars."

"You have done excellent work mending his leg," Aurelia said. She stared at her child and inhaled the odors of lilies and straw which filled the back garden of the House of Maximus. The small farm pen beyond the wall of the courtyard held her son, a bed of hay and a very young fawn which returned a worried stare at Lucius.

He stroked the animal's head and calmed it with his touch as much as with a set of wooden splints which he had wrapped around its hind right leg. Without looking up, Lucius said, "The fawn's leg will mend now, will it not, Mother?"

"Yes, you are a gifted healer, Lucius. I am very proud of—" she broke off.

A dark shadow covered all three of them and blocked the sun as a huge form bent over their conversation. "And what have you here?" Horatius bellowed. "You cannot do this to a wild animal! If it cannot fend for itself, it must die!"

"No, *Pater*! I found him in the field, alone and without his mother. He could not walk because of a broken leg," Lucius protested. "He needed my help."

"The only help it needs is not from you or any of us!" Horatius shouted. He stepped over the courtyard wall and shoved Lucius aside. His two large hands wrapped around the animal's head.

Again, Lucius said, "I have splinted his broken leg. He will recover because of me."

Horatius closed his grasp upon the fawn's head, jerked it up from the straw and disregarded the screams of his son. "I will do what we did when I was a boy and we came upon hopeless creatures such as this," he said.

"No, no, no, no!" cried Lucius as if he knew all too well what was happening. "Noooo! I am a healer and I have cured him."

Horatius looked down at the fawn whose eyes froze upon him in horror; then still grasping its head, he gave its dangling body a quick single jerk. A crack, like a dry limb breaking, came from its neck as the fawn gave a soft whimper and its swinging body fell limp.

Once more Lucius cried, "Nooo! I could have helped him recover. I am a healer." He began to whimper more loudly than the fawn had.

"Your son performed an excellent deed, splinting the fawn's leg, Horatius," Aurelia said. "Even if it could not return to the forest, he could have made it his own."

"You are wrong and you know it. It would never have walked or run as it should have," Horatius said. "I did right by killing it."

"No, you did not," Lucius sobbed. "I cared for him. I knew what to do."

"No, you are a soldier and as a soldier, weakness must be shunned and snuffed out whenever it emerges," Horatius said.
Lucius grew quiet and bent over the dead animal, listening for any breathing. He whispered, "Perhaps in your world but not in mine."

CHAPTER THREE:
A FINE SOLDIER?

"For I also am a man set under authority,
with soldiers under me…"
— Luke 7:8

…kindly remember how to be heartfelt and caring, not just strong and brave to impress your comrades or commanders. You were falsely dedicated to Mars.

With all my love and greetings,

~Mother Aurelia

"**R**emember, legionaries, you were dedicated to Mars!" Lucius looked up from his mother's words and heard the paraphrase of his father's now echoing from the mouth of his commander, Tribune Flavius. At eighteen, he had filled out to a muscular stature, trading his tussled brown hair for a short Roman cut and his boyish face for deep-set penetrating brown eyes.

The Empire had trained his young strapping body to be a fighter for Rome, outfitting and commissioning him as a "centurion" to lead one hundred young legionaries, not much older than he was. The *Legio XII Fuminata,* the "Thunderbolts," a name from Emperor Augustus himself boasting its strength and toughness as a terror to any opponent, was his legion and now his destiny.

Once their training ended, that legion marched North, then East—from Italia to Illyricum to smash a tax revolt, a recurring problem from the barbarians of that region. Sometimes these rebels simply demonstrated, stopping work in their towns and frustrating the proconsul. Sometimes they only refused to pay the taxes. And sometimes they took up arms. North Illyricum chose this last act of defiance.

So, Lucius marched with his one hundred, now a fast-march, into another nameless town. He smelled it before he saw it, odors of urine, feces and rotting food began filling his nose, then the streets which stretched between the close dull tan rows of houses and shops. The people with their children stared without jeers or comments from their windows and doors. Their gaunt faces and spindled bodies, covered with frayed robes and tunics, were the epitome of prisoners who had no hope of release.

Lucius' eyes tried to ignore them, remaining straight ahead on the long line of bobbing Roman helmets; but he still caught enough of all the squalor on either side—and beneath his sandals. The Emperor never saw this, never saw how his subjects lived so far from him in his retreat of marble and endless flowers, his remote palace on the Palatine in Rome.

Finally, Lucius just closed his eyes and the scroll from his mother which he shoved with her troubling advice into his side satchel. His sandals stumbled and caused him to open a gaze narrowly fixated back down the line and on the transverse red plume of the centurion helmet out in front of him—Marcus Cornelius.

The square-jawed, darker-complexioned officer was the only friend which Lucius had taken from his training. He hailed from another town and another villa north of Lucius' own—Florentia. Though his father had also been a farmer, he had also served in Caesar's legions as an officer.

But Marcus was more sought after by the women, not just because of his chiseled face and broad-shouldered size but also because of his superior rank as *primus pilus,* first spear, Senior Centurion, at the front of any assault ahead of Lucius and all centurions. Their training had been entirely the same, but somehow Marcus had risen faster through the ranks.

And somehow the resentment grated in Lucius—then stopped—suddenly. There ahead in the street between Marcus' bobbing plume and the *century* behind him was a gap of ruts and hardened dirt which perfectly outlined a small form. A child of maybe five, younger than when Horatius had dedicated him to Mars, toddled into the street.

The little boy bent down to watch something between Marcus' unit and the one out before it. That something became so intriguing that he no longer noticed where he was or what was descending upon him—a Senior Centurion and one hundred legionaries in full armor and cleated sandals.

The boy should have moved but he did not, did not even look up. The *centuries* should have split apart but held fast in a solid wall of "Thunderbolts."

Then Lucius heard his friend's voice: "Forward!" Not "divide," not "separate ranks," just "Forward!" from Marcus. Lucius could counter that order, move his one hundred to the side around the boy. But what was a boy to Rome? Besides, the *century* ahead would get to the victim first.

All at once, hope shot out from Lucius' peripheral vision. A woman darted from the ranks of emaciated onlookers. Too late. The legionaries spun her aside like a top whirling away over a flat rock; and the little one vanished beneath the cleats of the bobbing spears and clanking shields of Senior Centurion Marcus' men. Like a roller on the ocean, their helmets rose then fell upon the dry road and the "rock" at the surface below.

Afterwards, Lucius did not look down when his own unit bobbed up then down as if they were crossing a small hill in a field— or a body? He felt something soft, then nothing.

Nothing but the sobs of a high-pitched voice, a whimpering which brought a shiver and a memory of a deer long ago. The sobs turned to shrieks as Lucius feet moved forward but his glance swiveled back.

A woman's bare head bent over a motionless heap between the units, her hair blowing back in the wind which had risen. She scooped up a bloody bundle and held out her son as if she were offering him to the gods, then screamed, "Filthy Roman scum! You take our money, our food and now our children! May the gods burn and bury you!"

Lucius stumbled and caught himself falling forward. Then remembering his mother's letter, he shoved the words aside with the slogan of Horatius, "For the Emperor and Rome." That motto felt as hollow in him as a stone tossed down a dry well.

CHAPTER FOUR:
A GAME AND NEW ORDERS

"If you love those who love you, what credit is that to you?
For even sinners love those who love them?"
— Luke 6:32

Most of army life was marches, fast and monotonous and slow, not like—. The bobbing helmets and the softness under his sandals returned, but Lucius let it drop into a cup of morning wine and stale bread. He had risen early from his cot to clear the center of his tent.

The men were coming, Marcus and others from his *century* with hopefully no stray talk of a dead local child. No…all focus would be on the "game."

How Lucius loved "the game" or *ludus latrunculorum,* as they called it in Latin, "game of bandits." A lone soldier with coins jingling in his belt pouch, shoved back the tent flap; and dust mingled with a heavy leather smell suddenly emanated from the entrance. The handsome face of Marcus followed this first soldier along with a third legionary struggling with the square *ludus* board and its raised squares. He dropped it with a thud in the center of the tent which Lucius had now cleared of armor, swords, stools and maps.

The first soldier warned, "Careful, Cestus, there are rocks beneath the rug there."

His comrade shrugged it off, as another soldier ducked below the tent flap and held a bag of clanking stones. He spilled it beside the board and round black and gray markers rolled into a pile.

Two more legionaries bowed into the centurion's tent, speaking in low tones as Lucius heard one say, "The centurion always wins." The other replied, "Perhaps not today." *So, a challenge is building to my past victories*, Lucius thought.

One more contestant came as coins rang on a lamb skin which Lucius put out beside the game board. All of the players, including Marcus and Lucius, crouched around the *ludus* board like school boys intrigued with a new toy.

The "battle" commenced. Black and gray markers were placed, then moved one at a time.

Cries burst like sparks from a bonfire, "Aw, not again!" And "I cannot fathom the Fates always tilting in his direction."

Lucius won so often that his pile of sesterces grew until it slid sideways in front of him. But as the markers flew more rapidly across each square something began flowing with every move—the luck of the centurion. His coins began to vanish as though they were sucked into a drain beneath the center of his tent.

Each time Lucius moved his black marker, believing he had outflanked his opponents, even his friend Marcus, a series of gray stones slipped around his piece. He was surrounded, first on two sides, then on a third by another opponent. At last the trap closed with a fourth block grinding in Lucius' ears as a legionary slid his marker across the *ludus* board.

Hemmed in! It was like a battle gone bad and he was the conquered one. Each time he had to pay, not one, but four opponents. Each time his body tightened at a quadruple loss. Each time his palms sweat as they counted out the coins to his men.

But his arms slapped the black markers down for a new round each time far louder than needed as he listened to fewer coins clank in the pile at his feet. His men, mostly, were scheming to destroy him.

Lucius' face reddened. Then bang! His hand grabbed the stone board, raising it and himself, spraying black and gray stones over every player. The men ducked to avoid the shrapnel spinning towards their faces. Lucius let two pieces strike his own chest as he slammed the *ludus* board down on the rocks beneath it.

Crack! It snapped in two. "Get out!" he shrieked. "All of you!" The legionaries quieted and shuffled out now like school boys punished by their headmaster. "He can't handle our wins even though we had to handle his," one said.

Only Marcus remained. "No time to salve your wounds, Friend Lucius," he said. "We must muster the men for a real fight."
Still, Lucius wondered if the "game of bandits" had not stolen more than his money.

CHAPTER FIVE:
AN ATTACK GONE WRONG

"Do not judge, and you will not be judged;
Do not condemn and you will not be condemned."
— Luke 6:37

No dreams had come. No visions had come. No letters from his mother either. His only succor had been the morning wine as he had slipped on his leather armor—one bowl for the endless buckles that had become harder to clasp with each sip.

Buckling his belt and adjusting his centurion's *gladius* had deserved a second bowl. He had consumed a third as he secured his baton and dagger and a fourth had quenched his lips at the adjusting of his transverse-plumed helmet.

After all, this was Lucius' first engagement so he had wanted some help, but nothing had come, except wine, as he stumbled for the door of his tent, attempting to avoid Marcus or his men. Would his *century* even be there for him after his "display" at the "game?"

So, here he was, his nose filling with the sweet aroma of swamp grass blending with the sweat of legionaries all around him. Lucius thought that he had heard one say, "Did you smell his breath? Too much for him today."

He dismissed it for the grass that again tickled his face and waved a curtain in front of his blurry eyes—from the "morning courage?" But even with his *century* around him, fear, not composure tore at him after—. That "game" had ruined him.

His feet sent a shiver up from their cold wet place in the murky water beneath him. He trembled as he waved a silent low signal down the line to his decurion and beyond.

All at once through the swaying tendrils of grass, he saw it—the red plume of his Senior Centurion. Marcus, perhaps his only friend or perhaps not after this morning, popped up then disappeared along with his *century* in the open meadow ahead. They re-appeared only to vanish in a fog that slowly cloaked them.

A shout pierced Lucius' ears from a strange tongue, followed with cries from three sides. The locals of Illyricum had also hidden in the tall field grass and rose like a phantom to strike using the field's misty cover. Lucius could count through the haze that they outnumbered their Roman prey by at least three to one.

But out of their cover, Marcus' men hurled spears upward like hornets swarming from a hive. Then their swords rang from their scabbards. Even with casualties among the rebels, who had screamed from the Roman spear assault, the push by the enemy caved in two sides of Marcus' *century* as falling legionaries piled on top of each other.

The mist rose like a curtain on a Greek tragedy, and Marcus only remained with a small contingent of soldiers. Lucius remembered

Tribune Flavius' orders, "Do not commence the counter-attack until I give the word." Had Flavius miscalculated?

Still, Lucius waited and tipped to his right. No order. He pressed his hand into the slimy grass of the trench to steady his sandals. Nothing. Through the tall waving blades, the helmet of Marcus was about to vanish in the charging waves of locals hacking at the remains of brave Roman soldiers.

"Now! Advance!" the voice of Flavius echoed across the field from behind Lucius. Roman eagles bobbed out of the ravine as the centurion pulled his sword and waved it overhead. But a charge turned to a slippery slide and a stumble when legionaries swept around and nearly over their commander.

Lucius saw his unit roar by him like billowing smoke leaving its fire behind. The rebels jerked up, spun back towards this surprise assault and ceased their onslaught on Marcus' legionaries. But as they were untrained fighters, these locals paused to allow the first of Lucius' men to join their shields and launch their spears at a full run. Whoosh!

Lucius stood up; and with his soldiers out before him, he saw a line of Illyricum's men drop and disappear onto the field, spears now pointing up like fence posts obviously in chests or backs. The remaining enemy line folded into a V-shape around two sides of the new Roman square but the enemy had been diminished.

Still shaking off the morning, Lucius finally re-joined the action and shoved through his men towards their front. Any worries about a first action, or about support from his unit, evaporated as a white-painted face popped up to his left. For an instant, the white spots of another creature shot through his mind—a fawn?

Lucius made a quick choice, not about healing but about harming, when he jerked his *gladius* from the belly of a barbarian where he had thrust it and raised it over the speckled look.

Then crack! The sword landed with a heavy blow. The spots fell from Lucius' sight, probably wounded but not dead.

Soon the crowding of the first contact with the barbarians dwindled even more as the enemy retreated. His men were not only shoving the opposing line back, they were pursuing them with or without their commander.

Then silence. Only the faint groans of the wounded broke the air as bodies, not combatants were piled around Lucius. His own *century,* the rebels, even Marcus and his men had bolted away.

Lucius was hemmed in by a "fortress" of dead and dying, his own and the barbarians', creating a wall all around him. Blood, gashed arms, and shattered legs were what he could see as the groans and the pleas of "Help me" and "I'm cut" floated on the wind.

Should he stop and attend as many as he could? What? No.

He was not the camp physician. But all at once, he was not alone. A shadow stretched beyond him. To his side was the speckled-faced barbarian, standing taller than he remembered and very much unwounded. The rebel raised his long sword and charged, ready to split this Roman in two.

At that instant, Lucius became Mars' servant again and drew back his *gladius,* swinging his horizontal blade forward and meeting the downward strike from his attacker. Blow followed blow, ringing the silence from the field. Lucius grew winded, but his opponent, with endless strikes on his enemy's short sword, did not.

Then the rebel raised his weapon to bring it down upon Lucius' head; but he left his own torso unprotected. The centurion's training commanded the moment.

Lucius swung his *gladius* out to the side and into the speckled-faced enemy's waist, not wounding the man this time but slashing him deeply with a thrust. He looked up with wide eyes, gagged, dropped his weapon over Lucius and fell.

None of the centurion's men had seen it. Everything fell quiet until Lucius said to himself, "I know where to catch up with my *century*."

When he arrived at the town, legionaries were running down vacant streets, kicking open doors and dragging out locals. Up ahead two of his men had missed a tiny hovel on the right. When he arrived at the low wooden door, it creaked open slowly.

A dark form filled the unlit room. Light from a back window silhouetted a helmet and a transverse plume. Lucius knew the square jaw of Marcus who put a finger to his lips.

A door beside the Senior Centurion swung out, a dark robe leaped with a shout from a woman's voice which said, "You filthy Roman scum! You killed my son and I will repay you!"

A hand raised above the robe, and a small blade glistened from the back-window light. Marcus' hand wrapped around the elevated wrist and shoved the knife back toward his attacker.

"Aagh!" a woman's voice shrieked and the robe collapsed to the floor.

"No!" Lucius heard his friend say. Then Marcus added, "I did not mean to kill her."

"But she meant to kill you," Lucius said. The spirit of Mars continued from his last engagement. "What's one more barbarian death to the Empire or to Caesar!"

Marcus just stared at the dead woman. "Look at her eyes," he said

Lucius said, "No concern of ours." Then he paused, looked down towards the face with its set stare. It pierced him like the knife now pierced her heart.

They were the color and shape of the eyes of his mother—Aurelia.

CHAPTER SIX:
GRIM NEWS AT HOME

"Why do you see the speck in your neighbor's eye,
but do not notice the log in your own eye?"
— Luke 6:41

The dream returned to haunt him: first a fog swirling and damp which made him strain to see what was there. Darkness framed the silvery mist until it outlined a specter of a woman. She lifted both arms in front of her and a long sword, a barbarian *rhomphaia,* flashed in the light.

The woman began to circle the weapon and lowered it in his direction, finally flinging it at him with all her fury. Lucius awoke— with a tunic drenched in cold sweat. Where was he?

Not where he had dreamed—not in Illyricum, but home in Tuscana. Attempting to forget his dream, no, attempting to bury his first engagement, at least the dead child and murdered woman who would not remain buried, he tilted up on his bed and rose, stumbling for his sandals.

As he shuffled out of the sleeping quarters and across the room, the generals and legionaries of the atrium frescoes grimaced at his every step. They appeared to be prophesying the behavior of his father.

Yet, when he arrived at the *triclinium*, the plate of grapes, bread and cheese along with a cup of wine did not mimic the angry mood which he expected. Instead, the room was more like twilight than early morning, more like an "end" than a "beginning." Horatius was looking out the window towards the courtyard, and he was staring in a kind of eternal frozen grief.

Without turning toward his son, he said, "She did not write because she had become too weak. She died a fortnight ago."

Lucius coughed but softly, not wanting to interrupt his father. "No physician could break her fever. She slipped from me like a morning mist," Horatius continued.

Lucius was computing the time of a "fortnight"—during the Illyricum campaign, maybe the very moment of the attack upon Marcus from the woman.

Thoughts removed him from his grieving father and sent him back to his commander's words: "Centurions and legionaries, we have been victorious for Caesar and Rome. Two thousand of the enemy lie slain." Lucius thought, *Two thousand plus two more, a son and his mother.*

He reached for last night's dream but it would not come—only another woman, a prostitute who had spent the early part of the evening with him. A chestnut-haired woman with bronze skin and ebony eyes, she had slipped into the villa after Horatius retired. Lucius needed comfort, not sex. When they finished, he shoved her with a thud from his bed to the floor, like a sack of grain slamming down on a wagon bottom.

Kill a woman, or hurt one, what was the difference? Lucius rationalized. *Unless that woman was his own mother.*

Horatius brought him back to the present, back to the *triclinium,* "Steward Demetrius tells me that you are departing from me. I had wished that you might remain longer to be here in my mourn—." He covered his emotions and said, "But you must do as you are ordered. Where are you to be sent?"

"To Palestine, to join the *Legio X Fretensis* in Jerusalem."

"That place is the filth pit of the Empire. Who did you cross to suffer *that* assignment?" Horatius said. His father did not wait for an answer, but stepped out the door from the dining room into the courtyard and its morning sun.

After he was out of sight, Lucius began to sob, but stopped. Another's sobbing grew louder than his own and intensified—from the garden. It came in the tones of Horatius.

Suddenly Lucius felt a hand on his shoulder, and he recognized the bony fingers of the Steward of the House of Maximus, Demetrius. He whispered in Lucius' ear, "Master Lucius, you would not have believed how tender your father was with Mistress Aurelia. He sat at her bed and made certain that she wanted for nothing, neither food nor drink. He was a dear 'physician' to her every hour of every day."

Lucius' eyes filled with more tears, not simply for his mother.

CHAPTER SEVEN:
NEW POSTING, NEW PROBLEMS

"…give to the emperor the things that are the emperor's,
and to God the things that are God's."
— Luke 20:25

Lucius smelled roasting meat mixing with the oil of burning torches in the hallway as his sandals slapped the stone floor deep inside the bowels of Jerusalem's Fortress Antonia. The march to Palestine went without incident until one monotonous month after another carried him to "the holy city," as the locals called it, to be posted here at the Proconsul's fortress overlooking the Temple of the Jews.

Only when they were on patrol did any Roman even glimpse the Jewish sacred site from above on the towers of Governor Pilate's fort. Otherwise, Lucius' life, every soldier's life, was *below* in the barracks.

And there, the monotony of his journey ended when he heard the slapping of his sandals, interrupted by the voices of his men. They grew louder and clearer, rising into some sort of verbal combat.

"No, *born as he should be—a true messiah*—his mother brought him forth in a humble place—that he might become *savior* of us all to bring peace on earth and good will to everyone..." the voice trailed off but remained firm.

"So, *you* say, Publius, and that might fit Emperor Augustus but Tiberius is *no* god! He has abandoned the Empire and gone to Capri! He deserves neither loyalty nor divinity!" another voice disputed.

"Every Emperor *is* a god. They protect us and save us no matter how humbly born. They deserve allegiance and worship!" the first voice argued.

The original debater was driving his point to its mark as if it were a sword. "How else can we die for them?" he said.

"Not me!" the other said. "I intend to live, Emperor, god or no. I am serving my time in this pit of a posting and heading home! That's it!"

"Then, you cannot call yourself a son of Rome. You coward!" Publius shouted.

Suddenly Lucius heard nothing. Silence snuffed out the verbal battle. Then thud! Something heavy hit a cot, and wood snapped like someone breaking twigs for a campfire. Lucius knew what the scene was before he encountered it.

As he walked through the doorway, legionaries leaped from cots and camp stools and slung arms across chests in a salute. They formed a line as straight as fence posts, mostly in tunics, though some in far less. The victim of half of the fight lay in a pile of broken wood and covers, naked, but with a gash dripping blood into his eye.

Lucius extended a hand to him as he said, "Men, assume your previous position, but prepare to listen!" He glanced at the naked man, rubbing his wound while feigning a weak salute with the others.

"You might want some cover for these orders, soldier," Lucius said, trying to choke back a laugh. He was also attempting to develop more rapport with these men after the loss of loyalty in Illyricum. The *Legio X Fretensis* reputed to be more combative as he had just experienced second-hand; so no *ludus* games with these soldiers.

Elsewhere in the barracks, tunics slipped over naked bodies, followed by quiet. No further debates about emperors, worship, loyalty or military service came from this *century*. Lucius thought, *Better save your anger for real enemies, fellows.*

He did not look up from his orders but said. "Might want to reserve some fight for the knife men out there. Those Jewish *sicarii* will not bother to debate whose god is with us. They already have one, not ours, by the way." He glanced up and waited. Low laughter cascaded down the barracks.

Lucius thought, *Now they are with me.* He said, "We have orders for Galilee, a little hovel named Capernaum. The Proconsul is coordinating with the local King there, named Herod, to suppress would-be rebels *and messiahs.*" A head shook in agreement at the mention of "messiahs," possibly from the "Emperor defender" in the earlier "debate."

The aromas of cumin, garlic and bread, filled Lucius' nose and he added, "Take your mid-day meal and prepare to move out."

He scanned down the line of young faces barely younger than he was until he got to a legionary who had not yet dressed. "You might want a little more protection for this march, legionary."

Laughter again rippled through the barracks, but Lucius

wondered if this also meant loyalty. Could any Emperor heal the brokenness which haunted him from Illyricum?

No room for maneuvering meant overwhelming odors of local bodies, the smell of sheep and goats and the stifling smoke of ovens cooking the day's catch from the Sea of Tiberias or "Lake Gennesaret" as the locals called it. Small towns like Capernaum bordering the lake had nothing to offer except trouble for Lucius and his patrols. Narrow streets crammed with vendors' stalls meant the Jewish rebels, *sicarii,* aptly called "knife men," moved in between legionaries and ripped Roman stomachs with small sharp knives so swiftly that the attacker vanished before the soldier hit the ground and bled to death.

Yet, after several months, Lucius and his men shoved forward on another patrol down that Capernaum *agora,* looking as conspicuous as ever in red tunics and a transverse-plumed helmet on their centurion. The market was even worse today because some were shopping for one of their local Jewish holidays—Passover. He took the rear, put the bodies of his young legionaries between him and the decurion whom he sent to the front of their thin line. Silver iron helmets bobbed through the black and brown robes of locals on either side of the street as Lucius darted his eyes around looking for any sign of potential attack.

But the action was not up ahead. From behind, shoving bodies into him and his line, came a wave of Jewish voices shouting in perfect Greek, "Make way, make way for the elders of the synagogue." Lucius turned back from the line of soldiers in front of him.

Brown and black striped robes were cutting a path through the wall of shoppers. They were men with ivory prayer shawls and gray-flecked beards searching the crowds for something—or someone.

Without warning, they broke their step and jerked to such a halt that those in the rear of their group bumped up against the men at the center. A man with very white hair and a tooth missing from his mouth spoke for the contingent. "Master," he pleaded, "a Gentile has a sick servant—fevered to the point of death. Come at once and heal him."

At first, Lucius could not see who was being petitioned as the bodies between him and the "elders" covered the one that they called "Master." Then a head moved left while a couple of bodies shifted to the right and some robes stepped backwards toward his patrol.

A man was standing at the side of the street, about thirty in age, and dressed in a charcoal robe with an ivory head covering similar to the elders. But he had a peasant's bed roll for travel slung over his left shoulder and one other item which betrayed his vocation—a bag hung from his right side, a pouch usually carried by Greek cynic teachers for begging.

He did not speak even as the elders and the crowd around him quieted. So, the initial petitioner grew impatient and barked his words like a dog pleading for table scraps, "Master, come quickly. Though this man is a Roman and a centurion, his servant should be healed."

At the mention of "centurion" by the elder, Lucius perked up and held back one of his men who had pushed around him. What would be the outcome of this?

He heard whispers from the shoppers—words and titles floated through the air. "Jeshua ben Joseph." "The Nazarene." But when some said, "The Messiah," and "the Savior," Lucius' thinking returned to the debate among his men months ago at Fortress Antonia. *Should these titles for an Emperor apply also to a cynic? Who is this?* he wondered.

While the centurion *here* was trying to determine why a centurion *somewhere else* might be asking for assistance from one like this local, another elder said to the "Master," "He is worthy to have you do this. He loves us. He has given a huge sum for building the synagogue where you taught today."

The Nazarene did not speak but gestured to the elders to lead the way to the one in need. Behind him seemed to be a group of his own— "students?" Some in the crowd called them "Followers" and even spoke names like "Petros," "Johannus," and "Andros" as if they knew them.

No sooner had the teacher and his Followers begun to move than others came up behind the elders to add another act to the drama. They pushed through the striped robes up to the Nazarene himself. A younger man with light brown hair and head uncovered, perhaps another servant of the centurion in need, looked down then up and said, "My Master says, 'Do not come under my roof for to you I am an enemy. But just speak a word of healing and my servant will recover. For I, too, am a man set under authority—a centurion named Sibelius, like yourself, Rabbi. I, too, give orders to soldiers and servants alike.'"

Lucius thought about himself, then about this fellow officer whom he did not know but who apparently had some wealth. That centurion was paying homage to a local as if he were a—a Roman— royalty even. Yet, all that Sibelius had and all that he was could not heal his hurt—nor the illness of a favored serv—.

The Nazarene interrupted Lucius' bewilderment and spoke, "Never among my own people have I found such trust and such acceptance." He bowed and whispered something in the young servant's ear. Lucius could not hear what he said.

Suddenly beyond this second group of petitioners, a third "elder" came with the same striped robe, ivory head shawl and graying beard. His face betrayed his news as he shouted, "He recovers. The servant is healed."

Lucius stopped any further advance toward the group; instead an "assault" was roaring through his head: a "savior" and a "messiah" humbler than the great Augustus? Yet, he does more than *rule* the world; he heals it and welcomes the adulation of all no matter what their need or what their background is. What kind of ruler is *this*?

A darkness engulfed Lucius and the street. Above, storm clouds were shrouding the hot Capernaum sun and its hovels. The weather was about to change and Lucius was not certain that it would be for the better.

As he marched his men out of the *agora* and onto the open road towards their barracks, he looked down at the tall grass waving in the wind. There it was! He had not seen it for fifteen years, not since his dedication in Aesculapius' Temple—a shiny black form slithered from the dirt into the grass. It had to be a snake.

CHAPTER EIGHT:
A NEW CITY, AN OLD FRIEND

"He said to her, 'Daughter,
your faith has made you well;
go in peace.'"
— Luke 8:48

"**C**apernaum is his," the light brown-haired speaker said. Fog swirled around his face and robe and out into the darkness. Lucius walked with him but held his silence.

"Jerusalem is his," the speaker pressed on. The words drifted away with the mist and Lucius said nothing trying to concentrate only on the young man's appearance.

"Rome is his," the fellow said. And with this declaration, he paused and things blurred into haze and dark.

His head dropped and with his face to the darkness, Lucius shouted, "No, no, no, no, no! All are Caes—." He looked up. Everything about the speaker transformed.

A scruffy beard, dark piercing eyes, and hair, covered with an ivory shawl, sharpened for Lucius' eyes as the servant of Sibelius dissolved into Jeshua ben Joseph, "the Nazarene"—and "Messiah?"

"No, no, no, no, no!" someone was shouting in the corridor of the barracks here in Jerusalem.

"No, no, no," Lucius said and awoke. "I never want to see *him* again. Never!"

After shaking off his dream, he felt the cold wet night tunic wrap around him on his cot. A quick breakfast of sour wine, bread and cheese, a switch into his red Roman garment, his armor, sword, dagger, and baton followed with a splash of cold water onto a flushed set of cheeks, chin and forehead.

He hoped that it would all help to eliminate—nothing. Perhaps a walk through the streets of his new posting—"the Holy City"—would clear his head.

Transverse-plumed helmet? Yes, a centurion needed to let the locals know who their real "messiah" was—Caesar and no one else. He pulled the head gear on and adjusted it front to back along with the chin straps. Then out of Fortress Antonia Lucius went—alone.

He glanced up at the gold leaf atop the Jewish Temple. As he passed, the sun flared in his eyes from a harsh glare off its cornice. Hopefully there would be no surprises—and no unexpected encounters on his quiet stroll.

The narrow street swarmed with shoppers at local stalls, buzzing with buying and selling, the aroma of leather from sandals, fish salted and hanging and meat cooking and held up for purchase. Not like yesterday when it all stopped—for—for *him*. Again, it was about the one whom Lucius did not want to see.

Then, business had ceased and dickering turned to shouts of "Hosanna!" or "Osanna!" or whatever slogan the locals cheered.

Then, bodies were no less squeezed against each other except that they all did a pivot to face the street and the rider who waved like a Caesar home from his conquests, but on the back of a donkey not a stallion. *This* was not Lucius' "messiah," but it was theirs—these Jews. He was the Nazar—.

Ah…suddenly up ahead a Roman, not the Nazarene, suspended his obsessive memories. The transverse plume, the square jaw and the bronze complexion could be "yes," then "no," then "yes" it was—Marcus Cornelius. The Senior Centurion had turned back to the red line which he was leading through the dark-robed barrier of customers blocking the market. Lucius noticed *him* but Marcus did not see his old friend.

Marcus' Romans began shoving forward once more, and Lucius took advantage of the column's lack of progress. He slipped along the right side of vendors' stalls shoving by a wood worker, nudging around a woman with a dark veil and nearly bowling over a small black-haired boy who spun back to his mother as a Roman centurion whisked by him.

Marcus' back was turned as he was trying to cut his own way forward with his baton. Two hands grabbed his shoulders in what his old friend intended to be a warm greeting and a surprise all at once. Instead, Marcus jumped as though he had been assaulted and unsheathed his *gladius,* dropping his baton in the crowd.

"What in Hades!" he shouted.

Lucius smiled and said, "Senior Centurion, how splendid to see a familiar face." Marcus' face did not return the warmth.

After explaining how he and his men were victims of a zealot assault just outside the city—slings and stones, not *sicarii* knives—the stress of Marcus' eyes matched his words and warnings. "Use Latin, not Greek," Lucius heard him say. But little else.

All Lucius knew was that his friend had just arrived and had been greeted with a deadly "welcome" from unseen terrorists, Jews having murdered two of his men. Still, for Lucius, Illyricum returned. Marcus might have other reasons not to be welcoming as Lucius now remembered how most of his friend's *century* had been sacrificed, how a woman had attacked him and how Marcus had turned the attack back upon her, killing her by mistake. All at once Lucius recalled a final detail: he had tried to calm Marcus only to receive a fist in the mouth from him as a reward.

So, Lucius offered an explanation for their ironic new circumstance: "It seems that Flavius got his way with both of us and here we are in 'the Holy City' as the locals call it."

"I have another name for it," Marcus grimaced.

They moved forward and talked, Marcus finally persuading his reckless friend to switch to Latin so no more of the crowd would take an interest in this Roman reunion. As Lucius pointed out Jewish customs, including their Temple rising ahead, he broke sentence and said, "They worship an invisible god who became visible yesterday with a donkey ride into—."

From a street on their right a mob composed of mostly black-robed men with white ivory shawls on their heads blew towards the two friends in an interruption which swirled like dust before a desert wind. The black robes shoved a blanket with bare feet protruding from the bottom but nothing else exposed. The feet danced up as they struck the hard, uneven stones of the street, but the mob continued pushing it, turning right and heading back from where Lucius had come earlier that morning.

The two centurions looked at one another, then ahead at the men and marched double time to catch them. The race wound through other market stalls, less compacted with shoppers as Lucius and Marcus closed in. The street opened up back at the origin of Lucius' morning stroll—at the Temple and a set of stairs with a crowd of a couple hundred at its base.

The hustling robes seemed intent on rushing their covered "business" right past, but the fast pace had separated the mob into a right and left group. The left group pushed the bundle ahead trying to clear the stairs and crowd as the right group attempted to close the gap with them. The half with the covered mystery feet stumbled and fell forward unfurling their prisoner like a bed roll, its contents spinning out onto the pavement.

The mob hushed. The crowd at the base of the stairs hushed. But a figure seated on one step above it all simply stared.

Lucius recognized a shapely curve, a naked bare back and the reason for everyone's focus. A woman lay on one corner of the unfurled blanket completely unclothed, covering her front with her right arm as best as she could.

Instead of her, Lucius pointed to the figure on the stairs and whispered to his friend, "It's *him. The Nazarene. Their messiah.*"

That very one, whom at least one of the Roman friends did not want to see, now panned the crowd with a warm half smile and eyes which seemed to welcome his listeners, the black robes, the two Romans behind them and the woman who was both prisoner and victim. She dropped her arm to expose herself to this teacher.

The Nazarene held his stare upon her as well as the rest. The woman said nothing. Then a black robe stepped out from the mob and shouted, "Rabbi, this woman was caught in the very act of adultery. The law according to Moses says because of her sin, she must be stoned but what say you?"

Marcus had also focused on the bronze, compromised body and at the angry words reached for his baton which had been lost back in the market. Fumbling for his sword hilt instead, he stepped forward as if to intervene. Lucius threw an arm across his stomach.

"Let this be, Centurion," he said. "That man is a Pharisee. He will have you up to Proconsul Pilate on interference in local affairs." Marcus halted.

Meanwhile, the Nazarene was writing in the thin layer of sand on the wide step in front of him, such large letters that even the centurions could read them upside down and from the back of the audience. The Greek letters read, "Where is the other sinful party in this? Why have you not brought him?" Lucius read it in low tones as if his friend were illiterate.

"Let him who is without sin be the first to throw," the Nazarene brought Lucius back to the long black hair and bare back in front.

Clunking sounds pounded below the mob as rocks thudded from their black robes and onto the street. Then one and another, a third, a fourth and finally several shawled men drifted away back down into the market where they had come from, leaving the crowd and the two centurions as the only onlookers for this spectacle. Its center of attention rose and snapped the cover off the pavement, wrapping the blanket around herself as if it were a gown for an elegant dinner.

"Woman," the Nazarene said to her. "Where are your accusers?"

The woman turned behind her, glanced around and said, "Nowhere, Rabbi."

Then he said, "Neither do I condemn you. Go your way. Use no one and let no one use you in a sinful way."

She tightened her wrap at her arm pit but looked up. Lucius was staring at her but her eyes were not on him. She was engulfing his friend with the longing eyes of a lover. Had she heard the words of the teacher or was there more than Lucius knew? She strolled away in the opposite direction but a perfume of cinnamon and cedar filled his nose.

The stairs of the Temple were also empty. The one, whom Lucius never wanted to see again, the one, who now haunted his nights and harassed his days, that "Messiah" was gone.

CHAPTER NINE:
THE THREAT OF ANOTHER EMPIRE
AND ITS FOLLOWERS

"The good person out of the good treasure of the heart produces good, and the evil person out of evil treasure produces evil…"
— Luke 6:45

They parted ways after both left the stairs of the Temple. Marcus had men to bury, one or two, maybe more, from the zealot attack—the slingers outside the city walls. Lucius now recalled dead bodies, being jostled by the soldiers in Marcus' patrol as he had surprised his old friend.

One stared up with eyes set but unclosed, his head swaying back and forth while the legionaries struggled to push through the shoppers, and the other soldier with a pebble-sized hole in his forehead from the stone which smashed into his skull. Dead men killed by another "messiah" for another empire. *Time to root them out,* Lucius thought, *all of them.*

But for present, he heard his cleated sandals scrape on the steps down to his quarters in the Antonia. He looked down and caught the heavy odor of burning oil from the torches leading to his doorway. Suddenly a smell of wine and cheese eclipsed it, and Lucius looked up into the face of a brown-haired nineteen-year old soldier still in his red tunic from morning patrol.

The legionary's face, flushed red from wine, went firm with a salute over his chest as he said, "Sir, we have a prisoner. From the Jewish zealots. We have gotten nothing from him. Would you prefer to interrogate?"

Lucius rubbed his eyes, glanced down and said, "Where is he?"

Their sandals tapped the stone floor down the hall; and Lucius following let his nose fill with body odor, cheese and wine from the men's quarters. There was something more, the stink of sweat and blood.

The centurion slipped off his red-plumed helmet but otherwise looked very much the commander back from his morning walk when he came through the door. Helmet or not, the men dropped plates and wine bowls on their cots and stood to salute.

A small group were in the center of the room and something—or someone—was behind them. A man, if you could call him that, knelt with head bowed, blood dripping red spots from his stringy hair onto the floor. Whatever the men had been trying to learn from him had been done through an extreme method of interrogation—a beating.

Lucius moved through the circle sniffing the source of their methods and wondering if the men had now involved their commander because of his rank or because of his healing skill. Often, they would come to Lucius with headaches and hangovers, flesh wounds and rashes. They brought slaves from the Fortress, their women, their whores, and one brought his "boys." Now they brought this—

"Zealot," a legionary from the circle said. "We chased him through the city last night. He nearly escaped."

"What makes you believe that he is a 'zealot?'" Lucius said.

"Sir, we believe that he travels with a leader called Theudas from across the Jordan, a tax-revolt leader who has been eluding us for months," a young voice said behind their centurion.

"Very well. Let me question him," Lucius said.

Two legionaries from the circle jerked the man to his wobbly feet. They scraped his sandals across the floor of the barracks smearing his blood behind him as it continued dripping from his hair and face. Lucius followed the entourage which hesitated, uncertain as to where to take him.

Lucius commanded, "To my quarters, legionaries."

The familiar leather scent of his camp stool and cot filled Lucius' nose, and he said, "Sit him there."

"On your cot, sir?" one legionary questioned.

"Yes," Lucius said. He did not wish to antagonize his men, but they had involved him, had they not?

The soldiers dropped their prisoner onto the bed with a thud like a heavy barrel thrown onto a dock. They stepped back but remained in their centurion's quarters as if they had something to guard.

Lucius removed his leather armor, dropped his helmet onto his bed above the man and threw his sword and belt over his camp stool. Kneeling down, he lifted a swollen face, felt around the prisoner's lip and right eye, then pressed on his bloodied head wound. The man winced.

A stoic appearance from Lucius did not betray his concern for the wounds which he had examined. He felt the zealot's chest and concluded from his groan: two broken ribs. The men had been thorough in their "methods."

While the legionaries watched, Lucius rose and crossed to a wooden cabinet. The small doors creaked open as he reached for some gauze, ointment and heavier bandages. Kneeling down, the centurion became a physician, poured ointment on the gauze as the air filled with the scent of aloes. He dabbed the gash at the man's eye, as well as his lip and head wounds.

"Sir, you should not be aiding the enemy like this," one of the soldiers protested.

Lucius agreed but something within him had aroused another *psyche*, another "soul," as the Greeks called it. Without turning, the physician in him said, "And what use will this prisoner be to us if he is too damaged to speak, or worse, if we kill him?"

Silence filled the room once more. Only the voice of Lucius broke it with a soft word to the prisoner, "So what is your name, Zealot? And who is your leader?"

The prisoner fumbled through swollen lips and said, "By—my b—bame—name is Simon. Though sombe in our community call be Simon the Zealot. I trab—travel with the Nazarene."

At the sound of this name, Lucius jerked back from the man's bloody cheek, but managed not to show his shock. His memory from the Temple stairs split open in his head as if a giant wave had crashed against a break wall at sea. This "messiah" was everywhere even when he was not here.

The centurion never turned to dismiss his men, but they turned and clicked their boots towards the door. One said to the other in a whisper, "We'll gain no information now. Our centurion is a *woman*. A coward."

Something deep inside of Lucius said, "You are a gifted healer. I am very proud of you." The legionaries were correct. It was a woman whom he was hearing, not a soldier. The scent of hay and a young fawn rose as he remembered the deer with the splinted leg and his mother's words from long ago.

A sigh exhaled from Lucius' mouth and nose, and he fell back on his knees staring at the bleeding soul who had dropped his head. It was not a fawn, but a man. Was Lucius a soldier or a "healer?"

Their "centurion" had better change his methods, at least his "soul," or he would lose his men's trust here in Palestine like his gambling had lost their respect in Illyricum.

CHAPTER TEN:
NEW ENEMIES AND A NEW PRISONER

"He said to them, 'But who do you say that I am?'"
— Luke 9:20

D ays of endless patrols passed like waiting for wine to age. The markets jammed with customers, the Temple filled with worshipers and Pharisees, and harlots harassed with their street walking, inviting his men to return when they finished their rounds. It all had the sameness of whitewash. If his men grew dull, Lucius grew duller, often missing details of a menacing glance from a dark-robed Jew near a vendor's stall or the hidden hands of a frayed-tunic on the street corner hiding something in the folds of his garment. But nothing happened.

They had released the prisoner Simon on "not enough evidence" to imprison him since the Nazarene was not Theudas or any of the other endless rebels railing against Roman power. Lucius strolled on, his men forming the usual thin red line ahead, silver helmets bobbing. Then there it was!

On the righthand street corner, where two perpendicular white stucco buildings met, a pointy cap popped up. The man was bearded, dressed in a longer tunic with a wide belt and a long *rhomphaia* dangling from it. This was a warrior or soldier, not a zealot, but a threat from some other "empire," perhaps to the East beyond the Euphrates.

As Lucius studied the "threat," his men, looking for closer problems, bounced ahead and ignored the "warrior." A group of ivory shawls shuffled in front of the stranger and blocked him, causing Lucius to raise up on his toes to see over them. The Pharisees passed and nothing! The pointy cap had vanished or had not even been there?

His patrol bobbled on through the last narrow street of market stalls. Aromas of leather sandals, wine skins hanging in the late morning sun and lamb roasting on stone grills mingled in Lucius' nose, then faded into burning wood. The smoke rose above the Jewish Temple walls—sacrifices to their god—invisible and non-threatening, or was he?

Shoppers diminished and the street widened out as they patrolled past the Temple wall. Up ahead, there it was again! A second pointy cap with a long brown and olive-green striped tunic, but with the same long sword on a wide belt. This one wore closed sandals as a warrior might use to ride. He scanned the crowd heading up the steps where the Nazarene had sat days earlier. Again, a small group of women stepped in front of him and blocked Lucius' view; the pointy cap descended behind them and disappeared. When the women turned to ascend the Temple steps, there was no one.

Who were these strangers? Spies? It seemed so to Lucius but they were not very covert if they were. Much like that threat from the

Nazarene being hailed as a "messiah" when he openly rode into the city a few days back. Should he alert the Proconsul?

No, Pontius Pilate was as squeamish as a lamb with a wolf ready to pounce on it. He was a governor caught between the Jews of this land and his Roman authorities who hated his lack of "competence."

He changed his mind as often as the desert winds. "The Gray Janus," the legionaries called him, because of his hair color and his two-faced approach to decisions, looking both ways to the locals and to the Emperor before he judged. Every *sicarii*, every zealot, every priest was not just accusing Rome; they were accusing *him*—Pilate himself, or so he thought.

The Nazarene was real but if the pointy caps were not, Pilate would blame the legion, the legionaries and their centurion, Lucius himself. Like Pilate, Lucius himself was caught between every leader, every empire and his own Roman one. Lucius was a "Janus" all his own.

The patrol and the phantom strangers from the street ended as always in the dim torches of the Fortress. He dismissed the men and found his door which welcomed him with its creak to the darkness of his quarters. He threw off his transverse-plumed head gear, sword and sword belt, and finally his leather armor.

His cot welcomed his bored but worried body as his eyes fell closed. He thought about a bowl of wine but did not need it. A deep sleep brought an eerie black escape.

Out from the dark appeared a shadow with no face except for a dusky light above. It had one of those! A pointy head, no, *cap*! The cap approached Lucius, but its countenance remained shadowed and its head covering extended down over its ears.

Then in the dim overhead lighting, Lucius discerned hair, long raven hair. The face, still shadowed, appeared to be a—a woman? But it transformed, blurring then sharpening into a bearded image, horrible with hair now stringy and dripping with sweat and cheeks bruised and bleeding.

Lucius himself was now raising his own hand with something in it, something which he could not see. He struck the face again and again. A roar of voices cascaded behind him saying, "Give it to him, sir! You're now one of us!" Lucius raised his arm once more and brought it down but then saw the face dimly lit from above.

Was it Simon the Zealot or his "messiah?"

He brought his arm down across the face with a thud. A thud banged his door and Lucius blinked, woke up and wondered where he was. Bang! Bang! Bang! He raised up on his elbows and looked toward the outline of his door lit by hall torches from the outside.

"Enter!" he shouted. The door creaked open and exposed the silhouette of a young blond man in a red tunic.

"Sir," the soldier said, saluting with an arm over his chest. "our later patrol has received another prisoner for our cohort to deal with. Orders directly from the Proconsul." Lucius recognized the voice of his decurion, his second in command.

He paused and thought about the pointy caps. He reached for his dream but nothing returned. Perhaps he did not need to report the street strangers to Pilate. Perhaps the Governor was already responding to the threat on his own.

CHAPTER ELEVEN:
JUST ANOTHER EXECUTION?

"So also when you see these things taking place,
you know that the kingdom of God is near."
— Luke 21:31

The arch opened out into the bright sun causing Lucius to squint as he marched into the courtyard outside the men's barracks. When he finally adjusted to the glare, he saw a man with stringy sweat-drenched long hair strapped to the flogging post. His face remained hidden but the hair stirred something from Lucius' memory. He pushed it aside as a legionary was pulling a robe from the prisoner's shoulders.

Lucius shoved a path through the catcalls of his men. "Give it to him!" "Dirty filthy Jew!" "We'll show you what happens to rebel kings!" The shouting rippled to an uneasy quiet as their centurion approached the front.

The prisoner's face stayed covered by his hair, and a legionary drew back the "cat," a short leather whip laced with iron barbs on each lash. Crack! The whip tore the exposed flesh from the bare back, but its victim simply jerked without a scream. Crack! Another lash spattered blood over the legionary and onto Lucius' sandals.

"Would ya' like some of this action, sir?" he said.

Lucius recognized him by his voice as much as by sight. He was the one who had called his commander "a woman" and "a coward." But what harassed Lucius more was the burning question: who was this prisoner? Simon...again? Or...a pointy cap, or some other zealot?

A soldier from the crowd shouted, "Let the Nazarene know what Rome thinks of his kingdom!"

The Nazarene? Lucius knew from *him* only healing, forgiveness for a whore and the gentleness of a zealot turned into one of his students. But rumors of another "kingdom" were also part of Jeshua ben Joseph's reputation. Lucius took the cat from the legionary and held it. His palm began to perspire.

Shouts roared up behind him: "Do it, Centurion!" "Let the dirty Jew have it!" "Stripe that back!" "See if the Jewish bastard bleeds like us!"

No, Lucius thought, *no kingdom but Caesar's.*

He drew back the cat. His arm flew as if he had let it swing forward on its own. He remembered: the dream had come back to him. But the lash ripped the bare back so hard that its skin and blood splattered him and the man beside him. The Nazarene now jerked, but did not scream.

Instead, inside Lucius, a voice screamed, "Damn these men! Damn this soldier's life! Damn Pilate! Damn Rome!"

And each time he heard a "damn," he brought the cat down harder across the Nazarene's back. All at once through the screaming in his mind and the catcalls of his men, it came: a whimpering, not around him but in front of him—from the Nazarene. The prisoner's back shook with sobbing. Lucius thought he heard words.

From the whipping post, the prisoner said, "Forgive this. Forgive them all."

Lucius paused his arm and panted. How could anyone "forgive" this? How could anyone accept this? But he shoved it aside. He thought, *Got to win the men over. Got to show them that their centurion is no coward, that there is no king but Caesar.*

Suddenly a hush rippled over the men and they came to attention. A shadow fell upon Lucius and he looked up at the square jaw, bronze face and plume of a Senior Centurion at his side. Marcus had come into the courtyard.

All Lucius could think to say was "Want some of this, Senior Centurion?"

Marcus batted the whip from his friend's hand, then said, "Enough! This sickens me."

A clunk banged in Lucius' ears as two legionaries dropped the *patibulum,* the crossbeam for crucifixion, between the two centurions and the Nazarene. After that, the voices and smells of bodies pushing and shoving each other eclipsed and overpowered Lucius, Marcus and the execution party snaking through the markets of Jerusalem toward Golgotha, a hill called "the Skull" by the locals.

The air became hot after they lost the shade of the city and climbed the rocky mound beyond Jerusalem's walls. Then everything stank with death and rotting flesh as their climb wound up to a level summit.

A rack for crossbeams already held two other victims, and the men laid the Nazarene down against his own *patibulum.* Lucius handed two spikes for the prisoner's wrists and feet to his Senior commander.

Marcus looked at them but did not take any, not at first. Regardless, Lucius began to pound one into the Nazarene's wrist, feeling a jerk but no scream from him. Then he stared down the crossbeam to his friend. Marcus was still hesitating.

He hesitated with the nail from Lucius. But trying to bring a blow down, his hammer glanced off and the Senior Centurion backed off like he was the one struck, not the Nazarene.

Watching the mistake, Lucius felt anger, not sympathy. After all, his friend had embarrassed him in front of the men, batting the cat from his hand. He yelled, "Let me do it!" Stepping over the outstretched body between them, he grabbed the hammer from Marcus, who was rocking back and away from the cringing hand of the Nazarene. *What is wrong with him?* Lucius thought and he did not mean the Nazarene.

When he gave a sharp blow to the spike, the prisoner jerked and this time yelped a little. Again, Lucius wondered what the man was made of just as he had wondered when they had striped him. But what puzzled him more was Marcus. Where in Hades was he? Gone.

Lucius scanned the men, the onlookers, some just cresting the hill, and the women who stood close to the rack. His men were lifting the prisoner into place between the two others. And still, Marcus was nowhere—but there!

He stood a little way down behind the crosses, talking to someone as if they had been on a casual stroll in a garden. The high pitch of a woman's voice made Lucius wonder if it could be—. It *was* the very whore whom the Nazarene had rescued earlier that week from her own execution. His friend was more interested in her than in what they had been ordered to do.

Only the deep low voice of another returned him to the summit. "Forgive them," it said. "Forgive them all," the Nazarene repeated. Ignoring this invitation, Lucius' body stiffened, his face reddened and he flung the hammer toward his friend, hoping it might hit him.

It fell short, barely bouncing against a nearby boulder, and rumbling. Rumbling? Thunder? The air changed from the rotting odor of death to garlic. Lightning was tearing a slate-gray sky in two. And a howling roared into Lucius from a rising wind. Rain was coming as a few large drops slapped his leather armor.

He fell and when he tried to stand, he stumbled again as if he were trying to balance himself in a wagon being jerked forward and backward at the same time. Earthquake! Everything shook and tilted.

The onlookers had ceased talking, and even the women near the base of the cross no longer sobbed but looked toward the Nazarene. They were jostling or falling. Some even dropped to their knees. Lucius blinked through the dust. This was "forgiveness?"

Suddenly something struck his foot and Lucius looked down then up. A drop of blood had fallen from the Nazarene. His head with a prickly crown on it had sunk into his chest, but all at once he raised his face with eyes wild and wide. He whispered in a loud croaking voice, "Finished!"

"Finished?" Lucius questioned to himself. Yes, it *was* "finished." His job here was "finished." He looked down and Marcus was ascending the hill away from the whore. His friendship was "finished." Nothing more was to be done.

Lucius looked back to the "messiah" on the cross and he was certainly "finished." So, scanning the hill, he wobbled up to his feet and did what the moment seemed to demand. Lucius "finished." He ran.

Let the men clean this up. They were eager for a kill. Let Pilate clean it up. He defended himself at all costs—even more than the empire. Let Marcus clean it up. He outranked him, always would.

Lucius stumbled back, back down Golgotha's rocks, back through Jerusalem's darkened streets, back to Fortress Antonia, back through the torches which gave its tunnels more of an eerie light than usual. He slammed the door of his quarters open, heard it bang against the wall, and shed his gear, all of it, dropping onto his cot and closing his eyes. At least, he had beat the rain with his retreat back to Antonia.

What he now remembered he dreamed. He saw the face of Simon the Zealot, blur into the bloody beaten face of the Nazarene. The words "Forgive them...forgive them...forgive them...forgive them" echoed over and over as if they were shouted from a deep well. He panned down to the base of a very high cross, an adder slithered around it and vanished.

Bang! Bang! Bang! What Lucius remembered more than the hill and its horrors, more than his dream, was the next hours and days. Bang! Bang! Bang!

A legionary did not even wait for his knock to be recognized but bolted through his door. Lucius propped up on his elbows, rubbed his eyes and thought, *Here comes some kind of cut about my escape from Golgotha.* But the silhouette of an armored and helmeted soldier even forgot to salute as he filled his centurion's doorway.

"Sir, we are ordered back out to the hill." he said, breathing as if he had been running.

"What? Why?" questioned his commander. "No, let the man die."

"He's dead, sir."

Lucius glanced down and then up. Thought to himself, *Already?*

"Pilate wants a guard posted," the blond decurion shouted coming in to his centurion behind the legionary.

"For a dead man?" Lucius said. He chuckled but inside he was saying, "That old Gray Janus is never satisfied."

The two thieves on the side crosses were squirming in pain. Lucius heard his decurion order the legionaries, "Just break their legs so they die faster."

Someone had died fast enough. The rancid smell of it cascaded down through the darkness, but in the twilight, the center *patibulum* held nothing, nothing but the ropes to lower the victim, nothing but the *titulus* above where the Nazarene's head had been. Pilate's words were on it, "This is the King of the Jews."

"Where is he?" Lucius said. "Where did you put the body?"

"A short way from here," a legionary said.

"Gets around for a dead man," Lucius commented on the soldier's words.

The soldier along with another led their centurion down the back side of Golgotha. They picked their way gently among the sharp stones, one scraping Lucius' calf. He could just barely make out the men in front of him as darkness was ending the day. Or had it ever left from the afternoon?

Up ahead in torch lights, Lucius saw several Jewish servants, some appearing to be women from the higher pitch of their sobbing.

The face of a gray-bearded man was about to order a bolder to be rolled across the cavernous opening of a black hole.

"Halt!" Lucius shouted still descending from the last of the rocks of Golgotha.

"Do you have the one who is called the Nazarene?"

"What remains of him," the gray-bearded man said squinting to examine the Roman who approached him with three other legionaries.

"Let me be certain of that," Lucius asserted. Why? He had never seen much of the man in life, how would he identify him in death?

He grabbed a torch from one of the servants. It hissed and crackled as he questioned, "In there?"

The gray-bearded man nodded towards the gaping hole in the side of another small rocky mound. Lucius plunged the torch into the opening and followed its lead. Thank the gods they had not covered the dead man entirely, at least not his face.

The set eyes, the ashen skin and the stringy hair made Lucius halt and stare. He inhaled as though he were breathing his own last breath. The beard and the dark hair all confirmed the Nazarene's identity.

Yet, Lucius nudged the lifeless shoulder nearest to him and pulled down a strip of burial cloth. The stripes on the back were full proof, no doubting who had given the man those wounds, at least some of them. This "messiah" was dead, but what about his kingdom?

Lucius' thoughts ran through his mind like the fast current of a raging river: *What kind of king had he executed? The words, "Forgive him" and "Forgive them all" rang inside him like a hammer striking an anvil. The sobbing at the whipping post was not from weakness and fear but sorrow for the attacks and the attackers. And finally, the pointy caps may or may not be real but if they were, how many more empires would challenge Rome and accost Lucius himself?*

"Sir, is it the Nazarene?" a legionary asked, bringing Lucius back.

The centurion was certain that his face was grayer than the dead man whom he had inspected. "Yes," he said, backing into the shadows and out of the torch light around him.

He turned and exited the entrance to the tomb. Outside he searched the mourners and found the gray-bearded Jewish elder who seemed to be in charge.

Lucius said, "And you are?"

"I am Joseph of Arimathea," the man said. "The Proconsul gave me—"

"Yes, yes," Lucius cut him off. "Just close it up."

The cover stone took four strong servants to move it even rolling downhill in the dimming torch light. Clunk! The sound of finality and death caused the sobbing women and the friends of Joseph to hush and stare.

Dead, Lucius concluded, except for one last assurance.

He stared at the rock and then said to Joseph, "We have our orders from Pilate as well, Pharisee. We are to stay and keep guard."

"Of course," Joseph agreed. "Do not want any grave robbers." He dropped his head and ushered his entire party away, leaving the Romans to whatever else had to be done.

Only one torch remained, making Lucius appear even more ghostly than the one who had just been buried. "We secure the tomb entrance," he ordered and then added, "No one sleeps tonight. No one!"

The soldier's hammers recalled his own at the crucifixion as Lucius watched his men pound iron spikes into the hard Judean earth. They lashed cords back and forth across the huge cover stone and pulled the ends around those spikes so taut that no one could snap them, not without a sound.

In his hands the wax bent and began to heat as Lucius took the torch flame and smeared a large mass at the "X" of the ropes. His hands stuck to the rock and he tore them from the waxy mass. Then from his satchel, he retrieved the seal of Proconsul Pilate. Rome would tolerate no disturbance at the grave of a rebel. He shoved the signet so deep into the wax that it scraped the rock beneath.

Handing the torch to his blond decurion, he said, "Light a fire. It will be a long night." His second-in-command saluted and abandoned his commander to darkness as he gathered the men and ignited a pile of brush and wood.

Like most days of military life, the next morning was a warm spring day which melted into a hot sun upon the tomb of a man who would never see it. The grave was so silent that Lucius heard bees buzzing among the flowers all the way back to the rocks of Golgotha.

The seal at the tomb remained untouched though when he inspected it, it grew soft from the heat of the rock behind it. Legionaries left as replacements relieved them to suffer the heat of the day, then the cool of the evening when the sun began to set. But Lucius never left, never gave the duty to his decurion or any other officer.

He remained, through the guard changes, through the bees buzzing and relinquishing their humming to crickets. He remained through the tedium and the monotony of time. He stayed as the second day melted into the glow of a red-orange sunset retreating behind the dark gray clouds of night. How many more days would be like this one?

He did not know but he did not rest, never slept, only roused the men every time one of them slid down to close their eyes in the cool darkness.

An insect buzzed in Lucius' ear as the cool breeze of another morning brought his hand up to his ear. His eyes blinked then squinted and blurred with the scene ahead.

Thank the gods, he thought, *is this a dream? Or are they still asleep...asleep as he had been, now defying his own order. Damn!*

But worse than this: the scene at the tomb caused him to shiver as he rose on what was a warm-turning-hot day. He could cover for his own disobedience rising before any of his legionaries, but nothing could excuse this!

Ropes were snapped like overfilled fish nets and strewn across the hard sand on either side of the opening. And the opening was open at the tomb! The seal was cracked, shattered like smashed pottery and the rock, which took four men to move the short distance downhill, was up hill! The black hole behind it stood as vacant as on the night when they had filled the grave; only it was more haunting. Lucius wanted to go there, go there before the men did—and yet not.

He rose so slowly that he was not sure that he was standing, but he was. The birds sang but with tweets sharper, shriller and more piercing than the previous two days. It was as if they had to sing a song ordered by someone else. The sun was warmer, too warm on his skin. It was not just another spring day. The air was sweet, as fragrant as his mother's garden back home in Tuscana.

Then it crashed in upon him: he had slept, his men had slept, but the Nazarene's men had not. If his "Followers," as the locals called them, had not rescued their "messiah" *from* death, they had rescued him *in* death.

Lucius grabbed his sword hilt to minimize its noise and stepped rapidly to the gaping hole of the grave. Suddenly, by instinct, his sword rang from its scabbard and he pulled out his baton, but looking back the men slept on. And as he crossed the threshold, he realized that he had no torch.

It did not matter. The inside had its own dusky twilight, a soft glow, not bright like outside but a glow like early dawn or a fading sunset. The aroma was not the stench of death or the acrid frankincense from anointing a corpse, but an even sweeter floral perfume than outside, like inhaling a stand of pomegranate blossoms in spring.

Lucius re-adjusted his eyes to the soft glow and gasped, gulping like a child horrified by darkness. On the burial platform was nothing! No body! No Nazarene! He looked to the floor and bent down feeling around. Still nothing. His body shivered and his hand jerked back from the cold floor.

As he rose to stand again, he realized that he was panting as if he had been fast marching. His breath came in short puffs which he could *see*—steam coming from his mouth. He had returned his sword to its case and when he reached for it, it stuck frozen in its scabbard. The cave had not been this cold two days ago when they buried the

Nazarene; and outside the day was warm, very warm; but the tomb was like an ice cave in winter back on his family farm in north Italia. The walls, the rock and the burial platform had a glistening light frost on them—like *another* place, but not this place.

Then Lucius saw the covers from the body of the Nazarene, folded neatly on the upper corner of the bier. The napkin which had been over his head was rolled as someone might have prepared it when they were ready to use it, not when they had already done so.

Grave robbers would not take the time to be so neat. They would throw the grave clothes aside or take them with the body.

What in Hades *was* this? The centurion shivered again, not just from the cold. He said to himself, "Who is this? Whose empire has he come from?"

"Pardon me, sir." a legionary's voice said behind him. It was the soldier who had called him "a coward." "Sir," he continued, "did his men steal his body?"

Lucius did not answer immediately. Then without turning, he shook his head and said, "I do not know."

"Sir," another voice now joined the first soldier. "I forgot to tell you. We received word from a messenger yesterday. Your father has died at your family villa in Tuscana.

Lucius stared straight ahead into the soft glow and the ice cold.

CHAPTER TWELVE:
COMFORT FROM A FRIEND

"When the Lord saw…he had compassion
…and said… 'Do not weep.'"
— Luke 7:13

T he letter on his table dampened his spirits more than the gloomy torch light in his quarters. Lucius opened the scroll again to make certain that the news was true.

To Lucius, Son of Horatius,
From Villa Maximus,
Your father passed to the Elysian Fields yesterday.

Lucius noticed the date. It was a month ago, maybe even longer. Letters took so long to arrive in this part of the Empire. The sound of his father's wailing at the death of his mother haunted him, and he began to cry. He read on:

We buried him with honor in the family crypt and mourned
your absence as well as his death. As chief steward, I will
manage the villa and farm for you. But sole ownership and
all final decisions pass to you as the heir of Master Horatius.
We look forward to your return as early as possible. May
Mars be your protector in every campaign.

From the hand of your loyal servant,

Demet—

A gentle knock interrupted his re-reading. Marcus entered and saluted as Lucius dropped the scroll on his leather bed table and returned the salute. He stood, rubbing his eyes so as not to reveal his tears.

"As you were, Centurion," Marcus said, sitting on a small camp stool and motioning his friend to do the same. "Know that all of us in the Cohort grieve the death of your father with you, Lucius. I understand that he was a loyal and brave Centurion like yourself."

"Yes," said Lucius, wondering when the reprimand would come about his retreat from Golgotha.

"I am grateful for the men—and for yourself," he added. Was he "grateful?"

Lucius moved his eyes to the torch behind the Senior Centurion so that Marcus might not see any hint of anger in them—or guilt. They knew each other from training outside Rome, from the action in Illyricum and finally from the posting here in Palestine. His friend was always skilled at knowing Lucius' moods. Yet, Marcus' sympathy might be his apology after abandoning the execution of the Nazarene for a conversation with the whore.

The Senior officer broke the silence between the two comrades. "The Proconsul sends his condolences for your loss. And—," he said.

"And what?" Lucius broke in.

Bang! Bang! A knock came at the door. A young legionary did not wait for either officer to recognize him. "Sir, we must make haste to the Proconsul at once," he insisted.

Without acknowledging the soldier outside, Marcus said, "Pilate orders you to his study immediately."

"For what matter?" Lucius' voice filled with anger which now he did not try to hide. *So, this was not a sympathetic visit,* as he suspected. His face lost its warmth if it ever had any.

"About the Nazarene, I believe," his commander said sounding official again.

So, Lucius' abandonment of his men at Golgotha was about to be "handled."

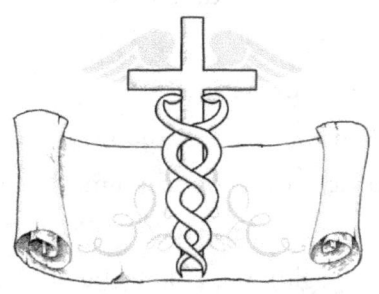

CHAPTER THIRTEEN:
LYING FOR PILATE AND OTHERS

"No prophet is accepted in the prophet's hometown."
— Luke 4:24

"**Y**ou will do as I order you, Centurion Lucius!" Pilate insisted.

Lucius looked down. He had arrived on the upper level of Fortress Antonia in the cramped study of the Proconsul, a writing table and some stools consuming most of the room amid its limestone walls. Pilate himself remained seated behind his desk.

Men in black robes with ivory shawls crowded on one side, and they allowed the two Jews in lighter robes, obviously priests from the Temple, to speak for them. On the opposite side of the table were the legionaries from the morning guard at the Nazarene's tomb. The "Gray Janus" was positioned between—fittingly, thought Lucius.

As centurion in charge, he had attempted "honesty," not embellishments in the questions from the Governor and the Jewish leaders. He explained, "Sirs, two nights ago the tomb was sealed and

68

untouched. Two mornings later—open. No body. But grave clothes so neatly folded that it looked like a corpse had never been there."

"Or taken!" one priest said, wiggling his finger at Lucius. The man smelled of wine. "That Galilean imposter claimed all sorts of powers including messiahship over our land. We have no king but Caesar!"

Lucius thought, *Are you certain?* Memories of gentle Simon as a "Zealot" flooded back into his mind. The scene of Centurion Sibelius' servant healed from a distance loomed up, along with the forgiveness for Marcus' whore at the Temple stairs and finally the ice cave which had been a tomb. His body shivered even in the stifling heat of Pilate's quarters. "Imposter" is not the word which Lucius would choose.

"I draw no conclusions about him nor his kingdom. I was present at his burial by one Joseph of Arimathea, and two mornings after I found nothing in the same tomb."

"Because his Followers removed it in the night," a second priest said. He now pounded a bag of coins on Pilate's desk that he had drawn from the folds of his robe. "Here," he added. "This is one thousand sesterces for you and your men, Centurion. Spread the obvious news of grave robbing throughout the city and we will all be satisfied. We cannot have his men saying that the Nazarene 'lives.'"

"Lives?" Lucius thought about that word. How? The man was dead when Joseph and his servants laid him in the tomb; Lucius had inspected the body carefully. No, what happened after *that* was not grave robbing. Lucius was certain of that.

Pilate now injected himself into the debate. "Centurion," he said. "Go and do as these leaders want. I command it, and I do not want any further troubles from you, from the people and definitely not from this Nazarene." The "Gray Janus" was as two-faced as always, taking the Jewish not the Roman position on this one.

"But—," Lucius tried to speak.

"No," Pilate concluded. "We are finished here."

Lucius thought to himself, *No, we are not finished. The men may take the bribe, not me.*

Lucius knew what had to be done. No more two-faced traps laid by the "Gray Janus," at least not for him and not for his men if he could help it. To quote the Nazarene, he was "finished" with Pilate, with Pilate's lies—maybe even the Empire which they served.

CHAPTER FOURTEEN:
FREEDOM FROM ONE EMPIRE

"So Pilate gave his verdict that their demand should be granted."
— Luke 23:24

It was damp and reeked of urine, feces and mustiness. The walls were dripping moisture and the floor was cold with the only covering at night being a single frayed woolen blanket which smelled like sweat. At the window were bars blocking the only daylight from above while the heavy door opposite that portal closed with a creak followed by a ferocious clunk. Lucius could not believe that he was *here, here* in Pilate's prison.

Pilate should have been here. His comrade, if you could now call him that, Marcus, should have been here. But here *he* was, perhaps where the Nazarene had been just weeks before. And that was not the worst of it.

Two worries haunted his thoughts: first, how did the Proconsul know about his plot? And the second was even more troubling: how did Marcus know about his plan and why did his friend betray him?

Lucius ran the whole affair through his mind over and over. After the priests offered the thousand sesterces to lie about the body of the Nazarene, he and his men took the money and left Pilate's study. Perhaps that act was his first mistake. From the beginning he and the men should have refused the deception and its the bribe.

Instead, Lucius ushered the two legionaries out onto the street, away from Pilate's study, their barracks, and the Fortress where everyone had "ears." For the first time, the centurion studied his men, boys really, not much younger than he was, age nineteen perhaps. Their heads barely filled their silver iron helmets.

"Listen to me, soldiers," Lucius said. "If we spread these lies for the Jewish leaders and Pilate does not defend us, it will be only a matter of time before the Nazarene's men catch up with us. We have already interrogated one Simon the Zealot from his men and others will follow, putting a quick knife to your bellies and mine."

At the sound of the Nazarene's name a man slowed his walk around the upper end of the Temple. While looking straight ahead, he appeared to lean it in their direction. Even the street had "ears." Lucius moved the men around and behind a brace of the Fortress, but another slave in a dark tunic wobbled with his bundle of wood and passed too near.

Lucius dropped his voice to a whisper and said, "The Nazarene's men might be far fewer than Rome's but they move in secret and they outmaneuver our might with their stealth."

Again, a man from the street appeared to alter his course toward the legionaries at the base of Antonia. He actually halted and feigned adjusting his head shawl. So, he might hear their conversation better? The street was no more secure than the Fortress.

"Janus," Lucius said to the soldier now shaded in front of him. "Follow me into the Fortress. You as well, Ludinus."

His sandals slapped down the stairs to the lower levels with the sound of two other pairs of boots behind him. Lucius shoved open the door of his quarters and motioned with his hand toward his cot. He surveyed the torch-lit corridor and waited to listen for chatter from the men's barracks. The silence and the vacant hallway were both a stroke of good fate. Everyone was out on patrol.

He closed the door gently behind him, the two soldiers still standing by his bed. "Sit," he ordered as he pulled up a stool for himself. Lucius slammed the bag of coins from the priests on his leather bed table as a thud followed with the jingling of the money.

"We are not spreading any rumors, legionaries," Lucius said, removing his helmet and tossing it onto a blanket on the floor. "It is time to end this drama with the one who truly must die and disappear—not the Nazarene, but the Proconsul."

The soldiers' eyes widened and they drew back into their helmets. Janus rubbed his hands and they began to perspire so he rubbed them again. Ludinus shuffled his feet scraping his cleated sandal boots across the floor.

"But sir, that is treason," he said.

"Yes, we can't even speak of it let alone act against the Governor," Janus said. "Besides, we have taken their bribe."

Footsteps grew close to the door, then they stopped and suddenly hurried toward the staircase. Lucius put his finger to his lips and stepped lightly to the back of his door. When he was certain no one was there, he turned back to the men.

"We took their bribe but not their lie. I do not want you dead in the alleys of Jerusalem because of a falsehood," Lucius said. "So, are you with me?"

The two legionaries looked at their commander as young school boys might gaze upon their teacher for protection. They shook their heads in agreement.

"Then here is what we will do," Lucius said.

They had arrived early in the judgment hall, before the Proconsul. The weeks since their initial planning brought others into the plot, at least two more. Lucius held a red cape, looked around the hall. Only Pilate's empty judgment seat was on the dais.

The centurion's hands sweated as he spread the "shroud" over the seat and backed to the left of it. The large doors to the public entrance were open but no servants had come in for the day and no one, not even passing soldiers, observed his deed.

Ludinus came in from the public hallway, followed by Janus. Two other legionaries entered from the left door on the platform and nodded to Lucius. He pointed to the latch at the middle of the side entrance and one of the soldiers threw it into the locked position. Then he joined Ludinus, Janus and the third legionary on the main floor below.

Lucius felt droplets trickling down his temples as a tingle began at his spine and stiffened in his neck. Janus nudged the right entrance door away from the wall and looked behind it. Then he disappeared into its shadow and created a rumbling sound from the back.

All at once, from the right-hand door of the platform a figure entered, not Pilate. It was Marcus! By all the gods, what was he doing here? He was not assigned to this public duty. But here he was, hesitating on the dais.

The righthand door swung open again and Pilate entered before Marcus could even acknowledge Lucius. The Proconsul looked ahead past the Senior Centurion to Lucius, then his eyes darted to the guards on the floor below.

The legionaries each held a *pilus*, not a sword, which Janus had pulled from behind the righthand door. Ludinus and Janus swung both public doors shut with a loud final clunk, and the latch scraped into place as Janus locked them.

Pilate pulled up his toga and positioned himself in front of the judgment seat but his eyes widened as he fixed upon the spears and the legionaries now aiming in his direction. "Now!" shouted Lucius. The men hesitated but finally released their weapons in unison as though they were in full combat.

When the spears whooshed through the hall, Marcus leaped towards the Proconsul, flattening him to the floor of the platform. Two spears banged into the judgment seat, burying themselves into the red drape and pinning it to the wood beneath. Two other weapons struck the wall beyond the chair and showered splinters and plaster down upon Pilate and Marcus as the other legionaries who were part of the plot hurled their weapons toward the dais.

Lucius paled with the horror at what these misses meant and as the righthand door to the dais slammed open again and a contingent of ten legionaries led by another transverse-plumed officer charged onto the platform.

Marcus extracted himself from the Proconsul and ran towards Lucius who was trapped by the latched door behind him. He drew his *gladius* on his friend and their swords rang one against the other.

From the corner of his eye, Lucius now caught the rescue squad, surrounding Ludinus, Janus and their two accomplices with swords drawn. They were outnumbered.

Lucius ordered, "Stand down, men." His soldiers dropped their swords and they rang against the stone floor. Their commander's sword followed as it clanged below the platform.

"So," Pilate said, as he adjusted his toga and sash back to some semblance of authority. "Centurion Lucius, you thought that you would send me to the Elysian Fields along with the Nazarene. But it is not so."

Pilate was panting now and trembling as though he had been in a severe cold. He shouted, "Remove Centurion Lucius and his plotters to prison, Centurion Sibelius! Put them in the same cell that held the Nazarene. We shall deal with them later."

Marcus showed no emotion as he passed Lucius to the sword of Sibelius; but at the name of the "Nazarene" Sibelius' eyes drooped as if it meant something just to him. He and three other legionaries marched Lucius and the four plotters out the righthand door off the dais.

Over his shoulder, Lucius heard Pilate say, "Kill me, would they? They will all feel the might of Caesar and Rome for their treason." The sound of ripping and the fluttering of a heavy cloth followed this indictment.

"They will not wrap me in that filthy funeral pall," Pilate shouted. The shroud had been removed from the judgment seat. But the pain of Marcus' betrayal remained in Lucius.

He worried about his men. Where were they held and how could he help them? Would Pilate torture them into a full confession of the entire scheme? Lucius' mind fretted with these results of his disastrous plot, and more.

Marcus may have been the footsteps which he had heard outside his door when he had talked with Janus and Ludinus in his quarters, or perhaps his friend turned betrayer listened in at some other time when the plotters enlisted the aid of the two others in the men's barracks. If only he had locked the door on the right side of the judgment seat.

No matter. No men. No friend. No empire, at least not Rome's. No, here he sat on the other side of it all, here in Pilate's prison. Whatever side that was.

Never had Lucius felt so hollow and empty like a dry well. The stern image of Father Horatius flew through his mind. At least, he would not bring shame on him or his family name—with—with this treason.

A rat scurried through the sun beam from the grated window above. He saw why the creature had run since the shiny scales of a slithering undulating black cylinder caught the same beam. A black snake had scared it.

CHAPTER FIFTEEN:
A NEW ACQUAINTANCE

"Blessed are you who weep now,
for you will laugh."
— Luke 6:21

Lucius scratched on the cell wall with a stone—one for each sunset which he saw as the day's light dimmed in the window above him. And the days rolled on one piling on another. A month melted away.

No torture came. No execution—not his at least. He was still uncertain about his men. Yet, the loneliness was torture enough, especially as the boredom of his isolation threatened to unhinge his thinking.

The cascading heat of summer from his window surrendered to a damp cold of gray winter when the light did not come—only clouds, and wind. It howled, and the sky closed into a slate darkness like the day when he had crucified the Nazarene. The lines of walls and floor snuffed out into an early night.

Lightning split the darkness with momentary flashes, followed by a rumbling that vibrated even the rocks around him. It rolled away like the drumbeat of a departing army on the march, and the jagged lightning repeated its rapid flares. So, Lucius was not certain that he saw it.

But he heard it. And he smelled it—a perfumed sweetness which held a twinge of aloe. Then he heard it once more. His cell door had creaked open and banged against the wall.

The huge guard for his cell filled the doorway, standing head and shoulders over Lucius because of his muscular arms and legs. His scruffy beard bobbed up and down his red tunic as he rolled something, or actually someone, with one arm in front of him, like an Olympian releasing a discus.

"There you go!" he bellowed. "Your fate to be put with the one who tried to kill the Governor. The lightning flashed and exposed a colorful robe which winced with an "awgh" as it struck the stone floor beyond Lucius who drew back and inhaled in fear.

Another bolt of lightning exposed a short but ghostly figure. The man stood, shaking off the dust of the floor, and straightened out his robe. As the guard bellowed a laugh and grabbed the door from the wall, he swung it shut with a clunk, Lucius was still uncertain if he was not dreaming.

The face which he saw was ruddy with a neatly trimmed gray beard. His hair was straggled and he shoved the tendrils back under his head shawl. The lightning flashed and sparkled the colors of his silken robe, stripes of red, green and purple under a silver head veil.

The stranger gasped when he discovered that he was not alone. He stood silent until the next flash revealed the bearded and emaciated face of Lucius.

"Allow me to make my introduction," the new prisoner said, bowing as if he were addressing a noble man. "I am Caduceus. Yes, yes, like the serpent-covered staff of Hermes or Aesculapius. I am physician to Herod Antipas. Or I was—" he broke off. "Never mind. And you are?"

Lucius did not respond, but fixed on the visitor's every word. He was still uncertain about whether the man was real. At least, his perfume filled the air and felt real enough.

"Lucius Maximus," Lucius said. "Formerly of the Italian Cohort, Centurion of the *Legio X Fretensis.*"

"Oh," Caduceus said. "A Roman in a Roman prison? And how did one such as you come to such a demise?"

Lucius did not want to share his story of the Nazarene, nor the plot against Pilate, nor anything else.

"And who are you that I should reveal myself?" he said.

A huge flash lit the cell and exposed the two of them opposite each other. A rattling rumble shook the rocks in the walls and the loud whisper of rain splashed a small stream below the window.

The stranger seemed more willing to speak than Lucius was. Although Lucius knew that Marcus and his men often called him "the Mouth" behind his back, isolation had blunted this trait. So did the specter of a stranger in the lightning around him.

"As I have told you, my name is like that of the staffs of the gods Hermes and Aesculapius, depending on which you prefer, though I profess belief in neither of those imposters."

The little man paused, adjusted his silver head covering and added, "Of course, I am Greek, Egyptian and a bit Jewish on mother's side certainly. I have been educated in the medicinal arts at the great school of Alexandria."

Again, he stopped as if waiting for some question from Lucius, then said, "And that is how my troubles came to be. I served in the court of the proconsul of Egypt. When he traveled here to Palestine, the great Herod learned of me—"

"Hey, ya' keep it down in there!" the huge guard bellowed banging on the cell door. "We're tryin' to sleep out here. But not all o' us so don't go plannin' to escape. Ha! Ha! Ha!" the laughter and his words trailed off as he strolled away.

Caduceus lowered his voice just above a harsh whisper, "Herod Antipas wanted me for his court physician. I was that skilled. But then I failed to relieve his aching stomach and his pounding head."

He paused and appeared to be waiting for his Roman cell mate to react. Lucius remained in fixed silence, but revealing no emotion.

"I attempted to work every cure," Caduceus continued. "But that was my sin. I merely worked to cure the king, not to heal his Excellency. Every elixir, every herb, which I poured down his throat, aggravated his symptoms. If only I had known—" He broke off, staring into the light flashes illuminating the gaunt wreck of a man in front of him. The rain was now diminishing to a tapping on the window ledge above.

Caduceus spoke in such a low tone that it either bordered on fear of the guard—or perhaps a reverence for something else. He said, "If only I had been a physician in the manner of the one whom I now serve. Believe me, *there* was a healer—for the blind, the lame, demons. Every remedy gushed from him like a spring bursting forth from a desert. Evil, sickness, demons, even death ran from him as a legion before a thousand Parthian warriors."

The stranger stopped suddenly and looked up, realizing his audience. He chuckled and said, "Oh, my apologies, Roman."

Lucius did not show offense at Caduceus' humor since he was wondering more about the "healer" who had so fascinated this physician. Instead, Lucius emerged from the shadows of his side of the cell into the new moonlight flickering in and out of the clouds as they dispersed from the passing storm.

"Who has such power to subdue every disease and demon?" he asked the stranger.

"You have not seen him then?" Caduceus continued whispering.

Lucius repeated, "Who?" He knew that he spoke too loudly.

The latch clanked at the cell door and the heavy portal creaked open in an endless screech. It banged against the wall.

"That's it then. Do I need to teach the pair of you 'ow to lower them voices of yours?" the huge guard said, legs apart and hands on his hips.

"No, legionary, we were just sharing how fortunate we are to be granted another night of life in Pilate's prison," Lucius said. He knew how inflated the pride was in these prison guards.

"We will now sleep and let you do the same."

The guard said, "Humph!" His hands left his sides and he spun around grabbing the door with his right hand, screeching it shut with a thud and a shaking that matched the earlier thunder.

"Who?" Lucius whispered again to the physician. "Aesculapius? My mother dedicated me to him when I was a mere boy."

"Noooo…" Caduceus drew out his rebuff. "Have you not heard of the one called the Nazarene?"

Lucius hoped that his face did not reveal his shock. He looked beyond the stranger to a silver black snake slithering into the shadows near the door and vanishing. Then he said, "Tell me more about you—and about *him*. What has become of him?"

CHAPTER SIXTEEN:
THE DIFFERENCE BETWEEN CURING AND HEALING

"Now there was a woman who had been suffering
from hemorrhages for twelve years; and though she had spent
all she had on physicians, no one could cure her."

— Luke 8:43

"I will not tell you about him but you will dwell in his kingdom," Caduceus said. He spun around until his robe blurred into one continuous color like a child's top, and he chuckled with the sides of his silver head covering flying out from his shoulders.

For Lucius this only meant one thing—rescue. Herod would not allow his best physician to sit in Pilate's prison. He might even use the Nazarene's men to launch an escape. So certain was Lucius of the possibility that he quit scratching lines on the prison wall. This hell would end soon so why count the days, weeks and months?

Days came and went and with them entire months, or so it seemed. At least, the wait was not boring since the isolation had ended. The time filled with "patients" for the "doctor." Each entry was almost the same. The cell door banged to one side, two smaller guards would enter with some "case" and the large guard would direct them to Caduceus.

First, they carried in a man, if you could call him that, since the face and arms were barely attached to his body. His odor preceded him and overwhelmed Lucius' nose even as he sat across the cell in its shadows. The flesh on the poor victim's body was being eaten away in large sores and boils. "Leprosy," Caduceus pronounced. "Best throw away the rags which you used to drag him here."

The guards dropped him to the floor along with their own rags and covered their noses in retreat. Before the large guard left, Caduceus said, "I will need my satchel." The huge guard grumbled something to his subordinates and one brought back a leather bag, dangling it toward the physician while still covering his nose.

After the door slammed, Lucius could hardly believe that Caduceus touched the man's arms and hands so freely. He must have known that lepers were "unclean" and untouchable.

Then the patient looked up into Lucius' eyes and the centurion gasped. The man had no nose and his eyes were sunken into their sockets, but the face made Lucius gasp for another reason—the beard and straggling hair were those of someone whom the centurion knew from a recent execution. Could it be?

"Guard!" Caduceus shouted. He had only poured aloes and a creamy ointment on the patient's sores, nothing else. The door swung open and the guards took their time protecting their hands from the arms and legs which they now grabbed to carry the poor leper out.

When they disappeared into the shadows of the hall, the large guard shoved a small form into the cell. A lame boy bounced ahead, steadied on a makeshift wooden crutch. Lucius wondered, *What is a child doing in prison?* "See what ya' can do for the likes of this one," the guard said as he grabbed the door and pivoted it closed with a bang.

"Come, little one," the physician beckoned. "Let me examine your leg there."

Again, Lucius thought, *Why not give his place to an able-bodied man? A crippled boy cannot do much for anyone.* A memory of the one from Illyricum loomed up, the one he had marched over.

Caduceus touched his calf and felt all the way up to his hip. From his satchel, he pulled a leather strap and two short sticks and wrapped the straps around the curved shape in the boy's leg. Then taking a knife, he cut some length from the crutch.

"You are very caring to a child," the boy said and Lucius noticed a drop fall from the little one's eye.

"It is a privilege to serve you," Caduceus said as if he had just helped King Herod himself. "Guard!" the physician called and the patient disappeared.

But the parade did not stop. Instead, two smaller guards brought in a man whose eyes were glassy and milky—obviously blind. After pouring some ointment in each eye, Caduceus had him removed, and a man with a hacking cough entered. He was spewing up blood and spitting it across the floor. The physician called for another satchel and poured a liquid down the man's throat that smelled like pine oil. Next came a paralytic dragged in by two others and one of the guards. After a brief stay, he was followed by a legionary in only his red tunic with sweat so bad he must have been consumed with a high fever. When the guards pulled him out, Lucius thought, *Enough of the sick and dying. Where is our rescue?*

The door swung open and no one was there, not at first. Lucius began to raise up, believing that this was the moment and he must be prepared to go. Instead, the guards appeared arm-in-arm with a prisoner who had blood running down his face and arms, his head drooping deep into his chest. The huge guard filled the door behind them.

"Just fix him well enough so we can crucify him tomorrow," he said. The guards dropped the victim onto the stone floor like a sack of grain on a loading platform and he groaned. Then the soldiers all turned their backs and walked out, slamming the door with its usual clunk.

Lucius rocked back into the shadows and watched Caduceus as he rolled the patient over, listening to his shallow breaths. He moved an ear to his mouth and nose, feeling with his hand around the man's ribs. The fellow groaned like a sick cow.

"Broken," Caduceus concluded. "More dead than alive," he said to himself as he crawled to his satchel, retrieved some rags and bound them around the man's chest. The physician went back and pulled out a small jar, unstopping the top and pouring its contents onto another cloth. The cell smelled of mint. Dabbing around his eyes and arm wounds, Caduceus worked on every wound.

The patient opened his eyes and said, "Why do you do this? They will kill me tomorrow. I am a Samaritan and a rebel." Lucius was thinking the same.

Caduceus said, "You are a child of God. Our Lord and King, the Nazarene, welcomed one like you into his very kingdom when he was dying on his own cross. I now do the same for you."

The man, who had been shivering, relaxed as Caduceus held him in his lap like a mother might hold her ailing child. The labored breathing became more even and he stretched out his arms. Lucius let the calm of the man touch him as if he were watching a Greek tragedy, the light engulfing both the patient and the doctor from above. He forgot about a "rescue."

Bang! Bang! Bang! The large guard pounded on the door and bellowed, "Are you finished, physician? We have others."

"Give me a little longer with this one," Caduceus said. Then looking into the man's face, he promised, "The Nazarene will receive you into his kingdom—his Paradise, as he calls it—if you want that. Even tomorrow he will make you live as he lives."

Lucius halted and his meditating on the doctor and patient exploded with the words, "as he lives." Suddenly it flooded in from all of the patients in all of the days; Caduceus always spoke of the Nazarene as if he was still here.

The guard pounded again and shouted, "You are done. We have brought many over these last days. We have two more."

Last days? How many days had it been? It seemed like all of these patients had come on the same day, or had they?

There was no time to count as the door unlatched again and swung back banging off the wall. The two guards jerked the man off Caduceus' lap and slid him out the door while the large guard stepped into the shadows of the dusky light of evening and two figures hurried by him into in the cell. Whether it was the same evening which had begun with the leper, Lucius could not say.

Yet, the next patients were unbelievable: what were they doing in a hole like this? A woman, older and dressed in a dark brown robe with a black head veil guided a bent-over younger woman in gray robe and maroon headpiece. By the size of the younger's stomach, she was very pregnant, or was she? Why would a pregnant woman be *here?*

Lucius thought of the woman killed in Illyricum and did not think that she deserved the services of a physician. Nor did this woman. A midwife could deliver her child unless she had some other malady.

Caduceus guided the pair to the fading light in the center of the room as the door swung shut with its customary slam. The woman in gray jerked up and Caduceus felt around her stomach. He looked at the older woman and said, "Not long."

Motioning to them both to sit, the physician said, "Our Lord, the Nazarene was born in a cave without midwife or physician. So, a prison may be a better birth place for your sister."

At these words, Lucius remained in the shadows, but a wave of cold rose from his waist, up his back to his head. When he exhaled, steam came from his mouth, as it had at the vacant tomb of the Nazarene. It was not because of the cold stone wall at his back.

The women and Caduceus did not even notice the other prisoner in the cell and what was occurring with him. After chatting so softly that Lucius could not hear them, the older woman and the physician wobbled the pregnant patient to her knees, then to her feet. She shuffled on the arm of her sister to the door, and the older woman knocked for the guard.

They stepped out into the shadowed hallway and the door closed more softly this time. Caduceus searched for a pair of sparkling eyes from his cellmate. He approached Lucius and said, "So what do you think from what you have seen these last months?"

Months? The centurion hoped his shock did not show as he tried to decipher what had happened in what felt like a day, not more. Then he whispered what was truly on his mind, "Where is our rescue from this torment? Where is the kingdom that you promised?"

"My good boy," Caduceus said, "you have lived it. It has been all around you these last weeks." He gestured wide with his arms and with his robe fluttering out from his sides.

Then he added, "The Nazarene's Kingdom is here. He has told us that the least, the lowly and the hurting *are* his kingdom. It is they who rescue us from the powerful and the unjust when we receive them in him. Tomorrow you will be rescued even more when you, not I, will do his healing."

Lucius now pulled his emaciated body into the dim light of a rising moon and said, "I was waiting for his rescue, not further burdens and torments. I am a soldier, not a doctor. I cannot cure the likes of these as you have done."

"Again, my son, you have not seen much saving from sickness and death these last weeks. My work has been mostly curing, well, with the exception of the Samaritan, perhaps, and the last woman. I have not healed as you will now do. Soldier, ha! Your mother dedicated you to Aesculapius, did she not? You will do greater works than I have even with all of the secrets of Alexandria which I possess."

A guard knocked on the door with a low recurrent thumping. He did not reprimand, did not need to; and when he stopped, his steps tapered off down the hall and away. The two cellmates knew that evening had come and quiet was to be kept.

Lucius lowered his voice to a whisper in the darkness, "I cannot do this," he repeated.

From the darkness near the door, the physician's raspy voice said, "Tomorrow."

The moonlight from above shimmered on an undulating body of silvery scales as a snake slid into the shadows beyond Caduceus.

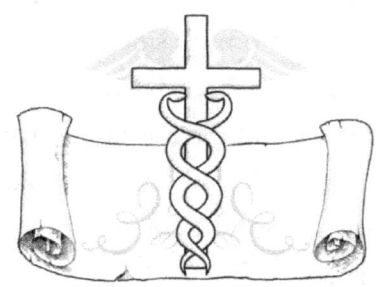

CHAPTER SEVENTEEN:
GREAT AND BELOVED WHAT?

"Fear seized all of them; and they glorified God, saying,
'A great prophet has risen among us!...'"
— Luke 7:16

Lucius turned the words of Caduceus over and over in his mind as he awakened, "Tomorrow you, not I, will do the Nazarene's healing." Just because his mother had interrupted his father's destiny for him, did not mean he would be anything but a soldier. Ah…but then Demetrius had told him the worst secret of all: his father had become a healer for his mother.

His mind was deceiving him. Prison life, the long days of isolation, the arrival of a madman were all driving him to insanity—.

The latch on the door interrupted with a clunk as the big guard swung the door around and shoved a gaunt man in rags into the dawn light of the cell. "Here ya' go," he thundered. "First one." He spun back around and exited with the swinging bang of the door.

The man stood there shaking like a wet dog as Caduceus, not Lucius, said, "Friend, are you hurting anywhere?"

With a face fissured from dehydration, the fellow croaked, "I am terrible weak, and I cough blood all day…" He could not finish but began barking like a dog with a series of coughs until he choked.

Over his shoulder, Caduceus said toward Lucius, "Now, physician, what will you do with this poor victim."

Lucius felt a shiver run through him and said, "I-I will relieve his cough. I will try to increase his rations. Rest. Rest. He must rest." All of this he spoke to Caduceus as if the man were not there.

"Yes, but what does this poor soul *need?*" Caduceus said still examining the man. "You have not yet asked *him* or examined him for yourself."

"I need to rest and sleep," the patient croaked. "My cough comes and goes."

"Oh," Lucius said.

A hard knock broke off the instruction as it pounded on the door. "We have others," the huge guard roared. "Get on with it."

"I need more time," Lucius shouted back.

"But you will not have more time," Caduceus criticized. "Other patients with other needs will come and press in upon you. They, not prison guards, will demand immediate assistance."

The door unbolted and the large guard stomped into the cell, his two fellow soldiers blocking the entrance behind him. He jerked the gaunt man up with one arm and said, "Time to go."

Caduceus intervened, saying, "Here now, let him take this with him." He handed the man a vile of some liquid as the big soldier yanked the croaking fellow out.

Behind them one of the smaller guards pulled another man into the room, or rather limped him in. Lucius observed that he was very lame. The guard shrugged and exited, slamming the door behind him.

The bald patient hopped and banged, hopped and banged on his makeshift crutch. Lucius helped him to the floor and stretched out his lifeless left limb. The man groaned and looked beyond his examiner to Caduceus.

"Kindly let him, not you, assist me," he said, preferring the true physician as Lucius now thought.

Afterwards the rest of the parade of patients continued with the same results. Another man with a broken leg dragged in on two bent wooden crutches. Lucius applied splints to his injury but made them too loose. The fellow rose, wobbled, lost balance and shouted "Awg!" He fell forward with Caduceus catching him before he hit the stone floor.

When Lucius re-positioned the splints and tightened the bindings, the man's foot turned blue. The physician teacher's silver head covering shook a "No" in obvious disbelief.

Then followed a man and a boy with horrible rashes on their arms. Lucius pulled Caduceus' bag over and retrieved a lotion that smelled like frankincense, poured its contents on their limbs and the pair howled, "It stings!"

On it went. Sores were not relieved, coughs were not silenced, headaches continued to pound. Worse yet, a rage rose up Lucius' back and reddened his face.

"It is enough, my son," the teacher physician said, putting a hand on his student's tightening shoulders. "We will try tomorrow."

The guards knocked and handed each prisoner the evening meal of moldy cheese, stale bread and sour wine. It was then that Lucius paused and sucked in a quick breath. He spotted it for the first time.

Caduceus never diminished, never grew thinner, never became emaciated as Lucius had. If months had passed on this meager fare, why had the stranger continued to remain untouched by the lack of food?

Lucius also noticed that his teacher did not even consume the entire meal. From the chunk of moldy cheese, he broke off the outside green decay.

Lucius said, "Why do you do that?"

"I save it as an application for wounds," Caduceus answered. "It makes them close up faster."

The student felt his stomach churn, not from the bad food nor from the stranger's behavior but from the disasters which *he* had inflicted on so many. He wanted to shout, "I am no healer!" but there was now snoring rippling across the cell as the room fell into the dusky light with the approaching night. Caduceus was already asleep.

Lucius wondered, *Will my talent for medicine ever improve? It cannot become any worse.*

Time passed or stood still. Which way it was Lucius could not be certain. Was only a day gone or perhaps it had been a month? Yet, nothing changed: every patient was sicker than the last, needing more from him—from them. The student doctor felt worse than the people whom the guards brought in. And his teacher always had to interrupt, offering some other lotion, or powder, or syrup, or wine.

"Perhaps I am not what my mother intended—" Lucius broke off his excuse.

The guards were pounding hard and rapidly on the door. A shriek like a harpy from Hades exploded in the hallway. The cell door swung open.

The woman in the dark robe with the brown head shawl from before led her sister, bent over completely, through the entrance. "She is back!" Caduceus shouted with excitement. "And ready!" "Ready?" Lucius questioned.

Before his teacher could answer, the young pregnant woman howled again and tumbled to the cold floor nearly dragging her sister with her. The guards formed a barrier at the open door and stared.

"Sirs, some privacy," Caduceus ordered. "Kindly dismiss yourselves."

The men shuffled out, the door banged shut, but Lucius wanted to join them. Instead, his teacher shoved him toward the women.

"Now," Caduceus said, "We will observe what you have learned, physician! We are about to bring new life from the Lord." He snapped Lucius' blanket from the far side of the cell, motioned to the older woman and together they rolled the pregnant patient onto it.

"Noooo," Lucius shouted. It was too late. Blood, fluid and "new life" was pouring out of the younger woman. At first, Caduceus was at her legs, but then he turned to his student and said, "You do this."

Lucius' face went pale and dropped as he raised both hands in a sign of refusal. "Not me," he protested. "I know nothing of women's ways."

The pregnant woman was now pushing hard as Caduceus grabbed his student's tunic and yanked him down between her knees. "Talk to her," he ordered. "Speak to her about what is happening, son."

At once a baby slid out on to Lucius' blanket with all of its red bloody smell of life. Her sister shouted, "You have a son, my beloved." Caduceus thrusted a knife into Lucius' hand.

"Cut the cord," he said. "Then make certain that the mother is fine."

The older woman cradled the infant into her dark robe and took it to a bucket of cold water, which Lucius did not notice that they had. The newborn squealed and cried as the mother insisted, "Let me see m' baby." Her sister brought the child back clean and still whimpering and placed it in the younger woman's arms.

The cell door whooshed over all of them with a quick wind and banged against the wall as all of the guards stormed in. The huge guard was behind the other two and he was dragging his left leg, blood spurting from it and something silver and metallic protruding from the calf.

"Aahg!" the large soldier cried. "Get her out of here," he bellowed. "Get them all out of here!"

Caduceus and the older woman let the mother remain on Lucius' blanket, handing the corners to the smaller guards who dragged her into the hallway. Her sister scurried out behind them like the rat which Lucius had seen his first day in prison.

The huge guard roared, "That dirty zealot stabbed me and I killed him." He looked around at Caduceus and Lucius and shouted, "I should run you all through!"

Then he wrapped his hand around the silver end sticking from his calf and jerked it out with a scream which would have deafened even the baby who had just been born. Blood shot out sprinkling Lucius and the floor.

With wide horror-filled eyes, he boomed, "If you're a doctor, stop this!" He flailed around and the sharp silver blade slashed the cheek of Lucius who grabbed for his face and shrieked "Aww!" blood running down to his chin. Seeing the guard off balance, and the other two guards still gone, he bent down, charged and head-butted the big fellow onto the floor.

For an instant, Lucius did not look for Caduceus, He did not think about healing or medicine or the Nazarene, except that the moment had come. He was certain that "the rescue," which the Nazarene would bring, was about to unfold.

The guard looked up from the floor, blood still streaming from his leg with Lucius now above him. Both of their eyes widened.

"I know what you need," Lucius said. He paused. Then he kicked the bloody knife to the shadows at the back of his cell.

"Enemy or not, I know what you need," Lucius repeated. "Lie still, or you will bleed to death here in my cell."

The huge man puffed hard, a groan following each breath; but he did not swing at Lucius and dropped his head back to the floor. The centurion, now turned physician, dropped to his knees and shoved the "patient" over on his right side, applying pressure to the slice in his leg.

"Caduceus," he said, "do you have staples in your bags?" His teacher shook his head "yes."

Lucius said, "Good. Give me all that you have and plenty of bandages as well."

Caduceus smiled and dragged both of his satchels to his replacement and his patient. He handed each staple to Lucius, who pushed them in around the wound one at a time. As the man continued to whimper, Lucius said to the huge guard, "The worst is over now." He pulled white bandages from Caduceus' bags and unrolled them, wrapping them over the wound and staples, layer upon layer.

The guard relaxed his breathing, then grabbed his "physician" by the arm, but not in a manner to harm him. Rather he said, "You could have escaped and let me die. You could have hated me and yet you have healed me. You *are* truly a great and beloved physician— blessed by God."

Caduceus was up and spinning his robe into a blur of colors, practically singing, "My son, you are no longer a soldier. Your work is greater than mine. You are a healer in the kingdom of the Nazarene."

Lucius looked down at the blood on the floor flowing towards the door. The black snake slithered through it becoming just as red as the blood and heading toward the shadows.

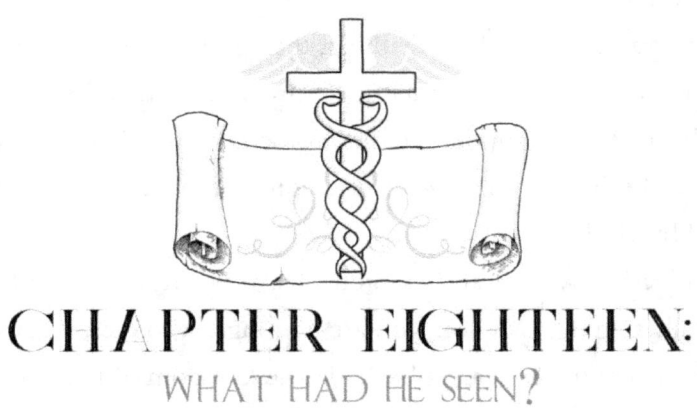

CHAPTER EIGHTEEN:
WHAT HAD HE SEEN?

"The Spirit of the Lord is upon me,
because he has anointed me
to bring good news to the poor."
— Luke 4:18

Lucius blinked at the dim morning light from the window above as it outlined shapes and objects in his cell. The cold slab beneath him reminded him that he had no blanket. He focused forward towards the door and listened to—nothing. There was no snoring, no breathing from anyone but him.

He strained his eyes once more toward the door and sniffed the air. It held the same mustiness as always. No blood. No perfume. No odors of birth or anything else. He focused on the shadows.

Then he whispered, "Caduceus?" Nothing.

"Caduceus?" he searched again. The stranger was not there. No silver head covering. No striped robe. No bag of medicines. Perhaps the guards had removed him last evening after——. But his blankets were not there by the door. It was as if——.

Lucius broke his own thought and sprang to the door, pounding on it again and again. No response came. He banged once more. "What d' ya' want?" the voice of the huge guard roared in contrast to his softer tone last night. *Maybe he does not want to show weakness to his men.*

"I said, what d' ya' want, prisoner?" the guard roared and grew louder than before.

Suddenly the bolt screeched back and clunked, and the cell door whooshed wide with its customary bang against the wall. Two guards charged in with their large bearded commander following.

Lucius did not look up but down toward the large man's leg, his left leg. He did not limp, did not show any sign of a wound and there were no bandages. His large frame stomped on the slab floor behind his men, unhindered as it always had been.

Looking between the first two soldiers, Lucius addressed their commander. "What have you done with the prisoner Caduceus? Herod's physician? Where is he?" he said.

"Who?" the angry big man said. "There is no one here but you. And ya' alone. Remember that," he said, his beard bobbing with each word.

"No, he *was* here. You brought us the sick from every cell in the prison," Lucius insisted.

The huge guard roared with a laugh which jiggled his stomach. "Ha! Ha! Ha! Yes, I am running a temple to Aesculapius here—a healing sanctuary. That will be a story for the Proconsul."

Lucius looked down then up, his eyes drooping and his face contorting all at the same time. He wanted to leap at the man, but with the passage of time and lack of food, he knew that he no longer had the strength for an attack. Only silence followed.

It was broken by the big guard saying, "I dunno who ya' think's been here but there has been no one 'cept you in this cell. No Caduceus. No patients. No other prisoners. No one, ya' hear me, no one these last years."

Years? Lucius knew for certain now that this demon of isolation had deceived him There had been no Caduceus, no patients and no "healing" of this large bully who now mocked him. Was the whole dream just a dream or had it truly occurred? The pain of his loneliness crushed in upon him worse than all the ridicule which he had just endured.

"Guards, about face," the commander ordered. He turned and they turned, stomping out, the door swinging shut with what felt like a final bang.

Lucius turned to the back wall and saw his scratches on the stones. They tapered off. He had forgotten to keep the tally. Reaching up to rub his emaciated cheek, he suddenly felt a scab and a light sting.

Yes! A slash was there where he had received it recently from the feel of it. In the shadows of his cell, he heard a familiar voice, the tone and words were his teacher's, as Caduceus said, "You must rise above your pain. Let your pain become your passion from now on. But remember this, my son, if you do not know that you need to be healed, you cannot heal."

A pounding came at the door. The big guard bellowed, "Tomorrow two more will join ya'. I don't think either is named Caduceus. Ha! Ha! Ha!"

CHAPTER NINETEEN:
AT LAST, FELLOW PRISONERS

"...your faith has made you well;
go in peace."
— Luke 8:48

The day began where it had ended the night before, not with his guard's taunts, but rather with questions now haunting Lucius because of that taunting. These doubts flew at him like bats swarming from a cave: had he truly been here for years, not days or weeks? Had Caduceus been a mere dream? And the worst, was he going mad from the isolation?

Before he could know any answers, a bang pounded against the door. "Get back!" the big guard shouted. The latch clanked and screeched in its chamber, and the door creaked open and slammed against the cell wall.

The two shorter guards pushed two men, bound at the wrists, into the center of the morning light from above. The first was an older fellow with a longish gray beard and disheveled graying dark hair. His eyes were kindly and sparkling. His garments were a long robe of brown, tightened at the waist with a leather belt like a workman might wear to draw up his clothing. His sandals were frayed and had seen some walking perhaps from prolonged journeys.

The guard shoved him forward and untied his hands which he now rubbed from the soreness of his bindings.

Behind was a younger face with a clean-shaven beard, and hair tossed about his head like wind-blown shrubbery. His robe was gray and frayed and his sandals also bore the worn straps of long journeys. He glanced beyond his companion at Lucius who noticed that the younger man's eyes were deep-set and bore a worried look.

The second guard unbound the younger man and leaned around toward Lucius, saying, "Here are your new cell mates. More real than the others you've been telling us about."

Both men squinted at the light, attempting to adjust to their surroundings. The guards turned, stomped out and swung the door shut with its creaking latch and customary thud, as their sandals grew softer with each step down the hall.

When they were gone, the older fellow moved toward Lucius and said, "My name is Petros, though some call me Simon. I am a fisherman by trade but now I fish for men."

His companion stayed behind him and said nothing so Petros added, "This is Johannus. He is also a Follower."

The word "Follower" caused Lucius to sit up and then crawl into the dim morning light. He was uncertain whether his mind was not tricking him again so he remained silent.

"Friend," Petros said, "how long have you been here?"

At last, Lucius said, "Too long."

Petros said, "Who are you and where are you from?"

Caduceus had fooled him before so again, Lucius did not want to answer. But his loneliness overwhelmed his caution and he blurted out, "My name is Lucius Maximus, formerly of the Italian Cohort."

The older man said, "Oh, a Roman from the garrison here in Jerusalem. A Roman in a Roman prison. Must have committed a capital offense." Johannus remained focused but quiet.

Once more Lucius did not want to reveal anything further so he chose another path for their conversation. "Tell me," he said, "do you know a man named Caduceus, a physician to King Herod? I believe he is also a Follower as you call yourselves."

Petros peaked his eyebrows and seemed to be thinking. "I know—" He turned toward Johannus. "We know no one by that name. But there are now many of us," he said.

Johannus also shook his head "no." He also furrowed his forehead as if he were trying to recall someone.

A bang on the door made all of the prisoners jerk. "It is time for the mid-day bread rations," he shouted. "I will bring it shortly so remove ya' selves to the back of the cell."

When his steps tapered off outside, Lucius found himself wanting to touch the robes of his new visitors, to make certain of them. Instead, he motioned for them to sit.

"How do you know this man?" Petros said, sitting first. Johannus looked at his companion and then at Lucius and sat behind the older man.

"Caduceus?" Lucius questioned. He wanted to tell them the whole story, say that he met him right where they were sitting. But if these two were specters as well, he would appear more foolish—if not mad.

Instead, he reached out a bony hand, feeling the coarse cloth of

Petros' robe. The fisherman smiled. Then Lucius reached around him toward Johannus and twisted his gray robe between his fingers. "Real," he whispered.

"Yes," Johannus said, "we are prisoners for the Nazarene. The High Priest Caiaphas of the Jews sent us to the Governor who has imprisoned us."

All at once the door swung open as a guard brought a bucket of water and a very dry crust of flat bread. He dropped the bucket with a slosh out of its sides onto the stone floor while he tossed the bread in the center of the three prisoners. It bounced and sprayed crumbs on them.

The guard laughed and said, "Eat hearty, men." Then he retreated out the door along with another guard posted there.

Lucius waited until the door closed. He could not say why— perhaps it was the loneliness of these years in prison, perhaps it was the madness of his "visions" if that is what they were, or perhaps it was just having others to talk to at last. But he blurted out his story about Caduceus like it had all truly happened.

The strange man in a striped robe and a trimmed beard of gray, purporting to be physician to King Herod had simply appeared. His wisdom and knowledge of broken bones, debilitating rashes and leprosy as well as coughs and fevers were without question. His birthing techniques outshined most midwives.

"But," Lucius finally said, "he knew stories of the Nazarene from *his* healings to the—the cross." He paused, bit his lip and withheld his own involvement in that murder.

"But then," Lucius added.

"Yes?" Petros pursued.

"No one knew that Caduceus had even been here. And he was—was just gone—," Lucius said.

The prison door whooshed open and banged against the wall, nearly shoving Johannus to the floor. Two guards struggled in, holding up their huge commander, angrier than ever. His legs dragged behind him and the two attendants could hardly keep him upright as they slid him along the cell floor.

In the giant man's right calf, protruding from it, was something silver and metal, glinting in the afternoon sun. Blood shot from the wound, spraying Johannus and the floor.

"Damn zealot!" the commander shouted, "he stabbed me. I'll kill him."

Lucius knew the whole event and had seen it as clearly as it was now unfolding before him. Except Caduceus was not here—not this time. Lucius pushed between Petros and Johannus to the three guards who did not prevent him from getting close.

He ordered, "Get me bindings and bandages and bring a flask of wine, none of that cheap vintage that you serve us either."

One guard ran out the door as Lucius helped the other lower the injured giant onto the floor. Blood formed a red pool beneath his right calf, and he moaned with pain.

The guard returned with u-shaped metal sutures, bandages and a small flask of wine. "Make him drink the wine," Lucius said, "all of it." He slipped the leather belt from the commander's waist and shoved it toward his mouth.

"Bite this!" Lucius yelled. "I need to extract the knife." As he pulled the blade out, another shot of blood spurted to the floor and spattered Lucius' tunic.

"Awww," the wounded commander shrieked dropping the belt from his mouth. "I'm dying!"

"No, you are about to live!" Lucius said. "Give me the sutures." The guard passed one to the prisoner, now become their physician.

The first staple drew some of the wound together as Lucius pressed it into the man's flesh. He groaned but in such a low tone that Lucius thought, *The wine is working.*

The second and third staples went in and with the fourth staple, the giant's eyes were now closed. His chest moved in a slower rhythm.

"His breathing is calmer," one of the attending guards said.

Lucius was too busy winding the bandage around the man's calf to notice. At first, it was bloody but soon the outer layers remained white as the flow had ceased.

Lucius ripped off the excess bandage and said to the guards, "Let him rest here." He touched the bandages on the commander's leg, smeared his fingers through the pool of blood on the floor and rested his palm on the rising and lowering chest of the giant. It calmed him even more. Lucius thought to himself *This is all very real and yet I have seen it before—even though some parts are different.*

He lifted his hand off the chest of the commander and rocked back upon his knees, staring towards the door of his cell. Over his shoulder, he heard Petros say, "I do not know who you are, Roman; but I do know that you apparently have been healed when you heal others. You have the very spirit of your teacher, Caduceus, who was possibly a visitation of the Nazarene himself. *He* has made you a great and beloved physician in his kingdom."

Johannus added, "Petros is correct about you. You are no longer a centurion of Rome. So, would you like the Nazarene's washing?"

Lucius paused and thought, *No longer a centurion for Rome? Had the Nazarene become a god? Had he come to him as Caduceus?*

Lucius looked at Johannus and then turned to Petros. He shook his head in a "yes."

The older Follower said, "Guard, could we have some water? Our bucket here is empty?"

Petros had made sense with what he said about Lucius' vision, his healing and his life. Something *had* healed in him as he ministered to his enemy who still lay unconscious in their cell. A prisoner no more, Lucius had crossed into a new—new world, no—a new kingdom, releasing all the anger toward his father, toward Proconsul Pilate, even toward his friend, Marcus, wherever he was.

Petros stood above him with a handful of water splashing from the new bucket which the guards had brought. "Receive the washing of Jeshua Christos, the Nazarene," he said as he spilled the handful of liquid over Lucius' head.

The "great and beloved physician" smiled, water trickling down his temples. Rising without a word, he ambled toward the shadows of the darkening cell. At first, he felt cold, breathing steam, like he had that morning at the empty tomb. Then a glimmer of warmth came, beginning at his feet, moving up his calves, then his loins and his back into his face and head. He was not burning up but the wave warmed him like an infant might feel when cradled in the arms of its mother.

After a while the door swung open and the guards returned for their commander. Petros and Johannus breathed deeply from the other end of the shadows in the dusky prison light. They had fallen asleep.

But Lucius wondered what he had done or what had been done to him. A silver moon rose high in the window above and lit the cell as Lucius drank in its silence.

Suddenly the door swung wide again and banged against the wall as a torch entered followed by a decurion, not one whom Lucius knew. He stood at attention and saluted towards the back of the cell and at its most emaciated prisoner. Petros and Johannus awakened and gasped.

The decurion saluted again, clanking the leather of his armor and sword belt, then said, "Centurion Lucius Maximus, Legate Vitellius of Syria and Palestine has removed Pontius Pilate as Proconsul. All perpetrators against Pilate stand exonerated. Lucius Maximus, you are to be freed and restored to your command as centurion in the Italian Cohort of the *Legio X Fretensis*. Hail Caesar!"

He saluted a third time and said, "You will be freed tomorrow at sunrise." Finally, the legionary pivoted without any recognition from Lucius; and guided by his torch, he exited, swinging the door shut with a clunk behind him.

Lucius wondered if the soldier was real or not, but on the floor in the moonlight was his proof—a dropped dagger—often carried by decurions.

In the beams from above, a *serpens,* the Latin sign of healing, was wrestling with itself. The snake tugged and pulled against its own covering as a new *serpens* slipped from the scales of the old.

CHAPTER TWENTY:
BACK ON THE MARCH

"Return to your home, and declare
how much God has done for you."
— Luke 8:39

T he march north from Jerusalem along the *Via Maris* felt familiar, comfortable—but also distant. Why?

After all, even at age twenty-three, Lucius could still lead a fast pace with a patrol of ten men, all younger than himself. His unit comprised a signifier with the emblems of Rome and the *Legio X* out ahead of them, seven legionaries, a decurion and their centurion—their re-instated centurion.

Lucius' commanders, Tribunes Commodus and Tacitus gave him a month to rebuild his strength with a proper diet of meat and vegetables and the proper re-training in combat drills with *gladius* and baton. The tribunes were respectful but pushed him hard to return to the field to lead patrols like this one as zealot "activity" in Palestine had increased.

If only Lucius could now retreat into the monotony of his sandals slapping the road, passing sandy beaches and coastal hills. He could not. Everything felt as if the world had never been like this before but now was more "engaging." The birds in the few trees no longer chirped; they sang. The waves on the sea to his left no longer crashed; they kept time better than the men's marching feet. And the day was not just warm and sunny; it was fresh with a salty air filling his nose and refreshing his step. It was all like that day—that day when he had first stepped out from the empty tomb.

But something had not changed; and that something had begun in prison. Was it Lucius' healing? He had offered a solid arm shake to Petros and Johannus as if he were bidding farewell to a fellow Roman officer; and he promised to write these new friends. But what occurred in the hallway was even more remarkable.

As Lucius approached the exit, led by a guard, the odors of oil burning from the hall torches and the musty dinginess of the dark passage were filling his nose. He hoped this was all for the final time. Suddenly that familiar darkness became more threatening as a huge shadow was bearing down upon them.

The large guard filled the passage and had stepped into the path of the two oncoming men. Lucius felt the scar on his face and said to himself, "Here it comes again, one last tirade if not a swipe at me."

The giant stopped and his face drooped as he brushed by Lucius' guard, raised his hand and placed it gently on the newly restored centurion's shoulder. Then the commander said, "Accept my gratitude for all ya' healing to my leg, Centurion. Or is it Physician?" He smiled.

"I hope as well that you recover all of your strength," Lucius said looking down at the man's bandaged leg.

He paused, stared intently at Lucius, and said, "And accept m' regret for slicing ya' face."

Lucius tried to withhold his shock but thought, *When had he done that? Was it proof that Caduceus was not a dream or vision?* He shook his head with a "yes" then moved forward with his guard around his former patient.

"**S**ir, the men need to rest and take water," the decurion brought him back to the *Via Maris*. Dust filled his nose and made him cough as the ocean crashed in his ears and the wind had come up.

Lucius swallowed and choked out, "Halt! Take water!" Up ahead he saw that the signifier was encountering someone on the road.

Men in tunics, slaves probably, were blocking the way. He could not explain why but ran to them, leaving his patrol behind.

As he approached, the signifier said, "Sir, this local seems to know you."

The patrol had now closed the gap to the tunic-clad men who smelled of sweat and dirt, farmers for certain. Though they had scruffy beards, one at the front had a neatly-trimmed face and a better-made brown tunic, not frayed like the slaves. He looked familiar.

Lucius ordered, "Decurion, clear these Jews from the road."

The man with the neat beard stared at him and said, "Pardon, Centurion, but there are no Jews here. No Jews, no Romans, just men."

Lucius did not offer any response but instead revised his order. "Decurion," he said, "move the men out around these men."

The patrol followed the signifier and the decurion, fast-marching off the road into the sand and around the locals. Their centurion held back until his men were well ahead and out of earshot.

He put his hand on the arm of the brown-clad man and said, "Marcus, you are more correct than you know."

Without delaying for any response, he ran to catch his patrol as his old friend stood staring from behind. Lucius wondered what had become of Marcus. He looked the picture of a land owner, perhaps even of some wealth, with slaves. He thought, *Marcus has left the army and I am still here.* Yet more than his good fortune, what troubled Lucius more was his friend's openness to all people shown through the warmth which Marcus had shown him. That spirit lifted his spirits even though Lucius had no understanding for it.

The evening fires poked holes in the black night as the sea crashed behind their camp. Their march had ended for the day, still along the beach. Lucius sucked in the salty air then threw the flap of his tent aside and entered, lighting the oil lamp with an ember from one of the camp fires. It sputtered into a dim light on his writing table.

He looked out at the men still moving about their bed rolls and fires and then sat upon his small stool. The scroll which he had left at sundown was still there on the table and he unrolled it, lifting his stylus out of his camp sack along with his ink flask.

Dipping the stylus into the flask, the words flowed from his memory, words which Petros had shared and Johannus had agreed to. They had given Lucius the sayings and the endless stories of the

Nazarene's life and healings. Lucius paused for a moment and looked up again, amazed that the one who had been such a threat to the empire which he still served, the one whom he had executed, now filled the scroll panels before him and now fed the hunger of his heart.

His stylus scribbled on until the light grew dimmer and he heard the lamp crackle and spit as though it might go out. His legs and arms ached with the day's march, and he stowed the stylus and ink flask back in his pack, then extinguished the flame with a quick puff. Laying back on his cot, he heard the men speaking in low tones outside; but inside him, he wondered if he was still the Roman that they were.

The walls of Caesarea rose up over them as they passed through its southern gates. The guards on either side saluted by drawing their spears to a full stance of attention. Lucius had not been here often so he had to recall streets and public buildings for where he should direct his patrol.

Yet, it was not getting lost which bothered Lucius; deeper thoughts distracted him. The memories of the huge angry guard who had sought him out and apologized, not to mention the encounter with Marcus and his strange "welcome" to him, to all people really. It was not the threat of zealots and *sicarii* in the narrow streets; it was "others" simply standing on the corners.

There in one small square, at a market stall and along the wider streets, Lucius saw those strangers again. Men in pointed caps, long tunics and with long swords surveyed the crowds but studied the

Roman troops even more. They were still here after his prison time, still watching like vultures perched above some prey.

Lucius thought that by their dress, they must be from somewhere to the East out beyond the deserts. They were some sort of spies and made no attempt to hide their identities. He had been in prison and they were still watching or perhaps had never left.

One riveted his eyes upon Lucius and stroked his beard. He never diverted his glance so Lucius returned the stoic look believing that the stranger must certainly be the soldier of another empire, not Roman, not his. But maybe Lucius was not even part of his own empire either. Whom did he truly serve?

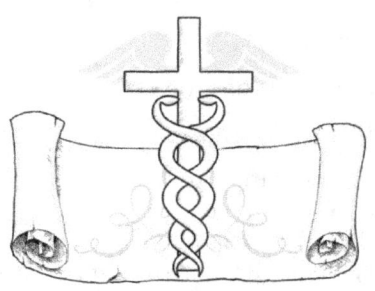

CHAPTER TWENTY-ONE:

AN ENEMY REVEALED

"They said, 'Lord, look, here are two swords.'
He replied, 'It is enough.'"
— Luke 22:38

Rumbling thundered toward him like an approaching storm, and he could taste the dust thrown into the air even though there was no wind. What was happening? Lucius could not see it through the sand making its own cover.

Then came faces—angry faces, thousands of them swarming upon him like hordes of locusts. Their stingers fell from the sky, wave upon wave. His hand moved to his sword, and Lucius drew it with a ring against the angry faces, against the stingers, in a battle. He looked at his hand on his sword and it dissolved into two—two hands—not of a man, not his fingers, but the hands of a woman.

Hands shook him awake from his dream. The musty smell of the barracks in Caesarea filled his nose along with the sweat of a legionary shoving at him.

"Sir," the soldier said, "you must rise. We are ordered out."

Lucius grabbed his red tunic, donned his armor and strapped on his *gladius* in the dim morning light. His days in Caesarea had been short, but long enough for him to learn that Legate Vitellius of Syria had appointed Marcellus as Proconsul after removing Pilate. Vitellius hoped for more peace "at home" in Palestine from zealots, *sicarii* and all of the Jews.

Lucius would soon know the reason. The legionary who had stirred him was correct in his awakening. Their cohort of six hundred and all of its six centurions were ordered out by Tribune Tacitus and "out" meant to the "frontier"—the lands beyond Palestine and the Jordan to the East. Enemies from over the Euphrates had harassed the Empire in the past, and they had returned. So "out" they went.

In his years in the legions, Lucius had more experience with Gaul, Germanica and Illyricum, not with Arabs or whatever was out there in the desert. Yet, fear of the unknown was not the worst of his worry.

The blistering sun caused his throat to parch and his entire body to sweat, drops streaming down his back and chest. The heavy chain armor, which the commanders ordered him and his men to wear, made the desert heat twice as unbearable. Why had they demanded the extra cover?

The metal not only turned every man's body into an oven, it also slowed their march to a crawl. If attacked, the men could never pursue the enemy rapidly.

Yet, here they were marching through the stifling humid air of Galilee into the baking torrid dryness of the desert beyond. The only relief was that Tribune Commodus knew each and every oasis for water as well as encampment.

One night after leaving the green of Galilee, the cohort bivouacked under a canopy of swaying palms. Lucius' decurion with the black tussled hair entered his tent and saluted with an arm to his chest. His centurion almost ignored him, lost in his work at a small writing table.

When he finally looked up at the young soldier, Lucius realized that his scroll was very exposed and contained his continuing journal of the Nazarene. Even if the decurion could not read, Lucius did not want to explain where he was spending his evenings.

He rolled the scroll shut, closing it with one stroke under the light of his oil lamp. "Yes, decurion," Lucius said.

The legionary responded, "Sir, if I may be so forward, what are we doing in this hostile border land? I know stories from my grandfather about vast horsemen from the East who defeated our legions fifty years before the days of Augustus. More than six legions were sacrificed because of foolish tactics. We are not made for this—"

Lucius interrupted, "Decurion Marius, our commanders know the country and the enemy. They will protect us." The words felt hollow even as he spoke them.

Another centurion entered behind Marius and said, "Centurion Lucius, we are summoned to the Tribune's tent."

"Tomorrow we divide the cohort in two," Commodus said. "Three centurions will take three hundred men and march onto the plain below us here while you other three centurions will march your men into the hills above,".

Lucius saw with the Tribune's gesture that he was in the "plain" group. He despised these divisions of armies. His reassurance to his decurion felt like even more of a lie than before. It was all another front, another battle, another victory, or not—for the Emperor. But what truly haunted Lucius was what defeat did Marius know from his grandfather that he did not?

Commodus continued, "Keep alert, Centurions. We will *not* have the result from these barbarians which they gave to Crassius some eighty years ago at Carrhae."

What result? For the first time Lucius asked himself the question which had never come to him before: Was this fight necessary? Or was it just another plan of the few to control the many? This was the theme of his empire—perhaps of every empire.

The oil lamps and torches around the tent were snuffed out by the hands of the slaves as the Tribunes bade their farewells for the evening. Lucius stepped out into the cooler desert night with its thousands of stars. *They say the heroes of battle are gathered there in those lights,* he thought as he observed the sky, *But I do not want to be among them.*

Lucius took the wide end of the formation—the outside, more vulnerable position to protect his men. His chain-link armor pulled his tunic down his back so that the links at his throat nearly choked him. It not only weighed on him but caused him to sweat again all over.

The *century's* drums pounded in his throbbing head and echoed off the hills to Lucius' left. They marched, descending down the ground which was drier than his trust in his Tribunes' strategy. His men looked more parched than he felt, clanking in their own heavy armor. What was all of this torture for?

Further and further their sandals at first dug into the sand and then slapped against its hard surface. Lucius hoped that their fate would not be that of those legions from eighty years before, dying in this demon of a desert.

He looked up and the glare of the sun hid the men of the two *centuries* ahead, blurring them with its brightness and its wavy heat which incinerated everything. To the right there was nothing, no sign of the rest of the cohort from a foolishly divided army, and no sign of the enemy, whoever these barbarians were, either.

"Hold up!" he shouted.

"Hold up!" another centurion repeated. A third centurion echoed the same command.

"Refresh, men," Lucius ordered. The other centurions repeated the words. Armor clanked as the men first stopped and then raised their water skins, mouths open for the warm liquid as it also doused faces and chests. Bronze skin sparkled in the shimmering heat, but it was the wind whistling in Lucius' ears which caught his attention.

Glancing around, he realized that they were at the bottom of the plain, the lowest part and the most vulnerable. Again, the wind deafened all other sounds as Lucius stoppered his water skin, stiffened—and then, listened. Had he heard it? It pounded now and wind did not pound. It rumbled in a manner which he knew from somewhere when he had heard it before—in a dream?

He blinked through the dust and blurry heat waves obscuring the ridge to his left. The dust vanished so that Lucius could not even be certain that it had appeared. Then a cloud swirled up over the ridge once more and it was not from a hot wind.

A pounding not only returned, it intensified and hammered like the chariot race of a hundred drivers. Only this hammering became so rapid that its shadow darkened the blue sky. The darkness began to cover the Romans on the plain and formed a rapidly moving peril pressing upon them.

Lucius saw the reason: below the dust and above the thunder, strange tongues shrieked with a unified shout. Horses and riders had crested the ridge above the *centuries* and now swarmed down like ants abandoning their nest. Lucius estimated one hundred riders, maybe two hundred even.

The foreign tongues screamed again and the phalanx of horsemen bore down towards the plain. At first, the riders displayed no weapons then swords were raised and flashed.

"Sound the alarm!" Lucius shouted as the trumpeter blew his circular horn. "Shields ready," their centurion ordered and the men brought their heavy covers around facing the onslaught. He had never been in a cavalry fight before as Gauls, Germans and the barbarians of Illyricum only fought on foot. His neck tightened and his back stiffened.

"Shields around," another centurion commanded up the line. But beside him he heard Decurion Marius sneer, "So this is protecting us?"

Meanwhile the horsemen pressed the attack down the ridge, flowing toward the wall of Roman cover like a fast-rushing stream surging toward a dam. Lucius waited and waited and waited for the lead riders to be close enough to see their faces beneath their pointed caps.

Pointed caps? He was beginning to fit the pieces together: pointed caps in Jerusalem, pointed caps in the markets of Caesarea and pointed caps sweeping upon them in the plains beyond the Jordan. No time for any other discovery as his orders were now crucial.

"Throw spears!" he shouted. The two other centurions echoed the same command, "Throw spears!" A hail of Roman javelins whooshed out from behind the shields and filled the air. But the line of horsemen rushing toward them as an unbroken horde suddenly shocked the Romans.

They split. They divided like a seamless garment ripping in two from top to bottom. With two swirling groups, riding to the right and left, they opened a vast empty hole directly in front of the Roman line.

The spears of Lucius' men and all the other units pounded into the vacant spot with a nearly unified thud. All but one. "Awww," a pointy-capped horseman cried as a spear found its mark in his chest and he toppled from his ride.

Again, Lucius wondered: who were these soldiers? Suddenly from up ahead a fellow centurion gave him his answer. "Come on, brothers! Let's give these Parthians a taste of Roman steel!"

The entire half cohort clanked up from behind their shields and lunged forward like a red wave running across the sand. The Parthians did not confront this counter-attack, but each branch of cavalry shocked the Romans again.

They wheeled in reverse and began riding away back up the ridge in a two-pronged retreat. Somewhere they sheathed their swords as Lucius drew his, circling it in the air and encouraging his men to pursue the horsemen.

Then the victory turned to terror. Parthians, both right and left bands, pinched their knees against their horses and pivoted around in their saddles like a gate swinging backwards on a post. Each man now had a bow, notched perfectly with an arrow aimed over the top of the Roman onslaught.

A twang of strings gave way to a whistling hail of arrows which darkened the blue sky once more. The missiles arched up and then dropped into the front and center of the charging legionaries.

At least fifty Romans dropped when the arrows found their marks in faces, eyes, necks and shoulders. Other arrows bounced off Roman chain mail as these intended targets kept charging. When Lucius passed his decurion, Marius looked up just in time to receive a missile to his face. The legionary dropped to the sand. His eyes set and he gasped as he fell, but there was no time to stop for him.

One band of Parthian horsemen had double-backed from their retreat and pressed a charge directly toward Lucius' men. This new assault with bows leveled forward did not use the retreating scheme from before but rode headlong toward the Romans. They fired another barrage straight at the unprotected legionaries.

Seeing this barrage, Lucius gave the order, "Tortoise shell!" The men threw their shields up, around and over the top of themselves. Arrows pierced the makeshift Roman cover or bounced off like rain on a tile roof. The riders roared around the Roman square and ended up, dividing themselves, half in front of the protected legionaries and half behind them.

"Trumpeter, sound the alarm!" Lucius shouted. The man raised his circular horn and gave three quick blasts which echoed across the valley. Without waiting for reinforcements which he had now called for, Lucius saw an advantage.

"Head toward the horsemen on the ridge in front of us," he shouted, raising his sword and circling it in the air. An arrow whistled from above him but landed with a thud at his left foot.

"Go!" he shouted again. "Do not remain here!" His men, some now shedding their chain mail, charged the rise toward the separated group of Parthians. The horsemen tried to turn back and repeat their pivoting tactic like before, but the Romans overwhelmed them too quickly, pulling riders from saddles and toppling horses onto the hard sand. The smell of horse flesh filled the air as the animals shrieked in terror.

Lucius followed his men but paused half way up the ridge to make certain that most of his *century* had swallowed up and overtaken the enemy. At that instant hoofbeats pounded the hard sand behind him.

He turned backwards as a rider was bearing down upon him. Pivoting sideways, Lucius dropped his *gladius* and reached out with both hands to grab the horseman bobbling directly at him. His hands latched onto the rider's belt and long tunic as he ripped the Parthian off his mount slamming him to the hard ground.

Expecting the adversary to charge him, the centurion pulled his sword from the sand and stepped back circling his weapon. The Parthian never moved but unsheathed his long sword with a ring. Lucius ran toward him, bringing his weapon down against the *rhomphaia* in continuous lethal hacking.

Though the man returned the attack upon Lucius' blade, he remained in place like a statue. As Lucius replied with his sword on the Parthian's, he glanced down and saw why the rider did not move. Blood was running down his left leg and out from under his tunic.

Finally, a thrust from the centurion rang against the long sword and sent the barbarian reeling backwards to the sand, groaning in pain. A Roman spear protruded from his thigh. The shaft had broken off but it pinned his golden tunic to his leg.

His garment together with his silver pointed cap and metallic leather sandals let Lucius know that this was no regular Parthian cavalryman. This victim, whoever he was, stared up wide-eyed and panting, then he tossed his weapon to the ground and surrendered.

Shadows surrounded the pair. Lucius smelled horse flesh and heard the snort of a mount. He looked up, keeping his sword trained upon the barbarian, as a circle of Roman armor and red tunics encompassed them. One legionary was holding the reins of a black horse shaking its head up and down, proudly like Alexander the Great's *Bucephelus*.

The voice of Tacitus boomed over Lucius' shoulder. The Tribune in a golden helmet said, "Romans, we have won the day. You have vanquished the Parthian barbarians. The other half of our cohort overran their camp and took their horses and their slaves into captivity. This is a great victory for Legate Vitellius and Emperor Tiberius. Your centurion here, Lucius Maximus, has captured their leader, Commander Mithradates, and his horse." The proud stallion snorted again and whinnied.

The Romans all around shouted, "Lucius! Lucius! Lucius!" Then they cheered, "Hail Caesar! Hail Vitellius! Hail Tiberius!" Finally, the men screamed that strange name which Marius had learned from his grandfather so long ago, "Carrhae! Carrhae! Carrhae!"

But Lucius backed away from his victim still bleeding on the sand and thought of him more as a wounded man rather than as a prize of war. Again, Tacitus said, "Take this prisoner to the camp physician so we can question him, then crucify him."

Now Lucius spoke and said to his commander, "Sir, bind him but give him to me, not the camp physician. I can hea—attend to his wound."

"Very well, Centurion. As the hero of today, he is your prize but we want to interrogate him after he is worked on," Tacitus said.

Lucius saluted, sword still in hand, and said, "As you order, Tribune."

But he questioned within himself, *Marius, my tussle-haired decurion, did not want this battle. Mithradates, wounded and now captured, did not want this battle. My own men, even cheering me as a "hero," did not want this battle. What would Caduceus want?*

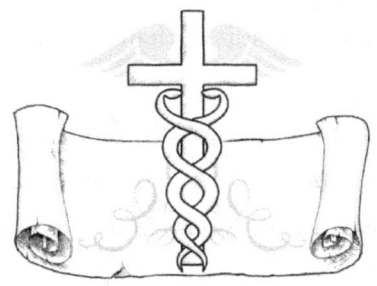

CHAPTER TWENTY-TWO:
HEROIC TREASON

"When the centurion saw what had taken place, he praised God
and said, 'Certainly this man was innocent.'"
— Luke 23:47

W inds rustled the palm branches above the Roman encampment at the oasis. They should have refreshed Lucius, but they blew from the East and the desert so they only oppressed with their scorching heat.

As he walked up a ridge of hard sand, the staples in his satchel clanked against his hip. Hearing a snort to his left, Lucius smelled the Parthian horses tethered in a line, spoils of the battle as Tribune Tacitus had announced. Lucius fixed his memory on how far up the hill this tether line was—for later.

Thank the gods that *they* had ceased as he neared the edge of the Roman camp. He paused and listened. Moans and cries of the wounded still on the battlefield no longer harassed his ears. It was an eerie silence.

His sandals scraped the hard surface again as he ascended toward a lone Roman guard, the legionary throwing hand over chest in a salute. Lucius approached a new tether line. This one consisted of Parthian prisoners, not horses.

At the upper end, which wound forever from the largest man to the furthest and smallest figures across the hilltop, was Mithradates scorching in the sun. His tunic had dulled from its earlier golden sheen and his pointed cap was missing. Matted black hair, tangled in sweat and flattened against his head, framed a square-jawed and handsome face, withered with furrows from long exposure to the sun. His beard glistened from perspiration as he sat bound with chains around his wrists and ankles.

He blinked when Lucius covered him with his shadow. Then he looked up with a contorted face, panting like a hunting hound just ending its chase. Lucius stood with a full water skin at his side along with his medicine satchel. On his other side and covering his *gladius,* was a smaller wine skin. All of this burden had slowed his ascent to the Parthian commander, who was turning and gazing down toward his captured army and trying his best to ignore the approaching centurion.

Regardless, Lucius waved a greeting and moved in front of the prisoner. The blood-soaked bandages on Mithradates' calf had dried, and Lucius reached for the wound causing the Parthian to groan. The centurion felt the hot wind blow across his sweat-drenched tunic, chilling him.

But the real heat and chill erupted from the Parthian when Mithradates turned and said, "I spit on you Romans!" His Greek was perfect causing Lucius to wonder where he had learned it. He looked up from his examination of the wound and offered a questioning stare.

"I learned your language from a Roman whom my grandfather captured generations ago." The prisoner paused and then added, "We defeated you once at Carrhae."

Carrhae, Carrhae, Carrhae, Lucius thought. He was tired of hearing the name which he had not even known before his own battle with these Parthians. But Mithradates would not let him forget and winced as Lucius pressed his calf.

He said, "We destroyed you once. We will do it again, Roman. All the way to Anatolia and Palestine."

Lucius responded, "Perhaps, but not today, not with this wound."

Gently unwrapping the bloody bandages, which he had applied on the battlefield, he made the Parthian jerk once more. "That spear head must be removed," he said, "immediately."

"Why? So you can kill me tomorrow," Mithradates bellowed. "If not with thirst today." His voice grew raspy.

"Drink this," Lucius said, handing him the cool water skin from his shoulder.

The Parthian unstopped it. Water splashed into his mouth, then over his face, hair and beard. Lucius pulled the smaller wine skin from his other shoulder and handed it to the prisoner.

"Here, drink this as well," he said.

"What poison is this?" Mithradates said, shoving the skin back.

The guard from the end of the tether line sprang up the hill and interrupted, leveling his spear point at the Parthian's face.

"No need for that," Lucius insisted, and the legionary backed away.

"You can stand down," his centurion said.

Lucius turned back to his patient, wind now blowing even Mithradates' matted hair across his forehead. He answered, "It is wine mixed with gall. It will deaden your pain."

The centurion turned physician handed the skin back and said, "We gave this to the Nazarene when he was dy——." He cut off his own words thinking that this was not the best timing for discussing dying.

"We have better herbs and libations for pain in my empire," the Parthian said with clearer speech from his earlier drink.

Lucius did not explain either his own interruption nor about the Nazarene. "Make your own choice on the wine, but the pain will kill you, if I do not," he said. He continued holding out the skin in silence.

Mithradates dropped the water vessel, mostly empty. He jerked the other skin with his shackled hands from his "physician" and sipped at the unstopped opening. After wiping his mouth and grimacing at Lucius, he closed his eyes and lay back on the hard sand.

Lucius pressed around the wound again, believing that Mithradates was sedated. A spurt of blood shot to the ground. This told him that he had to remove the spear in one quick jerk or risk an even more rapid bleed-out.

Lucius grasped the broken shaft. A stream of sweat trickled down his back. He pulled back in a swift yank as Mithradates let out a shout. The wine had not yet fully quelled his pain.

Blood shot to the sand and spurted over Lucius' tunic as if he were a butcher.

After grabbing the wine skin from his patient's hands, Lucius poured it on the bloody calf, then pulled the staples from his satchel.

They went in easily, suturing together the edges of the torn skin. Mithradates winced but did not scream. The wine and gall were finally taking hold.

He remained on the sand, eyes still closed; and Lucius felt his chest, Mithradates' breathing becoming slower even as his physician began panting like a nervous dog. Suddenly Lucius thought of the last time when he had done this procedure.

Beyond the tether line he was certain that he saw *him*, his multi-colored robe blurring as it spun. Caduceus was there and dancing, celebrating as he had done with the healing of the guard in Pilate's prison.

All at once, the dancer became only a Parthian soldier, chained and standing to stretch in the hot sun, nothing more. Lucius had not realized that he had been on his knees against the hard sand and that they had begun to hurt. He rocked back and rested, his own breathing slowing to the pace of his patient's.

Reaching out his fingers, he smeared them with blood from the ground. The blood of the Parthian was the same as Roman blood, the same as Jewish blood, the same as anyone's blood. All bled the same and needed the same healing, enemy and friend alike. Had not the Nazarene welcomed his enemies as he bled all over them?

Yet, even as a healer, Lucius was now feeling *that* healing in himself with a new purpose growing inside him. Instantly it cut off. A dark shadow engulfed both him and his patient.

Tribune Tacitus peered down and did not even demand a salute from his subordinate. He said, "Centurion, let me know when he is awake, so that we can get on with him."

Lucius thought, "Get on" with another crucifixion, another enemy, another victim of Rome's empire. Mithradates groaned as the sedative was releasing its grip on him. But the sedative of violence from Rome was also releasing its grip on this centurion.

Even with Tacitus' repeated demands, Lucius was hatching a daring and dangerous plan. The exact position of the horse line came back to mind in him.

For better than a week he trekked up the rise to the prisoners. The oppressive heat never abated, but at least even with the parching sun and confining chains, Mithradates' calf stopped bleeding.

The forest of crosses with Parthian victims on them increased beyond the tether line as the row of prisoners diminished. Mithradates stared in that direction, but it was Lucius who began the day's conversation.

"Are you able to stand?" he asked.

Without looking at him, Mithradates said, "Why? So you can crucify me next?"

"Perhaps," Lucius agreed.

The Roman glanced back toward the single sentry and the line of horses below him. His palms moistened with sweat as he thought, *What am I planning? I am a Roman. This man is my enemy and would kill me without hesitation. But...I am also a Follower...of the Nazarene.*

The Parthian looked back and up, squinting his eyes in Lucius' direction. Returning the stare, Lucius seemed to see someone else with a dark beard, ebony eyes and an ivory prayer shawl—the face of the Nazarene now eclipsing Mithradates.

Lucius whispered, "I will return tonight."

Mithradates furrowed his forehead. He did not speak.

The night wind rose, first gently like always, but soon it began to howl like a wolf on the hunt, and from the East—off the desert. The coolness was refreshing but the whistling was more welcome. It would disguise sounds and talk. It was the cover which Lucius needed.

As he crept up the ridge in the moonless night, he noted the single torch at the first tether line. The guards, three of them, were chatting and laughing between gusts, their helmets glistening in the dim light. They were all on the far side of the horses, which snorted and ignored them.

A black muscular stallion, not the horse which his men had captured from Mithradates but a fast-looking ride regardless, caught Lucius' eyes as it was silhouetted about four, maybe five, animals down the line. He heard his sandals slap the hard sand, felt his palms moisten and moved opposite the sentries, putting horses between him and them.

Counting to himself, he whispered, "*Unus, duo, tres, quattuor*...my mount." The horse snorted but remained quiet as he slipped up next to its nose, rubbing its head and offering it some grain from his satchel. The other horses were just as silent as the one which he had chosen. His hands slid down to the tether line and untied the reins so easily that Lucius wondered why any of the horses were still there.

A gust came up to a perfect wailing howl in his ears. The sentries moved away further down the ridge for cover, and Lucius slipped the black stallion out of the line to where the saddles were stacked up the hill. He slid one over the mount and whispered to its head, "Shh, shh, shh. That's a boy."

132

Removing a large water skin from his one shoulder and a satchel of bread, salted fish and dates from the other, he slung one on a hook on the right side of the saddle and the other on a hook at the left. The horse remained silent as it blinked its eyes to the sand-filled gusts.

Lucius looked up and back, the guards' voices came and went through the wind. "No one should be out—" the voice dropped to a mumble in the wind. "Right, so why…we…here," another soldier agreed. Their words all faded as Lucius led his ride away and into the darkness up the ridge.

At the top through the squalls, he heard the intermittent clanking of chains as he blinked his eyes from the blowing sand and approached the second tether line. The snort of a horse caused Mithradates to stand, alerting the lone sentry who moved toward him in the dim torch light. It played into Lucius' hand.

Hoping the horse would not run, he dropped the reins and patted his nose once more. The stallion stood as still as a rock. Lucius sprinted up the ridge on the balls of his feet, not even hearing his own steps. He slipped his sword from the scabbard without a sound.

All was so quiet that he heard the rustle of paper in the leather satchel that remained over his right shoulder. The legionary was still up on the ridge, ordering Mithradates to sit. Lucius turned his sword sideways, moved up behind him, waited for a howl of wind and brought the weapon against the man's throat, ramming a fist into his mouth to prevent any cry for help.

His eyes bulged out, then closed as he collapsed into Lucius' arms and dropped to the ground. "Next time I must train you better," Lucius whispered. "Never turn your back to the boundary of an encampment."

The centurion searched the guard's belt for keys and scooping them together on their ring, he cut them loose. Trickles of sweat ran down Lucius' temples as he jangled them toward a standing Mithradates. The Parthian blinked against the sandy wind, but Lucius pulled up his wrists and inserted a key in the lock, snapping it open. He bent down and did the same with the commander's ankles.

Mithradates rubbed his wrists and smoothed the skin on his shins, realizing that he was now free. He did not attack or try to overpower Lucius.

Instead he said "Why are you doing this, Roman?"

"Because I am no longer *that*—a Roman, that is," Lucius said. Reaching into his satchel, he pulled out the paper which had rustled all the way up the ridge.

"Here is the story of the one I now serve," he said. "Take this account of the Nazarene as my gift." Mithradates slipped the scroll from Lucius' hand.

"And something else," Lucius said. "The world does not yet belong to Followers like me. You will need this." He flipped his sword from the handle to the blade end and stretched it toward the Parthian.

"Come. Your ride is down the hill," Lucius said. "Can you mount a horse?"

Mithradates nodded, but taking the sword, he sheathed it into his belt and then brought his hand to the Roman's shoulder. "I cannot believe that a Roman does this. You will be remembered by me and my people."

He started to wobble behind Lucius who looked at the long, silent stares of the other prisoners behind them. The centurion smiled and then furrowed his forehead.

"I wish that I could release you all," he said.

But Mithradates commented, "You have done a great work, Physician. I have a gift for you as well. My personal servant remains somewhere in your camp. You will know the slave when you two meet. That slave is yours and no one else's."

He smiled as Lucius joined the walk behind him through the howling wind. When they reached the black stallion, Mithradates threw himself up and over the saddle, examining the water skin and food bag there. Then he reined the horse around and galloped into the blowing darkness.

Over his shoulder in the dimming torch light, he swiveled backwards and waved, raising the scroll still in his hand letting it flutter in the wind. Lucius waved as his former prisoner and patient disappeared. Then he dropped down the ridge avoiding the guards and the horse line.

The howling wind had stopped.

The wind from the desert had stopped. The wind inside Lucius had not. He had just committed an act of high treason—releasing an enemy prisoner—and not just any prisoner, the commander of the Parthians.

What had he done? Why not go back and release them all? What empire did he serve? More questions than answers resounded in his head.

The voices raged back and forth inside him. Or was it the voices which he now heard ahead in the light and over the crackling of the camp fires? He slipped back into the scene beyond his tent.

His men had not missed him. Thank the gods! They were circling around two large fires, drinking, shoving and swearing at one another. Their fires roared and snapped covering the noise of Lucius' sandals sneaking in from the darkness.

He drank in the image of legionaries, most in tunics, some with helmets cocked back on their heads. Others had armor partially laced up. Most were drunk, wine skins being raised and shoved toward one another.

But in the center was a dark bundle, shorter than most of the soldiers and covered with a hood. The men pushed it and spun it, each taking a turn at taunting the small form.

"Shove that slave to me!" one legionary shouted.

"No, I deserve it. I captured this prize when we overran the Parthians. The slave is mine," a second helmeted man asserted.

"In na munner do ya' have a right to dis prize of Mithradates himself," a very drunk soldier now shouted.

Lucius was about to turn and retire to his tent but hearing the name of the prisoner whom he had just freed, he stopped and stiffened to attention, fixing upon a fourth drunken legionary who had just entered the "contest" for the bundle. He wobbled toward the dark robe.

"Let's just see what we 'ave here," he said with a laugh, grabbing the slave with both arms from the back. Together they stumbled into the fluttering light. All at once Lucius' eyes went half way down the dark robe to its sleeves.

Arms and hands were sticking out. They were not those of a man but those of a—a dream. Was it what Lucius thought that it was? The drunken soldier dropped his grasp and backed up. Then he grabbed the hood of the robe at its back and yanked it down.

Even between the heads in front of him and through the bodies silhouetted from the fire, her deep-set eyes sparkled. Angular cheek bones gave her a shadowed but enticing face as trusses of raven hair cascaded down either side of her face and tumbled around her shoulders. Mithradates had not said that his slave was *a woman.*

But Lucius knew two things: this had to be the gift which the Parthian wanted him to have and from the sheen of her skin, she had not been just a slave. There was something more to her. She held another secret.

Heads bobbed back and forth in front of the centurion as he began to move forward. Her form appeared and then disappeared as bodies leaned left and right, trying to steal a better look. Catcalls now rose along with whistles from men who had not seen a woman in weeks.

"I'll take her!" one man shouted.

"That wench was worth the battle. I need my bed warmed tonight," another added.

"No ya' don't. I am the *signifier.* I take all the risk of attack at the front. Give her to me," he said.

Lucius continued to press ahead as legionaries recognized their commander and either saluted or stepped aside to make way. The last of the men finally divided at the front near the fire. The jeers shut off like water dousing a raging inferno. Soldiers fell into an uneasy silence, and the crackle of the camp fire waited for someone to give this scene a voice.

Lucius stepped up to the woman and the man wobbling behind her. Even drunk, the soldier paused then saluted with a shaky hand over his chest. He held the pose.

"I will take her," Lucius said. "She is mine."

From his right in the circle, a decurion said, "As hero of our battle and the captor of Mithradates, Centurion Lucius Maximus is correct. She must now be his."

Lucius thought to himself, "If only they knew." He was not certain that she could understand him, but he pointed toward his tent and said to the black-trussed face, "Go."

Somehow he knew that she would never belong to him, but he followed her to his quarters.

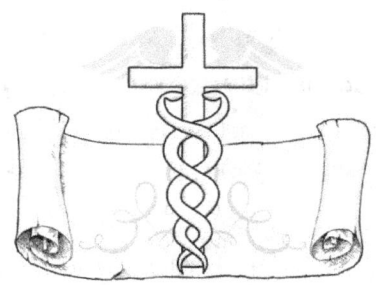

CHAPTER TWENTY-THREE:

NOT JUST A SLAVE

"While they were there, the time came
for her to deliver her child.
And she gave birth to her firstborn son…"
— Luke 2:6

The scorching heat of the Idumean desert faded, though it still suffocated Lucius every step. The drums, pounding out the march of his century—boom, boom, boom—vanished, though his head throbbed with every beat. The dust stirred from the units marching ahead in the cohort, though it also disappeared as Lucius ignored the sand gritting in his eyes.

Even the loss of twenty of his own men and the Parthian crosses looming up as the Romans left the enemy prisoners to die while the cohort abandoned the oasis did not disturb Lucius. Everything melted into *her.*

His century marched outside the other units. Boom! Boom! Boom! The drums kept their pace fast and slow—double march and rest steps. And she, the "gift" of Mithradates, marched alongside them, but just beyond, as she kept the pace, her bronze ankles and bare feet slapping the sand as fast as any of Lucius' legionaries and slowing only when they slowed. She never stumbled, but she never spoke. She was just there—present.

He thought that she might be deaf or a mute. But she kept stride with the drums, her feet prancing out every beat. Once when Lucius looked in her direction and quietly said, "So, there you are," under his breath, she turned with a wondering look.

Then suddenly he allowed his focus to change to the legionary up the ranks, the one who had been the sentry on the prisoner line. The soldier was limping and breathing hard but the march was not fast. The loss of Mithradates had not gone well for some Romans.

A few days back when the "escape" of the Parthian commander was discovered, Tribune Tacitus called Lucius and the four sentries to his tent. Tacitus was already deposing them as Lucius arrived. The "hero" centurion slipped into the officer's quarters, its walls whipping in the desert wind, as Tacitus was whipping up his own reasoning on the "disastrous escape."

"It is clear," he was saying to the guard whom Lucius now watched ahead in the ranks and whom he had nearly suffocated with his sword, "that somehow someone from the Parthian ranks surprised and overpowered you, attacking you from behind and seizing the keys to the prisoner."

As Lucius saluted and remained quiet, the Tribune turned to the three other guards.

"And what have you to say?" Tacitus' face reddened as he demanded more than questioned with his words.

One of the sentries said shyly, "Sir, I saw a red tunic about—about the height of the—the centurion here leading a horse out of our torch light. But I thought it must have been a prize of battle for one of you officers."

"Enough!" Tacitus shouted. "Next you will have me believing that Centurion Lucius here is a traitor who releases the very Parthian whom he captured. Of all the foolish explanations!"

Lucius shifted his feet on the tent floor, but remained flat-faced, staring at the Tribune.

"I just wanted you to hear what happened with one of your men," Tacitus turned and said to him. "We know Centurion Lucius was back with his *century*—suppressing a riot around one of Mithradates' slaves. He was nowhere near the prisoners."

The Tribune paused, looked at his centurion and half-smiled. "Though I wish that he had been."

No, you do not, Lucius thought, remaining stone-faced. *At least, I am not a suspect, but someone is and someone will pay for my deceit.*

Now that "someone" was dragging his boots up ahead, and Lucius knew that this legionary had received a severe flogging for Lucius' lie and *his* treason. Perhaps all the guards had.

Tacitus not only accepted the justification which Lucius never had to make. After the Tribune dismissed him and over his shoulder on his way out into the blowing desert wind, he heard the commander say, "Your foolishness has cost us *his* heroism. I did not want to expose him to more from you four, but I should let *him* flog you."

Lucius returned to his tent to find his "excuse" sleeping at his door. He stepped over the slave to get some rest of his own.

She had begun to snore—loudly, sucking in each breath like a female lion. He lay on his back, feeling every bulge and ripple in his cot. He turned to his right side. She snorted and quieted, then snorted again. He felt the bulges in his blanket under him and rolled to his left.

He thought about his legionary lashed for his treason.

He tossed to his back again and worried about the soldier who had seen his theft of the horse. What if the story was backed by one of the others? Would Tacitus come for him?

Then he fell asleep through the snoring of his slave and through his fear about his own treason—about letting others take his punishment. He dreamed through it all.

At first, that dream made him smell the death all around him, from the crosses at the end of the camp. He heard it: the ringing of a hammer upon the nails. Another cross went up and another Parthian groaned in death, and another, and another.

Then the face of the sentry from his *century* popped into his face, and Lucius smelled the sweat of the soldier as he put his nose up to Lucius and shouted, "Traitor! You should be flogged, not me. You should be crucified, not them."

Then Lucius looked away to someone else in a brass helmet as Tacitus' eyes narrowed right in front of his. He bellowed, "Traitor! Your men have suffered instead of you. How much did the Parthians pay you?"

Finally, Lucius looked away and up to a voice that cried from a black horse rearing up, "Ha! Ha! Ha! Traitor! Roman, you are not one, are you? You belong nowhere; you have no empire."

"No, no, no," Lucius cried.

He was shaking on his cot, or someone was shaking him with an angular face, two penetrating blue eyes staring down at his. His slave was trying to pull him up. When he stood and looked around, he saw that his scrolls, his packs, his bed roll for quick marches, everything was neatly packed and stacked by the door of his tent. She had secured it all, then had awakened him. Again, she did not speak but pointed outside.

Lucius heard the clanking of helmets, armor, swords and bundles. The auxiliaries and the legionaries were breaking camp. So, without a word to her, he laced up his armor, belted his *gladius* at his waist, secured his baton in his belt and felt his cold helmet with its transverse plume on his hand. Then still with nothing to her, he brushed by and became part of the march which he was now on.

The sun had shifted to the East, to their backs as they were heading back to Palestine. Was this campaign over? Was the threat gone—for now? Lucius did not care. What he did care about was her.

If he had ignored her when the cohort broke camp, his eyes moved back to his left once more, to the flowing black hair streaming out from the chiseled cheeks, still stepping off the march like a proud mare.

When they reached the Jordan, the units halted. Lucius leaned down and scooped up a handful of the water, icy cold and running faster than it looked on the surface. The men picked their way in, some wobbling, soldiers splashing as they lost their step on the hidden rocks below. They rose to the shallows of the opposite side.

Alongside them she stepped in, then swam, ending up ahead of her master as she regained her footing and rose also onto the other side. The water flowed from her robe in a personal falls flowing along her body, splashing down into the river. She shivered and then shook herself like a horse shedding moisture when it rises out of a stream.

But what Lucius noticed was that her frayed brown robe hugged her wet body, revealing her form. It invited him as did her bare feet, still not bloody even from walking through the sharp, rocky river bed. Her "womanliness" held him; but suddenly his desire for her shifted to who or what she was.

She did not carry herself like a slave, a Parthian perhaps, but she was both an alien in his land and perhaps in her own. With all of this mystery, she never complained, never offered a word, not a groan, even when ignored or worse.

Some days later as the march turned North, a muscular, black-haired centurion named Flavius dropped back along the line. Lucius did not know why, but as the officer cut between his slave and him, the burly soldier gave her such a strong shove that her steps slipped against the sand and made a scraping sound tumbling her headlong onto the ground. The centurion continued to fall back, as Lucius and the cohort moved on.

In his peripheral view, Lucius saw her, limping but not complaining, not even moaning as she jogged to catch up to him. It was as if the act had never happened. Soon Flavius returned back up the ranks and once again moved in behind her, preparing to repeat the same shove? Lucius was uncertain.

But he slipped his baton out of his belt; and crouching down, Lucius aligned himself with the men to become invisible. He held his baton at ankle height. Flavius pounded the ground with his jogging and turned toward the Parthian, leaning out to shove her but ignoring his feet and the bar at his shins.

Thud! His legs tangled in the tightly held baton and shot him forward like a catapult launching a stone. He went head first onto a sharp desert rock. "Aagh!" he screamed as he disappeared from Lucius' view—and the Parthian's as well.

They moved on like before, snubbing the fallen Flavius. Except she turned and smiled towards her master. Lucius nodded back, catching sight of the fallen Flavius to his rear, pulling himself up and wiping the blood from his chin.

After crossing North through the green of Galilee, towers and walls rose in the path of their march. Behind him, Lucius heard a legionary say, "Syrian Antioch."

The distance closed as the shade of the walls loomed up to their front and Flavius of the split-chin shouted "Halt!" "Halt!" another centurion cried. "Halt!" Lucius yelled.

The entire cohort rippled to a stop like some undulating snake. Lucius thought that it was the only sign of a *serpens* which he had seen for a while. The guards at the double-door gate drew back their spears and saluted. The Roman troops wound into the dark shadows of the inner city toward the market areas.

As they arrived at their barracks, larger than those of Fortress Antonia in Jerusalem, Lucius and the Parthian followed the sounds of the men, yelling and sifting out their quarters down the dark halls. Through the ranks came someone who should not have been there.

A bronze tribune's helmet was winding past the bodies of the soldiers along the wall. The torch lights flickered and glistened off the brass as it brightened then went dull again. Finally, a body taller than Lucius halted in front of him.

This was not good news. Perhaps Mithradates' escape had turned against him. Lucius stood still but shifted his sandals, scraping the limestone floor. His slave had gone ahead somewhere out of the way.

This time it was not Tacitus. Tribune Commodus drew close, and Lucius saluted. The Tribune had wavy black hair and deep brown eyes. His square-jawed face always conveyed a serious tone.

He said, "Centurion Lucius Maximus, you are no longer posted to the *Legio X*."

Lucius said, "Tribune, where should I now report?"

Commodus dropped his voice and looked down then up, saying, "Nowhere. Legate Vitellius will no longer pursue a campaign on the Arab frontier—." He broke off, glanced down the hall toward Lucius' slave and lowered his voice further. "Nor against the Parthians. We no longer need as many officers. The Emperor is grateful for your sacrifice with his legions. Remain on call but please vacate your quarters here the day after tomorrow."

Commodus turned and scraped his boots on the flooring without further comment. His steps echoed down the vacant hallway. Lucius had forgotten to salute as the Tribune exited. Why bother? He was leaving the army—or it was leaving him. Where would he go? What would he do?

His eyes moved back in the other direction where his slave stood outside the door of his now "temporary" quarters. For the first time in the flickering torches, he noticed her eyes were not blue. They were the color of the sea on a bright day.

Behind him, he heard voices, probably of legionaries. One was just saying, "There are Followers here. They live in the north part of the city up the stairs leading out of the market plaza."

He looked at his slave again, wondering if they would accept a Parthian. When he turned around behind him to see who had spoken, no one was there.

Lucius worried whether Commodus' words were just an excuse for a centurion's treason with Mithradates. The tribunes would never be able to explain how a hero freed his own captive so just rid the army of the problem. All of these fears plagued him as he followed her up the wide stairs.

He had no thoughts about what lay ahead—another world, another "kingdom," another empire. They came to a set of large rough wooden doors. Lucius knocked. Nothing.

He knocked louder. His speechless slave gave him a glance like "I do not know if anyone is here" as she shrugged her shoulders.

Suddenly one side of the huge wooden doors creaked open by itself. They shuffled in, Lucius entering first to be certain that all was safe. There were no guards, no gatekeepers. Nothing but a wide courtyard opened up in every direction with remnants of a fountain, now dry, at its center. On each side was a three-story set of limestone rooms rising and partially shading the courtyard.

Lucius coughed as the smoke of cooking fires wafted into his nose and mouth from two or more ovens on the lowest levels. The aromas of fish grilling and meats searing for some sort of mid-day meal filled the air. Tables were set with cups and bowls in the yard with far too many places for one family.

People were coming and going as though it was a city within a city. If these were the Followers, their clothing was modest to poor—

frayed dark robes, workmen's tunics, the head coverings and the veils of laboring women who baked, wove linens or even worked some sort of fields somewhere. It was hardly the attire of kings, queens or the military of any other empire.

One thing was certain: they lived *together* in this community, and they relied on each other. Some clustered on balconies, in twos or threes; some stared at the strangers who had just wandered in without any announcement. Even the children ran by, unattended, paying more attention to each other than to the new arrivals.

Finally, a bearded man with a belted gray robe approached and smiled, raising his hand as he spoke, "My name is Barnabas. I am a leader here." He stroked his sandy brown beard with his other hand as if he was trying to recall something about Lucius.

"We Followers live here together in the love of the Nazarene," he said, stretching out his hands toward the balconies. Lucius was not certain but the man's peaceful behavior felt truthful.

Barnabas added, "And who are you?"

Lucius explained himself, feeling embarrassed for the first time, at the name "Roman." He ended his introduction with the words which he felt would bring him credibility, "Baptized by an Apostle named Petros in Pilate's prison." He did not share his story about executing the Nazarene as he was not certain about which Followers had been where in that rabbi's life.

Instead he added, "And I am a healer—a physician."

Barnabas' eyes widened. "Good, a friend of Petros is our friend," he said. "We have need of your gifts of healing."

Lucius and his slave settled in to two rooms at one end of the first floor of the complex. Dust hung in every crack of the limestone; but his slave, whom he had begun to call "the Parthian" since she remained silent about her identity, opened windows, swept floors and gathered cots, stools and a writing table for each of them.

Her master set aside his red tunic, armor and *gladius*, opting for an ivory robe belted at the middle and a medical satchel of ointments and sutures over his right shoulder. His sandals were simple walking footwear, not the cleated boots of the military. A well-trimmed beard covered the scar from his days in prison. He had changed, at least in appearance, to a physician.

As for his own history, Lucius never told Barnabas or any of the Followers about his life as a centurion. For all they knew, he had been a traveling doctor, trained in Egypt or apprenticed by another physician for all of his nearly thirty years. So, on his third day in the "Rooms" as the Followers called this community, Lucius tailed a young Follower, a teen named Timotheos, with a striped-robe, brown hair and clean-shaven face. Timotheos toured the Roman through the interior of the complex with its apartments and storage closets until they arrived at its clinic also on the far end of the first level.

The room was too dark for Lucius' comfort and it was starkly furnished with only a few cots, most patients having little more than a blanket on the floor. Some attendants appeared to be giving elixirs, libations or only water. Others placed cold damp cloths on fevered foreheads or massaged aching joints. No one was in charge.

Following a few introductions, Lucius went to work at once after Timotheos released him. Over the next few weeks, he prescribed ointments for wounds and severe rashes, applied splints to broken legs and bound deep cuts with metal sutures as he had used in the army and in Pilate's prison. Nothing was too difficult but nothing was more than what Caduceus had called a "cure."

Each morning "the Parthian" awakened him and by the second week had begun following him to the clinic. When he finished his own rounds of about thirty patients, he began observing what Caduceus had celebrated, but with her.

She still did not speak but she comforted, hugged and welcomed patients of any background or illness. She moved freely among Greeks, Jews, Samaritans and one Parthian as if they were from her own empire and were as healthy as she was. Even dreaded lepers did not repulse her and she always found extra bread and dates for them. Her technique dismantled him as she served the hurting more effectively than Lucius did.

Then one quiet afternoon when the stench of the fevers, the wounds and the unchanged dressings suffocated Lucius and when only a few patients were lying in the shafts of light on the limestone floor, the huge wooden door swung wide and banged against the wall. It reminded Lucius of his cell door in prison.

That memory snuffed out quickly as a woman tumbled in held up by another older matron. The first woman shrieked, "Help me! My insides are ripping apart!"

The older woman wore a charcoal veil covering her graying hair. She was struggling to help the one in pain, even to walk, as the afflicted woman folded over and nearly fell. Her guide looked up at Lucius and calmly said, "They told us outside that you were a physician of some skill. Can you help us?"

Shrieks came again. While Lucius was searching for a response to these new arrivals, the gray-haired woman said, "I am her sister. She is about to give birth."

Finding nothing else to say, Lucius directed the pair to a corner with a low cot. "The Parthian" assisted the older sister in embracing the pregnant woman as if to say, "You will be fine. We will care for you both and for your baby."

Falling back onto the cot like a stiff board, the younger sister tossed with every contraction. But Lucius only studied her and stroked his chin, trying to remember what Caduceus had taught and shown him about birthing. Nothing came, and it was too late to work his mind back into some sort of step-by-step process for bringing new life into the world.

Instead, the mother-to-be thrashed on the cot so hard that she bounced it up and down, its legs tapping on the floor over and over. Her sister looked up with a panicked face crying with tears in her eyes, "Physician, kindly help us. I fear that something may be wrong with her child."

Suddenly the shrieking stopped, while the pregnant woman rested, worn out by her pain and panic; but Lucius knew that the calm was momentary. The physician in him stooped down, spread her legs and pinched the hem of her robe with a finger and thumb, pulling it back. The infant was not crowning. Something *was* wrong.

To his side, "the Parthian" was staring at him, at the woman on the bed and at her sister. Lucius nodded to his slave, rose and stepped back. She knelt down between the arched legs, now quivering, as her sister held her shoulders up.

The Parthian leaned around and focused forward, pressing her own lips together, saying, "Whooo…whooo…whooo," and demonstrating with this exhaling how the birthing mother should breathe.

At once the patient took short puffs of air but continued to moan through each one. Feeling between her legs again, Lucius' slave reached for something. Her face contorted as she pulled her kneeling body to one side, then shifted it to the other. Her hands moved in deeper as she grunted.

The woman shrieked from the procedure. Lucius had begun to doubt that he had made the right decision in turning this birth over to a foreign slave. But without a break in her work, the Parthian looked over the knees before her and kept saying, "Whooo… whooo…whooo" in short breaths. The hurting mother-to-be mimicked her.

The Parthian pulled an orb from the mother. A tiny shoulder followed. The air around smelled of blood and birthing fluid as a male infant emerged into the slave's arms.

She cradled it and rubbed it until its cries drowned out the mother's. The Parthian motioned to Lucius for a knife and cutting the cord, she slipped around the exhausted mother, laying her child in her arms.

The woman looked up through tears and a large smile. She tried to speak but her exhaustion stole her words. Her sister pushed her graying hair back under her veil and said, "You are a beautiful and gifted midwife. What is your name?"

In perfect Greek, the Parthian said, "I am called Axsen. In my tongue it means turquoise." Lucius thought, *Of course, her eyes.* Then she added, "The child was turned in the wrong position. I know since I have delivered many children among my people in Parthia."

Lucius' eyes widened and he inhaled. It was the first time that he had heard from her in the four months since he had freed her from his men. Unlike the sister here, he had never asked her name nor anything about her, assuming that she could speak neither Latin nor Greek.

She had understood everything that he had said for four months! She was not just a slave.

Deep inside himself he heard Caduceus say again, "Remember that curing is not healing."

He scanned beyond Axsen and the woman with her new son to the room itself. There was no sign—no *serpens*. There was no snake.

He looked for Caduceus, somewhere around the clinic among the faces of the attendants, but there was no one even looking his direction, except for Axsen's turquoise eyes. She had found her voice, but he had not found his.

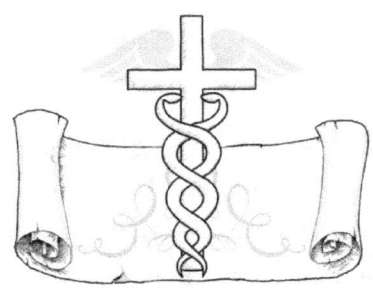

CHAPTER TWENTY-FOUR:
A NEW PRACTICE WITH NEW PATIENTS

"Jesus said to him, 'Receive your sight,
Your faith has saved you.'"
— Luke 18:42

The latch felt cold though he knew that the day would not be as Lucius listened to the door creak to the clinic. He moved into the area with the cots which he had now obtained for all of the patients in the "Rooms." His thoughts were still stinging from yesterday and why Axsen had never spoken to him.

A patient said to someone beside him, "I heard that he died—in his sleep, I believe."

Lucius thought that he meant another patient; but when he scanned the room, no one was missing from last night.

Finally, the first patient said, "When you're the Emperor, you are lucky to die that way. I hear that it happened two months ago. So, Gaius Caligula is Caesar."

"Yes," the other said. "It's why Vitellius withdrew the army from the desert frontier."

And why the army no longer needed me, Lucius thought. Axsen had not come with him this morning. There were no further births with children turned the wrong way. She was not needed as much. Nor was he.

Other physicians had come to Syrian Antioch. He was more of an overseer than a healer. It made Lucius feel like the morning, hazy, damp and dull, like the stone floor beneath his feet.

As he made his way between more cots, someone else was talking. A woman leaned over to another beside her. She looked wrinkled and older perhaps more than her years; but she was just saying, "I am blessed to be here. In Ephesus there was no care like this."

Lucius repeated the word in a whisper to himself, "Ephesus." Then a voice interrupted, echoing off the limestone walls. He looked up to a bare head in a dark robe. Someone older was at the lower end of the clinic speaking to the patients and attendants gathered around him.

Barnabas was preaching and reading from a scroll by an author whom Lucius did not know. He said, "So, the Apostle tells us, 'Let no evil talk come from you but only what builds another up so that your voice gives grace to all who hear it.'" Barnabas paused and then added, "Brothers and sisters, find your voice in the Nazarene. Blessings to you all."

Those who were standing shuffled out, returning to their care for the patients. Barnabas looked up and down the room. His eye caught Lucius.

"Physician, may I have a word?" he said.

Lucius replied, "You seemed to have a lot of those this morning." His comment sounded as cutting as his centurion's sword, even to Lucius himself.

Barnabas' sandals slapped down through the clinic into the hazy light but his face became shadowed as a cloud moved over the sun. He said, "I must abide by my own message."

The Leader looked away and then back. He said, "I know you. I know you from your other life." Lucius froze and paled.

Barnabas continued, "You have covered yourself in your beard, your long robe and your physician's satchel, but I knew you the moment when I met you in the courtyard."

"And who am I?" Lucius dodged the discovery.

A young brown-haired attendant came up to them and said, "Josephus, you are needed at the entrance."

Barnabas nodded, the attendant exited and Barnabas seemed to read Lucius' face. He said, "Yes, I am someone else, too. And that is how I know you, centurion. You were there when we buried *him*. Perhaps you remember me as Josephus of Arimathea."

Lucius remained riveted on this man who knew his history. He made no comment but his past was overtaking his present like a wolf running down a lamb.

"Do not trouble yourself," Barnabas said. "I will not share your secret here. That is for you to reveal in your own time and your own way." He paused, his face wrinkling into a warm smile. Finally, he said, "You can live in the Nazarene's kingdom but you cannot hide in it."

Another servant with deep brown eyes and a gray tunic approached and interrupted Barnabas, "You are needed at the gate."

"Yes, yes," Barnabas said. "In a moment. Leave us." The slave departed into the glare of the lower doorway and out of the clinic.

"I did not want to bring you pain. I came to tell you that the Followers in Ephesus need a physician—and a healer. Go to them," Barnabas said. "Bring the Nazarene's healing to them and you will be healed."

Suddenly Lucius observed that the face which he had first seen in Barnabas was not younger with a sandy beard. It was the one here now with a gray-streaked beard and graying hair growing lighter in the returning sun. Barnabas, or Josephus, was even older than Lucius remembered from the burial of the Nazarene. But he was whom he said he was—Lucius was certain.

"The woman with you is a great gift. I can reason from her eyes upon you that—that she loves you very much," Barnabas said. "Is she a Follower?"

"No," Lucius said.

A third attendant came and said, "Brother, we need you at once."

Barnabas ignored the plea and said, "Think about my words." He put a hand on Lucius' shoulder, and departed this time, following the attendant down through the cots and disappearing out into the glaring hazy sun.

Lucius did not need to think about the second time that he had heard the word, "Ephesus." He gathered up his physician's satchel and never spoke a "Farewell" to the other healers.

Axsen met him at the door of their rooms. "You are home too soon," she said. "Is something wrong?"

"No, Axsen," he said. "Something is needed. Then he looked deep into her eyes and said, "Ephesus. We are sailing to Ephesus."

"You cannot find your voice if you do not know what your voice is saying." The words echoed inside Lucius. His body rocked one way and then the other. His mother spoke the words, "You have a healer's voice. Use it." Suddenly a face blurred into the bearded, silver-veiled head which he knew from prison—Caduceus smiled and pointed. A final face arose on his right side. His body rocked back in the other direction.

The face said, "Ephesus. You have a home in the Nazarene's kingdom but you cannot hide in it." Lucius' body rolled again. And he awakened on a deck, his ship rolling in the waves of the *Mare Nostrum*.

The captain of the small grain vessel shouted, "Ephesus! We have arrived in Ephesus!"

Axsen stood looking down at Lucius. She said, "The last stadia were disturbing with large waves pushing us into port, Master."

Lucius looked back up at her, smelling the salt air and blinking his eyes at the bright morning sun. He sat up and glanced around at the ships ahead and behind theirs. At least, the rocking had stopped.

"Let us take our baggage and find our way to the Followers," he said. "I have heard that the Nazarene's mother lives here among them," Lucius said, making casual comments to his slave.

Axsen appeared to ignore him and searched the deck for all of their bags and satchels. Her Master acted differently than most, reaching around her for the heaviest and largest bundle. They dragged themselves and their belongings to the dock, Lucius paying the captain the remainder of their fees.

"How will we find the Followers in all of this—this confusion?" Axsen said. Dock men, slaves, sailors and some women were conversing, unloading ships, and recording cargoes. The docks were larger than Syrian Antioch and far more crowded.

Lucius asked a dock worker, "Where would the Followers of the Nazarene be?" The man in a frayed tunic shook his head that he did not know. A woman, who was trying to entice a captain from the boat behind theirs, also shook her head "No."

Again, Lucius moved down the dock, struggling with the heavy bundle of his and Axsen's goods. He got up close to a slave in a dirty and thread-bare tunic and repeated, "Where are the Followers of the Nazarene?" The slave shrugged his shoulders.

A man in his early thirties with black Greek hair and a short beard paused and cocked his head. Lucius did not notice him, but his slave did. She ran down the dock and planted herself directly in front of him, dropping her baggage on the pier.

Before she could ask, he said, "No, I do not accept offers from women, even one as beautiful as you."

Axsen ignored his misunderstanding and said, "My Master and I are searching for the place where the Followers of the Nazarene reside and work."

"Ah," the man said. "Why did you not say so? My name is Tychicus and I am one of their leaders. I will take you to them."

Lucius had now caught up to them and had deposited his bundle on the limestone. "I am Lucius. This is my slave Axsen. Perhaps the Follower, Barnabas, wrote to you about me. Or you may know him as Josephus."

"Ah," Tychicus said. "Josephus told us that he was sending a physician named Lucius Maximus. We could not believe that a Roman would be a healer for us. You look more like a soldier to me."

Hopefully Tychicus did not know Lucius' past, but it seemed that Baranabas/Josephus had not exposed his secret. "Let us go," he said. The colonnaded road up from the docks created almost a forest of limestone pillars on either side of their walk. It led to a large three-arched gate. But before they passed under, a structure on Lucius' left caught his attention.

Nothing was around it and the windows were dark, some even covered. It was beige limestone and appeared to be an abandon warehouse. For all of the traffic which had suffocated the docks, no one was here. He wondered why.

Tychicus returned to him staring at the building and motioned him forward to where Lucius' slave was at the arches. The shadow of the port gate darkened their journey for an instant and then passed quickly overhead and behind them. Ahead on the road, a glistening street crossed their path with its marble surface running left and right.

They turned right onto the Marble Street and rose toward what seemed to be a plaza of temples. Before they arrived at the first temple, Tychicus turned into a house which needed some repair, shutters falling off the windows, the door missing at least one board and only the most rough-hewn benches and tables inside.

Followers seemed to be congregating and conversing in two's and three's. Lucius was panting and finally dropped his bundle as did Axsen with her two smaller bags. The room was dark even with several open windows to the street. Tychicus motioned them to a door at the end.

Tychicus ordered a young Follower with blond hair and dark brown eyes to give Lucius whatever he needed and to show their healing area to him. "We will take care of your baggage," the young man said. "We need you at once."

He ushered Lucius and Axsen into the small wing of the dilapidated building. The door groaned and nearly fell off its hinges when the blond man opened it into a room which smelled musty and stale. Like Antioch when Lucius first arrived, there were only two or three cots and the remaining half dozen or so patients had a blanket each.

Lucius hardly had time for his eyes to adjust to the dim lighting when a gray man, both in hair and skin tone, used crutches to drag a bent right leg towards him. The physician in Lucius sized up that he was a work man or from the muscles in his arms, a soldier. He had set many limbs in the army and at Antioch; but this man's condition appeared too severe.

The weathered fellow looked the physician up and down as the blond Follower slipped around them and Axsen and exited out the moaning door. "Let me see your leg," Lucius begged but his tone was doubtful. "What is your name?"

"My name is Marius!" the man bellowed. "I served in Caesar's legions in Macedonia and Gaul. I've seen more fights than you will ever see. I don't think ya' can help me!"

"I cannot help if you will not let me examine you," Lucius protested.

"My friends told me that the Followers had healers but I can hear the doubt in ya' voice," he bellowed. "I don't think ya' want to touch the likes of me."

Marius spun on his crutches and shoved Axsen aside so hard that she hit the wall with her back and groaned, "Aagh!" The thud of his crutches was pounding hard and quick as he slammed the door behind him, splintering another piece of it with his exit.

Lucius thought, *Welcome to Ephesus.* But he stepped to the wall at the door and reached around Axsen lifting her by the shoulders into the dim light. He straightened her ivory robe and checked her head and back, looking her over for any possible injury.

"Master, I am fine," she insisted. "But let me say that I believe we need more space."

Before Lucius responded, the door groaned open slowly and he positioned himself between Axsen and the possibility of the return of the angry soldier. It was not him.

The new patient stepped in gradually feeling his way towards whatever was in front of him. He tapped with a stick on the limestone floor, inhaling the breath of Lucius before him. His tunic was dark and torn at the bottom.

"I am blind," he complained. "My eyes burn like fire and my sight is blurry at best."

He paused then added, "I went to the Temple of Aesculapius, and made my offering to the god but nothing happened. Then I stopped at the new foundation for the Temple of Roma, but they told me to leave, that Emperor Caligula could do nothing for a non-Roman."

At first, Lucius thought about the words, "Temple of Roma." When was either Rome or the Emperor a god to be worshiped, let alone heal?

He rubbed his hands together and his palms grew moist. Then Lucius glanced toward Axsen as she dropped her face in what seemed like doubt, if not sadness. There was nothing from her.

"What is your name?" Lucius asked.

The blind man said, "Bartholomew."

"Are you Jewish?" Lucius said.

"On my mother's side."

Lucius thought, *Why not go to the rabbis?*

Instead, he said, "Here among the Followers of the Nazarene, you are welcome. There are no Jews, no Greeks, no Romans nor Parthians." He looked at Axsen. "Just children of the one true Lord and his empire. We are all the same."

"Can you help me?" Bartholomew begged.

"Come with me," Lucius beckoned. Axsen followed, remaining silent. The physician took his patient to a window, swinging back the shutter with a loud squeak. He positioned Bartholomew in the light, then pulled his medical satchel from off his left shoulder. Extracting a small stoppered bottle from it, he opened the flask and poured a tiny bit of liquid into each of the man's eyes.

Bartholomew said, "Ahhh, that relieves the sting."

But Lucius was remembering an account of the Nazarene where Jeshua had told a blind beggar, "Go and wash in a sacred pool in Jerusalem." There was no pool here in the house of the Followers, at least not any about which he knew.

"Close your eyes," Lucius ordered. "Be silent." He put his fingers on the man's eyelids. Then he closed his own eyes and muttered something that neither the man nor Axsen could hear.

"Now open your eyes," Lucius said.

Bartholomew blinked, then shielded his eyes. "It is so bright! It is too much!" he shouted. Looking out the window, he screamed, "I see the street, I see the people, I see everyone moving and walking! I can see!"

The other patients in the room began murmuring. "This man is truly a physician," one said. "He does wonders," another added. "He is a miracle worker," a third said.

Lucius ignored them and responded, "You are not just cured of your blindness. You are *healed* but not from me, rather from the Nazarene."

Axsen stood more fixed and silent than before. Tears were running down her cheeks. Lucius stepped back from Bartholomew and from the window and wiped something from his own eye. A moist drop glistened on his right cheek in the light.

Lucius' slave now stepped close to him and leaned in, whispering, "You are truly a great and beloved healer whom I do not understand."

During all of this, the doorway to the clinic had swung open, and Tychicus stared in. He said to the blond Follower beside him, "Does the Apostle know about this man?"

Lucius looked at Bartholomew, then toward Axsen and said, "We need more space."

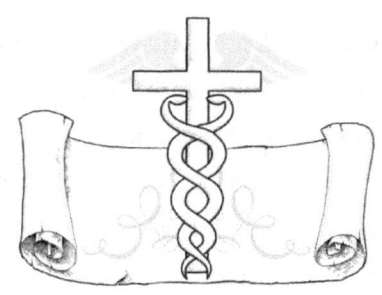

CHAPTER TWENTY-FIVE:
EMPIRE OF HEALING

"As he approached the gate of the town,
A man who had died was being carried out.
He was his mother's only son, and she was a widow..."
— Luke 7:12

Lucius' sandals slapped against the hot marble pavement as he passed the Agora with its market stalls and merchants. Odors of roasting pork and fish aroused his nose, reminding him that he had not eaten since early morning. A bag of coins on his belt clanked against his leg, but they were not the entire sum which had arrived from Italia, from Tuscana to be more specific.

The scroll in his hand was partially open and he re-read the words as he walked:

To Master Lucius, son of the late Horatius Maximus,
I will do as you order and prepare all of the documents for the sale. All
is well here as I have kept your farm in a good state even though....

Lucius glanced up as the stalls of the Agora vendors yielded to the temple section of Ephesus. Hammers chiseling large blocks of limestone drew him toward a foundation in the center of several small columned buildings. The builder held a scroll and waved his hand, directing slaves as to the exact placement of a row of stones.

A crate sat off the road with a familiar head and raised hand protruding from the top slats of wood. The curl of hair on the figure's forehead and the finger pointing up were undeniable—Caesar, Augustus' likeness to be exact.

Bartholomew was correct. This was to be a worship center like no other to the "genius" and spirit of Roma. This was how the Emperor controlled Asia. Lucius had seen no armies, no legionaries, at least not many, on Ephesian streets. "Worship" and a Temple to Caesar maintained the authority of Rome and the *Pax Romana*; but the peace was always peace through force and violence.

"Magnificent isn't it?" the architect said behind Lucius. He looked down at the money bag on Lucius' belt. "I am sorry. You will need to come back to make a donation. The priest may return soon."

"I do not wish to make an offering," Lucius said. "This is not my empire. I am about to invest in the empire of my god."

The builder's eyebrows raised, but Lucius never apologized. He brushed the architect's scroll aside with his scroll and his sandals continued slapping the Marble Street as he ignored the long low wall of this newest monument.

Again, he looked down at the words on the page which he unfurled to the glaring sun:

> *...though you are absent since your father's death, we have longed for your return to see the place of your birth one last time, before it is no longer yours. I am certain that it will...*

Lucius looked up, wrinkling the scroll together as a shadow covered his path. He had turned left without even thinking and was approaching the arch with its three gates opening to the ports. He could hear the waves crashing the docks and smell the salt air filling his lungs.

The shadow of the arch sped by and opened out to the limestone road which ended in the piers. Yet, his goal was not the docks but just before them to his right as his money bag clanked louder against his thigh.

He unfurled the scroll one last time and re-read:

> *I am certain the farm will bring seventy-five to one hundred talents. As soon as I receive the funds from the sale, I will remit them to you.*
>
> > *Your humble servant,*
> >
> > > *—Demetrius*

"The funds," as Demetrius, his father's trusted steward, had called them, arrived at the same time as this letter which was to precede them. It was a typical problem of the mails and shipping in the empire.

Still, Lucius had not brought all of it with him from the quarters of the Followers. He did not want to pay more than was necessary for the transaction about to occur, even though he was certain that he would pay too much.

"This warehouse is a fine structure," the little man droned on to Lucius. "It is spacious and secure and dry for storing any cargo."

"Come with me," Lucius ordered. The bright sun of the docks faded to a large, musty shadowed room. A door creaked in Lucius' hand when he shoved it open and ushered the land merchant into the subdued quiet of the limestone structure.

The Physician stretched out his hands. "This warehouse leaks like a linen cloth in a pouring rain. It is damp from the ocean breeze and it is as large as a chariot arena," Lucius criticized; but to himself, he thought, *I saw it my first day in Ephesus and it was as perfect then as it is now.* He would never let the land merchant know this.

Instead Lucius said, "I will give you forty talents for it and no more." His bag contained sixty but no use letting the little man know.

The land merchant was dark-complexioned with a stubble beard and brown hair covered in a loose head shawl. His robe was long, black and so wrinkled, that Lucius was certain that he must have slept in it. But he was alert and a tough negotiator, countering with words laced in the foulest wine breath, "I can take no less than fifty-five for it, not a sesterce less."

"Forty-five," Lucius said. He grabbed the bag at his waist and jingled it, then added, "I have nothing more or the sale is terminated."

"Done," the merchant said, shaking his head and pulling out a scroll from a satchel which Lucius had not noticed until now. The despicable man was so sure of the sale that he had already prepared the proper contract.

The Physician and the Followers would have a large splendid new space for the Nazarene's healing.

He was as proud of it as any action in his time as a soldier. Bartholomew, Axsen and a number of Followers along with their Physician moved into the musty leaking warehouse on the docks of Ephesus.

Axsen found bedding and cots so that no patient would rest on a blanket or worse yet, on the cold floor. At the Agora, she purchased cabinets for covers, bandages and bowls and cups. A small room at one end required the re-hinging of its door to provide a study for her master. But her crowning achievement was a writing desk and a set of shelves where scrolls and records could be placed and accessed from pigeon holes.

As thorough as her accomplishments were, they were counter-balanced by Bartholomew who had nowhere else to go so that he continued on here in the new clinic. Through his whiskers and from his flaxen brown robe, he whined about everything: the leaky roof with every rain, the musty smells, the complaining patients and the lack of medicines. Lucius thought that someone who had regained his sight as Bartholomew had should be grateful for even the smallest triumphs, but no.

And there was the Physician himself. When Lucius was not making rounds on patients or answering the questions of Axsen and other Followers, he was writing—again—another journal about the Nazarene. It was to replace what Mithradates had taken back to Parthia.

He had wanted to contact the Nazarene's mother, "Mary" was her name. She had come to Ephesus from Jerusalem before Lucius and with the Apostle Johannus, the same Johannus who had shared a cell with Lucius and Petros. Then one day Bartholomew, always the bearer of bad news, let Lucius know, "Mary had died."

"No use to search for her," he said.

How did Bartholomew know? Johannus had given the previously blind man the Nazarene's washing before Lucius had healed him.

So, Lucius would learn of the Nazarene's birth elsewhere. Instead, he wrote what he did know—the stories from Petros and other Followers, the miracles and the healings of course. And remaining as honest as he could, Lucius included the Nazarene's execution, the death which he had caused. But he never spoke about it to the others, not even to Axsen.

Yet, in between writing, bandaging and healing he watched—her. She did not move among the patients; she glided with a soft touch and a caring hand on a shoulder or an ointment on a wound, always with an encouraging word. The patients searched for her almost more than the Physician—more than Lucius himself.

The more he studied her every move, the way she pushed her hair back on her shoulder or wiped a tear from a child's eye or dressed a leper's sores, the more Bartholomew watched him. Finally, he said, "Physician, you are in love with her. She is your slave and can be nothing more to you."

Lucius said nothing. Each day he moved on among the cots as the beds filled in the hall, from ten to fifteen to twenty to over forty. People told him that they had abandoned the Temple of Aesculapius in favor of what not only the Followers but the whole city called "the Healing House of the Nazarene." Illnesses like leprosy and "the fevers" entered this former warehouse; but those maladies disappeared from their victims as everyone departed with health and renewal from what had become a sacred space—everyone, that was, except for one.

One day as Lucius stood watching Axsen, she rushed to someone else who had stumbled to the dockside doorway. A black form stood barely balancing herself, silhouetted and shrieking, "Where is the Physician? I am in pain." A veiled robe hobbled in, trailing a stream of water behind.

A woman's voice screamed again, "I am about to deliver. Have mercy on me and show me to a bed." The woman shoved between the close cots of patients, disregarding them. She knocked over a man attempting to rise on his crutches throwing him back onto his bed. Pushing forward further, she nudged a patient with a bandage over one eye but still lying on his cot.

Finally, Axsen wound around other attendants and through the cots, grabbing the woman as she was about to tumble onto a third man. This mother-to-be, looking up at Axsen with a face wrenched in pain, appeared older than she possibly was. The Parthian said, "Come with me," and ushered her to a corner bed across the hall.

Lucius had fixed a rope around the top of the area and reached for a blanket hanging to one side. Beyond the flaxen smell of the cover, he recognized the odor of birth fluids and followed Axsen and the new patient as she tumbled onto the private cot. A servant drew the curtain more completely around the birthing area but winced as the woman cried, "Help me! I beg you!"

The Physician eased her over on her back and knelt at the end of the bed between her knees, parting them. But as he began to reach in, the mother-to-be looked to her left and shouted, "No, *her!*" toward Axsen.

Lucius backed away and stood, motioning to his servant to move into his place. Axsen knelt down between the woman's legs and rolling her robe up, she maneuvered her into a squatting position face down on her knees.

She reached into the darkness under the dangling robe and glanced up at her master, shaking her head and then throwing it to her left for Lucius to come beside her. Her voice whispered, "I do not like how the infant is positioned. Something is mistaken here."

Then Axsen said in as soft of a voice as Lucius had ever heard from her, "Now, my mother, I must have you push hard." The sweat-covered woman groaned, "Aaagh!" as Axsen reached both hands around something and pulled it from the mother.

The form was covered in blood and fluid and smelled of birth, but there was nothing else, no whimpering and no cries. Again, Axsen glimpsed at Lucius and again she whispered, "The child is stillborn. It is gone."

Tears filled Axsen's eyes as she looked at Lucius' face, tears also rolling down each of his cheeks. As if nothing was amiss, she rose, cutting the cord and carried the newborn off to a bucket of warm water brought by one of the attendants. The woman had rolled onto her back, breathing in exhausted puffs.

"Is my child just—just quiet?" the new mother said.

"I am afraid too quiet," Axsen said, returning the small lifeless body to his mother.

"Aww!" the woman shouted. "I cannot endure this! This cannot be! My child cannot be—be stillborn."

Axsen wrapped an arm around the shaking shoulders of the mother and held her through each sob as she cuddled her motionless infant.

Lucius engulfed the scene with blurry watery eyes, uncertain of how to assist or what to say. Then suddenly he looked up and rubbed his face as if the answer had come—not in a cure but in a healing.

Before he could speak, Bartholomew stepped around towards the cot and whined his own advice, "Take the child now or she will become too attached to it."

Axsen ignored the words and said to the woman, "What is your name?"

Tears ran into the mother's mouth as she coughed then stuttered, "M-M-Mary. My name is Mary."

Lucius knelt beside the women and placed his arm over Axsen's on the woman's shoulder. He looked into the face of the dead baby and said softly. "Ah…like the mother of the Nazarene. Her name was also Mary."

Mary stopped crying and lifted her tear-stained face to the Physician with what seemed to Lucius to be a questioning look. His bearded face became firm but with drooping, kind eyes fixing upon hers.

He said, "Yes, you know that she lost her son, not once but twice."

The woman did not speak but waited. "She lost him once to a Roman cross and then a second time to the Nazarene's kingdom when he left her, left all of us," Lucius explained.

"But how do you know this?" the mother said, looking down at her son, then up at her doctor. "You are just a physician."

Lucius stared toward the curtain and then back to the mother. "Because I was there. I took him from her. I was not always a doctor. I was once a—a soldier. I crucified the Nazarene."

Bartholomew froze and stared at the Physician. Axsen fixed on him and not on the mother. Outside the curtain, every noise, every low voice ceased. "Healing House" became suspended in silence at the words of the Physician, or soldier, which was it?

All at once, the mother filled the vacuum saying, "But he came back to you and to us."

"Yes," Lucius whispered avoiding her face. His breath became cold in his mouth as he remembered that spring morning at the tomb.

The mother added, "And when he returned, he didn't kill you."

"No," Lucius said, rubbing his moistening eyes.

"He didn't kill you, so you could become *our* Physician," the woman said.

A wind rippled the blanket around Axsen and the mother. It allowed the light of a nearby window to shine on the water bucket which Axsen had used to wash the dead child. Lucius caught his own reflection, but suddenly it was not his likeness. The well-trimmed beard, a striped robe and the gray-streaked hair were someone else's—Caduceus' image sharpened in the liquid.

Bartholomew broke Lucius' concentration and said, "She scares the others, Physician. Let us bury the child and let her be gone."

The Physician focused on Axsen holding the woman tighter and countered, "Let her hold her son as long as she wishes and let them remain here."

The mother had gone out, bearing her dead infant to the street and the docks. She disappeared so completely that Lucius thought she might not have been real. But Axsen had held her, Bartholomew had whined about her and the other patients had whispered to one another as she departed.

Axsen and Lucius worked the rest of the day ministering to every hurt and every illness, while the sun dipped low and orange into the West. That night they did not return to a small cottage which Lucius had purchased after opening Healing House. Both slid down the wall at one end of the clinic and observed the patients beginning to lie down and sleep.

"Did it disturb you to be so truthful today?" Axsen asked her master.

"No," Lucius said.

"I believe that the one needing healing became a healer to *the* Healer," she said.

"Yes," Lucius whispered pointing to a patient who had put his finger to his lips to silence the pair.

"Please be quiet," another patient demanded.

"Do you like what you do here?" Lucius said dropping his voice and moving his lips close to Axsen's ear.

"I like it well enough," she answered.

A breeze blew through the open shutters of the clinic and the night torches fluttered. Lucius concentrated on how glistening the black hair was beside him and how her eyes sparkled, as always, like two rare jewels.

"But you should be somewhere else?" the Physician said.

"I should be here. I am yours," she said softly.

"You mean that you are my slave?" Lucius defined.

"No, I mean that I am yours," she responded, moving along the limestone up against his side.

He felt her softness, the warmth of her bronzed arm in the dim lighting. A tingle of pleasure ran up his back to his neck and hair.

"But who are you, Axsen?" he said, wanting to move behind the Parthian mask. There was more. He knew that her life, her connections were somewhere else and remained hidden to him.

She turned her face toward him and moved close to his beard, riveting on his dark eyes. "I am yours and only yours," she said. She pressed her lips onto his, taking his face into the long fingers of both her hands.

"Oh, please silence your words," a patient complained close to them.

Axsen backed her head from Lucius' face. She whispered, "I am drawn to a Healer who even allows himself to receive healing from his patients." She pressed her lips onto his again and nuzzled under his arm, leaning her head against his chest to feel his breathing.

Bartholomew was darting from bed to bed and stopping only at a servant here and a Follower attendant there. Patients were now rising on their cots and some were retreating from off their beds backing into those around them. Others scanned the room with searching eyes to discover what the disturbance was.

Lucius' eyes opened to all of this as he gently slipped his shoulder out from under Axsen's head, resting it back against the cool limestone wall. She continued sleeping. He stood and watched the panic of Bartholomew, not certain if it was his usual behavior or a situation which needed attention.

"They brought in a boy with fevers. He has a thickness of tongue and he aches and—and he will infect everyone," Bartholomew announced to a slave next to him. Lucius knew that it might be a simple coughing spell, but there was no way to be certain.

"Let me examine him," he said, surprising Bartholomew from behind. "Where is he?" Bartholomew pointed to yesterday's birthing area, the blanket partly hiding a man in a dark brown robe and maroon head covering.

As Lucius rounded the curtain, a younger woman stood beside the bearded man. She wore a frayed, worried look in a frayed gray robe and black-veiled head as she looked towards her son, breathing rapidly and lying on the cot where only yesterday another mother had lost her child in birth.

Lucius nodded to the parents and then knelt to the boy who groaned but never opened his eyes. He pried the child's mouth open and the tongue was indeed swollen along with a face and forehead that was beginning to cause sweating and shaking over the entire small body. Bartholomew was correct, but Lucius did not want to alarm all of Healing House.

He had seen an incident like this before but some time ago. It had not begun with someone from the docks or streets but within the clinic itself when rats had run unhindered from the ships and adjoining warehouses. Patients contracted "fevers" whenever the animals were near their cots or even bit them.

Lucius did not know if the rats were the cause of those fevers, but he ordered the attendants and slaves to move patients and beds to one side of the hall and the rats to be killed. They barred the doors and shuttered the windows for weeks while they washed walls, floors and bed linens with clean sea water. The brine smell stifled every nose so intensely that it was difficult to recognize where the beach ended and Healing House began. Yet it had worked; the illness had not returned from outside—until now.

All at once, the curtain rippled in the corner of Lucius' eyes, as he recognized the ivory robe and black hair of Axsen coming around behind the parents. She did not know what was happening to the child, but she ushered the mother aside and put her hand on the woman's shoulder.

"What are his symptoms? How long has he been like this?" she pressed.

Lucius suddenly saw the boy's eyes blink and open in slits as he groaned again upon his cot. The Physician exited and returned with his medical satchel, reaching in and pulling out a small stoppered jar. Raising the child, he poured the contents into the boy's mouth and worried about himself, Axsen and everyone if this was the return of "the fevers" from the rats.

But as Lucius said, "Lie back down," a bigger worry came whistling through the window beyond the curtained area. A smell of burning pitch followed a bright flash and intense heat causing the father of the boy to shout, "Watch out!" at Lucius and the small patient.

The Physician thrust the boy from the cot and a ball of flaming pitch replaced him. Blankets burst into flame, but Lucius looked up and out the window as a voice screamed, "This is for those who defy Rome's gods, Aesculapius and Apollo! Healing does not come from the Nazarene but from Caesar."

The perpetrator spun around and limped away around the building and towards a crowd on the docks. "Tend to the boy!" Lucius shouted towards Axsen.

She had grabbed another blanket and beat the cot with it. When the flames turned to smoke, she ran to the other side of the bed and lifted the child whose arm was now smoking.

"Bartholomew, assist Axsen for me!" Lucius ordered. Then the physician, returning to his centurion ways, bolted beyond the curtain and shoved his way through cots and patients, nearly knocking two attendants to the floor. At the doorway he scanned the walkway along the docks, realizing that the flame thrower did not run, but limped down the street pushing workers, slaves and merchants aside, trying to lose himself in their chaos.

Lucius kept him in focus and began sprinting towards him, closing in, a barrier of bodies bobbing back and forth, revealing the limping man then covering him again. He hobbled as fast as he could but the waves of people were beginning to lessen.

Truly the man looked familiar as Lucius narrowed the gap. A weathered gray look with graying hair stirred in the Physician's memory.

The last bodies dwindled away between the two of them and Lucius was now certain of his identity. "Halt, Marius!" Lucius leapt up and fell upon the limping man as Marius looked up into the pouncing face of his attacker. They slammed to the limestone pavement and into the shade of the arched gates along the port street.

Lucius rolled the man over onto his back and grabbed his arms behind him. "You injured a boy back there, soldier," he said as he lifted the assailant and dragged him back down the docks to Healing House.

Bartholomew met them at the door. The entire clinic choked with smoke and the odor of burning pitch.

Bartholomew said, "We got as much smoke out as we could." He pointed towards the smoldering cot and there was no boy on it. Instead, Axsen and his mother embraced the small patient.

"I have the mother and father at peace," Axsen whispered to

Lucius but she added, "Their son's arm is badly burned." She had left the parents and made her way through the hall to her master.

Lucius jerked Marius' arms up behind him and bound them with a cord which one of the slaves had now brought him. "Bind his ankles, too," he said to Bartholomew. "We'll dispense with him later."

But dispense how? The Nazarene had said, "You will be hated by all because of my name." The empire which Lucius now served was a kingdom of healing ruled by the Nazarene; and it would receive the same violent response as its crucified king from every other empire. So, the Marius's would not be one; they would be legion.

The Physician glanced down toward Axsen and raised his eyebrows to know if she were injured. She shook her head in reply seeming to indicate that she was unscathed. But he examined her up and down to be certain as the flaming ball had barely missed her on its way to the cot.

Suddenly she returned his concern and half smiled, responding, "Physician, if we work any closer on these cases, we should certainly be married."

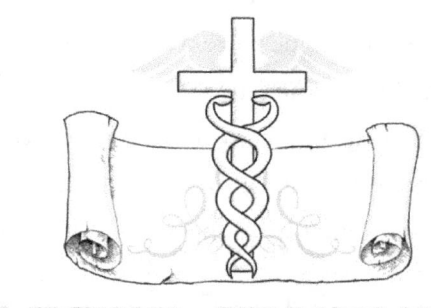

CHAPTER TWENTY-SIX:
A SIMPLE MARRIAGE BETWEEN UNEQUALS

"Jesus said to them, 'You cannot make wedding guests fast
while the bridegroom is with them, can you?'"
— Luke 5:34

A plain face with dark brown hair tilted up towards Lucius. The eyes were kind and appeared approving when they moved so close to his that he could feel her breath. Aurelia, his mother, said, "You are such an honorable son to me. You have done precisely what I desired for you."

A shove came erasing the face and replacing it with another—a puffy, whiskered one with a graying Roman haircut. The mouth curled in anger and said, "You are weak—a woman. Of no use to me nor to Rome." The words growled out of Father Horatius like a bear.

Another face eclipsed the second but remained shadowed so that Lucius was uncertain of it. The half-smile was surrounded by a well-trimmed beard and eyes which brought compassion like—like

Caduceus. As it stepped into the light the beard grayed into the face and the face withered into the gray of Marius who did not speak but simply stood before him as if he were waiting for something.

Lucius spun backwards and the shape of a woman emerged in sheer ivory robes. Her hair was light but he could not discern if it was because it was illuminated from above or if it was golden. Her eyes were also darkened, presumably by the same light but she invited him to be with her.

She said, "I am yours. I will be your wife."

Lucius breathed out, "Axsen." He blinked and opened his eyes to the burly sandy beard of Bartholomew who was shaking him. Was Lucius dreaming or was it some sort of vision?

"Wake up, Physician!" Bartholomew shouted. "You are to marry today. Though I remain warning you that you should not marry her until you have freed her."

Lucius realized that he was in his study at Healing House and that after a sleepless night, he had rested his head on his table while continuing more work on the Nazarene's journal. Odors of urine, aloes and brine swirled in from the main floor of the clinic until Bartholomew walked over and gently latched the door.

Then he said, "Axsen is a slave and Romans do not marry their slaves. Postpone the wedding today. Free her first. Besides, she is not a Follower and the Apsotle Paulus tells us not to be yoked to unequals."

Lucius raised up into the light streaming in from the window to one side of the room, then said, "Here we are all the same. In *this* empire there are no freedmen or slaves, Jews or Gentiles. You know this, Bartholomew. Regardless, my love of the Nazarene will make her a Follower."

But there was another argument which Lucius withheld from his trusted attendant. He recalled a scene from two months ago: Marius had burned the little boy in his attempt to torch Healing House.

Lucius had not only caught him and brought him back; he made the scoundrel confront the boy and his frightened parents. Once he had Marius bound, he pulled him through the cots and patients and motioned the family of his victim into his study. Lucius was about to close the door when a shadow pushed against him.

Axsen had followed them into the room. When the Physician finished with the family, he instructed them to see Bartholomew for some food and for a closer examination of their son's bandages. The boy was feeling as light-headed from his fever as from the attack, but the parents slowly led him out the door.

When they were gone, Lucius said to Marius, "Who are you? You have seen the fear which you have brought to these sad people? What defense do you make for yourself?"

"My actions need no defense," he blurted out pulling against his bindings and realizing that they had never finished securing his ankles. "I serve the one true empire—Rome! This—this kingdom of the Nazarene is a sham. He is no king. Hail Caesar!"

Before Luicius could counter, Axsen stepped around her master. Her turquoise eyes flashed and fixed on the lame man so viciously that Marius had to look down. When he glanced up, her look had not altered.

Her full fury unleased and she said, "Go ahead and justify your foolish empire and the weak, immoral fools like Claudius who rule it! But tell me this, have you ever seen the power of the Nazarene?"

Marius shook his head "No."

"Then you best know that I have seen it and felt it with more force than Rome could ever muster in a thousand years!"

"Where?" the lame man whispered.

"Look around out there in the hall, Marius," Axsen said. "Rome makes us one, if you can call us that, with armies, soldiers like you, slaves and force. Its power does not free; its power enslaves both rich and poor alike——."

Forget Marius. Lucius' memories of his own sins on behalf of Rome interrupted. He saw himself and another woman in Illyricum whom his friend, Marcus, had killed. Axsen did not know about her. But she did know about another image which came to him: the Parthians writhing on their crosses at the oasis when he and his fellow soldiers left them to die. She was right: Rome was force, all force, and he had been a full participant.

The door of the study creaked open and a brown tunic entered in the person of a slave who said to Lucius, "Physician, what should I do with the boy and his father and mother?"

Lucius replied, "Are they comfortable? Did Bartholomew not attend to them?"

The slave bowed but added, "They are Samaritans. Are we to help the likes of them?"

"You know that we heal all," Lucius said. The servant bowed again and retreated out the door.

"Did you hear that, Roman?" Axsen said to Marius. "That is the first power of the Nazarene. He heals all. *All.* Rome is only for Romans. It oppresses the rest of us to keep that power."

"Perhaps," Marius said. "But I was not healed."

"It is because you wanted a cure, not a healing," Axsen said.

"I am a Parthian and yet, I have seen with my own eyes a man healed of blindness from the hands of this man," she added grabbing Lucius' arm. "His healing hands are empowered by nothing except the spirit of the Nazarene. You can 'Hail Caesar' all you wish but Caesar cannot make a blind man see and Caesar does not see the world with love. I have seen this. Have you, Roman?" "Roman" came out as if she were spitting poison from her mouth.

The lame man admitted that his own friends had all abandoned him. He had no one. "It matters to no one what I think," Marius confessed.

"It is time, Physician…regardless of what I think" Bartholomew interrupted Lucius' memories.

Even with his thoughts of the pathetic and suspicious Marius, Lucius returned to the present and wondered more about her. *For weeks when we first met, the woman would not say a word to me, not even her name. When she unleashed like a cornered wolf on Marius, it was about the Nazarene. What a mystery! Why not marry her?*

He swung the door open and a slight breeze entered from the clinic. The Physician looked into a brass plate which Bartholomew held up before him and stepped out of the safety of his study. He had shaved and trimmed his beard before his nap. His hair was cut to a proper Roman length with bangs adorning his forehead; and he donned an ivory tunic cinching it with a new leather belt.

The beds, blankets and patients had all been pushed around to the sides of Healing House. Up front, towards his study, a small table had been set with a cup of wine and flat bread on a red clay plate.

Lucius waved to the slaves and attendants gathered mostly towards the front doors of the clinic. They were waiting for her. As he wound his way through the beds, patients stretched out a hand to their doctor or they raised a friendly wave if they were too ill to sit up.

"Yes," one said behind him.

"Should have happened months ago," another agreed.

From down the hall, a third shouted, "You are a blessed man, Physician! May the Nazarene give you and the woman a long life together and with us."

Lucius breathed in and coughed at the air, again odors of salt brine, aloes and urine choking him. Then an aroma of lavender floated over the entire clinic, causing him to look up to the main entrance.

A woman's form was silhouetted there in the morning sun with a glare around it as if the light were emanating from her. She moved forward into the dimmer glow of Healing House. A black mane of curls framed her face and forehead with the remaining hair pulled back into a bun on her head. Her turquoise eyes found Lucius and her ivory robe, gathered at her waist with a white cincture, swished just inside the door as she waited.

Bartholomew came up behind Lucius and the Physician said, "She looks like one of the angels who announced the birth of the Nazarene."

"Still," Bartholomew said, "remember that you are the only Follower in your couple."

Instead, Lucius remembered her confession to Marius. The Physician broke from Bartholomew and nearly pranced to her.

"Blessed morning, my dear one," he said taking her long fingers in his. She leaned forward and kissed his lips. The room stopped.

He guided her to the table and he stopped. Bartholomew had positioned himself to one side but he was not the Presider. Too many protests from him about the marriage prevented that.

Another moved out from the attendants and down through the cots at its edge. Though he was clean-shaven like a Roman and not as withered or gray as he had been since the Followers offered him a better diet of lamb and vegetables, his eyes and brown tunic could not hide his previous life as a soldier. He nodded to the couple and limped around them behind the table.

Lucius' dream returned as he instantly recognized Marius. Axsen's confession had proven too convincing and Marius succumbed to the Nazarene's washing and to long periods of instruction which gave him leadership status among the Followers. Yet, he was not healed of his lameness and some among the Followers wondered why. He motioned for silence in the room and a hush fell as he waited for all eyes to turn forward.

"Our Lord and Master, the Nazarene, has said, 'And the two shall become one,'" Marius said. A collective sigh arose from the patients, slaves and attendants. Bartholomew looked on with a furrowed forehead. Lucius was not certain if Bartholomew's behavior was about Axsen or about the Presider.

Inside himself the Physician's elation turned to worry, like the cloud now covering the sun. He was not bothered about Marius. Would Lucius ever "be one" with this Parthian or would she always be mysterious—and separate?

INTERLUDE

(72 C.E.—REIGN OF VESPASIANUS)

"**B**ut I thought *you* married the Physician, *avi,*" Anoys said with her pale blue eyes growing wide at me. Her bronze face twisted into a look which told me that she thought that I had led her and her cousins into a lie. They all stopped fussing with their cloth dolls on my atrium floor as the sun grew hazy above them.

"I did—almost," I hedged shifting on my round-backed Roman chair.

Miriam shook her brown hair and said, "*Almost* is *not* married!"

"No, it isn't," I agreed. My little ones sent my mind backwards to my early days in Ephesus. My memory fixed upon his chiseled brown-haired face when he had said, "Will you marry me?" I did not know the Physician's history and no one had told me about Axsen. I did not know why.

We had seen one another more than once, more than many times, as he made the journey from Healing House up the street through the three-arched gates to the Marble Street, the temple district and the Agora markets and finally to where he had settled me and the grandmothers of these three girls playing at my feet—in the Terrace Houses.

He loved to walk with me through my small atrium with its frescoes and its center pool or out through the cozy park which lined Marble Street and led back to the markets. After he proposed, his life burdened with the patients who filled Healing House and spilled over to the Followers' meeting place just below my home.

These became victims as a drought led to starvation, famine and all of the diseases which went with them. Unlike the past, Lucius could no longer speak of his patients coming to him in sickness and leaving renewed and well. Many died and his heart died with them.

So, when I set our wedding, I determined to make the day a renewal which would contrast to the rest of his sad work and his melancholy life. My atrium exploded with the fragrance of roses, hyacinths, and poppies in every corner. It was as if the characters in my entry room frescoes appeared to be hiding behind floral fortresses. I left nothing to fate and joined my kitchen slaves in preparing the best calves, lambs and fowl for my guests.

The aromas of these fine meats and dishes flowed like a river from my kitchen and triclinium, nearly snuffing out the floral scents in my atrium. If I had spent a night with one Follower named Apollos in Corinth, I was certain to be with the Physician for a life time.

Truly the day was uninterrupted by my Love as Lucius was not only fighting the effects of the drought on his patients but had gone on one of his short journeys. All would go to chaos at Healing House whenever he was absent. So, while I was ordering my slaves to move couches and chairs, serving tables and plates, I imagined him, upon his return, commanding Bartholomew and Marius to attend three and four patients each. He had no one else other than a few slaves and attendants from the Followers.

As for me, I had Phoebe, my long-time friend from Cenchreae near Corinthia. She was such a blessing, knowing where to place tables, flowers and serving plates.

"I like this home more than Corinthia," she insisted. "Though it will be crowded with everyone whom you have invited," she admitted, brushing back her black hair as it fell across her face from all of the work.

"It is fine," I said. "I want to share my joy with everyone. All of the Followers here who have welcomed me and to the entire city beyond."

Men of some stature in Ephesus arrived in white togas after mid-day. The slaves plied them with wine. Some of my women friends from the neighborhood came in their best *stolas,* these robes of maroon, green and blue belted with metallic cinctures at their waists. Their hair was twisted into tight buns at the back of their heads with curls dangling down the sides of their faces.

By the early afternoon a Presider had come from the Followers in Antioch, a man whom I thought my husband-to-be knew, one Barnabas, a travel companion of the Apostle Paulus.

Phoebe was correct as all of my guests jammed my atrium and dining area until no one could move. But if the flowers, the food, the guests and the Presider were here, "the guest of the day" was not.

We waited, we waited and when the afternoon drifted into the longer shadows of early evening, we waited for no one else except

Lucius. My stomach began to swirl and my palms moistened. I knew that he knew what day it was.

I nudged a path through the triclinium, smiling and greeting each guest, a toga-clad business associate in front of me, one of my women friends in a shimmering blue *stola,* smelling of cedar and cinnamon and dozens of others. A head bobbed in front of me and parted to offer me a way to the atrium. I shoved two tunic-clad Followers aside nearly knocking them into a bank of red and white roses. They smiled and stepped aside.

I went for the steps to the upper street level and my entry door to the outside. I thought, *These are the steps where Lucius had first brought me and my daughters and granddaughters to descend down to a dim musty entry room on a dark and frightening night, leaving my old home of Corinthia in a whirlwind.* I was alone then but now I thought, *Alone no more, I hope.*

My foot slipped off a step as I reached the top and regained my balance just in time to turn and see all of my guests below. They were beginning to gossip.

"Is the Physician ill?" a tall blond woman asked.

"The Physician?" a man said beside her. "I have never seen that man ill even for a day."

"Where is he then?" a third woman, a Follower, said, "He certainly did not forget his own wedding this time. I know that he didn't the first time. I was there."

And I knew what had happened as he had told me and I assured him it would not be his fate again; but my worry was now with him, not with Axsen. Crowds were hurrying home for the evening meal. But for me there was nothing and no one. What had happened? I needed an explanation.

I turned back in to the torch lights which the slaves had lit in my atrium. I scanned my company again and I felt the trickle of perspiration down my back moistening my ivory robe adding to my sweating hands. I sighed.

Then feigning a pent-up cheerfulness, I shouted to the guests below, "My groom is delayed. Let us enjoy more wine and the wonderful small fowl which my kitchen slaves have roasted all day."

Suddenly these memories broke and the interruption of my great grandchildren brought me back to the present, mostly because of a question which my guests from the past could have asked.

Livia said, "So, did you ever marry Lucius? Or did something happen to him?"

I was grateful that she had not inquired about her own grandmother nor the grandmothers of her cousins which I had all but forgotten on my wedding day. I panned across the faces of all of my babies, my dear *puellae:* and I stopped at the bronze look of Anoys.

I said, "That is the remainder of my story. And the most critical part for you, dear Anoys."

"Then tell us, please, *avi.* Don't be so mysterious!" Anoys insisted.

PART TWO

AFTER THE APOSTLE

(44 C.E. TO 70 C.E)

CHAPTER ONE:
A STRANGER'S VISIT

"You also must be ready for the Son of Man
is coming at an unexpected hour."
— Luke 12:40

"He has shown strength with his arm, he has scattered the proud in the thoughts of their hearts. He has brought down the powerful from their thrones, and lifted up the lowly; he has filled the hungry with good things, and sent the rich away empty."

L ucius re-read the words and laid down his stylus on the writing table. The wood of the desk drifted into his nose along with the mustiness of his scroll about the Nazarene. He reached for the wine cup sitting to one side of the parchment, took a swallow and then put a piece of fish into his mouth from the plate next to it. The breakfast was cold from the time he had given to his writing.

A shadow covered him, and he thought that Axsen had come through his door open to the chatter and the ward outside. He looked up.

Bartholomew was above him, reading the words which he had penned. "What do these thoughts mean, Physician; and about whom are they spoken?"

"They are for Romans, emperors and even religious authorities. They describe their ultimate end," Lucius explained.

"But such writing is treasonous. Who spoke this?" Bartholomew said.

"They are the words of the Nazarene's mother about her son and his kingdom," Lucius responded. "Treason or not."

All at once a breeze banged the shutter on the study window and rustled the scroll before its writer. A voice whispered, "Someone— someone—." It cut off, but Lucius was certain that he had heard it.

"Someone, what?" he asked.

"What someone?" Marius said as he crossed the threshold of the study and eyed both men.

"Nothing," Lucius said and swept the scroll into a cylindrical curl as Marius looked over at the words upside down. Lucius spun backwards on his stool and shoved the parchment into a pigeon hole in the cabinet behind him. Marius stared at where the work had been placed—in the center. Why?

He avoided the suspicious man. Axsen, wearing a gray work robe and leather apron, had come into the clinic. She eased her way between the cots, offering a morning greeting to each patient. Her eyes met her husband's through the study door; and she conveyed a quick smile, her turquoise look refreshing him like a pool of comfort in the desert of his early morning writing and the chatter of his two attendant magpies.

Lucius watched her and pondered about the years since their wedding. She had become a partner, definitely not a slave and not merely a wife. Though her patient care was "clinical," he learned much through her about herbs, elixirs and the mysteries of medicines from the East.

When he faced renewed cases of pain, she offered the secret of an anesthesia, a medicine called "laudanum." She even warned about its excesses saying, "You must use only a small amount. Too much will bring death."

Yet, as they ministered together, Lucius knew that *his* was a more "complete" healing, touching not only body but heart. Every bone set, every pain relieved, every rash soothed was not because of his curing hands, not because of faith in their Physician, not even because of faith in the Nazarene but rather all was a healing freely given from the Nazarene himself.

"Nooo...Aurelius," Axsen cooed to a little brown-eyed boy just outside his study. "You must keep that dressing on your arm one more week at least."

The tone recalled the night before when he felt the same power in her love for him. What he studied here by day, he experienced with her by night, her body warming and disarming him in the cottage which they had away from Healing House. Her love did not steal his strength; it renewed it.

The patients, the cases, they all folded into one mission of love, not only inspired by the Nazarene's love but by theirs. He certainly was not stifled by the worry of Bartholomew—that Axsen was not a Follower.

Clang! Clang! Clang! Suddenly a flash from the open doors on the street erupted like a summer storm outside the threshold of

Healing House. Lucius diverted from the shape and softness of Axsen as a gray whirling flurry of clothing bolted from one side of the entrance to another.

In the adjoining window to the side of the doors, the brown shape of a pointed head covering bobbed with every blow of a *rhomphaia* upon someone beyond Lucius' view. Ring! The next strike of the long barbarian weapon came against an invisible opponent.

"You filthy Roman ass! Your empire will be overrun," the barbarian shouted as he swung his sword against "the filthy" whoever he was.

Lucius jerked up from his stool and panned across for Axsen. She was gone. He shoved Bartholomew and Marius aside and bolted through the beds, covers and patients as he sprinted to the entry doors. Where was she?

Arriving at the street, the barbarian, at least two heads taller than his Roman opponent who wore nothing but a black tunic and sandals, was banging his long sword off a *gladius* held crosswise to him. As the pointed cap rang his weapon down for what appeared to be a fatal blow upon the older man with gray hair, it glanced off and sliced a gash into the Roman's sword arm.

"Aaagh!" he shouted. But Axsen saw an opportunity. With the huge barbarian off balance at the edge of the street, she ran at him with her entire body and rammed him so hard that he not only stumbled off balance but slung his *rhomphaia* into the air. It rang onto the limestone street barely avoiding its owner's head when it fell against the hard stones.

"Parthian pig," Axsen yelled. "Can you not see that this man is older than you? Your empire is not welcome here. Get out of this city before I alert the Proconsul."

The "Parthian pig" panted as his eyes widened at the Roman being rescued by a—a woman. Lucius smiled and waited in the doorway to be assured that his wife was not about to become the barbarian's next victim.

The pointed cap gathered his gray robe and reached for his sword. He waved an angry hand, not a sword, at this new opponent and said, "Not worth the effort."

Axsen had moved on to the bloody upper arm of the older man, taking his other hand and pressing it against the slash. She grabbed his weapon and led him towards her husband.

"Come with me," she ordered as she smiled at Lucius and escorted him into the clinic. "I have some laudanum which will ease the pain. I can suture your wound."

Lucius watched and wondered what manner of wife he had. Or did she have him?

"**W**hat happened out there?" Bartholomew asked as Lucius, carrying the *gladius* which Axsen had given him, walked back into his study.

"Just another day among the Ephesians," he said. He did not want to arouse concern about the return of the Parthians on the eastern frontier. It was not just another street scuffle.

Bartholomew suddenly said, "Regardless, Physician, we need more income as those we heal cannot pay us." He gestured to the study door and the beds beyond.

The talents from the sale of his family villa in Tuscana were drying up like a wadi in summer. Enemies from without were not as troublesome as the enemies from within Healing House.

"Nor would I want them to," Lucius said coming back from his thoughts about the Parthian, his wife's boldness and the older Roman which she was treating, gently dabbing the sutured wound on his arm.

Marius said, "So where do we secure the funds for your work, Doctor?"

"Not my work," Lucius corrected. "The Nazarene's."

Marius was continuing to focus on the scroll in the cabinet behind Lucius' desk.

"Someone—someone close to you—" a voice breathed.

"Someone?" Lucius said.

"What?" Marius said.

"Husband," Axsen's voice interrupted, standing at the threshold of the study. "Someone is here to see you. He says that he is a Follower whom they call the Apostle."

The "Someone" which Lucius had heard calling to him was not her voice.

"**M**y name is Paulus. I am an Apostle for the Nazarene," the stranger said. He was short, a head and a half shorter than Lucius himself, and older, his beard and hair were graying into the forties, at least ten years older than the Physician. He was wearing a black robe but it was not threadbare and his head was covered with one of the long prayer shawls worn by Jewish Pharisees or rabbis.

"I am from Tarsus and a Jew," he said. "Though I am a Roman citizen like yourself, I hear. Since Damascus, I am now a citizen of another kingdom, that of the Nazarene."

Damascus, Lucius thought, *What about Damascus?*

Paulus filled the silence and said, "I see what I have heard about. You are indeed a healer—a physician of the first order, Lucius Maximus."

Lucius paused then finally said, "So others say. But I am also a soldier." Then he blurted out, "I may be a healer for the Nazarene; but know this, Apostle, I also crucified him."

Out in the clinic, patients sat up on their cots. Attendants stopped bandaging wounds or giving water or cradling fevered heads. All chatter clipped off into a quick uneasy quiet, waiting for the next response.

"Oh," Paulus said. "I only tried to kill his Followers. You have outdone me. Good!"

The Apostle smiled and stared into Lucius' face.

"The Nazarene can use both of us," Paulus continued. "I want to speak to you about that. Let us talk privately."

Lucius dismissed Marius and Bartholomew. He thought about Axsen and watched her as she had returned to the Roman fight victim. Then he closed the door to his study and invited only the Apostle to be seated.

CHAPTER TWO:
TROUBLING DEPARTURE

"Now when these things begin to take place,
stand up and raise your heads, because
your redemption is drawing near."
— Luke 21:28

"Why must you go with him?" Axsen pleaded. Tears swam in her eyes. Turquoise began to melt into red.

"The Apostle has a mission for sharing the news of the Nazarene in the north and east of Asia. He has requested me to bring the Nazarene's healing with him," Lucius persisted.

"Did you not see the fight yesterday, husband? Tensions are rising on the frontier here. My people are harassing again," she said. Her eyes dropped to the floor, then looked up at him.

"But there is something else with you. I know it," she said.

Lucius averted his eyes from her face, too inviting with its tears. He said, "We also need more support for Healing House. Our Followers here do all that they can, but they do not have enough to

203

help us, especially with the famine. Look at the boy just outside my door, Axsen. He can barely stand from hunger."

"How will running off with the Apostle help?"

"I want to feed those who come for healing. We need more funding for food and med—" the Physician said, pausing.

"Are you ready for the journey, my beloved doctor," a stranger's voice boomed through the door of Lucius' study. The Apostle, dressed in a coarse brown robe with no shawl over him and a large travel roll on his shoulder, filled the threshold.

Axsen's eyes widened. Her husband had already packed his medical satchel and flaxen bag for the trip. He grabbed each and crisscrossed them over his shoulders. From a hook at the wall, he reached for his belt and strapped his centurion's sword around his waist.

"I will miss you every hour of every day," his trembling voice said. He scooped her up into his muscled arms and offered a long kiss. Then he backed away with tears filling his eyes now.

"Care for everyone as if we were both here. But watch over Bartholomew and do not allow his complaints to rule your decisions. Also be mindful of Marius. I do not tru—" he broke off.

Her head cocked at this last order. Two others came up behind the Apostle. A balding man stood over Paulus on his left while a teenage boy in a red, blue and green-striped robe wore a serious face behind the Apostle's right.

"Allow me to introduce our travel companions, Silas here," Paulus said gesturing to his left. "And young Timotheos of Antioch," he said pointing over his shoulder on his right.

Lucius remembered Timotheos from his own days in Antioch, but not well. He looked back at his study and as the men turned and snaked through the beds, he wondered, "How long will I be gone? What will be left of Healing House when I return?" Even more worrisome, could Axsen carry on without him?

The barren hill country of Asia rolled out before them like a rippling brown ocean. It all appeared the same, scrub trees, stubby oaks and hard sand, beaten and baked by the blinding sun. They had left the coast days ago, pushing inland through small villages and poor, famished people.

To the Apostle, it was like a paradise, an "Arcadia" as the Greeks called it, of new acquaintances and believers in the love of the Nazarene. Silas and Timotheos were more silent and never commented except about the weather or the small offerings of bread and dried fish from the locals. Lucius wondered what he was doing there.

The towns could not support the work which he had done in Ephesus, and he had only splinted a small girl's leg who had fallen down a rocky dry creek bed. He explained to her parents how long to use the splints, but he was uncertain that they understood.

Still, they wanted to pay—a few sesterces which the Physician recognized as all that they had. "I cannot take this. The healing from the Nazarene is without cost except in love for all of you from me and the Nazarene," he said. The man and his wife offered a humble meal of crusty bread and watery lentil soup instead.

Lucius smiled, but he also felt their ache at wanting to provide more. Asia would provide an unconditional embrace from its poor, but no help for the poor of Ephesus nor for Healing House.

Besides the girl, there had been only a few other patients including assisting Paulus in circumcising Timotheos whose mother was Greek but who had become a Follower in Antioch. Lucius questioned the Apostle about this Jewish ritual but all Paulus said was "I believe trouble may be coming up ahead in the larger cities with Jewish populations." Then, why not Lucius, too? But he did not ask.

Out on the journey again, the winds began to trick Lucius' thoughts. "Someone," a voice whispered. "Someone—someone close to you," the air swirled in his ears. *"Someone" what?"* he said to himself. But the Apostle heard him.

Paulus said, "Someone what, Lucius?"

"The wind has tricked me into believing it speaks," Lucius said.

"Oh," the Apostle said. "Like the Spirit."

A small city called Derbe gave them one Roman convert, named Gaius, a small wizened man with great wrinkles in his face and a red tunic from his service in the military, but not much else, no funds or time for any clinic to be established. They lasted in the town one day and marched on the next morning to a more formidable city which Lucius did know.

Lystra was a Greek center of some means in its time; but at the outskirts of the Empire, its time had faded. Augustus had made it a Roman colony like Corinthia and other Greek towns, but this outpost had veterans from Roman legions for citizens. A few Jews had also built a synagogue.

That dingy little limestone hovel was the very place where Paulus wanted to be. Lucius was amazed at his change one morning when the Apostle appeared from the bushes refreshed after a bath in the adjacent stream and dressed in black robe and ivory prayer shawl like the moment when Lucius had met him.

He led the group, Silas, Timotheos and Lucius following,

through the market stalls and past a water fountain to a narrow street with few buildings. They pushed their way through thirty or so Jewish males, dressed like Paulus and congregated outside of one structure; and then they entered the dark, torch-lit auditorium with benches and a rostrum adorned with only a leather seat.

The Jewish men filed in, leaving the women and a few Romans and Greeks staring through the odor of a cedar screen at the back. This included Lucius, Silas and even the newly circumcised Timotheos. "Gentiles must not pollute our place of worship to Adonai," a Jewish leader said to the Apostle.

Paulus' sermon was more like a lawyer convincing a group of witnesses that the Nazarene was "the Messiah" and "the Suffering Servant" of their Scriptures. When he finished, the audience paused as if they were uncertain about what to say next.

Then the questions hurled at Paulus like exploding cinders from a volcano.

"How can one such as you tell us that the Servant of Isaiah is this—this Nazarene?" one young black robe shouted.

"Yes, and since when does the Messiah arise from Nazareth? We know that he comes from the tribe of Jesse," another countered.

The room descended into chatter and shouting. Lucius' mind drifted but he was certain that the Apostle was not in any danger from these debaters. He inhaled the cedar smell and backed out from between Silas and Timotheos. Easing between the black robes of three women and the gray fraying tunic of a Gentile, he vanished out the door of the synagogue into the full heat of the afternoon.

He wanted to see Augustus' city for himself so he strolled back across the marketplace towards the temple district. The monuments were smaller than in Ephesus, a row of columns supporting a granite structure to Apollo, a white single entrance shrine hailing Aphrodite and then came an open space with a long, wide disturbing foundation like he had seen in Ephesus.

A workman caught him staring and stopped with an admiring grin. "I know it is not the temple to Roma which Ephesus has, nor Corinthia. But we'll make something of it for the glory of Emperor Caligula there," he said pointing to a white marble likeness radiating in the sun at the road's edge and looking more like a fake Augustus with short-cropped hair and raised right hand.

"I would not know. That is not my king nor my kingdom," Lucius confessed. "I am a Follower of the Nazarene. I serve his kingdom."

"Oh, one of those," the workman in his dirty tan tunic said, shaking the dust from his hair. "But you must admit, sir, that our empire protects yours."

"How so?" Lucius questioned.

"We build roads for your travel, raise armies for your protection and foster business for your support even here at the farthest reaches of Rome's rule."

"Perhaps," Lucius consented. He halted.

A pointed-capped warrior said, "That depends on whose empire you belong to." His Greek was perfect but sneering. He reached for his long sword, pulling it to the edge of his scabbard.

"Excuse me, Parthian, but you best remember where you are," Lucius intervened.

"And who will remind me? Not the likes of you," he snarled.

Lucius thought that Axsen was correct, that tensions seemed to be rising as these warriors were not the "spies" moving and hiding among the crowds as they had been years ago. With the one some months ago engaging in a fight outside Healing House and this man, they were visible and pushing in along the edge of the frontier.

"Sheath your weapon, soldier," Lucius commanded.

Instead, the Parthian pulled it with a ring. Suddenly he stopped. His eyes widened in shock at discovering the *gladius* of Lucius already at his stomach. The warrior jumped back. Sweat trickled down Lucius' back. At last, the pointed cap walked backwards, escaping the reach of the Roman sword and turning away into the smoke and incense fumes of the other temples.

The workman said, "Much appreciation. Can I repay you?"

As Lucius shook his head "no," a thud came from where "Caligula" stood. A clunk followed the noise of a rock crashing against an even harder stone and ending in the sound of someone smashing something like an alabaster vase. The Parthian roared in a bellowing laugh, "Ha, ha, ha." He re-sheathed his sword

"Caligula" stood beside him but only from the shoulders down. The "emperor" was completely de-capitated..

"You must pay for that, foreigner," the workman shouted at the Parthian.

"It appears that we are even, sir. My empire has now protected yours," Lucius interrupted. "But perhaps you can charge the repairs to *his* empire."

When they reached Troas on the north coast of Asia, a letter was waiting for him. At the docks Timotheos handed it to Lucius while they waited on the Apostle to speak with a boatman.

"I am sorry that I forgot to give this to you," the young Follower said. "It was given to me by a Follower in Lystra. "It must have arrived when we were visiting the synagogue."

Months had passed and they had moved too fast to send word back to Axsen, but also Lucius had not heard from her. Salt air filled his nose as he inhaled the ocean and listened to its waves at the port; yet it was the parchment and its mustiness that returned him to the news in his hand. The intermittent scents of lavender revealed the author even before he opened it. It was from her.

> *To my beloved Lucius,*
> *All is not well here at Healing House. I am alone as Bartholomew has traveled out into the city and beyond to secure more funds since our last talents are all that we have left. Marius has disappeared and no one here or among the Followers knows where he has gone.*

Lucius heard the chatter between Silas and Timotheos. They were growing impatient and wondering what the Apostle planned for Troas and beyond. He looked back at the page.

> *I feel your love all around me and the love of the Nazarene as well, but I cannot work with these hardships much longer. Kindly quit your journey with the Apostle and return to me and Healing House. Also, I must say that your large scroll is missing. I have searched all of the cabinets in your study and elsewhere in the clinic. I have discovered nothing. I feel that all of this sounds distressing but I must remain truthful with you, my beloved.*
>
> > *From the hand of your loving wife,*
> > > *~Axsen*

210

Lucius' eyes filled with tears as he slammed a hand to his sword. "Marius!" he whispered. "I must return home at once."

"Did you say something, Physician?" Timotheos said. "Your news was from home, I assume?"

Before Lucius could answer, the Apostle had returned. His forehead furrowed, and he did not wait for questions from his companions.

"That boatman wants far too much for a passage to Macedonia," he said. "We will spend a day or two here in Troas and then move on to the northwest into Mysia."

"The very frontier of the Empire?" Silas said. "What will protect us there?"

"Silas, have faith," Paulus smiled. "The Nazarene is our guide. Besides, as I always say, 'Be subject to the governing authorities.' The Romans have kept us safe through Galatia and Phrygia where we came from. They will be our friends on the edge of the empire."

Lucius was not certain of this, now finding a side of the Apostle which he had not experienced before. Paulus had not seen the headless "Caligula," had not confronted the Parthian who had defaced it and had not read a plea from a frightened wife about a husband's continued absence. It was time to go—but back to Ephesus.

A soft-spoken innkeeper offered a room in Troas but they all had to share it. The Apostle snored like an old ram so that Lucius stared at the moonlight on the ceiling. What should he do: let them all know of the distress of Axsen in Ephesus and secure passage home? A few healings, some small donations amounting to a few hundred sesterces and no clinics begun in any of the towns, not even the large cities like Lystra and Derbe, were the outcomes of this "mission" as the Apostle named it. He would not be missed.

He drifted off. Everything descended into a smoky darkness. A light caught the haze from above as a figure stepped into it with a well-trimmed beard, streaked in gray. His robe was striped in brown, green and white and his head was covered with a metallic wrap.

But the voice was the same haunting tone which Lucius had heard in his study, on the road and now in this dream. "Someone," it said. "Someone close to you will—" the voice tapered off.

The figure stepped out into the light and Lucius knew who it was, not the Nazarene but Caduceus. His teacher fixed on his student and his eyes drooped in kindness. When his face rose from his chest, the robes and head covering were the same but the face blurred and sharpened into *HIS OWN*—the face of Lucius.

"Someone close to you will betray you," his own voice said.

A whizzing sound flew over Lucius' head spiraling down past his right ear. Phfft! A long shaft stuck at the feet of Caduceus-become-Lucius. Then, phfft, phfft. A second, a third shaft hit to the right and to the left of the man in the light. At last, phfft, phfft, phfft. Lucius ducked as shafts rained like a spring storm and landed all around Caduceus/Lucius. Some caught the light more than others. Arrows.

Finally, a sound screaming like a hawk attacking its prey began far up in the darkness above him and then spiraled down towards his head. Before it landed, Lucius awoke and sat up on his cot. He stared wide-eyed into the moonlight but only heard the breaths of Paulus.

The morning awakened them all with the early red sun off the eastern-facing window sills. Lucius formed his words about his wife's letter and about his dream of impending danger. But everyone was missing from the room. They were out in a room at the front of the inn, sharing a breakfast of bread and wine with the innkeeper.

"Ah, Lucius," Paulus greeted as he looked up and saw the Physician walk in. "Have some breakfast with us."

"Certainly, but first, I must speak to you, perhaps in private," he said.

"Of course, but let me share with you the dream which the Nazarene sent to me in the night," Paulus said.

Overriding the concerns of Lucius, the Apostle pressed, "You know that we were preparing to travel to Mysia. But last night I saw a man of Macedonia coming from the East and waving to me. He said over and over, 'Come, all of you, come over to Greece and help us.'"

The eyes of the Apostle drooped in a sad look of caring as he concluded to Lucius, "How can we not answer that plea immediately? But, Physician, you wanted to say something to me?"

Now Lucius looked at the floor. The arguments of safety and the distress of Axsen vanished like the orange sun turning to its mid-morning gold. "Nothing, Apostle," he said. Lucius spun around and returned to their room to pack—for Macedonia, not Ephesus.

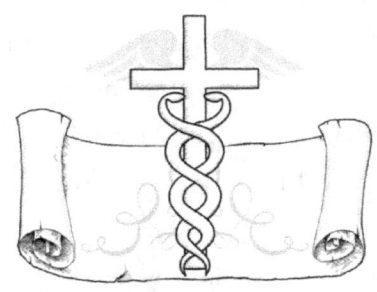

CHAPTER THREE:

THE FIRST OF THREE WOMEN OF MACEDONIA

"And he said to the woman,
'Your faith has saved you; go in peace.'"
— Luke 7:50

"**W**e agreed to fourteen more days!" a woman's voice shouted.

"The Proconsul finds the time unacceptable. He cannot delay longer with you!" a man's voice barked in reply.

Lucius heard the dispute echo along the water before his traveling companions did. The group had found safe passage on a lower-priced merchant ship, hauling grain from Troas to Macedonia, docking first in Samothrace, then Neopolis and finally sailing into Philippi.

When they strolled through the limestone city, named for the father of Alexander the Great, Lucius, the Apostle, Silas and Timotheos passed its limestone walls, small and great houses, some even constructed in marble from the sheen, and a large theater at one end, capable of seating thousands.

At the center of the town, Philippi's Forum called them with its flavors of roasting pork and fish from the vendors' stalls. Paulus was hungry so the entire company purchased some meat, cheese and a bowl of wine each.

"We must find the place of prayer," the Apostle said, wiping his chin from its pork juice.

He shouted, "You there!" A leather vendor in a stall close to them perked up. "Where's the place of prayer?" the Apostle asked.

The man, dressed in a brown tunic, fine leather sandals and a leather apron shrugged his shoulders. Nothing came from him.

Silas went in another direction and was returning to the group. "I have it," he reported with a smile. "Out beyond that western gate and beyond what the locals call the 'Colonial Arch.'"

They all felt the quick passing coolness of the Arch's shadow as it passed overhead and ushered them to the rushing sound of water. The River Gangites guided them on a more northern trek.

Lucius smelled the perfume of wild flowers as they walked, but this was Greece, not Italia, and he could name none of them. The scent of cedar up ahead mixed with the floral odors and finally overwhelmed them as he saw high cypress trees waving in the breeze along the river bank.

Then he heard it, the breeze had voices or did it? After all, locusts were chirping in the smaller trees. They whined with an endless chorus over the rushing river next to them.

Then yes, no. The locusts whirring rose, then fell to nothing and stopped. The voices did not. It was the male voice which bellowed and echoed through the silence.

"I will arrive at your home in the city, the day after tomorrow. Have the Proconsul's robe or—" the male voice paused.

The woman's voice did not. It assaulted.

"I cannot have it sooner than promised!" she countered. "I am missing three workers."

The man said, "You have already received payment."

Between the voices ahead, volleying back and forth, Lucius heard his sandals and those of his companions slapping on the small pebbles of the river bank as they pushed through the tall reeds blocking their view. Two figures emerged, then disappeared behind tall green stems. The reeds slapped his face so he pushed them to his right and left.

He halted. Paulus and the rest halted.

The two debaters appeared at last on a wide bank of pebbles. The male voice had his back to them, a soldier, alone, but with centurion rank as his transverse red plume showed. Facing them was the woman's voice, dressed and belted in a rich red purple robe, a purple head veil covering her black hair with streaks of gray slipping out. The creases in her face revealed that she was older, in her forties, at least the Apostle's age; and the furrows contorted as she spoke.

Beyond them was a sort of "factory" for purple goods. One slave woman was smashing a pestle into a tub and cracking the mollusk shells covering the ground beneath her. Another younger woman displayed arms of purple to her elbows as she dipped and re-dipped fabric into a large tub. Steam and the pungent odor of vinegar billowed around her. Two other slaves, men with large muscles, drew out huge twisted purple cloths from a vat that rinsed them to the shade which they chose for their final tint. At the end was a small young woman who stood in the river and spread out the ends of dyed fabric to cleanse each item. She wobbled in the current.

Lucius had never seen an operation like this. But the woman, who appeared to own and direct it all brought him back with her next attack on the lone Roman officer.

Her finger banged against the centurion's leather chest plate. "If you come, you will receive nothing! Tell that to the Governor!" she shouted. It caused her opponent to back up.

"Do you hear me?" she said as she moved into the Roman's face and as he kept retreating step by step without turning away.

The centurion was consumed by her onslaughts. So, Lucius stepped out from his companions and into the view of the woman. His sandals made no crunching on the pebbles nor the mollusk shells strewn all around the river bank. He put a finger to his lips as her eyes caught him over the officer's shoulder.

The Physician stepped almost on his toes as the argument before him continued to cover his approach.

"Look at my slaves and workers," the woman continued, still pushing the centurion in reverse. "They work as rapidly as they are able."

"The Proconsul does not care. He will shut down all of your work here and your business. You will have nothing!" the soldier shouted down at his attacker.

Lucius disappeared behind him. He slipped his own *gladius* from its sheath without a ring. Then kneeling, he held the blade horizontal to the officer's legs.

He re-considered the possibility of injury to the man. So, as the centurion reached Lucius, he spun the blade with the flat side toward his victim. The last thrust came from the woman—in words not weapons.

"Nothing!" she screamed. She banged her finger on his chest, sending him backwards. "I will give you nothing no matter what you and the Proconsul threaten."

The centurion stepped backwards and into the barrier behind him, transverse plume wobbling and then tumbling down over Lucius' tightly held sword.

The Roman looked like a turtle which someone had flipped onto its shell, and he shouted, "Aaww!" He had fallen onto a bed of sharp broken mollusk shells thrown out all over the beach. They stuck in his hands, arms and calves like thorns from a rose bush.

Lucius re-sheathed his sword as the Apostle, Silas and Timotheos ran up and halted, choking back laughter. The woman leaned over and inspected her fallen opponent.

But it was Lucius who said, "I believe that you have harassed this merchant enough. Why not take your wounded pride—and your other wounds and return to her at the time you have threatened her with?"

The Proconsul's centurion was picking shells from his arms, hands and legs. He pulled himself to his feet.

Ignoring Lucius and his companions, he shouted to the woman, "I have no regard for your rescuers here. I will return the day after tomorrow to your home!" He spun around and limped and groaned up the beach.

"Are you unharmed, woman? Or mistress?" he questioned leaning in as if searching for a name.

"My name is Lydia from Thyatira though now from Philippi here. I am a purple merchant," she confirmed.

"Oh," Lucius said. "Are these workers yours?"

"Yes," she said. "They assist me with dying, drying and cutting purple cloth here." She looked away towards her operation at the river's edge, then said, "Though perhaps not much longer."

"That officer is from the Proconsul's personal guard. He came for the Governor's new toga and cloak. The agreement was for fourteen days from now—not two days. If I do not deliver, I will lose my slaves and my business—my entire liveli—" she paused her explanation.

A shriek pierced the air from the Gangites. The silhouette of a woman with long black hair strung wet across her face, bobbed up and waved with both arms. The girl at the farthest end of the line had fallen and vanished below the current. Her head popped back up as she washed further down river. Then she disappeared again.

Lucius did not wait for another scream. He cast off his travel robe, kicked his sandals to the beach and unfastened his sword belt.

He sprinted to the water's edge and bound up a rock overhanging the river. Raising both arms, he dove towards the current sweeping the slave under for a fourth time. As he bobbed to the surface, the cold water chilled him; but ignoring it, he scanned the rushing river. A contorted face appeared just above the water, and the woman coughed out the muddy flow of the Gangites.

When the face sank, Lucius plunged beneath the rapids. The other workers were now screaming from the shore.

"Keep your head up, girl!" one vat keeper shouted.

"Help is coming!" another screamed.

"Save her, stranger!" a third yelled.

"Oh, not Miriam. She is my best worker," Lydia cried.

Timotheos said to Lydia, "If anyone can get to her, Lucius can. He was once a centurion."

Lydia's eyes widened as she looked at Timotheos.

At last, Lucius began stroking against the river and towards the shore. A half-submerged form floated behind him as he dragged the slave girl into the shallow, calmer water where the other workers now gathered.

"Come quickly!" he yelled to Lydia and his companions. "She is injured! Bring me my satchel."

Lydia, the Apostle, Silas and Timotheos arrived as Lucius knelt over Miriam. Her eyes were closed and her breathing was shallow. A deep gash on her forehead oozed blood like a leaking wine skin.

Silas slung Lucius' medical bag around to the Physician. Without glancing up from his patient, he said, "Forgive me, Mistress Lydia. My name is Lucius Maximus. I am a Healer for the Nazarene. These men with me are my travel companions, Paulus there called the Apostle, his friend Silas and young Timotheos."

As he wrapped strip after strip of bandages around Miriam's head, Lucius said, "I believe that we can assist you in your problem with the Proconsul."

"Then come home with me," Lydia invited.

"**S**he rests calmly, but I am fearful about how serious her injuries are," Lydia said.

Lucius had dried off, bathed and re-dressed into a linen tunic which the owner of the house had provided from her husband's garments.

House slaves were lighting the night torches in Lydia's atrium. The home was expansive extending back from the street and Philippi's Forum with this entry room not only large, but laid with marble flooring to the center pool. Frescoes enlivened the walls with stories of the past in Greece, not Rome. The one covering the entire lower wall was Alexander the Great, astride his black stallion, *Bucephelus*, defeating the Persians. The conqueror looked even fiercer in torch light. He was not unlike the owner of this house earlier today.

"My husband bought this home from a Greek merchant. He died a year after we moved in," Lydia explained. "We had no children. My slaves are more like children to me. I will not let the Proconsul take them, nor my home, because of his foolish impatience."

Lucius studied her dark sparkling eyes. He settled himself into a curved leather Roman chair and drank in the paintings on the walls, halting at Alexander.

Then he said, "Paulus is a tent-maker by trade. He knows how to work with fabric. I learned colors, dying and shades from my mother in Tuscana. The other two of us have strong backs to move vats and mix dyes. Let us see what can be done for you."

"Ah," Paulus said, entering the large room, his voice echoing off its hard frescoes. "Is Miriam resting?"

"Yes," Lydia said as she looked up from another leather chair opposite Lucius. "But tell me about this Master of yours, this Nazarene, whom you serve. What is his teaching and where does he abide?"

Lucius could have told her all of the stories in his now missing journal. He thought about the healings, the feeding of five thousand poor and his own hand in the Nazarene's death.

Instead, Lydia carried him back to her story. She did not wait for answers to her questions.

She erupted, "I am hurt in my soul. I am alone. I lash out in my anger—like today with the Proconsul's centurion."

Lucius cleared his throat and was about to respond, but it was Paulus who filled the pause which she had left them.

"Then have this mind," he said. "Have this mind *in you* that was in the Nazarene who though he was in God did not count this status to be gained but emptied himself and became a servant of all, even to death—death even on a cross."

Lydia fixed on the Apostle but yawned. She said, "Tell me more tomorrow. We will speak over our work at the river."

She looked over at Lucius, then said, "I can be as humble as your Nazarene at least to thank you, Physician, for saving me from that centurion and for rescuing my Miriam from drowning."

Then she asked, "Are you married?"

"Yes," he said, "and I must retire to my room and write to my beloved." He thought of Axsen. He had not written to her, nor she to him since her letter had been handed over by Timotheos at Troas.

He had been gone from her over eight months.

"Here. Take this purple-trimmed toga for the Proconsul. There is none finer in all of the Empire," Lydia said, handing the white and purple-edged garment to the centurion at her door. She allowed him no further entrance, forming a barricade with her body.

Still as he turned to leave, a down-turned mouth adorning his face, she stopped him.

"Wait," she commanded. "And here is a purple *stola* for his wife." She spun around to Timotheos behind her and pulled a woman's robe from his hands.

The centurion's arms still held out the toga so she plunked the dress on top. He turned again, grumbling to himself.

"Ah, wait, Roman," she said a third time. "I am not finished." Silas was behind her on her other side. She turned and reached back for a garment from him.

The officer swiveled around one more time.

"Here. Take this royal cape with you as the Proconsul also agreed to. Would not want the poor Governor to become cold and sick this winter," Lydia said.

She plopped the cape on top of the stack, still held out by the centurion. "That is all. You may go," she dismissed him.

As he turned to the street and the heat of the Forum, she added, "Tell the Proconsul that this concludes any further dealings between us. Let him find another purple-maker in Philippi—if he can."

She slammed her front door with a bang nearly shoving the transverse plume into the street. The bright sun shut off but not her laughter from inside her house.

"**D**id you not see his face? He couldn't run from you any faster," Timotheos laughed towards Lydia.

"Well, yes. Have some more roasted pork and pass the sweet meats around again. You Followers have definitely earned it," she said.

Miriam was up from her bed and lay on the couch at the end of the table in Lydia's triclinium. She reached to her forehead and touched the bandage, then winced.

"Are you feeling better, my daughter?" Lydia said.

"Yes," the slave girl responded. Her voice was soft and weak.

"Good. It is my delight to see you up and here at table with us tonight," her mistress affirmed.

"And now, Paulus, may I call you this?" Lydia asked.

The Apostle nodded.

"I must say that your words about the Nazarene have not only convinced me, but so have your courage and love for a stranger such as I. All of you saved my business and my dear Miriam," Lydia said, looking to Lucius during the last part of her words.

"I would like to become a Follower of this Nazarene. I want his washing—for me and for my entire household," she gestured to her slaves.

The next sound which Lucius heard behind him was the sloshing of liquid in a bowl. A blond slave girl, not more than fourteen years old, brought a large bronze basin into the dining room.

The water splashed first over Lydia with the Apostle saying, "I wash you in the name of the Nazarene, Jeshua Christos. Become his Follower and his servant." One by one the slaves followed in a parade along the triclinium table.

Lucius thought that Macedonia was everything that Asia had not been from its welcome to its new community of Followers in Lydia's home.

He looked up and smelled the burning oil in his lamp broken only by the musty parchment before him. He had begun his letter to Axsen the day before but had been interrupted.

Lucius now read:

To my beloved Axsen,

We have received a glorious welcome here in Macedonia from an older merchant woman named Lydia—a purple dyer and—

A knock came on the door to his room where he had remained awake to write.

"Enter," Lucius said, expecting the night visitor to be Paulus or Silas, explaining the plans for tomorrow's departure. Instead, he looked into the dim light and tried not to show his shock. Lydia swished in, her hair down, gray-streaked and black-curled to her shoulders. She wore what appeared to be a night robe, not the purple of her work, but ivory linen.

"Kindly do not find me too forward, Physician," she apologized.

"Not in any way," Lucius countered.

"May I sit?" she asked.

"It is your home, not mine," he said.

Lydia spread her robe out over a curved leather chair opposite his and his writing table. The light played on her furrowed face; but Lucius could see that with her dark eyes, she was still a woman of high cheek bones and a small slightly upturned nose, and was very attractive.

She produced a leather bag from the folds of her robe. It jingled full of coins.

"Here is my gift to your—what do you call it—your Healing House."

Lucius nodded and smiled. She reached the bag across to his hand.

As the offering jingled, she said, "Fifty talents. I desire that it could be more. But then that was before I lost one of my best customers today by my own hand." She smiled.

Lucius said, "My deepest gratitude to you, woman."

Her forehead furrowed. She looked over into the torch light, fixing on Lucius' scroll.

"A letter to your wife?"

The Physician nodded a "yes."

"Kindly tell her what a blessed woman she is to have such a husband as you," Lydia said.

She looked down and then continued, "I know that you believe the residents of Macedonia and Philippi are very welcoming. Be aware, Physician."

She paused, then disclosed, "I also know that you are a Roman and a centurion, not like the one who has been harassing me. Take care of the Apostle who speaks too much and too recklessly—and the others of your companions."

Lydia rose and the light flickered upon her robe as if she were a specter, not their host. She swished to the door as quietly as she had entered.

The door creaked open and the ivory shimmering "ghost" disappeared into the outer darkness of the hall. Lucius fixed on the bag of talents which rested upon the table in front of him. He shoved the leather, the jingle telling him that it was real. So was its donor.

He could not yet return home, but he needed to finish his letter to let Axsen know.

CHAPTER FOUR:
THE SECOND WOMAN OF MACEDONIA

"'What have you to do with me,
Jesus, Son of the Most High God?
I beg you, do not torment me.'"
— Luke 8:28

The door closed with embraces and tears from Lydia. Lucius, the Apostle and the other companions reserved their damp eyes for the street as they inhaled the aromas of the Forum with its baking bread stalls and other vendors of roasting meat. Their exit from the woman Lydia was a contrast to that other departure of the Proconsul's centurion, nearly dropping his stack of robes from the purple merchant and her "helpers."

Lucius glanced at the deep violet fingers of Timotheos—an award from the dying vats but an honor for serving the Nazarene. It would take weeks for that tint to wear off.

The Physician also had his own reward. He had returned ten of the fifty talents to Lydia for a Philippi version of "Healing House," a clinic to begin in her home. He had trained Miriam to direct it.

So, the hazy day began as rewarding as their work had been. So much so that Paulus turned back to the group and said, "I want to find the speaker's rostrum here in the Forum and bring a word from the Nazarene."

No sooner had he spoken than a whirlwind broke upon them like a hot spinning dust storm from the desert. It twirled into the open plaza so fast, none of them could see the face, the bare head nor its robes. The "squall" twisted and gyrated towards the Apostle first, then around him, dancing to Silas second and then towards Timotheos. It saved Lucius for last, turning a path around him in the center and breathing "Aha, aha" into his face.

Then it zigzagged away towards a group of men on a street corner. Behind him, Lucius heard a voice say, "Let's hope she earns 'er keep today."

"Yeah," another said. "We need everything she makes just to support 'er."

As the "storm" slowed ahead, Lucius smelled the air. It had become foul like rotting meat instead of the baking bread and other cooking aromas from the market. He gagged, but then saw the stringy hair of a woman with sunken eyes painted yellow and orange. Her robe, which had spun into a blur, slowed to red and blue stripes, colorful but frayed.

"Let's see if these fine gentlemen give 'er anythin'," the same voice said behind Lucius. Were these voices her owners? If so, were they starving her?

As a Physician, he noticed her thin face and her arms like sticks protruding from her robe. "Gaunt" was too kind of a word for it.

Suddenly she shrieked at the men on the corner, "If you pay me a shekel, I will tell your future. If you pay me two, I will give you more." She laughed with a deep raspy guffaw like Medusa.

One man tossed a silver coin at her bare feet. "Aha" she laughed and spun around, then leaned her stringy hair and thin face toward the customer.

"Work hard, old man," she said. "You will not have long to work." She jerked the shekel from the pavement.

Paulus leaned over to Lucius and said, "What is wrong with her?"

"I am uncertain," Lucius answered.

"I am not," the Apostle confirmed. "She is possessed. And these men behind us control her and make money from the fortunes she tells."

All at once "SSSS" came from her mouth toward the men while her body arched like a snake ready to strike. The customers lurched back to avoid her, but she stood upright, then twirled and danced like a child's top, moving along the edge of the Forum, turning down a side street.

As she vanished, Paulus shook his head and broke from his companions, then climbed the steps of the rostrum at the far end of the plaza. He cleared his throat with a cough.

"You have seen the powers of darkness," he said, pointing to the street where the girl had disappeared. "Now hear of the powers of Light and Love."

He continued to preach and the crowd gathered below him, but Lucius drifted back to the whirling "storm," which had gone, not the crowd which now remained.

They had planned to leave Philippi but continued with the crowds who had begun to speak of "the Jews with a new message." Lucius chuckled at being grouped as a "Jew" with the Apostle and the others.

On the third day, Paulus climbed the rostrum once more. Hissing like a viper exploded from a side street, followed with an "Aha." Stringy hair flung away from the whirling face like tree limbs twisting in a storm.

This time the soothsayer's robe spun out revealing her thin ankles, hardly larger than the limbs of a young sapling. She stopped and stretched out a boney finger towards Paulus, then at Lucius, and finally shrieked, "These men serve the Most High God and offer you the saving of the Nazarene."

She hissed again and stopped, shouting at Paulus, "Now pay me!"

Lucius nodded a "No," and shoved her back from the rostrum. She vanished down another street leading from the Forum. He hoped nothing else would come of her, but also that nothing would happen to her.

When the Apostle finished his message and questions began from the crowd, a hissing returned. It exploded up from the back of the rostrum. A red and blue blur flew onto the platform towards Paulus, nearly shoving him off the front into a row of Philippians.

Behind him, Lucius heard the voices from three days ago. He glanced around to see three men, two in gray tunics and one in a long robe, all bearded and interested in their "investment" up front.

"Watch this," one said.

"Let's hope she shames 'im for us," a second one commented.

The third stayed silent but their soothsayer did not. On the rostrum with the Apostle, she laughed and shrieked towards the crowd, then grabbed the neck of Paulus' robe, hiked it up as if to hang him, and screamed, "You see, I told you that these men are slaves of the Most High God."

She paused panting and then shouted, "Now pay me, all of you for letting you know."

A silver coin spun from the crowd and stung the woman's cheek. "Aawh!" she cried. She released the Apostle's robe as she bent down to retrieve it.

Freed, Paulus leapt from the platform and tried to push through the bodies gathered below. They blocked his escape.

The "storm" jumped after him. When she hit the pavement with her bare feet, one cracked open and her blood oozed onto the limestone. She looked down and said nothing, spinning and smearing the plaza with her blood.

The crowd, unlike with Paulus, parted as waves might before the bow of a ship. "SSSS," she said. She whirled, she shoved her way back through the bodies and she ended up at the Physician.

Lucius backed away but her head arched toward his. Her breath stank of cheese and wine as she clenched her yellow teeth, batted her yellow and orange tinted eyelids and said, "Someone close to you will betray you, Physician. Darkness and disaster await you. You cannot escape!"

The gaunt face blurred in Lucius' sight. The stringy hair became gray-streaked with a bearded face. The soothsayer became a teacher. Her face flashed into that of Caduceus.

Lucius panicked, *How did this demon know him? How did it know his teacher?*

231

He flinched, bobbed backwards and was about to speak as she bent away and stretched out her hand for payment. A dark gray robe cut around Lucius and batted her arm away. Paulus, not the Physcian, shouted, "In the name of the Nazarene, be gone from her."

A gust like a roar down a dry canyon howled to a deafening pitch around the woman. A cone of black swirling dust blew her stringy hair up over her face until her eyes rolled back in her head and vanished.

Lucius covered his own eyes, but the Apostle stood as still and as straight as a column on a temple. The robes of the onlookers in the crowd swished backwards and up.

The soothsayer's hair dropped as the wind began to die. Her eyes shut. She fell to her knees, screamed "Aagh!" and listed to her right side onto the pavement, unconscious.

Everything stopped. No shrieking. No hissing. No wind. Only silence.

"Is she dead?" someone said.

"I believe so," another remarked.

From the group of three overseers, a gray tunic said, "She is of no use to us now. Get rid of 'er."

A second overseer said, "Oh, no, we are reporting this. This man has cost us!"

Lucius blinked his own eyes as the Apostle reached out a hand touching the hand of the "dead" woman. Her orange and yellow eyelids fluttered. Paulus eased her up to sitting.

A man from the crowd straightened his robes and said, "It is a miracle. She is raised."

Another said, "Who are these men? What is their power?"

The soothsayer rubbed her bleeding foot and opened and shut her eyes at Paulus.

"Where am I? What happened to me?" she asked. "Who are you?"

She looked at Lucius, then Silas and finally set her eyes on Timotheos. Her voice was calm as if she had awakened from a nap. But if she was composed, the crowd was not.

The three overseers pushed the people towards the Apostle, grabbing him. Silas was beside him and one of the managers went for him.

All of this happened so quickly that Lucius was wobbling and waving back and forth—confused like a night after too much wine. He was not dreaming, but the "warning" from Caduceus, conjured up through a demon, made him freeze with fear.

He could only watch as the woman's managers took the arms of Paulus and Silas and shoved them through the crowd.

Lucius and Timotheos sat at their camp fire on the edge of Philippi. The crackling popped in their ears. Smoke swirled and stung their eyes as it rose into the trees overhead.

Hermine sat on a log above them. She had cleared the orange and yellow make-up from her eyes, but still wore the striped robe. Her handlers had abandoned her.

"They can make nothing from me," she told Lucius and particularly Timotheos.

She fixed on the young Greek Follower, revealing her name, "Hermine," to him, asking about his home in Antioch and questioning about his family. Though the Physician had wrapped her foot, Timotheos bought her leather sandals in the Forum and was slipping them on her.

Lucius stared at them as Timotheos lifted her and supported her when she limped off beside him away from the fire. The day was warm and the Physician felt the sun through the trees as it caressed his shoulders.

He wondered, *Where are Paulus and Silas?* Lydia was correct. When he made sense of yesterday, the events returned. The magistrates under the Proconsul had condemned Lucius' companions to prison. Loss of "property" for whatever reason was as serious as murder.

These overseers had lost a valued commodity with Paulus' exorcism. So, Lucius' last view of his friends was a Roman legionary binding the hands of each one and pushing them into the surrounding crowds at the end of the Forum opposite the rostrum.

The Physician was remembering all of this and staring at the "commodity" and Timotheos when two voices buzzed behind him. The chattering grew louder.

Was it? No. Yes. He looked back towards the city. Paulus and Silas hobbled slowly toward his camp fire.

Before the Physician could ask about them, Paulus blurted out, "We were beaten with rods and imprisoned in stocks."

Lucius's mouth dropped open. As Silas turned toward the Apostle, red streaks seeped through his robe.

"Best let me examine you," Lucius said.

"Always the Physician," the Apostle exclaimed. "But let me share the rest of my story. The Nazarene sent a shaking, opening the prison doors." Lucius had felt nothing.

Paulus said, "The jailer himself became a Follower and we gave him the Nazarene's washing. Then they freed us. Our wounds are nothing."

As Silas peeled off his robe, and exposed deep gashes still bleeding on his back, Lucius said, "I would not say that, Apostle."

Timotheos and Hermine now returned to them. They looked wide-eyed at Paulus and Silas

"She wants to come with us," the young Follower said.

For Lucius again it was all happening too swiftly. He washed Silas' wounds with clean cold water, the Follower wincing with each dab of the Physician's wet cloth. Paulus babbled on about their "good blessings" as he called their imprisonment and beating.

Still, Lucius' mind ran back to Hermine's warning, really that of the demon which had possessed her. Smoke spiraled downward from the fire again and he coughed and looked away.

Who would betray him? He had been gone too long from Ephesus. Was something at home "dark and disastrous?"

He looked at the back of the Apostle. His robe was even redder than Silas'. It was soaked with blood, but it did not seem to bother him.

Just then Paulus broke Lucius' thoughts and said, "Tomorrow we move on to Thessalonica, then Athens and finally Corinthia, the best of all."

CHAPTER FIVE:
THE FINAL WOMAN OF MACEDONIA

"…(she) has chosen the better part,
which will not be taken away from her."
— Luke 10:42

The lightning flickered in the starless sky. Thunder followed, rumbling low against his ears and rattling the rocks along the road. The air smelled like pungent onions from the lightning, and the dampness chilled him even though it was a spring night.

His trek from the port of Cenchreae where Lucius now stayed among the Followers in this part of Macedonia, led from the house of Phoebe, a tall Jewish woman. It was more stadia than he thought or relished towards Corinthia, but at least the rain had stopped.

He had dressed quickly in his dark brown tunic with soldier's belt, sword and military sandals. Phoebe had awakened him in the middle of the night so that he was wobbling around and fumbling for each piece of clothing.

"An accident," she said. "A friend of mine named Chloe. Her husband is injured from the shaking we all felt today. Can you go to her in Corinthia?"

In the middle of the night? Lucius thought as the breeze to his back shoved him to the trade city. Corinthia. The name led him back to the last weeks of where the group had headed south from Philippi. After the beatings of Paulus and Silas, they looked forward to a better welcome in Thessalonica.

But that place ended in riots, too, when the Jews, then the Proconsul himself, threatened a Follower named Jason, charging him with treason. Tensions rose, especially when Jason at the words of the Apostle, was accused of swearing allegiance to another "king," the Nazarene, and not to Carsar. Jason posted bail and paid the bribe for the Apostle's freedom and his own.

Then as they escaped from the city, Hermine suddenly remembered that she had a family. Why now so many miles and days after her miracle in Philippi? She could not explain it to the companions, not even to Paulus who had healed her.

"I must return," she told Timotheos.

"But we need to go on," the Apostle said.

Lucius drew him aside, and said, "Give them a moment alone, Apostle." He pointed at Timotheos and Hermine as they now embraced.

She pressed her lips to the mouth of the young Greek.

Then, sobbing, she said, "C-c-come b-b-back for me."

Leaving her, the companions pressed on to Athens where Paulus found the speakers' rostrum near the Parthenon. It was a rounded rock of marble, polished by Greeks, then Romans and finally others who had ascended it to preach.

Philosophers there stroked their beards, questioned, then re-questioned the Apostle. Yet, it was all that they did—just listened and nothing further. When Paulus arrived in his story about "resurrection" and the Nazarene, the thinkers set their eyes along with their jaws. Athens remained unchanged and as hard as the marble mound which they reserved for new messages.

Suddenly lightning ripped a jagged blade into the darkness, returning Lucius from Athens to the present and the Cenchreae road. His cleated sandals splashed through the puddles while his sword slapped his side along with his medical satchel.

Passing through the gate of Corinthia, he arrived at the Forum, dimly lit and empty, a contrast to when the Apostle had spoken there earlier that day. Lucius paused, trying to remember. Then he saw the arch covering the Lecheion Road and leading to the north end of town.

His sandals clicked against the stone pavement, and he passed the Northwest Stoa with its covered market stalls. He inhaled the leather of sandal vendors and the final aromas of the day's cooked meats. Only a few Corinthians now crossed the closed square.

Suddenly a huge silhouette rose beyond the stoa to his left. The glow of a sacrificial fire flickered off the columns to Gens Julia. Like Lystra, only grander, Caesar put his mark with a temple to Rome into the heart of this commercial colony. Finally, after ridding himself of the Empire and leaving Caesar's "imprint," the dim lights of houses intruded on both sides.

Lucius turned onto another street and counted down, "*Unus, duo, tres....*" He paused with the odor of wood from a massive front door now filling his nose. This could not be it. Too grand. He knocked. A servant opened.

A woman half a head shorter than he was swished through the dim lighting from a cavernous atrium and came up behind the slave. Her round brown eyes caught the torch light. They peered out from an ivory veil covering wisps of blond hair. The high cheeks of her face and her fair skin were enticing

But that face suddenly twisted into anger. "Oh, these creditors will not disturb us any more tonight," she said, as she arrived at the entry.

Lucius stood on her threshold.

He said, "Excuse me, mistress. My name is Lucius Maximus. Though some among the Followers in Cenchreae call me Deacon Lucas. I am sent by the woman Phoebe. I am a healer for the Nazarene? Are you Mistress Chloe?"

Chloe's face untwisted and softened. She said, "Yes." Her eyes widened as she scanned up and down the Physician now standing in her torch light.

"Kindly enter. I am grateful that you have come at such a late hour," she said.

Dismissing the servant, she led the way across the front room. From other dim torch lights and the occasional flashes of lightning, Lucius could see the expanse of the atrium with its frescoes of Ulysses and the Aeneid. The house was larger than Lydia's, but he calculated that these women of Macedonia must be smiled upon by the Fates to live so well.

He smelled her husband before he saw him. As they entered a hall and turned left into a sleeping room, the pungent odors of sweat, urine and body fluids intensified. A bearded figure lay in the center of a large bed, the sheets soaked in perspiration.

The man's chest was concave, and his breathing was rapid and shallow. Lucius' sandals tapped across the room to the side of the bed. He moved his hands around the patient's stomach and up under his ribs. "Ummm," he said.

"His name is Alexandros," Chloe said, remaining at the foot of the bed. "We were walking in the Temple of Gens Julia when the shaking began. A slab of roofing slid from above and struck him in the chest."

Lucius did not look up, but noticed that her voice did not shake. She did not sob or cry. Why? Shock?

He laid down his medical satchel after slipping it off his shoulder. He unbuckled his sword belt and laid it aside.

Chloe dropped into a curved Roman chair, eyes fixed on the Physician, not her husband.

Lucius continued his examination; but from his side view, he saw her deep brown look sparkling in the torch lights. When she looked down and away, he drank in her form, belted at the waist, with arms as smooth as porcelain like a temple goddess.

She looked up and he jerked his glance back to Alexandros. Again, the Physician watched her from the side, but then it happened. The brown eyes grew lighter and became turquoise just for an instant, in a flash.

Chloe blinked, then with eyes closing, slumped over in her chair. Lucius raised up from Alexandros. He slipped over to her and sat her up.

"Mistress, you must get some rest," he said, kneeling down beside her chair. "I will be with him and send a servant to you if there is any change."

She blinked her eyes and nodded, then rose, shuffling out the door.

When morning peeked through Alexandros' window, Chloe stood in his doorway. She caught her Physician kneeling by the bed of her husband and mumbling a prayer. Lucius did not look up, but finally he pushed his elbows on the bed, raised up and turned to the door.

His face drooped when he said, "I need to give you my diagnosis."

She led him across the empty atrium as their sandals slapped, clicked and echoed off the frescoes. Chloe turned right down a short hall to a room, obviously a study, with a writing desk, a chair behind it, several other seats and pigeon-hole shelves emitting the musty scent of scrolls.

She waited for Lucius then shut the door behind them. Her porcelain hand motioned for him to take one of the chairs, then she sat opposite him.

"Your husband is near death. I can do nothing more," he explained. "I am not certain that I could have if I had come sooner."

He waited for her to cry or at least to begin sobbing. She did not.

Instead, her face set as if she were absorbing the news about a dying horse or a major repair to her house.

"Nothing more can be done?" she said.

Lucius shook his head "No."

A knock came at the door and Eurydice, Chloe's stepdaughter, pushed her way in. She was a girl in her teens with brown hair, wearing a red *stola* covered with a white drape.

She said, "Father's breathing is worse." She sobbed and then broke into crying.

Lucius continued at Cenchreae, except for the funeral of Alexandros. It was outside Corinthia in a pagan "City of the Dead" with a priest of Poseidon, bobbing his curved and pointed hat with every incantation. It was as strange as Chloe had been when Lucius watched her at the bed of her husband and when he had announced the man's impending death.

The Physician stood on the outskirts of the crowd. He wondered how a Jewess, whose father was a rabbi, could allow this ceremony. He also wondered who the strange group of stoic-faced men were at the front of the crowd. Chloe had said something about "creditors" the night when Lucius had answered her call for assistance.

Still, all of these questions evaporated as he studied her face in the hazy sun. Then the morphing occurred again. Sparkling brown eyes went into a blur and became turquoise, wisps of blond hair under her white veil darkened to black and the soft porcelain skin deepened to bronze. Axsen replaced Chloe.

His wife was there and not there.

As he smelled the sacrificial fires of the Poseidon priest, Lucius thought, *She will need protecting now*, and he did not mean Axsen.

"Would you like to remain for my evening meal?" Chloe said. "And would you like the Nazarene's washing?" Lucius said. They had come from another rough sermon by the Apostle, this time in her father's synagogue. Paulus, a Follower couple named Priscilla and Aquila and a few others had followed to Chloe's home but had now left. Only the Physician remained.

"No," Chloe responded. "I push men away. I am too angry."

"And yet, I am here," Lucius said. They were once more in her study. As he observed her, he thought again about how much she needed protecting. His look caught something on her writing table which he had not seen before or perhaps it had not been there.

A light sword in a metal sheath lay at the edge. Believing that it belonged to Alexandros, Lucius grasped it and pulled the weapon from its scabbard.

"I have seen these," he said. He smelled the forged steel. "They are light in weight but extremely sharp and dangerous in the right hands." Lucius paused.

Chloe's eyes widened now. She said. "Especially if the hands are small."

He realized what she meant but still asked, "Is the weapon yours?"

The door received a knock. Chloe's daughter, Eurydice, entered. *The child never seems to tire of interrupting her mother, especially when she entertains a guest,* Lucius thought but kept it to himself.

"Would you and Deacon Lucas like some wine?" she asked.

"Perhaps later…with our dinner," Chloe said. "We'll partake with you shortly."

Eurydice slipped out. He listened for her steps to fade beyond the door, then he felt a wave of both fear and boldness collide in him at once.

"I crucified the Nazarene," Lucius confessed.

"Then why do you still follow him?" Chloe asked.

"Because he forgave me," he explained.

His hostess cocked her head.

"And because—I know it sounds unbelievable—he did not stay dead," the Physician added. Suddenly the air around him became cold. He shivered at the memory of the Nazarene's tomb—empty and a contrast to Alexandros' pagan funeral.

"If this were not true," Lucius went on, "how could we Followers speak to you about him?" His face now fixed on her.

He was uncertain of her thoughts, but he sheathed the sword in his hands and placed it on her writing table again.

Chloe did not need protecting. She needed healing—from within. And perhaps he just needed to go home.

Paulus moved his preaching in Corinthia from the synagogue after the Jews turned on him. It was no surprise that after Derbe, Lystra, Philippi and Thessalonica, his mouth had brought trouble.

Still, in Corinthia, it was not a clean break with the Jews as two rulers of the synagogue became Followers: Sosthenes, a sandy-haired, now clean-shaven Jew, and Crispus, also a Jew but with a well-trimmed beard and dark brown hair. Even worse than their exit from the Jewish ranks was that Chloe's rabbi father knew them both.

Worse than this, the Followers of Corinthia jammed and pushed their way into Sosthenes' small atrium until....

...until the day when in that atrium, Chloe herself knelt by the center pool. The Apostle poured the water and gave the blessing, "Daughter Chloe of Corinthia, receive the washing of the Nazarene." Lucius, who knew her better than the others among his companions, could not say how she had succumbed to this change.

Yet, after this, the Followers abandoned Sosthenes' cramped quarters.

And the change led to the day when Chloe declared to the community of believers gathered in her atrium and triclinium, "My house is no longer the House of Chloe and Eurydice. It shall be the House of the Nazarene, open to all." The Followers cheered.

For all of this celebrating, Lucius had heard that the property had passed from her deceased husband to her. The Proconsul had favored *her*, not her creditors, in the legal transfer which made Lucius admit that Rome could favor the right people—even if that person was a woman. But what would happen when the word slipped out about Chloe's latest act: turning her home over to the Nazarene?

Lucius was about to leave after that announcement to the Followers when he saw her gliding through the crowd.

"I must go to the Apostle and Priscilla and Aquila in Cenchreae and let them know about your hospitality," he said as Chloe approached him.

"Then I will walk you out," she said. She was commenting on how quickly things had changed and how she, the daughter of a rabbi, had received the Nazarene's washing.

She ended at the front door saying, "And now here we all are." She smiled at Lucius.

The smiles soon faded as large shadows covered them at her entry. The gloom was not a cloud over the sun. A contingent of legionaries had filled Chloe's doorway. The officer in front sported a vertical red plume, which Lucius recognized as a tribune's insignia.

Something was amiss.

Chloe's face lost all color. Her brown eyes drooped and her forehead furrowed.

"Can we talk privately, Mistress Chloe," the Tribune said. Lucius was amazed that the officer seemed to know her.

He continued, "My name is Tribune Gaius Flavius of the *Legio IV Macedonia.*"

Chloe nodded her head to him and led the contingent through the robes of her guests who were gaping at them. Conversations ceased or dropped to whispers with pointing fingers as the mistress of the house and her military parade cut their way down the short hall to her study.

Some legionaries remained outside, but Tribune Flavius and a few others entered. The last soldier was about to shut the door behind them when Lucius slipped around and in.

Flavius removed his helmet and placed it on the desk. His temples were sweating under his gray-streaked Roman haircut. He chose the writing seat behind the desk and looked up at the "intruder."

"Does *he* need to be here?" Flavius asked.

Chloe answered, "Certainly. He is my advisor."

Flavius cleared his throat, then continued, "Mistress, we understand that you and your Steward engaged the Illyricum pirates some time ago. Legionary?"

A soldier stepped to Chloe's desk and produced a bag which jingled as he drew back the cords and opened it. He spilled the contents onto the table, coins jangling and banging as they fell.

"Rome will pay you one hundred talents to lead us back to the location where you engaged them," Flavius said. "We want to be rid of this menace to our eastern shipping."

Lucius intervened, saying, "Mistress Chloe is in a delicate state here. She raises a stepdaughter alone and manages her deceased husband's wine business without assistan—."

Now Chloe interrupted, gently placing a hand across Lucius' chest, "Tribune, I fought those pirates with my Steward, Scipio Africanus. May I bring him?"

Lucius did not hear the Tribune's response, but looked at the sword on the writing table. A round muscle on Chloe's arm slipped out from the cover of her robes.

The Physician knew that he had made the wrong diagnosis—she did not need protecting. But would she return from such a battle? Would any of them?

Over his thoughts, Chloe said to Flavius, "When do we depart?"

L ucius scribbled more notes with his stylus on the scroll before him. He was not composing a new journal of the Nazarene but putting down additional stories and sayings to include in what he hoped might be an existing journal. His eyes scanned the room from the small writing table in Phoebe's house.

Months had passed since Chloe had departed to hunt for pirates with the Roman fleet. In her absence, the Apostle himself still preached in Chloe's home with Sosthenes and Crispus, now as leaders of the Followers, welcoming each new washing until the community had nearly outgrown their new quarters. Even the frescoes of her atrium walls seemed to scowl as if to say, "A more powerful god than ours now rules this house."

Ever the cynic, Lucius broke from those thoughts, fearing that the good news of their work might not last much longer. He stepped from the quiet of his room and found no one at Phoebe's. Where had they gone? After finding only the house slaves, he sprinted for Corinthia.

The Forum was packed with Followers, Jews, Greeks and Romans. Up front Proconsul Gallio was on the speaker's platform, the *bema*, as the locals called it. Jews, dressed in their dark robes and ivory head shawls were debating with what appeared to be Sosthenes, Crispus and a group of Followers.

The Apostle was present. Anxious that his mouth would bring the trouble of previous cities, Lucius moved to the front of the crowd to restrain him. Then, it all exploded. An older rabbinic Jew struck Sosthenes, followed by two henchmen. The leader of the Followers was pummeled to the pavement.

Gallio sat silent, offered no assistance but merely watched. As Sosthenes lay there motionless on the Forum floor, the crowd began to disperse. Lucius followed the Apostle, Crispus, Silas and Timotheos as they scooped up the bloodied leader from the front of the *bema*.

Off to one side at the beginning of the street where the synagogue was, they eased him down. Lucius reached for his medical satchel and began applying ointments and bandaging wounds on Sosthenes' head and face. He felt along his twisted leg.

"Broken," Lucius pronounced though Sosthenes' eyes were closed and he was almost unconscious.

"I will set and splint his leg. Hold him in case he begins to wake up," the Physician ordered.

"Will he live?" the Apostle worried. "I cannot believe that the Proconsul would allow this."

Lucius could not believe that Gallio would not allow it. He remembered Pilate with the Nazarene. He recalled the impatience of the Governor in Philippi with his imprisonment of Paulus and Silas. Rome was Rome.

Then Timotheos, looking at Sosthenes' belt, said, "Wait! He is missing his money bag."

Lucius, certain that he had done all that he could for his patient, stood, grabbing for the sword on his own belt. He left his satchel beside Sosthenes.

"Care for him," the Physician ordered. "I'll go back to search for the bag."

As he rounded the corner and stepped into the wider part of the Forum, a new battle had begun.

"You should have let Rome honor you," Gallio bellowed, his voice echoing through the empty cavern with the crowd having dispersed completely. His comment appeared to be directed to the back of the Forum.

"No, I do not need that," a familiar woman's voice returned fire. "I have greater rewards than Rome can ever bestow for defeating some miserable pirates."

So, she *had* returned and she did not seem inclined to knuckle under to anyone's protection or favors.

Gallio furrowed his gray-haired forehead and glanced sideways at Lucius who had offered a centurion's salute to him.

"As you wish, Mistress," Gallio shouted. He rose from his judgment seat, sniffed and swung his toga out and around him, stepping to the back of the *bema* and disappearing with his two guards following.

Lucius fast-walked to Chloe. He wanted to embrace her but thought better given the defiance which had just poured from her.

Instead, he said, "Mistress, you cannot test the patience of the Proconsul like that. What does it harm you to let him honor you?"

Lucius could not believe that she had survived the engagement on the high seas, but he also could not believe what he had just heard from his own mouth even more. His words had become like Paulus, about "submitting to the authorities."

No words came from Chloe. Instead, her brown eyes melted from an icy stare towards the *bema* into a softer question directed at the Physician.

"Are you hungry, Deacon Lucas?" she asked.

Lucius nodded "Yes," but he thought, *She does not need protecting. Or perhaps she needs it more than she knows.*

He glanced back to the base of the *bema* where the blood of Sosthenes pooled up on the flag stones. No money bag was there.

The dinner in her triclinium came together swiftly, but it was only for two. They had surprised the servants by coming in so soon from the Forum. Her slaves scurried back and forth to the cooking area for plates and cups, wine and meats which had been prepared earlier that day. All of it was scrambled together and placed awry on the table.

She and Lucius lounged on couches perpendicular to one another. The conversation turned to the day's events.

"Sosthenes will recover but it will be a long healing," Lucius said.

"Oh," she said as though she knew more about the incident than the Physician did.

He did not say anything more. His face fixed on hers, her brown eyes, her blond hair once more, enticing him like the first night when he had come out of the thunderstorm.

His body stiffened and a tingle ran up through his back to his neck, flushing his face. Then he moved close to her, pressing his lips to hers. She returned the kiss. Lucius' eyes closed. But when he opened them, the brown before him altered into turquoise, the blond hair to black. The rounder face lengthened with a cleft in it. Axsen replaced Chloe.

He backed away with a jerk. "I can—can—cannot do this," he stuttered. "I am sorry but I cannot."

Chloe's eyes drooped and her forehead elevated into what seemed like a question.

"We leave tomorrow from Cenchreae port," he said. "I am returning home to Ephesus and Healing House."

"Who goes with you?" she said, possibly trying to cover her quivering lip.

"The Apostle, Priscilla and Aquila and Silas. Also Timotheos," he answered. "Our work here is finished."

Lucius did not mention Axsen. He had not told Chloe of her. He had sent three letters to Ephesus but had received none in return.

Lucius and his companions had been gone for over two years on a journey which was to last six months.

He rose from the couch without another word, but stood drinking in her face and her form one last time. Even the fresco of Venus on her dining room wall appeared to glare at him in the dim light.

They did not embrace at the front door and his departure felt more akin to an "escape" as he made his way through town, out the eastern gate and back to the Cenchreae road.

A breeze blowing toward the coast caused him to shiver and pushed him towards the ocean. Other thoughts pushed him even more.

Paulus had preached. Silas and Timotheos had moved the fellowship of the Followers to Chloe's house. But he had done nothing. No healings except for Sosthenes. No donations. No clinic for Corinthia.

He could just hear the Apostle excuse it all.

"I know this may seem like a dream to you, but you truly cared for a leader of the Followers in Mistress Chloe," he would say.

"Cared for" or seduced? He had not had any dreams these last months but she, and all of this, had seemed like living in a dream, or a drama.

Corinthia had been a Greek tragedy with Lucius as the lead actor. What would be the drama in Ephesus? What waited for him at home?

CHAPTER SIX:
A PAINFUL HOMECOMING

"Then Satan entered into Judas called Iscariot,
who was one of the twelve; he went away and conferred
with the chief priests and the officers of the temple
about how he might betray him to them."
— Luke 22:3-4

The torch lights barely showed the faces of his companions, the Apostle, Silas and Timotheos, as Lucius quickly bade his "Farewell" to them. He waved to Priscilla and Aquila at the rear of the boat since he had not known them very well even in the year and a half at Corinthia. The dusk fell and the shadows lengthened not only on the port of Ephesus but on his memories of his journey with Paulus.

The oil of burning lights mixed with the salt air while he grabbed up his travel satchel from the deck of their boat and threw it over his shoulder. Finally, he ran up the gang plank and onto the limestone sea wall pier, his sandals slapping the pavement as he sprinted.

Her turquoise eyes, the feel of her black hair and the smoothness of her bronze skin called Lucius like a siren from Ulysses. Before he turned left from the port road, he heard it, the banging ahead of him.

The silhouette of the warehouse rose in the dusk and a part of it was swinging back and forth in the dim single torch on its wall. As Lucius approached, "Bang, bang, bang" grew louder. One of the front doors was hanging by only a single hinge.

"Axsen!" he shouted as he dismissed it and ran for the entrance. Bang. Bang. Bang.

"Axsen!" his voice called again. He stopped at the threshold of Healing House or what there was of it.

A window beside the door was missing both shutters, laid against the wall where they had fallen. He yelled again, "Axsen!" The faces from eight, maybe ten cots, popped up like baby birds in their nests. No one said a word.

The light was dim from only two torches in the entire hall with other beds missing or stacked against the far wall and covered in cob webs. They had not been used for some time. A thin film of dust blanketed the floor. The odor was stifling and rank, like a dead body had not been attended to for some time, yet everyone appeared alive if you could call this living.

His eyes darted around the clinic. Who was caring for these few patients? "Axsen!" he shouted once more. "Bartholomew," he said a little quieter. And the name he hoped that he would not hear from, "Marius." Nothing. Gone! All of them.

There were not even any slaves present. He moved among the few beds where most of the patients seemed too sick, lying on their cots or just staring as if too weak, even after his entrance, to speak.

Lucius' breath shortened. His stomach churned. A man put his head over the side of his cot, coughed and spat at the floor. A child, a young boy, sat on his bed with his back against the wall, his mother holding a cup of water to his mouth saying, "You must drink something, my son."

Suddenly a man across the group leaned up on one elbow, looked at Lucius and said, "Adonai be praised. It is the Physician. He is home. We are saved."

Lucius was not sure. Before he ministered to anyone or called again for his missing staff, he crossed to his study. There pushing on the door, it collapsed off its hinges into his writing table. He looked at the pigeon hole cabinet behind the desk. His large scroll was gone.

Then throwing his travel satchel from his shoulder, dropping his sword belt with not only his weapon but his donation from Mistress Lydia and shoving aside a chair, he stooped down to a wood panel behind the table. He felt the splinters of the rough wood that seemed just like any other panel along the wall.

Pushing it back, the cover fell in and he said to himself, "Still here." A large scroll and a small money bag with three talents inside rewarded his search. No one had found this second copy of a journal about the Nazarene nor the coins which he had hidden for a moment like this.

Lucius rose, grabbed the money bag from Lydia and stooped down pouring its contents in with the hidden talents. He replaced the wooden panel and looked around as he stood again.

"Axsen, Marius," he said. Slipping over the fallen door, he was about to look up when a shadow as tall as he was nearly knocked him over into his writing table.

"Gone," Bartholomew's voice said. "They are gone, but you are home. Adonai, be praised."

Lucius said, "Gone where?"

"Of Marius," the Follower continued. "I am uncertain. It has been over a year or so and he went with some who claimed that they were the *true* Followers of the Nazarene."

"True Followers? What sort of true Followers?" the Physician questioned.

"They claimed that your Apostle has perverted the Nazarene's words," Bartholomew answered.

"Fools!" Lucius said, but he remembered some in Galatia who had debated with Paulus and hounded him all the way to Macedonia, about the need for keeping Jewish practices and traditions along with the Nazarene's teaching. Hearing this, Lucius wondered, *For what manner of life had the Nazarene healed them?*

"So, Marius had the truth and we did not?" he said. He also wanted to say, "Did he take my large scroll?"

Instead, Lucius pursued a further question which he did not want to ask. "And her? Where is Axsen?" he said.

Bartholomew lowered his head and looked out a window which had also lost one shutter and now exposed his study to the gathering dusk.

Outside in the clinic a hand waved from a cot. "Axsen, come and help me!" a weak bearded man echoed through the hall. "I need water and your kind touch."

Bartholomew broke from conversing with Lucius and ran to the water bucket, but said, "The man is fevered. I need to help," before he bolted away.

In his absence, Lucius wondered, "Where has she gone? How could all of this happen? How could the Nazarene's spirit be so perverted and poured out like water dousing a lamp?"

Bartholomew returned, stepping over the fallen door and resuming his conversation as if he had never paused.

"Two men came six months ago. They wanted to speak with Axsen and only Axsen. They looked like—like—like—." Bartholomew hesitated.

"Like what?" Lucius pressed.

"Like any of us, one in a workman's tunic and the other in a robe that was belted. Nothing else," the Follower said.

Lucius felt that Bartholomew was holding back and hiding some suspicion about the visitors. He waited and then said, "Go on."

"They did not kidnap her or force her. She seemed to know them. I am certain that she went willingly, as if she knew why they had come for her."

Tears welled up in Lucius' eyes. He said, "But you do not know where those men came from or what they wanted?" Her lack of faith in the Nazarene. Her unwillingness to take his washing. Her love of medicine but not of healing. It made sense.

The dream had come true. The warning of Hermine had been realized—perhaps at the very moment when Hermine's demon predicted it.

"No, Physician," Bartholomew said. "But she had one other secret which she did not want me to tell you. I swore to her that I would not break her silence and I cannot say it. Then she left."

Someone close to Lucius *had* betrayed him. Axsen had cut him like his own sword.

CHAPTER SEVEN:
"DELIVER US FROM EVIL"

"He said to them, 'When you pray, say…
And do not bring us to the time of trial.'"
— Luke 11: 2,4

Sawdust floated down in waves causing Lucius to sneeze as he gazed up at the army of slaves and Followers cutting new timbers and planks for the roof of Healing House. The doors and shutters were not the only damage from neglect—and his absence. So, workers crawled the length of the old warehouse like bees on a hive.

A Greek in a brown tunic stepped up beside Lucius. He unfurled a scroll with lines representing rafters, drawn and re-drawn on the parchment.

"I am Eutychus," he introduced himself. "Customarily I am a land merchant in Ephesus but I have also repaired many such buildings as these."

"And?" Lucius asked.

"Physician, you would do better to move from this one. Trust me, the roof will leak again and soon," he asserted.

Patients, the few remaining, had been moved to one end of the hall while the work continued. They endured dust and fragments of boards and tools tumbling on them along with the loud banging of endless hammer blows.

Lucius looked at them through the entrance without doors, then said to Eutychus, "What can be done?"

"Do you have three talents?" Eutychus asked.

The Physician thought, *Here it comes—a land deal. I am certain.*

The merchant said, "I have a vacant Terrace House on the Marble Street beyond the Agora. For three talents I could reserve it for you. The triclinium and atrium together are larger than Healing House. You could provide fifty beds, perhaps more, with no crowding, Physician."

He reserved the Terrace House without even seeing it. Eutychus had made the offer and Lucius slipped between slaves and saws, carpenters and hammers, to his roofless study. No one noticed him as he extracted three talents from the bag behind the wall which held a remaining twenty from Lydia's donation.

He placed the "deposit" in Eutychus' empty hand and said nothing to anyone, not even Bartholomew.

"This will do it," the Greek confirmed. "Pay me three more whenever you are able."

Lucius inhaled and sighed, his stomach churning. He had purchased a new "Healing House" without seeing it. But how could he dismiss the work of so many Followers? Besides would the Nazarene's clinic ever need to move to the center of Ephesus? Maybe not. Right now, Healing House needed healing.

The aroma of cedar beams in the ceiling and evergreen doors and window shutters in the rest of the clinic wove smiles among the patients, not to forget the quiet absence of saws and hammers. The hurting and diseased returned to Healing House from the temples, particularly from the shrine of Aesculapius.

After the work from so many Followers and helpers and the relief that all was finished, Lucius had decided to stay at the docks of Ephesus. Healing House was becoming known in its current location and moving it would be confusing to both the staff and the hurting. Perhaps he would negotiate a return of his deposit on the Terrace House—some time, but right now his healing work demanded everything from Lucius.

So, the Physician picked his way among the cots, setting broken and sprained limbs, relieving fevers and praying over blind children, their sight returning as he embraced each one. Even the cantankerous Bartholomew broke a half smile with his Physician back in place.

Yet, Lucius thought of *her* as they emptied the hall of broken cots, many of which she had found and dragged here. He touched them one last time as the slaves and attendants carried them out the front door. Where was Axsen?

As one evening descended, he finished his rounds, then slipped to his study, smelling the new wood on its door when he shut it. Feeling for the familiar panel near the floor behind his desk, he pulled out the large scroll.

He unfurled the parchment and inhaled the musty smell. No one knew about this second account on the Nazarene, not even Axsen when she wrote about the one missing from his study. Lucius scanned the miracles, the stories and the sayings.

Then he paused and halted at a passage which read like Ovid or Livy, only better. Rocking back in his seat, he said, "I will speak on this tomorrow to all of Healing House."

His head slumped forward and fell upon the words. His lamp sputtered and flickered out. The moon lit his writing table.

He dreamed.

First, turquoise eyes pressed close to his face and lips, saying, "I had to go. I am safe."

Soon brown covered turquoise and black hair turned to blond, a veil hiding its sheen.

"I know that you had to leave. But I am confronting grave danger. Come to me, my Love."

He looked above the eyes and hair; bodies pressed against bodies. He smelled the crowd and heard them, shouting a name, not hers.

"Lu—, Lu—. Lu—" formed on their lips. "Give us Lucius! You will not close this!" the mob shouted.

"Lucius," Bartholomew said, shaking the Physician's head and shoulders. "It is already mid-morning and Healing House needs to hear from you."

The aromas of baked bread, wine and dates covered the odors of urine and human perspiration in the hall. Attendants snaked among the beds, held up heads and fed the weakest.

Slaves brought cups of water. The murmur of chattering and the morning light streaming through the new shutters softened the scene.

Lucius stood at the door of his study and meditated upon it all, then raised his voice and said, "Let me bring all of you a word from the Nazarene."

A sudden flash of Axsen and Chloe made him pause. Were both in peril? Should he be content, presuming all was well and peaceful here when it was not—*for them.*

He forced his thinking back to Healing House. Nothing could be done—if his dream were even true.

So, Lucius switched from Physician to Preacher and said, "You are all the noblest, the highest, the best and the blessed in the kingdom of the Nazarene."

Heads bobbed up from cots like that first evening when he had just returned from Corinthia. He quoted, "The Nazarene says to you:

"Blessed are you who are poor for yours is the kingdom of Adonai.

"Blessed are you who are hungry now, for you will be filled."

Limp, step. Limp, step. Limp, step.

"Blessed are you who weep now, for you will laugh.

"Blessed—."

Limp, step. Limp, step. Limp, step. Lucius broke his speaking. "Limp, step" dragged in from the street and through the front entrance at the side of the clinic.

The face was clean-shaven, creased with lines but familiar with its gray-streaked Roman haircut. The robe was also like two years ago, military reddish brown. Marius had returned to Healing House.

They adjourned to Lucius's study. The Physician turned Preacher had cut his message short disappointing the eager faces anticipating every word. He felt more upset than his listeners, of that he was certain.

As he entered the room, his eyes went for the scroll exposed on the table. Moving around slowly behind the desk, he grabbed one end and rolled it into a tube.

"May I offer you some wine," he covered as he addressed Marius.

The cripple had noticed neither the scroll nor its contents. He shook his head "No."

He said, "Physician, I must talk with you."

Lucius stepped to the door, hearing the chatter outside, and shut it with the click of the latch. Then moving back to his seat behind his writing table, he put himself only arms-length away from the scroll but leaned toward it, like a mother eagle protecting her nest.

"Speak," he ordered.

"I know that some here speak ill of me," Marius began. "But I must say that I did not betray Healing House."

"Betray" made Lucius jerk but he tried not to show his visitor. He recalled his dream. The prophecy of the demon in Hermine returned.

"The woman Axsen," Marius continued, "gave me laudanum for my leg pain. It sickened me. We fought, and I left."

"Is that all?" Lucius said.

Marius remained standing and added, "No, I must share something more. As Followers, we must retain the customs of the Jews, including circumcision, and we must judge our communities by those practices. Their law and tradition will protect us from—from the authorities."

The Physician furrowed his forehead. He breathed in the new wood odor of the windows and the study door. His anger rose and reddened his face, setting his teeth on edge as he spoke.

"Why should we do that?" Lucius said.

"Have you not heard about the sons of Sceva the high priest?" the lame man asked.

"No," the Physician replied.

Marius explained that though the Apostle healed with handkerchiefs, aprons and mere commands so that even demons would be cast out of victims, such practices could have great risks. Some traveling Jewish exorcists, to be exact, encountered a demoniac at Ephesus port.

The man wore only a loin cloth, his body scratched with his own fingernails. He smelled of sulfur and growled like a wolf at every passerby. No one could contain him, and often he leapt on his victims throwing them to the pavement.

"And what is your concern in telling me about this sad case?" Lucius pressed.

Marius continued his tale, describing how the Jewish exorcists attempted to heal the pathetic demoniac. They were seven brothers, sons of a Jewish high priest named Sceva. When they heard about Paulus and how he could cast out demons with the mere mention of the name of the Nazarene, they abandoned their books, Jewish incantations and traditions.

GRRR! The demon-possessed fellow came at them leaping around as if he were a lion pouncing towards its prey. So, one of the sons of Sceva shouted, "I command you by the Nazarene, whom the Apostle Paulus proclaims, to come out."

A great wind howled through the entire plaza and frightened

onlookers who had gathered. The demoniac stopped pouncing, spun like a top, then fell as if dead. But the demon did not. A whirling column of smoke rose from the man, blocked the sun and danced over his body towards the first exorcist, leaping on him. The same smoky shaft whirled to the other six. Then a voice shouted, "Paulus I know and the Nazarene I fear but you seven are strangers to me."

"And?" Lucius pressed.

"And the seven sons of Sceva were infected with the demon, ripping off their clothing and shouting that they were burning from the inside out."

"Again, what is your point in telling me this?" Lucius asked.

"The magic of the Nazarene is dangerous without the traditions of the Jews connected to it," Marius asserted.

A knock rattled the door. Bartholomew stuck his head around but did not enter.

"My pardon, Physician," he said, "a new Follower whom I do not know wishes to speak with you."

"Kindly have him wait, Bartholomew," Lucius said.

His head disappeared out the door which shut once more.

"Tell me, Marius," Lucius returned to the earlier conversation. "Did the sons become Followers?"

"No," Marius said.

"Then they were attempting a cure, not a healing. You should know this better than anyone," Lucius said pointing down to the lame man's bent leg. "The Nazarene's work is not to be judged nor used as mere magic."

Marius was about to respond.

But Lucius went to the heart of the sin and its punishment. "The Apostle and I do not accept your teaching that Followers must become Jews, and be circumcised, before or after their washings. We are not welcomed into the Nazarene's kingdom to judge others and work magic in his name. The Nazarene welcomes us so that all we do in him is not magic but healing."

"Yes, Physician," the lame man relented. He paused and looked around, returning to Lucius with tears in his eyes. "May I stay at Healing House. I have nowhere else to live."

Lucius' anger eased along with the tightness in his body. He rose and walked around his desk, his arm extending across the shoulders of Marius.

"For as long as you wish," he said to the lame man.

Pulling the door open, Lucius ushered Marius back into the chatter of the busy patients, attendants and slaves in the clinic. Marius limped among the beds and across the hall.

A blond, square-jawed face met the Physician.

"Physician," the man said, "My name is Apollos. I am newly washed into the Nazarene by Priscilla and Aquila. Do you know them?"

"Yes," Lucius said. "But not well."

"Excellent," the blond man smiled. "I will not delay you. I bring an invitation from the Apostle. He wants you to join him again on another journey back to Asia and perhaps to Macedonia. What is your decision?"

This new Follower was more impatient than the Apostle himself.

"Tell him that I will give him my decision soon," Lucius answered.

Apollos nodded quickly. Before he could carry the message away, a dark form overshadowed them. Bartholomew stopped and filled in the silence.

"Physician," he said, "you are needed at the city theater. The followers of Artemis have attacked the Apostle and dragged him there."

At this news, Apollos bolted for the door.

Lucius watched him but said, "Attend to things here, Bartholomew, including Brother Marius, who has asked to stay among us."

"But Physician," Bartholomew protested, "is that wise, given how he deserted us?"

Lucius said, "And now he is back among us. The Nazarene welcomes all."

He returned to his study, grabbed for his *gladius* still sheathed on its sword belt. Buckling it on, he closed the door. Pausing before the new wood with a new latch, he secured the lock.

The scroll still lay on his desk. The Nazarene might welcome back his enemies, but he had also prayed, "Deliver us from evil."

"**G**reat is Artemis! Great is Artemis of the Ephesians!" a crowd roared deafening Lucius' ears as he pushed his way up through a tunnel into the seating of the theater. The structure accommodated nearly two thousand. It was a white gleaming pearl of marble at the end of the road leading from the port of Ephesus and ending at the Marble Street. But the Ephesians filling its seats today were not there for the typical tragedy; rather they gathered for a play that was tragically too real.

It was just unfolding. Below on the stage was the Apostle, bareheaded with other Followers at his side. He was silent now but

Lucius was certain that something he had said got Paulus where he was.

Beside the Apostle in a clean ivory robe was a younger man with a well-trimmed beard. A Greek in a brown work tunic, soiled with soot and pocked-marked with burn holes, stood to the right of the one in ivory.

The fellow in ivory was attempting to silence the crowd by shouting with an echoing voice, "My name—name—name is Alexander—ander--ander. The Apostle—ostle—ostle has not spoken against your god, Artemis—Artemis--Artemis."

Lucius' palms sweated. A tingle ran up his spine and stiffened his neck. Something from Paulus had angered such a large number of Ephesians.

The Greek workman shouted that very thought. "He has preached lies! Great—at—at is Artemis, goddess—oddess—oddess and protector of Ephesus. Kill the imposter—oster—oster from the false god—the Nazarene—ene—ene!" he shouted.

Lucius rubbed his hands together and observed the crowd around him.

A man in a frayed gray tunic yelled, "Bind the Apostle. Imprison him! He speaks heresy and falsehood!"

A second man in a long brown robe bellowed, "No, prison is too good for him. Flog him."

Another to Lucius' left said, "I know that 'Alexander.' He is not one of us. He is a Jew."

The workman now spoke so loud that his voice echoed more across the theater, "I am—am—am—Demetrius—Demetrius—chief silver—silver—silver smith—smith of Artemis—Artemis. The Apostle—Apostle—Apostle speaks against us silver—silver—silver smiths. And against all of us—us—us in Ephesus saying that—that gods made with hands are false gods—ods—ods."

"Then let the courts—courts—courts and the proconsul—consul—consul decide—decide—decide," Alexander echoed, interrupting Demetrius' rant.

"I dismiss—miss—miss this assembly," Alexander said.

Lucius thought, *Wise decision, sir.* A Jew had saved the Apostle. So, was Marius right? Were the tensions rising between the authorities and the Followers? Should he risk another journey with Paulus?

CHAPTER EIGHT:
A FOLLOWER RESCUED

"At that very hour some Pharisees came and said to him,
'Get away from here, for Herod wants to kill you.'"
— Luke 13:31

Years had melted one into another as did the reigns of emperors. Caligula was assassinated. Claudius replaced him but for how long. As if the tensions in the rule of Rome were not enough, Lucius was already in his late thirties and the journey with the Apostle felt slower, more tiresome, and full of constant doubts.

Yet, the cities of Asia blurred past as though he were running by the landscape on a fresco. They moved North where Galatia's familiar towns held some surprises.

When they passed the plaza in Derbe, Lucius saw something which he had not seen for years. A serpent, extended and black, slithered and disappeared into a crevice along the stony street.

He saw the reason for the vision. The glare of the sun hid them at first but there to his right were slaves, or perhaps attendants, carrying a man on a pallet to an old storage building. The Physician called to his company to pause. As he pursued the men and their stretcher, he broke from the brightness of the limestone road into the shade of a small room filled with beds.

"What is this place?" he asked a slave near the door.

"It is a healing place to the Nazarene," a young man with blond hair said. "It is similar to the one in Ephesus established by the beloved Physician Lucius Maximus, so they tell me? Do you know of him?"

Lucius smiled and did not reply but he wondered how this had come to be. Paulus' hand on his shoulder interrupted any introductions or further questions. The hidden "Physician" nodded to the slave and slipped from the shade back onto the sunlit street.

Moving on to Lystra, that old military colony, he and his companions were strolling through the temple district. The Apostle was chattering on about the endless pagan "foolishness" around them, words which Lucius was certain had been the source of the riot in the Ephesus' theater some time ago.

As they passed the Temple of Mars, a smaller shrine rose on the left, silhouetted by the morning sun. There was no priest out front and no statue of a god so Lucius wondered who was the "resident" of this small stocky row of columns.

All at once at its foundation, he saw it again, a brown viper crawled under the first step and vanished. Once more he drifted to the back of his group and turned left up the steps. The interior scene astonished him.

Though the smell was of sweat and human waste, the cots were arranged in orderly rows with slaves and attendants moving among them. Patients waved for help or were lifting their heads for water or perhaps medicines.

A young woman attendant in a gray robe stopped beside Lucius and asked, "Are you ill, sir? We are very crowded but we will find space for anyone as the Nazarene has commanded us to do."

Lucius did not answer at first, but then said, "I am fine. But what is this place?"

The attendant said, "It was at one time a temple to Aesculapius, the god of healing. Now it is a proper healing place, not to that imposter, but to the Nazarene. We have likened it to the one in Ephesus founded by the great and beloved Physician, the one whom they call Deacon Lucas."

Lucius sighed and tears filled his eyes. Even though he had done nothing in these towns on his first journey, the Nazarene *had* come.

Outside he heard Timotheos calling, "Lucius Maximus! Where are you?"

The attendant tilted her head to the side. She smiled as she had also heard the name.

"Are you—?" she broke.

"Deacon Lucas. Yes, I am," he answered and stepped out and back through the columns. The gray robe followed him and watched from the porch as Lucius descended the steps and re-joined his group.

Their journey sailed on to Macedonia bringing them to the familiar home of Lydia. Lucius entered first and was about to ask about the purple merchant when a slave named Clytemnestra answered his questioning look.

"Our mistress took ill, Physician. If only you had been here, Lydia might still be with us but she has gone to be with the Nazarene instead," Clytemnestra said with reddening eyes.

Lucius dismissed himself early from the evening meal and opened the door to his room. Sobbing over Lydia's loss, he lay on his small bed in the moonlight. What would now become of the Followers in Philippi? And worse, what would happen with the clinic which he had started by returning a portion of Lydia's donation?

Then he thought of the endless parade of patients certainly filling the cots at his Healing House in Ephesus. The last of Lydia's donations there had almost run out when he left; and, not trusting Marius, he delegated the final five talents to Bartholomew.

While he worried with tears running down his face, his eyes shut. The darkness became an escape into a dream, filled at first with a turquoise look and raven hair, bronze skin and a bold but inviting mouth. Then cedar and cinnamon scents replaced the turquoise, evolving into ebony eyes, the raven hair into blond with no veil covering as it was twisted up behind the woman's head. Her lips were open, not to a kiss but to a call in a silent voice.

He woke up. Then he dressed in a clean tunic. The morning had come, and he wondered what last night's vision had meant as it was more about Chloe than Axsen. Lucius looked at his travel bag and sword. They were nearly ready. A quick breakfast would be all that he would need.

On his way down the hall, he met Timotheos. "I must go," he said. "I must go directly to Corinthia."

"You cannot leave us now," Timotheos replied. "The Thessalonians are waiting for us."

In the dining room, Lucius said nothing. He let Paulus ramble on about the communities of Followers which had been founded in

Asia. The Apostle mentioned nothing about the clinics which Lucius had encountered, but it did not bother him.

Chloe was calling and he knew that with the death of Lydia, the silent summons in his dream—Chloe's open mouth—might not be for her need but for the needs of Healing House. After all, she had the appearance of an attendant at his clinic, did she not?

A journey of a week or better lasted only days as Lucius sprinted to Corinthia. Now his nearly forty years showed, causing him to pant and feel the aching stiffness in his legs. When the city rose like a white pearl ahead, he pushed himself into a painful jog and entered from the North by way of the Lecheion Road.

The familiar became strange as the streets in Chloe's neighborhood were bustling with no one. He passed closed doors as if everyone was somewhere else. Then he arrived and smelled the wood of her door.

It was the only one open. Lucius nudged it and let it bang on the atrium wall. He was about to scan the familiar and inviting frescoes of Ulysses and Jason and the Argonauts when a lone slave appeared in the entry room.

She shouted, "Hurry, Physician! Mistress Chloe is at the arena! You must save her! Go now!" Her face contorted and tears filled her eyes.

Without a greeting, Lucius threw his travel bundle and medical satchel at the slave's feet. He grabbed the hilt of his *gladius*. Stepping from the threshold back into the sunlight, he ran through his mind the way to the Amphitheater on the northeast end of town, hoping it was where the slave meant.

The limestone glistened in the morning sun as the huge arena rose and overshadowed his right side. He realized that he had not asked where Chloe was or how he would find her, but up ahead he heard the roar of a crowd shouting one name then another. So, this was where everyone was.

A man in a frayed threadbare tunic limped along the outside, panting as he went. Lucius caught up to him, hoping he spoke Greek.

"Where are the Followers?" he said as something told him not to name names.

The man pointed towards two entrances beyond the one where they were standing. Lucius charged for that arched gate, but continued to worry that finding Chloe might be easy but assisting her might not.

Then he heard the shouting more clearly as a chant, "Chloe! Chloe! Chloe!"

Lucius bolted up narrow steps to the second tier of seats. The chanting intensified, "Chloe! Chloe! Chloe!" He emerged from the shadows of the hallway and adjusted his squinting eyes to the bright sands of the arena below. Heads of the Followers moved side to side, sometimes exposing the action and sometimes hiding it.

Chloe was there in the center, her blond hair tied behind her head. She had no veil and wore only a light tunic with small sandals. A small sword like Lucius remembered from her study was swinging in each of her hands. Her opponent, a large muscular gladiator with a larger sword than hers, far out-classed her. Their weapons rang back and forth with Chloe sometimes falling back under the warrior's heavy blows.

Then Lucius heard what he had only questioned was the cause of this combat. Two Followers, both women, spoke back and forth.

The one was just commenting, "It's such a horror that Proconsul Gallio has made her fight for her daughter and for all of us Followers."

A sound like a precision clicking against stone rattled behind Lucius in the shadowed hallway. He recognized military boots pounding the steps from the lower level of the arena. He did not know why but he swung around to see Roman legionaries charging up single file because of the narrow passage.

They were coming at him and at this section of Followers. Lucius responded without thinking, more from reflex, as though he were back in combat.

He grabbed the *pilus* of the first soldier and ripped it from his hands. Putting it across the legionary's body, he shoved the man back into the soldier behind him. As they both stumbled, he fastened the spear into the gate holes at the top of the steps and formed a barrier.

The two men tumbled as he quickly reached for the spear of the second soldier and added it to the barricade. Meanwhile soldiers were plummeting backwards down the steps one onto another like the falling blocks of a child. Then the legionaries turned and retreated, but for how long?

Lucius rotated once more towards the arena where the gladiator now sat on the sand with two bleeding legs. Chloe was shouting to the crowds, "Freedom—om—om to all the Foll—llow—llowers from the Proconsul, by this document." She raised a scroll in her hand, her swords now gone with one plunged into the sand at her feet.

"She is a fool if she believes Gallio will keep his word, even written, to her or any Follower." Lucius said to himself. "Proconsuls serve only themselves, even in the name of Rome."

His sandals tapped along the aisle behind a row of seats beyond the Followers. He found another gate which he hoped the legionaries had not. Discovering it empty, he tramped down its steps to the lower level and out of the shadowed hallway back onto the Corinthian street.

The bright sun was high in the sky but still angled enough to silhouette two figures ahead. A familiar, small tunic was down on the limestone and held at spear point by a legionary. Lucius sprinted towards them.

The soldier felt something bang his spear, causing it to drop away from Chloe's face.

"I will take charge of Mistress Chloe," Lucius ordered to a shocked legionary who looked up the shaft of a blade to the handle of a centurion's *gladius*.

He herded Chloe's daughters, her servants and Chloe herself down the steep narrow stairway into the atrium of the Terrace House. He thought to himself, *I could never have moved patients in and out of this place. What was Eutychus thinking? No, I reserved this for her.*

As Chloe's family picked their way inside this new house by means of the dim light of Lucius' torch, he was recalling how close the Romans had been to their escape from Corinthia and yet how far away. When they had reached the port of Cenchreae, a Follower had told them that Gallio's lead centurion, Julius, had come with a detachment to Chloe's home shortly after they had all fled. The Romans had ripped through every bed cover, overturned every chair and table and defaced Ulysses and Jason on the walls with mud and stones from the atrium pool.

Believing that Chloe would escape on one of her wine ships, Julius had ordered his men North of the city to Lecheion port, not to Cenchreae and the East. Chloe had eluded the Romans, but her life in Corinthia was over.

Lucius knew this as his sandals slapped the stone floor across the atrium of what would become her new Terrace House. His hand swept the torch around its frescoes, illuminating their colors and figures. He said "I know it is not the magnificence of your home in Corinthia. Yet, I am sure that you will be comfortable here in Ephesus—and safe."

He paused, and his torch, which smelled of burning oil, crackled, filling the silence. Then he said, "I just need three talents from you and it will be yours."

Chloe motioned to her slave, who produced a bag. Her porcelain fingers drew out three coins and she deposited them in Lucius' hand. Then she collapsed, her robes and hooded cape becoming a heap in Lucius' arms nearly igniting as he thrust his torch to her daughter, Mara, and caught Chloe's limp body.

The interpretation of his dream was not fully correct. She needed *him* to make *her* safe, *but* did he also need her?

CHAPTER NINE:
A BENEFACTOR AND A TROUBLED RETURN

"And again he said, 'To what should I compare the kingdom of God?
It is like yeast that a woman took and mixed in with
three measures of flour until all of it was leavened.'"
— Luke 13:20-21

T
he cool salt breeze brushed Lucius' skin. The odor of the
day's patients faded into the perfume of her. This was the
second time when he had come to Chloe's and again, they
strolled into the grove of evergreens above the Terrace Houses.

These homes felt as if they were stacked one upon another, built
of white limestone and gracing the hillside above a ravine which
stretched back toward the temple district in Ephesus. Wealthy
merchants and government officials lived here, and made it all the
more desirable for Chloe and her family to move into a center
vacancy.

As they talked, Lucius no longer imagined turquoise eyes, eclipsed now by dark ebony ones beside him. He saw only Chloe.

As they walked, he threw quick glances in her direction, drinking in her round face with chiseled cheeks surrounded as always by wisps of blond hair under her veil.

Had she truly vanquished three gladiators in Corinthia's arena?

"I feel too far in years to fight like that again," she said, breaking into his thoughts. "Though it was a short time ago, I feel older than perhaps I should from such exploits."

Lucius said nothing. He wanted to move beyond her victory to his needs for Healing House. Lydia's donation was continuing to run as dry as a shallow cistern in summer heat.

Instead, she filled in the silence as they strolled toward the silhouetted cypresses to the torch lights being lit in the dusky Agora and the temples along the Marble Street.

"Did she truly abandon you?" Chloe asked. "Axsen, I mean?"

His current reality returned but not the one which he wanted. "It seems so," Lucius confirmed.'

"So, where did she go?" Chloe pressed.

"I have no way to know," he said. "Possibly home. Across the Euphrates."

"So, you are no longer married?" Chloe pursued.

"To some I never was. I never freed her from slavery but I still treated her as my partner. Yet she did not become—," Lucius stopped.

"A Follower," Chloe finished his thought.

"Sandals, Mistress?" a vendor from the Agora begged. The twilight had brought them to the edge of the markets which were mostly closed except for this merchant delaying the end of his day.

Chloe shook her head "No" and they moved on through the last chatter and torch lights of the vendors.

Lucius said, "Will you come to Healing House tomorrow? I want to share our—the Nazarene's—work with you." For all of their recent connections, he had never made the invitation and she had never visited.

"Of course," she said without hesitation. It made Lucius wonder if she wanted to see his ministry—or him.

Lucius slipped between the cots which were many, more than fifty now. Healing House had retained its full capacity, and more, under Bartholomew—even when its Physician had been absent.

"You will need to drink all of that, Publius," he said. "To stop your cough."

A little boy with brown Roman-cropped hair and rough dark eyes looked up and wrinkled his nose, saying, "But it is so bitter. It makes me cough."

A woman with the boy's same round eyes smiled at Lucius, then said, "I will make certain that he does as you say, Physician."

Lucius moved on.

An older man whose beard was graying and whose hair was disheveled waved and shouted weakly, "Over here, Physician." Lucius stepped across the clinic to a row of cots and took the raised hand and held it as though it were as light as a feather.

"Hermes, we will do all we can for you. Remember to pray as we did together yesterday."

Lucius caught someone in his side glance. A veil, dark round sparkling eyes and an ivory robe gathered at the waist, too formal for here, had entered the main doors.

He said nothing but Marius hobbled to his side. His Roman nose bent down and under his breath, he said to Lucius, "Someone is here for you, Physician."

Lucius did not respond. He continued his rounds, approaching a woman with a rounded stomach on a cot. She was panting and moaning softly.

She said, "I—I had—had—had hoped that Midwife Axsen would return for—for—for the birth of my baby."

Lucius observed that the one at the front door did not show any discomfort at this request. He said, "We all feel her absence." He felt the woman's stomach and concluded, "Not quite time yet."

Chloe continued to watch him without comment and without moving from her position.

He wove his way to a sandy-haired man bathed in sweat. When Lucius mumbled something in the man's ear, he relaxed but he appeared to be dying.

Then the Physician knelt at the bed of a woman in her twenties. Bandages covered her arms and legs. As he unwrapped them, Chloe gagged and choked. Rashes on the woman were oozing and filled with pus. The stench was like that of rotting meat. Another attendant bent over the woman and without reacting, began applying new wrappings to her.

Chloe gagged again, then bent over and vomited. Neither Lucius nor Chloe said anything except that she now wiped her mouth and covered her nose with her veil.

Finally, Lucius moved on, bowed his head and was gently touching the closed eyes of a man sitting on the edge of his cot. The Physician whispered, his lips moving in prayer. Then he stepped back.

The man blinked and blinked again. "I can see!" he shouted. "I can see!"

Lucius noticed that Chloe dropped her veil from her mouth, focusing at first on the formerly blind man then on his Physician.

"Come and help us," Lucius invited, at last turning toward her.

"No, I am not a healer," she said.

Looking away from the man whom he had just healed, Lucius realized that Axsen was certainly gone.

As they walked that night among the cypresses, she took his arm. In her other hand she held a small bag which jingled. She gazed at him more than he at her this time.

"Was Axsen very good at healing?" she asked, raising her eyebrows.

"She was," Lucius said, not wanting to explain the differences between "healing" and "curing."

"Oh, and now it all rests on you," Chloe said.

Lucius did not respond.

She said, "I have other ways to do the Nazarene's work," She thrust her jingling bag in Lucius' direction. The evening breeze fluttered her veil.

It was what he wanted but perhaps not so suddenly.

"Take this," she said. "And know that I also offer to handle your money for Healing House, if you wish. Remember that I directed my husband's wine business after his death. It survived even if he did not. It still does."

Lucius stopped their walk. He reached for the bag in her hand. All at once she stood in front of him. She raised her fingers up to his face stroking the cheek with the scar under his beard.

"I watched you today," she said gazing into his dark eyes. "You are an amazing man, not just an amazing doctor. You bring the Nazarene's healing to so many."

She pressed her lips to his and he returned the kiss. She backed away.

"I want to—" she broke off.

They had strolled to the temple section of Marble Street.

"Get out of Rome's Temple!" the priest shouted in his pointed red cap. "You cannot expect that from Caesar. He does not abide that sort of sacrifice from foreigners. He has his limits."

At first, Lucius thought the priest's attack was directed at them, so he pulled his face from Chloe and raised his eyes above her to the interior glow between the columns. The statue which he had seen years ago in its crate, Augustus with his hand held in some gesture of power and authority, was glowing in torch light at the back of the shrine.

Lucius thought, *Your attack could be for me as much as for that poor outsider. After all, Caesar has his limits but the Nazarene does not. The Nazarene's empire is limitless, and I am more than grateful to work for him.*

"Marry me," Chloe brought him back to her. "You work here. You live here. And I want my family to be yours."

Lucius heard himself say, "Yes." But was it possible?

CHAPTER TEN:
A WEDDING—OR NOT

"At the time for the dinner he sent his slave
to say to those who had been invited,
'Come, for everything is ready now.'
But they all alike began to make excuses."
— Luke 14:17, 18a

Waves played their rhythm on the pier outside the cottage which he and Axsen had bought near Healing House. The cool salt air relieved his tiring day without her at the clinic.

Lucius dropped back on his cot in the small sleeping room with only a bed and a chair.

Tomorrow would be for her, not Axsen, but Chloe. His wedding day had arrived and it would bring a new blessing which perhaps he required now. So, his eyes fluttered and closed with dusky light from his window as Lucius slipped into the darkness of a dream and then the light of a vision.

Axsen's face loomed up, stunning with her turquoise eyes and raven hair. It blurred into the brown of Chloe's eyes and the invitation, "Marry me." Then the face evolved, a beard forming under her veil and the dark appearance of someone whom Lucius did not know—or had forgotten.

As he was about to say, "The Naza—," The mouth on the face said, "He is mine and he is in danger. You must go to him now."

That face faded into black but the white marble of a *bema* platform slid before Lucius along with a thumb's up and someone who shouted, "You have appealed to Rome and to Rome you will go."

It all ended in a bright morning sun. Lucius fluttered his eyes again and heard the rhythm of the waves pounding the Ephesian pier. When he awakened fully, he saw the sun topping his window. It was high and the day was late.

He looked at his chair and the white tunic for his wedding. Under it was a gray one for the clinic, and he needed to go there before he went to her. As he raised up on his bed, his travel bundle and his medical satchel were fully packed as if he were leaving again. Had he done this last night or when?

Dismissing the mystery, Lucius grabbed the gray tunic from the chair and slipped out of his night robe and into his work garment. Healing House came up sooner than he expected but from that time, everything slowed. A baby had decided to be born gradually, a boy with a wheezing throat could not stop coughing, a paralytic required new braces for his legs and an afternoon burdened with hurts and patients sped away in time like a race chariot. The sun was shifting to the West and towards dusk.

There was no time to return to his cottage and the wedding

garment. His body stiffened with panic as he shouted to Bartholomew, "See to the patients and then come when you are prepared to."

His sandals slapped out the door barely missing two patients' beds as he sprinted to the port road, through its colonnade, its arches and its ascent up to the Marble Street. Lucius was panting now since the setting sun still warmed enough to send sweat trickling down his chest.

He ran through the temples and the Agora, vendors and stalls beginning to close as he brushed by a customer and had to grab for him to keep the poor man from toppling into a stall full of leather satchels. Finally, he came to the Terrace Houses and searched for hers in the center.

As Lucius approached the right door, he formed words in his mind, an apology and a hope that Chloe had kept the wedding to only her daughters and servants. His hand did not knock but shoved the entrance open. The wood creaked wide as did his eyes when it revealed the scene inside.

Followers which he knew, and some which he did not, jammed the entry room at the foot of her stairs. He inhaled, flowers, roses, hyacinths, lilies, all banking the walls and covering her frescoes. The aromas of roasted lamb, a calf and doves rose over the perfume of her décor. A slave woman in a white robe met him.

Lucius closed his eyes as he said to himself, "Oh, no, I am late. Way too late."

Behind her slave, Chloe moved up to him at the top of the stairs. Her blond hair was perfectly coiffed under her veil, her ivory robe was lined in golden trim and cinctured at the waist, outlining her inviting body.

She looked back towards her chattering guests and said with a grin, "My groom has finally come. The wedding can begin."

Her guests blossomed into a collective "Ah" and smiled upward to Lucius, sweated and wrinkled in his gray tunic from a long day at Healing House. He straightened upright and then spoke words which he had wanted to reserve for her in private.

"We cannot marry, Mistress Chloe, not yet. Someone is in danger and I must go to them as I went to you. I bid you farewell."

The chatter in the room snuffed out and the smiles of the guests extinguished to faces of shock and open mouths of disappointment. Lucius did not react and did not even embrace Chloe. His panic returned running through his body like the sting from a whip. But his dream pushed him more, out the door and back into the street.

To his back, Chloe said, "Has someone come to you with this news? I have heard nothing."

Lucius turned, walking backwards, and answered, "I have had a dream—a nightmarish vision."

CHAPTER ELEVEN:
A LETTER HOME AFTER
A PROCONSUL'S PRISON

"Go on your way. See I am sending you out
like lambs into the midst of wolves."

— Luke 10:3

The air was damp and cold even for an early summer day or was it from the cold limestone prison walls around him? Lucius looked at the hand of the officer and smelled the steel of his own sword.

"Here is your *gladius*, Centur—Physician," Tribune Lysias said.

Lucius, though in a simple tunic, saluted the superior officer with an arm across his chest.

"I appreciate your respect and release," Lucius replied.

"Do not be grateful to me. The Proconsul finds these religious matters trivial, but the Apostle must remain here until the Governor fully decides the matter. You know that he is a new appointee—this Festus," the Tribune said.

"I know this," Lucius answered. Yet, he wondered what would happen to the final face from his dream of several months ago and the vision which had ended his marriage to Chloe.

Stepping outside the high walls of the jail and onto the bright stones of a Caesarean street in Galilee, Lucius had no thoughts about where to go. At least his travel bundle and medical satchel had been returned with his sword, but they had been ransacked, having been searched by legionaries.

He strolled the *via* and turned into a low-ceilinged business, dark compared to the outside and filled with rough-hewn benches and tables, the whole room lit only by a lone window. The tavern had no patrons yet; so, the keeper motioned that Lucius could have any table.

"Beer," he ordered from the owner. Sitting towards the door, Lucius pulled a small empty scroll from his bundle to pen a letter back to Chloe. He had to explain the vision which he hoped he had interpreted correctly. His stylus scribbled:

To my beloved Chloe,

I must again express my sorrow about breaking off our wedding some months ago. Kindly accept my regrets if you are able to forgive me.

As the Apostle said before departing with us all from Ephesus, "It is more blessed to give than to receive." Yes, it was the Apostle who was in danger and who needed me. Though I did not know this upon leaving you, I know it from the events which I will now recount to you.

Lucius looked up at the sound of a pottery mug placed on his table when the tavern keeper returned. He paid the owner and thanked him, waiting for him to move back to his empty business. Then he wrote:

Amazing how one empire fights another to destroy the true kingdom of the Nazarene. A Tribune Lysias, whom even I did not know from my military days in Palestine's capital, had to rescue us from a mob attempting to kill us all, not just the Apostle...

Footsteps clacked in from the street and the eyes of two legionaries in red tunics without helmets greeted the tavern keeper. They appeared to be regulars, but they both began staring at the lone stranger seated at the back.

Lucius ignored them and continued to write more about how he had gotten there. His eye now picked up further down his page:

...at one point the Romans who held us were about to flog us. When the Apostle let them know that we were Roman citizens, the guards relented. I had to admit that Paulus' mouth finally worked for us and not against us...

Thinking about escaping the flogging, Lucius worried about how dangerous this journey had become. He scribbled on, but he felt the stare of the soldiers burning into him from up front:

...opponents remain to our kingdom which the Jews now openly call "the sect of the Nazarene." So, the Romans under a heavy guard of two hundred legionaries and two centurions escorted us back to prison in Caesarea until I was released.

The tavern keeper, a huge man with a leather apron and breath which smelled of stale bread and ale, returned to Lucius and attempted to read over his shoulder. The Physician rolled the scroll shut but the musty parchment smell remained along with the odors from the owner breathing down on him.

"I will have another beer," Lucius requested, and the keeper departed.

Recalling his place, he unfurled the scroll and wrote:

My Love,

I do not know when I will return to you or to Ephesus or to Healing House. There is a new Proconsul here, one Porcius Festus, replacing Felix whom the Apostle nearly converted to the Nazarene. So, with the Apostle still imprisoned, I must remain.

One last request from me. All of the Apostle's preaching here means the Nazarene's kingdom has become a threat to Caesar, not just to the Jews. Go to my study at Healing House. Behind my writing table in the middle of the lower part of the wall is a wooden panel. Push down and remove it and take the large scroll inside. It is a second copy of my complete journal on the Nazarene. Carry it under your robes to your home. I do not know who might be working against us, but I have my suspicions.

Keep the scroll some place safe, some place which only you know. My hope is that all is well with you, Chloe. My hope and prayer are also that we will marry when I return.

My love for you is strong, but my love for the Nazarene remains even stronger.

From the loving hand of your Physician,

—Lucius

Footsteps again strode into the tavern as Lucius rolled his scroll and recognized a group of Followers silhouetted and then made visible once more with the dim interior light. Leaving his bundle and satchel, he walked them back outside and discovered that one was heading to Ephesus.

"Take this to Mistress Chloe in the Terrace Houses," he said, reaching his letter to a man with a long robe and sandy beard.

"I know of her," the Follower responded looking around.

Lucius felt a tap on his shoulder. One of the legionaries from the front of the tavern had come out.

"Are you Lucius Maximus?" he said.

Lucius' palms grew moist, and his back felt stiff. He hesitated.

Then he said, "Yes."

"I have a letter for you from Ephesus," the soldier said. He was not young and from a scar on his face, he had seen a campaign or two. "I failed to give it to you when the Tribune released you."

Lucius opened the scroll and saw that it was from *her*. He wanted to retrieve the letter which he had just handed to the Followers; but looking in their direction, the men had disappeared as the soldier came up to him.

CHAPTER TWELVE:
NEARLY HOME

"Or what king, going out to wage war against another king,
will not sit down first and consider whether he is able with
ten thousand to oppose the one who comes against
him with twenty thousand?"
— Luke: 14:31

*…kindly return to Ephesus as soon as you are able. I know
that you meant well by me and that you had grave concerns
about the Apostle and his safety. I heard from a Follower who
came from Caesarea recently that Paulus is in great peril in
Jerusalem.*

Lucius looked up from Chloe's letter into the bright street. He
did not return to the tavern, hoping that his travel bundle and
medical satchel were still there. Her words were far more
critical as their letters had now passed much like their love had.

His eyes scanned down the page:

...I am not well, dearest Lucius. I have fevers, cannot eat and my nights are filled with endless coughing. Although Bartholomew has come nearly every day from Healing House to my house, I need your loving and expert hand. Come home. Return to me.

One other concern. Bartholomew has related to me that Marius has disappeared from Healing House.
From the hand of the one who loves you still,

~Chloe

Lucius did not worry that their scrolls had passed. Chloe was ill—perhaps very sick. The Apostle was going nowhere now in the protective custody of the new Proconsul. The Followers here in Caesarea could care for him.

He turned and re-entered the tavern, smelling its stale ale and musty wood. Grabbing his bundle and satchel, he headed out the door towards the docks. What had happened with Marius was far less troubling than Chloe's health.

Meeting a Follower on his way to the pier, he said, "Get word to the Apostle that I must return to Ephesus as Mistress Chloe has taken ill."

That afternoon Lucius booked passage on a wine ship which was sailing to Cenchreae but docking first in Ephesus. The aroma of wine from the *amphora* jars reminded him all the more that he must not stop at Healing House upon his arrival but hasten to the "wine merchant" in the Terrace Houses of Marble Street.

When he arrived, it was her words echoing in his ears, "I am not well...Return to me," which made him shove through the bodies along the pier. Dock workers, slaves and travelers bumped him with their carts and bundles.

"Hey, mate, watch where ya goin'," one fellow griped.

As his sandals struck hard against the stone road and led him to the warehouse area, the crowds dwindled to far less bumping and shoving. Shadows of large buildings hid him, and everything.

Suddenly a grab came from behind. A rough black cloth shrouded Lucius' eyes into total darkness. His sword belt and weapon slipped from his waist as his travel bundle and medical satchel were jerked from him over his head.

His wrists were forced behind his waist, bent and lashed so tightly that the leather ties cut into his skin. A voice shouted in a strange tongue. Another answered back and seemed to know what to say—and do.

Lucius was being "taken"—but to where and by whom? And why?

Two arms on each side of him grabbed his arms and dragged his sandals striking them at times on the port road with its rough cobble stones. The darkness around his face brightened and warmed him as if he were out in the sun, but that was all that Lucius knew.

Odors of salt air and wood and leather and fish from the warehouse district relinquished to hot and dusty smells. Then he heard it. He listened for it again as the arms continued to drag him and to rattle on in their strange language. A snort came a second time, then a whinny. And another snort.

Lucius smelled the pungent odor of a horse and straw. The "kidnappers" ripped his feet from the dust beneath them and dropped him down hard onto a saddle. His crotch banged the leather and he winced.

Other voices stranger than the first two shouted to each other. Lucius could not discern how many. His horse shifted and snorted again. A leather rope was lashed around his waist into his wrist bindings behind him and back out possibly to the neck of the horse.

Whoever it was had done this sort of tethering before. They were making certain that their "prisoner" remained in place. A whistle from someone ahead and Lucius jerked backward and then forward as his horse's hooves along with others pounded the hard ground. He coughed at the dust thrown up by his mount.

Again, he worried, *These marauders were taking him somewhere but where? And who were they?*

Lucius' knees pressed hard against the sides of the horse as it increased from a gallop to a full run. His back ached, not just from the fear of dismounting, but from the terror of what was happening to him.

The humidity of the coast left, and from the dust and dry heat he knew he was being ridden inland and East, but once more, *where?* The hooves pounded on and his shroud remained on so his direction was a mystery.

When night came, the coolness refreshed him slightly. His captors released his tether to his horse but not the bindings which cut against his wrists. Two large arms pulled him down to relieve himself and to sit, a pair of hands from behind him removed his shroud to eat some bread and dried fish and take warm water from a skin, again all from other hands and arms which revealed no identity. His back was always to the men beyond him still exchanging laughter in that odd language.

Day after day his horse pounded firmer ground in dryer air and hotter sun. Sweat trickled down his aching back and under his drenched tunic. One night after his meal and with blindfold removed, Lucius looked up into a starry sky and discerned the constellations determining that he was heading South into the desert beyond Palestine perhaps. The oasis looked familiar with its clear pond and crooked stream gurgling out the lower end. The grove of close standing palms rustling overhead appeared like one where he had camped with his cohorts years ago.

After endless days of more pounding and little rest, the galloping stopped—suddenly. Hooves and snorts continued but as if something was being decided. His captors were talking in low tones.

All at once the tethering to his horse's neck whipped off as two hands from each side lifted Lucius into the air and banged his feet against hard ground. The ties on his wrists snapped with a jerk, like a knife had cut them. Then nearly tearing out his matted hair, another hand yanked off his black cover.

Lucius blinked. His watering eyes blurred as he rubbed them with newly-freed hands and stinging wrists. He rubbed the cuts from the bindings and smelled the horse flesh around him.

Pointed caps, long robes and long swords were on every rider. Before him was a tall warrior with a silver cap and a long blue and green robe, cinctured at the waist with a belt and *rhomphaia* in a bronze sheath. His beard was black and his dark eyes were set on the prisoner as the armor clanked on his horse shifting back and forth in its halted stance.

He did not move his glare from Lucius as he spoke in near perfect Greek, not the strange tongue which Lucius had been hearing.

"Let us hope that you have done well in your search. Take him to our camp," he commanded, speaking to the two men behind the Physician.

As the two warriors who had been his captors seized his arms, a distant shout aroused the other riders. Pointed caps jolted backwards and the silver cap turned his head to listen.

He yelled, "We do not have time for him. We are under attack." Returning to the prisoner, he commanded, "Bind him to the oak here and then join us in the battle."

As the Parthians jerked his arms, Lucius turned in the direction of the first shout. Something was happening which concerned *them,* but not him, or did it?

The horsemen kicked up dust behind their lead cataphract and galloped down the knoll which retained only Lucius, the two Parthians and a lone scrub oak. Re-tying Lucius' wrists in front of him and doubling, then, tripling another leather line, the warriors bound him with arms on one side of the tree and legs fastened there on either side of the trunk.

They re-mounted their horses and something clanked from each of their saddles. Lucius, even with his face pressed against the bark, saw them, recognized them—bows with arrow quivers.

Below the knoll was a valley, gently rolling up to another rise. Lucius might not know where he was, but he became certain about who was here—not just Parthians. At least five thousand men, an entire legion of Romans had formed up into a square in the valley below.

The Romans faced away from where he was and from where the Parthians had been.

They were opposing no one—yet. Then he heard it but did not see it—the pounding on the earth directly in front of the legion like a great drumming. Only these drums now had hooves and riders.

At that moment behind him in the shade of the rustling oak, a voice said, "Centurion Lucius, is that you tied up there? I haven't seen ya for years. Do you remember me? Tacitus from your old *century*?" A legionary moved around him and into Lucius' line of sight.

He looked up and realized that the man claimed to be from *Legio X Fretensis* out of Jerusalem. The old legion he knew, but not this man. What was going on here?

"We are a scouting party," Tacitus said, now joined by two other legionaries in helmets and with swords. "Where is your armor? Did they take it when they captured ya?"

Was it true? Had his captors brought him overland from Ephesus all the way back to the desert beyond Palestine and Jerusalem?

Lucius did not know how to answer the legionaries so he just relented to their speculations about him. "I was their captive," he said. Still, he thought that he had no reason to know why.

One of the other legionaries moved to the opposite side of the tree and wielded his *gladius* backward banging the tether with a loud thud and freeing Lucius. Tacitus cut his wrist bindings with a small dagger and let his fellow Roman rub his wrist cuts.

If these men had served with Lucius, why were they not older? Even Tacitus appeared to be only eighteen or nineteen. Their appearance did not make sense but their rescue did.

All at once it came again but this time from an adjoining knoll to the right. Parthian horsemen pressed downward on the Roman square, perhaps another five hundred swelling the attack of the first group to one thousand riders.

Centurions shouted from the valley. A rain of spears whistled the air and spiraled upward toward both cavalry units. The riders reined up their mounts and rotated around bumping one another as they moved off to allow open ground between them and the Romans. Spears hit with thuds in the empty no-man's space between the opposing lines.

The Parthians, churning like waves in a storm, straightened out their charge from both the right and the left. The horsemen in the front of each unit released a counter attack of light spears now darkening the sky.

Shouts came from the centurions in the Roman ranks, "Tortoise shell! Tortoise shell!" One after another the commands echoed throughout the square as shields closed to the front, the sides and on the top of the legion. Spears hit upright leather covers with a thud or pinged off them like hail bouncing on a tile roof. One brought a scream sticking in a soldier who had failed to raise his shield in time.

Up above on the hill, the Romans, shaded by the oak, watched the engagement as Lucius said, "Do any of you have a sword?"

Tacitus thrust a spare sword in his direction but still held his own. Lucius did not know where he had gotten it as the other men still possessed their weapons.

At last one of the men shouted, "C'mon, lads, let's pour it to 'em!" All three soldiers bolted down toward the valley, leaving Lucius alone and staring.

Below, Parthians pounded the "shell" and rode around it as the Romans uncovered the top of the center section and *pili*, spears, whooshed out toward the warriors. Javelins landed in Parthian legs, arms, chests and horses which screamed as they fell, toppling their riders to the ground.

Then a maneuver unfolded which Lucius had not seen since long ago, perhaps in this very valley. The Parthians streamed back, retreating from around the Roman square and forming up in front of it once more. They split like a wave in a stream avoiding a log, one unit riding to the left and another circling to the right.

But this time it was not exactly as Lucius had recalled. This time each column formed a single line of horsemen as they rode up the right and left knolls. The smell of pitch filled the desert wind. A lone rider along each line ignited a torch holding it out from his horse.

The Parthian riders pulled their bows, notched their arrows and brushed the tips into the flames of the torch-bearing riders. Those single flames ignited into hundreds as the bowmen turned and galloped back down the hill towards the Romans.

The centurions in the legion ignored the danger and bought the ruse of the earlier retreat: they ordered swords drawn for a frontal assault. As the Parthian charge drew to within a stadia or less of the Roman line, it split in two and retreated again, flames streaming backwards.

Lucius froze and inhaled, eyes widening as his memory of this tactic unfolded. The centurions shouted, "Forward, men! Press the attack!" The Roman square crumbled and melted into a pursuit up the knolls in two directions. Legionaries dropped shields and dug boots into the hard ground of an upward climb. Centurions continued to rally them with shouts like "For the glory of Rome! We have the day!"

But Lucius said to himself on the hill, "No, you do not."

He began running down from the oak, waving his sword and shouting from behind the Roman charge, "Stop! Cease this! It is a trap!"

But the Roman charge was too far gone, and the Parthians knew it. The righthand horsemen swung backwards, flames streaming around with them. The other left-hand division did the same. Bows released a shower of fire almost in one simultaneous volley as the sky lit in a blaze of tiny flares like cinders shot from a volcano.

Lucius, standing half way down the hill, no longer saw it all as a soldier but more like a physician, more like what it would take to heal this carnage.

The arrows exploded as they dropped into the Roman advance. One man, then another, burst into flames as the inferno landed in their midst. Burning tunics and armor ran out of the ranks and attempted to extinguish themselves, rolling on the hard ground. Comrades patted flames on comrades with bare hands, screaming as they burned. As the wind shifted, the rancid odor of burning flesh began to fill the valley.

Suddenly a contingent of fifty or less were retreating, running up toward Lucius. He shouted, "Come and follow me up the ridge!"

Heading for the oak, his hope was that they could make a stand and head off any Parthian riders. But never looking back, instead of hearing the panting of retreating Romans, a worse vibration intervened—pounding hooves. The Parthians had cut off the splinter group and were moving between them and Lucius.

The entire action remained downhill, except for a lone rider who galloped toward Lucius. His pointed cap glistened in the sun as he flung away his bow and drew his long sword with a ring. The *rhomphaia* swung down and slashed in a gallop toward its victim; but the centurion in Lucius caused him to dip low and bring his *gladius* up with both hands.

As Lucius rang his sword into the blade above his head, he caught the Parthian off balance. The warrior wobbled on his saddle and fell sideways to the hard ground. He grunted and Lucius was on him. Their swords clanged again and again, each attacking then retreating, then slamming swords together once more.

Lucius' opponent was tiring as the Parthian loosened his grip on his weapon and the Roman struck a blow which sent the enemy's long sword spinning end over end until its point stuck in the ground with a thud. Turning his *gladius* to the flat side, Lucius brought it down on the warrior's head with a crack. The Parthian sank to his knees and fell to his side, unconscious.

Just then another set of hooves pounded toward Lucius. The rider wore a golden pointed cap, a multi-colored silver and copper tunic with a long sword which this warrior rang from its scabbard and swished over Lucius' head, barely missing him.

After the rider galloped by the Roman, the horse turned and rode back, Lucius noticed something, threw down his sword and grabbed for a thigh and waist which seemed too small for a soldier. He pulled the rider from the mount and threw this cataphract to the ground. The empty horse clanged its armor beyond them both as the dismounted Parthian and Roman stood up.

A circle of Parthian horses rattled their armor and snorted as they surrounded the pair. Lucius realized that he was trapped. He was a prisoner once again.

His opponent looked down, pulled off the silver cap, and *he* was not a *he*. Raven tresses fell to the shoulders, turquoise eyes widened towards Lucius' face as they looked at him and said, "Husband, how are you? I have missed you."

Axsen moved up to her husband and kissed him.

Palms swayed above him in the night desert wind. They rustled as the oasis spring bubbled over the chatter of the strange tongues and camp fires below Lucius. He wondered if this was not the same place where Mithradates had been years before, but how things had turned.

Now *his* chains jangled at the end of a long tether line of Roman prisoners with the Parthians as the captors. Now his hands began to sweat and he worried about whether these captors might remember and return the favor of crucifixion for him, for all the *Roman* prisoners.

The full moon blunted the stars above but it also illuminated the figure marching toward him with a bilious silver robe, shimmering and waving out from small sandals pattering the hard ground. The long black tresses blew behind the sparkling eyes as the desert wind continued to gust.

Axsen halted at the guard and spoke in Parthian to him, her form outlined by the leather belt at her waist which also held a long sword. At last, she spoke in perfect Greek and finally ordered the soldier, "Leave us!"

She moved up to Lucius and said, "Husband, you don't know how I've longed for your touch, the strength of these arms." She stroked his muscles with both her hands as Lucius had now stood to receive her. "And the caress of these lips." She moved her bronze fingers across his mouth, then kissed him.

Lucius backed from her with a brief image of Chloe's blond face swirling through his memory. "I cannot believe that you are alive," he said. He paused.

"But *who* are you, Axsen? *What* are you?" he asked.

She avoided his question at first, replying, "I had my men take you from Ephesus as soon as they could. We were among you there in Asia though not so obvious as before."

Lucius remembered that he had not seen any pointed caps at the docks as in the days when he had walked the streets of Ephesus in the past. *More mysterious and covert*, he thought.

"My men waited and watched at Healing House for over a year. They almost gave up, but I wanted to see you."

The guard had returned and stared toward the couple in the moonlight. Axsen stared back at him and he moved down towards other Roman prisoners.

Her voice dropped as she said, "I am not what you thought me to be—not a slave but a princess among the Parthians, granddaughter of the great Mithradates. When my tribe lost power, I was enslaved by that other Mithradates who gave me to you."

Another Parthian warrior was coming to relieve the earlier guard. He paused and spoke low to the one whom Axsen had ordered off. The soldiers exchanged places, but just to let them know that all was well, Lucius rattled his chains.

Axsen looked up while the new guard now moved down the tether line.

She said, "I make no apology for leaving Ephesus. The Parthians who came to Healing House told me that my people were on the rise but were in peril again. They needed me to rally them. My empire called."

Lucius looked down and said, "As empires always do."

"As does yours, my Love," she said. "I know this."

Again, Lucius jangled his chains and stepped back. He gazed into her sparkling eyes looking darker because of the moonlight shadowing them.

"I am giving you two gifts," she continued. "One will arrive back at Ephesus for you by way of my personal body guards. Bartholomew knew about it long ago. That gift will show you how much I love *you* and the one you serve—the Nazarene. The other gift will come now."

She produced a key which glistened, then silhouetted in the moonlight. She looked around and the guard had not yet returned. Inserting the key in the lock, it snapped open, freeing Lucius' wrists. Another key to his ankle shackles did the same for his feet.

"Here are water and some provisions," she said, slipping a small skin and a bundle from under the folds of her shimmering robe, suddenly thrusting them towards him. "Though we have won today, we cannot win this fight. Our empire is in turmoil beyond the Euphrates. Go back to your people as I must return to mine."

Tears trickled down her cheeks as silver moon beams flooded her face. She kissed him again.

Then the princess in her ordered, "Slash my arm with this." A small dagger came from under her robe and was shoved toward her husband. "I must convince my men that you overpowered me and escaped."

She looked down and then up and finalized her words, saying, "Farewell, my Love. You will always be in my empire of affections." She put her lips to his once more.

"I will always be a wife to you," she sobbed. "A short way down the hill you will find a horse saddled and waiting for you in the shadows."

Lucius ran through the brightness, looking for any cover from the full moon. He turned his head back towards the top of the hill with its waving palms. He had forgotten to take the dagger. He had forgotten to cut her, or perhaps he could not do it.

He looked again. She was slashing her upper arm with her *rhomphaia* and a squeal followed in a high-pitched voice. Then she waved, turned and vanished into the shadow of the palms.

"Did you know a legionary named Tacitus," Lucius asked as he marched alongside members of the Italian Cohort. He had abandoned Axsen's horse and re-joined the Roman lines, pretending to be what he was—not a retired Roman officer but a traveling physician.

"No, no Tacitus," the soldier said beside him. "Hey, any ya fellas know a Tacitus?"

"No," "No," "No," came back down the line.

Lucius pressed again, "He was with a small scouting party up on the knoll above you before the Parthian attack."

"We had no scoutin' party—at least none there," the legionary said. Lucius noticed that the man was rubbing his arm, badly burned to blisters. "Horror of a fight weren't it," the soldier said.

Lucius was about to ask the man if he wanted some help with his wound when a shout came from behind them. "Physician, we will need you to attend the wounded at the rear," someone commanded.

He halted.

The line flowed around him like a river of red ambling legionaries as Lucius allowed the back of the column to absorb him. The memory of his rescuers returned. He was certain that Tacitus had called him by name.

But no scouting party? So, who had been on that ridge and who had freed him the first time?

Axsen was right. His empire had been at work—not Rome's but the Nazarene's. So, what mysterious gift headed for Ephesus had *she* given to that kingdom and to him?

CHAPTER THIRTEEN:
"TO ROME YOU WILL GO"

"Now when these things begin to take place, stand up
and raise your heads, because your redemption is drawing near."
— Luke 21:28

L ucius stared out the front door of the cramped quarters and breathed in deeply searching for the fresh air which was heavy and humid. The musty cell had suffocated his night but the day appeared just as stifling with its hazy sky.

Through the bars in the door window, all of Rome stretched out before him. He had not been here since he was a boy with Father Horatius. Then, it was like a carnival with its jugglers, vendors of sweet meats, strangely-capped priests from various shrines and temples and its strolling senators in their white togas trimmed with purple bands. Now, it was tense like a panicked lion ready to pounce on him, on any Follower, especially the Apostle—Paulus himself.

It was fortunate that Paulus did not see what Lucius saw. Even here in Rome, the Apostle would just beam and smile each morning even in prison as though he had seen the Nazarene in resurrected flesh once again. He would greet the Physician with "Lucius, the Lord's peace be upon you. Today may be the day."

Lucius was uncertain about the meaning of these words until today when he grabbed the Apostle's arm and simply said, "Yes, hopefully the day for our freedom."

Now he continued staring out the front door as he recalled the memory of how all of this had come to be.

It seemed a lifetime had elapsed since his freedom from the Parthian kidnapping and the *Legio X Fretensis* march from the frontier beyond the Jordan back to Caesarea. Lucius had tried to arrange passage home to Ephesus through the Followers, but they were consumed with the fate of the Apostle still in prison at the orders of the Proconsul. They had urged Lucius to remain with them, so he did.

Paulus' hearing had come up before the new Proconsul, Porcius Festus, not Felix, not the one who had been favorable to the Apostle, not the one whom Paulus had nearly converted to the Nazarene.

On that day the *bema* was white hot from the noon sun but so were the tempers of the priests and high priest who brought their case to the Governor. The crime remained desecrating the Jewish Temple in Jerusalem, more specifically the accusation that the Apostle had brought foreigners, non-Jewish Gentiles, into the most sacred places. As usual, Paulus could not keep his mouth shut, but this time he did not preach about the Nazarene. This time he litigated his own case.

Lucius stood behind the Followers and shaded his eyes to watch the reaction of the Proconsul. The Physician did not know Jewish law, but he knew politics and power.

Under his breath, he murmured, "Give them what they want, Paulus. The Proconsul does not like them and hates their religion. We can be on our way if you do not make this a case against the Jews."

Suddenly like a volcano exploding, Paulus erupted with his back to the priests and his demand to Festus, "I appeal my case to the Emperor and to Rome. I am a citizen of Rome."

Festus jerked up in his seat like a twig snapped by a storm. His face relaxed from its previous twisted panic.

He shouted first at Paulus, then to the priests, "You have appealed to Rome, Apostle Paulus, and to Rome you will go!"

"No! It is unlawful!" a priest shouted.

"You cannot make such a judgment in a religious matter!" another cried.

The priests were correct about that. The case did not have to end with all of this drama; but with Festus' pronouncement, Lucius realized that his dream from years ago, the dream that had changed his fate and left Chloe without a bridegroom, had come true. "To Rome you will go."

So, to Rome Paulus went and Lucius went with him. The Proconsul wanted no more "troubles" from any of the Nazarene sect and ordered all of the Apostle's companions bound and sent to the Emperor with their leader, the Physician included.

The passage by sea was as harrowing as the judgment, taking place in winter when no one crossed the *Mare Nostrum*. They were shipwrecked off Malta but all were saved, finally arriving in the Imperial City, nearly seven years after Lucius had arrived back in Caesarea.

Paulus, of course, was overflowing with joy, not from their safe passage but from the blessing that he could now share "the good news" of the Nazarene's empire with the heart of the enemy's kingdom. "Right under the emperor's very nose," he had said.

With this thought, Lucius returned to the musty smell of the Mamertine Prison "under that nose." Ten more years had passed on top of their sea journey. If the Apostle's hair had turned gray to white, Lucius' was gray-streaked, a reflection which he could barely believe as he passed by the prison water bucket that morning.

Yet, in all of these years, two certainties were the same. The Apostle was brought up time after time to the emperor's assistants for hearing after hearing. Nothing changed. Secondly, letters flowed from Paulus to the world.

Often the odor of parchment scrolls overwhelmed the mustiness of prison walls as questions were answered and problems among the Followers were addressed in letter after letter "from the hand of the Apostle himself." Words of encouragement, love and thanksgiving traveled by Followers to Philippi, Galatia, Colossae and even Lucius' own Ephesus.

Yet, words went out but none came in to the Mamertine, at least not to the Physician. He wrote to Chloe many times in assurances which he shared with no one but her, to let her know that Axsen was alive and had kidnapped him and to let her know that the Parthian would "always be his wife," to quote "his wife's" words. He could never marry the beautiful wine merchant of Corinthia. But Chloe never wrote back; or at least he never received a response from her.

He wrote to Bartholomew time after time. His question was always the same: was there a gift from Axsen at Healing House? Silence. Nothing came from his clinic or his righthand assistant.

Why was everyone so silent?

In fact, Lucius had just finished a final letter to Chloe that morning when the Apostle came and put a hand on his shoulder.

Paulus was softer today and he was not certain why. Another hearing would mean another stay here in Rome and that was all.

Then the front door of the Mamertine creaked open, almost by itself. The duskiness from its barred front window shown on the stone walls, musty floors, dirty beds and small stools of a single room too small for the five prisoners confined there for so long. Uncertain as the fresh air felt, the open door offered a release from the cramped cell which had bound them for a decade.

But now the hazy sunlight brightened the landscape of a park with its cypress trees waving gently in the breeze over the limestone Temple of Castor and Pollux, a white-columned shrine to Jupiter and the beige war monument to Mars with its high-peaked freeze. The glare made Lucius blink and wonder: was this going to be only another hearing?

Legionaries poured in, crowding the cramped quarters to a near standstill. Two handed their spears over to their companions and pulled out clanking chains, about to shackle Paulus, Lucius and three other Followers waiting at the back of the prison.

The Apostle looked at the soldiers like a father might observe his own sons, then said, "I am not going anywhere, young men, except to be in the true empire with him. Do not bind me or any of these with me."

Lucius perked up at the words, "to be in the true empire with him." He knew that Paulus did not mean Caesar. All at once, his worry was interrupted by the legionaries laying hands on the Apostle from either side.

This did not feel like just another "hearing." After all, the emperors had changed some years before. Caligula went insane, pushing his self-worship throughout the empire, erecting temples and images of himself like the one which Lucius had seen "decapitated" by the Parthian in Asia. That mad emperor even demanded that his likeness be put in the Jewish Temple in Jerusalem, but King Agrippa had stalled on that installation.

When the empire had all that it could take of Caligula, soldiers assassinated him and Claudius, crippled as he was, limped to power. He did as poorly as Caligula, and his reign was reined in when his wife killed him.

It was Nero whom Paulus had seen several times in the last few years, sometimes with Lucius and the other Followers and sometimes alone. He became the hope for a better future, but all Lucius would say was, "We shall see."

Now smoke irritated Lucius' eyes and choked his nose as he shuffled out with the Apostle and the other Followers, surrounded by the red tunics and spears of legionaries. He had seen the glow out the front bars of the Mamertine for the last several nights.

A woman had come to the prison days before with her son, arms burned up and down. She told him, told them all, that the slums in Rome were burning. The only horror worse than the fires was the screams of children, trapped in their apartments or jumping to their deaths from third-floor balconies.

As Lucius lightly bandaged her child, she said, "Rome's mad emperor has burned his own people. This is no empire and there is no peace."

The Physician finished bandaging the burns and said, "I agree."

As he said his farewell to her and her son, he recalled his dream from the previous night. Crowds of people were pushing and shoving each other. They shouted, "Let him go. Give him to us." No one was given and the dream ended with the shadow of a small girl who never stepped out of the darkness. What did this vision mean and was it only about Rome's fires or did it also point beyond and back to Ephesus?

All at once that memory evaporated as the guards, Paulus and the rest of the Followers reached an end of the Forum below their prison. Lucius was in the rear and through bobbing heads he caught a view down to the other end.

A white marble seat was there. A small white toga with gold trim swished to one side of the chair and then slouched into it, an array of bronze armored and helmeted soldiers fanned out on either side. Lucius knew who they were—the Praetorian Guard with the Emperor slouching in the center. Nero was here.

This was no hearing. This was a spectacle to please the crowds, now cramming and shoving their way into the Forum between Caesar and the prisoners and straining for a better view of whatever was about to happen.

Suddenly Nero jerked up on his seat and shouted like someone who had lost all control, "They burned our city. Kill them. The Followers are killing us in the name of the Nazarene. Let us kill them." He laughed like a jackal over its prey. The crowd shouted, "Kill them! Kill them! Kill them all!"

This was no hearing. *This was an execution.* Lucius' eyes went wide. His palms moistened and his back stiffened.

The Apostle was jerked from Lucius and the Followers and bent over a block on a lower platform from where they had been halted. A silver sword rose, flashed in the hazy sun and fell toward Paulus' neck.

Lucius jerked backward and closed his eyes.

"Here is a centurion's sword," the officer said. "Follower or not, I know that you are a centurion of honesty and courage. My father served with you and told me of your bravery against the Parthians in the East."

Lucius studied the young centurion's face. His helmet with its transverse plume was sloppy on his head. *Twenty years old, if that*, thought the Physician.

"My name is Publius," the young officer continued. "My wife Lucinda is a Follower of the Nazarene. If I allow you to be killed, I must kill her, too. Besides, you healed her last year of stomach cramps and great body pain."

This soldier had come up behind him on the upper platform, just as the sword went up over Paulus' neck. He looked around, then slowly backed Lucius out from the rest of the prisoners toward a shady grove to the rear. Taking the Physician by the arm, to feign that this Follower was still in Roman custody, Publius fast-walked them both deep into a stand of fig trees away from the rest.

Lucius said to him, "I know what you are doing and I am grateful. But I cannot escape while the Apostle is sacrificed. I cannot do this."

The young centurion with blond hair curling out from under his helmet responded, "We cannot afford to have you not do this. You must escape. The Nazarene's healing must continue with you."

He paused and stared at Lucius, then he said, "Go now before they come to investigate us. Go anywhere—to Spain, back to Asia, anywhere but here. Rome is a cesspool. Nero is insane. We residents of Rome are not fools. We know that he ordered the houses of the poor to be burned to build new shops and monuments. He kills his own people. Blames you Followers and kills you for this. He himself will be killed."

Across the grove and Forum, Nero was shouting, now echoing with the distance, "Show—ow—ow us the head of the Apostle!—ostle—ostle!" There was a pause, followed by the crowd roaring its approval.

Nero's voice reverberated, "Kill—kill—kill the Foll—ollwers! Kill—kill—kill—them—them—them all. They burn—urned our city!"

"Go!" the centurion said motioning with his head. Lucius ran through the grove and out from under its shade into the back lower part of the Forum.

He said to himself, "So much for *Pax Romana*."

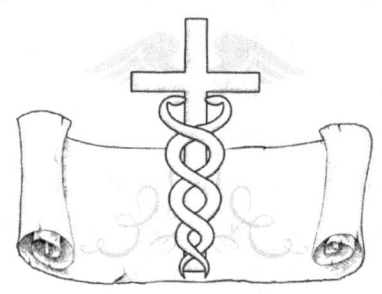

CHAPTER FOURTEEN:

A STOP ON THE WAY HOME

"As he came and saw the city (Jerusalem),

he wept over it, saying,...

'They will not leave within you one

stone upon another; because you did not

recognize the time of your visitation from God.'"

— Luke 19:41, 44

At Rome's port of Ostia, Lucius panted to a stop, then booked passage on a ship carrying leather goods to Cenchreae and the East. The Followers of Rome arranged it as long as he would carry the final letters of the Apostle to Philippi, Corinthia and beyond.

Lucius fell into a depression over his escape. Unlike the other rescue from the hill during the Parthian battle, Publius was flesh and blood. Lucius had felt the fabric of his red centurion's tunic to be certain, and he had pulled tight on the sword belt that Publius had handed him. Yet, this escape was more troubling than the one from

Tacitus or even the one orchestrated by Axsen. He felt guilty about why he should now be spared from the executioner's sword.

The rolling sea calmed him as the "deliveries" took longer than Lucius had planned. A stop in Malta which should have lasted weeks blended into over two years. The Followers whom the Apostle had left there after his ship wreck fought so fiercely with one another that Lucius thought that they were more poisonous than the snake which had bitten Paulus when he was detained among them years before. The story of the sacrifice of the Apostle finally brought the healing which their fellowship required. The death of Paulus became the medicine, the *serpens,* for the many, not just a few. Perhaps Publius was correct: perhaps Lucius was the balm for many of these Followers who needed many types of healing.

Boarding another ship, Lucius docked in Cyprus. Sergius Paulus, the Roman Proconsul whom Paulus had converted on his first journey with Barnabas, had died. He left a strong fellowship which defied the Empire of Rome for the kingdom of the Nazarene. They needed a healing center, and it took five years to set up and transfer to their able care. As Lucius departed at last for Cenchreae, he could hardly bid them "Farewell."

When he did sail into the Greek port, he was graying into his late fifties. He had sent many of the Apostle's letters ahead to Philippi, Thessalonica and even to Corinthia. Lucius added in the news that Nero had executed Paulus, but he avoided any words about his own escape.

"The Nazarene's call continues," he assured Cenchreae's Followers. The words rang hollow in a way which they had never sounded before.

When he finished with that announcement, he thought about the last time when he had stayed in Cenchreae, thought about Chloe, thought about her last words in her letter and about her cough, fevers and illness. They might be her very last words. Nothing more had come from her, nor from Bartholomew.

But a letter had arrived. From that young disciple of Paulus' who was now not so young, being nearly thirty and overseeing a shop in Syrian Antioch, came words which captivated Lucius,

> *...come, Physician Lucius, we need a healer like yourself.*
> *There is much good work to do here.*
> *From the hand of*
> —*Timotheos*

Lucius wanted to return home to Ephesus, wanted to ignore the plea, but no longer smelling the salt air, he was now turning in to a rancid swamp odor of river banks. His ship banged the dock—not in Ephesus, but south of there, on the Orontes River, in Antioch of Syria. It was not the passage which he intended, but it was the call which he had answered.

Timotheos did look older, truly more mature, as he walked the Physician across the complex in Antioch. Lucius needed to familiarize himself with it all again—the three-storied building, an old manor house, with people and families clustered on the balconies at each level. The courtyard still contained a small fountain in the center, Followers all around it, roasting meat on open fires, baking bread in bee hive ovens, weaving robes on open air looms and tying the laces of sandals. The aroma of smoke from their fires mixed together, a blending which Timotheos described and which Lucius was observing.

"We still live together in community here. Everyone meets everyone's need," the young disciple said. Nothing had changed from years ago.

Before Lucius could explain about the fate of the Apostle, Timotheos continued, "Come, I will show you our place of healing."

He pressed on with a purpose and with his red and white head covering appearing more like those from Asia or from across the Euphrates—more like a turban. His robe was also very colorful with green, purple and brown stripes as it swished through several adjoining rooms and doorways.

They reached a large wooden door with rough finish and Timotheos creaked it wide into a dimly-lit hall. Shutters on the windows located along one side were completely closed, the hall only lit with torches.

The fevered and coughing lay on cots among those with broken limbs and lepers with oozing sores. Nothing made sense to Lucius. But when he saw blankets, bedding and medicines all piled like trash, he knew why Timotheos had written.

After picking their way along the edge of the clinic, the young disciple spun back and smiled, saying, "We do a fine thing with our healing here, no?"

Lucius wanted to say "No, you do not." Yet, he did not want to be too forward on his first tour. He sniffed the stifling air and said, "I might have some suggestions."

A set of dark eyes, raven hair and bronze skin came up to them. Lucius thought of Axsen, but this woman was younger, not even twenty, and smelled of aloes and camphor, not lavender.

She said, "Is this the one called Deacon Lucas, the Physician, from Rome. I hear that you travel with the Apostle. When can you begin here?"

The next morning after he explained to Timotheos about the Apostle, Lucius nearly ran to the clinic. The young disciple was still speaking to himself and trying to imagine life without one of their leaders. Tears filled his eyes, but Lucius did not have time for details other than that Nero had killed him along with a number of others.

After all, this day would mean new procedures at the clinic. First, their guest Physician unlatched every shutter down the long wall and threw them open to the light of the dawn. Patients perked up as if they had just been awakened from a long sleep though many had been up for some time.

He wound around cots and beds, propping up heads to administer elixirs, smearing aloes and ointments on lepers' sores, splinting arms and legs and twisting elbows back into their joints as their owners groaned with pain.

Then he shouted, "You there! Can you help me move these patients into a better order?"

The dark-eyed woman from yesterday said, "My name is Rachel. And yes, I will help you."

By sundown, the fading light from outside softened on orderly rows of cots. Broken limbs and lepers were in proper lines but separated to one end. Fevers and coughs were squared off in the opposite section.

Lucius smelled the burning oil of the evening torches as they were being lit, and he felt as if not only the chaos of Antioch's clinic but also the chaos of his own past had begun to flow out of him. This was the first time that he had experienced any order for over a decade. The slaves continued lighting the evening torches one by one and everything was at peace until Rachel's voice erupted behind him.

"Come, Physician!" she shouted. "Come quickly!"

It was a plea, not a demand. Lucius shoved across the clinic to the far end. He discovered the reason for her panic.

A muscular man with short-cropped Roman hair, wearing a brown tunic, limped and shouted, "You dirty damn Jewish rebel! You dirty Sicarii! You'll slit my throat with a knife while I sleep. I'll do to you what I did to the others."

He drew back his fist and threw a punch towards a dark-skinned patient with a scraggily beard and a frayed gray robe. The victim jerked back onto his cot.

He looked up in surprise, not because the fist was about to strike him but because it did not. It had been grabbed from behind by two hands and twisted around the Roman's torso by Lucius.

The patient on the cot said, "You Romans starve us and take what little we have in taxes."

He had raised an arm in defense against the fist, but now shook it at the one whose fist had been rendered useless. The other was wobbling and about to speak.

Lucius spoke instead, saying, "Cease this! You will not defile the Nazarene's healing by bringing your hatred in here. Both of you know that all are welcome here! Roman, Jew, Sicarii or soldier!"

The warring men parted, the Roman falling back onto his cot two beds away and the Jewish Sicarii rolling away with his back to the rest of the clinic. As everyone returned to their tasks, slaves and attendants to serving patients, patients to their beds and their chattering about the fight which had nearly happened, Lucius wondered what was the reason for this animosity.

It felt like the same suspicions and hatreds which he had not seen in this part of the Empire for forty years. Or was it something more?

Rachel completed giving a cup of water to an old woman and re-wrapped a bandage around the arm of an ulcerated sore on another man. She sought out "Deacon Lucas" who had retreated to his thoughts and was writing in a corner lit by a torch.

"I must say what I know," she began. "Those two men will infect the whole clinic with their hate. They reflect the coming storm."

"What storm?" Lucius asked.

Rachel cocked her head, then replied, "Do you not know? My Jews have revolted against the Romans."

Lucius smelled the parchment of his scroll and said, "Romans and Jews have always had their differences but I agree that they cannot invade the Nazarene's kingdom here."

Rachel said, "Yes, but we will not be able to treat all of the victims from Galilee, Jerusalem and beyond."

Lucius nodded, rose and rolling his scroll, exited the clinic to return to his quarters. Just outside he realized that he had forgotten his medical satchel and went back to the clinic. Seeing it in the corner and feeling the day exhausting him, he slumped down against the wall. There had been enough "victims" today but what did Rachel mean?

Weeks turned to months in Antioch and the pull of Ephesus faded into the needs of patients here. Fevers, deafness, leprosy and wounds filled Lucius' days but his nights filled with the same repetitious dream. He feared that it had to do with the "storm" about which Rachel spoke so he almost hated to close his eyes—but he did.

At first, there were crowds, people massed, shoving and pushing each other, overwhelming some legionaries in front of them. They began shouting but the shouts were unclear and muffled.

Then a smile came up to his very face. It had a manicured beard which Lucius had not seen for a long time. The mouth in the center of the beard said, "Remember what I, Caduceus, spoke to you. Only the Nazarene's healing for your own life will allow you to heal others."

The face turned and the head had another face on its back, two-faced like the Roman god Janus. It was one which he had also known from long ago. This beard and hair were streaked with gray like his. The mouth opened and simply said, "I forgive you."

Someone was now shaking him. He thought it was her and said, "Rachel, I will be with you shortly."

"Physician," Timotheos aroused, "wake up. A man has come with his wife and a servant. They are victims of the war in Galilee between the Jews and Romans."

Lucius blinked. He looked down and straightened his tunic. Inhaling the odors of aloe and urine in the clinic, he rose. Finding Rachel, he leaned over to where she was and asked her to join him.

She dragged her left foot as if this crippling was not new. For the first time, Lucius saw that she limped. He could not believe after all of this time that he had not noticed it when they had first met.

He said, "Rachel, did you rest?"

She replied, "Yes."

Lucius hurried through the hallways and out the door of the manor house. He nearly ran across the courtyard, not knowing why he was moving so fast. Suddenly he turned and Rachel was dragging her leg behind him; but in front, Timotheos outpaced them both.

The young disciple pulled back one side of the double entry doors which groaned as Lucius filled the opening. A very familiar beard and dark hair, speckled with gray, dropped his jaw as he stood still at the door. His face reflected the image from Lucius' dream but from the traveler's frayed and disheveled robes, he had been journeying for quite some time. A man stood at his side and a donkey and cart with a bundle in it were behind him. Lucius' eyes widened.

Suddenly a righthand fist from the visitor swung at him and Lucius caught it before it landed a punch on his jaw.

Then he said, "And welcome to you, too, Marcus Cornelius."

Lucius wondered why he did not return his own punch, given Marcus' betrayal of him to Pilate so long ago.

"There, there, Machereus," Lucius said to a little boy with dark brown hair and big round eyes. The boy was crying at the ointment which the Physician had just applied to his arms. Lucius had just bandaged them and now patted him on the head as he returned him to his mother.

"Follow me," he said to Marcus who had been watching.

"Your wife, the woman Joanna, is in private quarters," the Physician said.

He began leading his friend, or betrayer, or both through the maze of rooms which adjoined each other in that part of the complex. He thought to himself as he led Marcus, *I can reprimand zealots and Romans for anger and hatred, but I cannot refrain from my own anger at the one who betrayed me.*

Just outside Joanna's door, Lucius halted. Marcus nearly ran into him since he had stopped so abruptly.

Then Lucius said, "Wait, I must say something."

Marcus lifted his eyebrows as if to be anticipating something.

Lucius added, "I cannot blame you for my imprisonment by Pilate any longer."

Marcus injected, "You have not been in the army then? That's the last I saw of you on the road by my farm in Galilee."

Lucius chuckled and said, "With this gray crown, I could hardly march for six steps now. No, I left the army years ago or it left me. I received the Nazarene's washing in Pilate's prison. I learned medicine there and have been traveling with the one whom the Followers called the Apostle, one Paulus of Tarsus, that is until the Emperor executed him."

"So, you did not attack and burn my farm or hurt my wife, Joanna," Marcus said.

"No," Lucius said, looking down and then pausing.

Then he said, "We have been holding baseless grudges and harboring angers as long as the years between us."

Marcus said, "I, too, know the Nazarene and he would say that such hatred will eat at us from the inside." He paused and his eyes reddened.

He said, "I forgive you, Lucius."

The words were again familiar, from a dream, as Lucius said, "And I you." He clasped the forearm of his old friend and fixed on his face.

Rachel limped up to the two of them.

"The woman, Joanna, is not doing well. She needs your attention, Deacon Lucas," she said.

The only part of the reunion more painful than the forgiveness which the two exchanged was the death of Joanna.

But even that sorrow held some mercy. After the funeral, Lucius said to Marcus, "That day after the Nazarene's death when Pilate sent us back out to guard the tomb of a dead man, something occurred which shook my soul. Pilate wanted us to lie about it and become victims of the Followers' hatred because of that lie."

"Yes," Marcus said.

Lucius breathed in, held it and then continued, "I only saw the empty grave and felt a cold like I have never felt before or since in that vacated tomb. I saw no one there, but your wife, Joanna, saw the Nazarene—*alive*."

As he left Marcus to mourn his wife, Lucius picked his way down a dawning garden path. Something slithered across it and into the grass—the shiny back of a snake shedding its old dead skin in the rising sun.

Lucius had come across the courtyard to meet with Marcus. The Physician inhaled the fresh morning air of what seemed like the first day of a new life. His friend did not share the same freshness and offered no smile even for a friendship redeemed.

Instead, Marcus said, "I must share something." He paused and drew Lucius aside to beyond where the Followers were cooking and working.

"Before she died," he said. "Joanna told me, not Lucius, not the Romans, but zealots burned our farm, kidnapped our children and grandchildren and attacked her."

The Jews had struck the farm of a Roman and justified it all as "the will of Adonai."

Lucius wondered about his own home.

Marcus added, "Legate Vespasianus and his son Titus have brought three legions from Syria, Egypt and Palestine into Galilee. I have seen them. They will not cease this action until they reach Jerusalem."

Lucius thought to himself. The Followers might be next. Chloe might already be dead. Bartholomew might be, too. Healing House was probably back to nothing.

He looked up at Marcus and said, "I must go home. Every empire except this one is ruthless."

That afternoon Lucius booked passage on a merchant ship bound for Ephesus.

CHAPTER FIFTEEN:
A FINAL HOMECOMING

"For nothing is hidden that will not be disclosed,
nor is anything secret that will not become
known and come to light."
— Luke 8:17

Antioch was so calming and full of forgiveness over the last months that Lucius did not want to depart. Limping Rachel and aging Marcus had formed into a new family, a sister and brother. Besides, what would become of his patients—many of them refugees from Vespasianus' war on the Jews.

Some had no homes and came covered with injuries, blistered with burns and wounds from fights with Roman troops. Others were thin and boney from hunger when soldiers—or worse, zealots—took sheep, grain and wine or what little else the locals had.

Healing from the clinic in Antioch was not just critical; it was vital. The story of the Nazarene was never more urgent—especially with the Apostle gone.

His old friend Marcus showed Lucius a scroll, his account of the Nazarene. Even as Marcus placed it back in a pigeon hole in the library at the Followers' compound, Lucius confessed to his own account about the Nazarene—if it existed any longer.

At the pier before departing, the sail of the merchant ship rippled and blew in the cold salty wind. Before he stepped onto the bouncing deck, Rachel came limping down the break wall faster than he could walk with two good legs.

Small paths of tears glistened on her cheeks. Her lip quivered as she said, "If you stayed, we might have done much healing together and—." She checked her next thought.

"I will remember all that you have taught me—especially that we do not cure, we heal in the name and spirit of the Nazarene," she said.

The other Followers had arrived. Lucius now wanted to embrace Rachel, but he took her hand instead.

"You are a fine and gifted healer, a blessing to this community," he said.

With the river waves slapping the boat hull, Timotheos said, "You have not told us, Physician. Who should be the leader for the fine healing place which you are leaving with us?"

Lucius paused. Marcus leaned his head forward as if to say, "We are waiting."

The Physician stared toward some of the attendants who had come to bid him "Farewell," then he turned to his right. "Rachel is the best one for your community. Let her lead you and shape the healing which you need here," he said.

Rachel's eyes opened wide and she bowed her face as she said, "Bless you, Deacon Lucas."

Marcus walked around Timotheos and whispered into Lucius' ear, "A wise choice, old friend."

As he moved back, tears filled his eyes and he clasped the forearm of his centurion comrade, then said, "Lucius, I promised Joanna that I would remain here. Kindly contact me if you are ever in need."

Lucius' eyes watered as well and he shook his head "Yes." He waved to Timotheos and the other Followers as the dock slaves brushed by him, loading the final cargo for Ephesus. "Cast off!" shouted the captain.

The bodies silhouetted and grew smaller on the pier, and Lucius fixed on Rachel, but thought of others. Turquoise eyes and a bronze face loomed up, then it re-formed into the round-eyed look of Chloe.

The stone wall of the pier protruded like some long finger into the harbor and blossomed into a fiery pink with the sunset. Behind him, the crew uttered commands to strike their sail, and it rippled down in Lucius' ears as it dropped against the mast. The boat drifted toward the moorings.

If this all seemed slow and relaxed, Lucius felt his body tighten like a deer ready to leap. He positioned his travel bundle, medical satchel and sword belt for a run, a sprint, not a stroll, to Healing House. The final coins for his passage jangled into the palm of the captain.

"My appreciation," Lucius said as he stepped on the creaking gang plank and felt it depress with his upward climb to the sea wall. The ending pink of the day felt renewing to him. He was "home."

The salty coolness and the dusk would allow him to rest at Healing House and refresh him for the reunions of a new morning.

Ahead the colonnade of the port road and the three-gated arch turned as rose as the pier had been. Before he went too far, he turned onto the familiar side lane toward Healing House, expecting to smell the aloes and camphor, the wood of the cooking fires for patients and the musty aroma of limestone walls and floors. The dusk replaced the pink sunset and he strained to see perhaps a torch or two at the front door.

Lucius' sandals slapped the pavement as quickly as his sixty-year-old legs would carry him. He looked down and then up—to nothing. The warehouse was dark, no torches at the door, no aloes or camphor, only salt air and a musty aroma of shuttered windows and closed doors.

The building was abandoned. He shouted, "Shalom! Is anyone here? Bartholomew?" He pushed each set of shutters which creaked but did not open. They rattled and echoed into the interior of the structure telling him that it was vacant. Was Healing House gone?

Lucius ran back to the front doors and nudged them, the right one creaking into the dark and cavernous room. It banged and reverberated off the wall.

"Shalom!" Lucius shouted again. "Shalom in the name of the Nazarene."

"Sha-sha-shalom," his words bounced back at him. Nothing else.

He left the door ajar so he could see in the fading evening light. Still nothing. There were no cots, none even stacked anywhere, no blankets, no jars of medicines, no staff, no patients and no Bartholomew nor Chloe.

Uniform steps slapped the pavement behind him.

"Physician Lucius Maximus," voices echoed through the empty warehouse. Lucius shook his head "yes" to faces which he could barely see.

"You must come with us," a helmeted silhouette said. Two Roman guards filled the doors and held spears toward him, blocking any escape.

With chilling from the dampness and less light than where he had come from the night before, Lucius was not certain about where the legionaries had brought him after they had manacled his wrists and ankles at a vacant Healing House. He knew it was a prison.

He knew that it was somewhere up in the heart of Ephesus but that was all that he knew. His bread was as stale and dry as his parched tongue. The wine in his bowl was more like vinegar and the lentil soup was colder than the limestone walls around him.

Someone had known about his return. He had sent word to Chloe and to Bartholomew but the letters must have been intercepted.

As the moonlight rose in his cell, how Lucius got there returned to him. The soldiers had marched him up the port road through the arch to the Marble Street. By the time they had reached the Agora, it was dark with only a few flares of light from one or two torches over the empty stalls.

Yet, they brought him beyond the markets, the temple area with its dimly-lit sanctuaries, even beyond the Terrace Houses where Chloe might no longer be living. Lucius had gone to a part of the city where he had never been—the Imperial Agora with its open court, its

Temple to Isis and the Odeion Hall used for hearings of the Proconsul—then beyond even that to a cold cell.

The dream came again, the one which had not come for a long time. His own face moved close with its lines of age, its gray-streaked beard and whitening hair. It blurred and re-sharpened into a well-trimmed beard and a younger face covered in a silver head piece. That face spun away into a dance which threw the man's robe into a fuzzy whirl of colors, all in another prison cell from long ago.

Lucius knew the dancer. He was alone and he was also a healer from long ago. He was Caduceus. He spun away and out of the prison into the daylight of a cheering crowd.

Then the morning beams awakened him with daylight, but with no crowd and with no spinning Caduceus. He was not in Rome or Antioch but here in Ephesus, in prison. The cold limestone walls were as musty as any had been throughout his travels, including Rome's Mamertine.

Lucius looked around for his travel bundle, medical satchel and belt. The legionaries had taken them all.

No one had come to tell him why he was here. The soldiers deposited him on the hard floor—alone. No Followers had visited and perhaps did not know of his return. Bartholomew was absent. Chloe, if she were even alive, might never have received his letters.

He stared at the sunlit square projected from his prison window onto the stone floor when the door banged open and swung a patch of shade over it. Red tunics and silver iron helmets with spears clanked in as two soldiers entered. One held a torch while the other clanged some chains in his hands.

The legionary with the torch said, "Lucius Maximus, come with us." Before Lucius could wobble to a stance, the soldier jerked him up.

He manacled the Physician's wrists and ankles, clanking the chains. But Lucius observed something else jangling on the man's belt, a ring of keys. It occurred to him that this time there appeared to be no Tacitus, no Publius and no Axsen to free him. This could finally be like—like the Apostle.

The legionaries led him up a flight of narrow stairs out of the dark and into the blinding morning of the Marble Street. Onlookers stared at the manacled prisoner, some with gaping mouths and others shaking their heads "No." They chatted among themselves and at first Lucius could not understand them.

But as the guards marched him by small groups of observers, every so often a person would break from the group and run off. He wondered about this even more as those departing increased to two's and three's and then more.

The Marble Street became brighter and so uneven that Lucius had to quit watching the crowds and concentrate on his shuffling sandals. From the heat rising through them, he guessed that it was perhaps mid-day, the time for Imperial hearings.

Then someone along the route said, "It's him. I am certain that it is *him*."

Another voice said, "Can you be sure?"

Both ran off.

The guards ignored the words as they guided Lucius south toward the Imperial Agora and its Odeion. They did not lead him through the courtyard and he wondered why.

Instead, they snaked up through a back door and onto a narrow staircase that climbed to a door and a hall which was dark except for a few torches. The soldier with the clanking keys bolted ahead to a second door which he opened with a bang onto a dais.

The other guard shoved Lucius ahead where he stumbled onto a curved stage of what appeared to be more of a theater than a court room. Below the platform and extending to a bright courtyard was an open space for viewers or petitioners but it was empty. Beyond it, a colonnade of Ionic columns divided the theater from the outside.

The interior was covered by a stone roof. A lone chair, large and wooden, sat on the stage. Guards with spears flanked either side and faced toward the colonnade. Between each set of pillars at the courtyard was a legionary with a spear turned laterally to shove back the chattering and roaring crowds pushing in from the Imperial Agora.

This could be where the onlookers had run from Lucius' street march. If so, the guards at each opening could hardly control them with their lateral *pili*. They did not seem to be the usual groups of petitioners, or theater goers.

Still, a drama might be unfolding but with Lucius as the lead actor. He hoped that it was not a tragedy as his eyes re-adjusted and blinked from the brighter courtyard to the dimmer interior of the theater.

Suddenly a door banged open from the far side. First, a brown-haired, middle-aged man with face round but lined by the dryness of the hot breezes of Asia entered, followed by two spear-toting legionaries. The first man was clean-shaven and wore a white toga trimmed in purple.

A voice at the front of the platform shouted above the crowd noise, "His Excellency, Proconsul Marcus Sullius Nerullinus, appointed by the Emperor."

Lucius noted that the herald had not mentioned who the Emperor was. Was Nero still alive? He looked down and when he looked up, Lucius did not see who the next person was, emerging from the same door to the right.

There was a dragging and shuffling, limp and shuffle, limp and shuffle. He stopped on the other side of the Proconsul's seat. Lucius caught short-cropped Roman-style hair, gray to white, and the man's tunic was also a fine fabric of gray.

A guard stepped between him and Lucius, then it was open, then another guard. Finally, it was open and he saw the man with a large scroll like the one which had been in the back of Lucius' study at Healing House years ago.

The Physician's back stiffened and his palms moistened for the first time that day. The roar of the crowd rose with the appearance of this new man, and he moved to the Proconsul allowing them to whisper to each other.

Proconsul Marcus dropped into his seat and waved to a guard. The soldier marched to the edge of the stage and banged his spear on the floor, shouting, "This tribunal of Proconsul Marcus Sullius Nerullinus will now be in session. Silence!"

The chatter of the crowd snuffed out to a whisper. The unknown man in gray remained partly hidden but he addressed both the mob waving back and forth in the courtyard and the Proconsul.

He shouted, "Prisoner Lucius Maximus, you are on trial for high treason against Rome and Caesar! My name is Marius Julius and I bring the case based on your own words in this document." He raised the large scroll.

Marius! Lucius thought. *So, the voices, the vision were real: someone close to me **has** betrayed me. Marius, the angry soldier, stole my scroll about the*

Nazarene. The Nazarene had his Judas and I have mine.

Lucius bowed his head as the guards on either side of him shuffled and clanked his feet forward. "Look at the Proconsul when you are addressed!" one said shoving him.

Marius also moved to the edge of the stage and unfurled the parchment in his hands. The size made it difficult for him to hold and he nearly dropped it.

Still, he found his place not too far along and said, "Let me read,

In those days a decree went out from Emperor Augustus that
all the world should be enrolled and this was the first census
when Quirinius was governor of Syria and all went to their own
towns to be registered.'"

Marius looked up and fixed on Lucius, "You are mocking the Emperor here and his power to tax his empire."

"I am not. The Emperor can do whatever he wills in his empire," Lucius countered. "There is no mocking in stating the historical record."

"Oh, no," Marius said, rustling the scroll to another portion, "Then allow me to read further,

While they were there, in Bethlehem, the time came for her,
Mary, to deliver her child and she gave birth to her firstborn
son, wrapped him in swaddling cloths and laid him in a
manger...'

"Whose birth is this, prisoner Lucius? It is not the birth of our most sacred emperor, Augustus, as we all know that he was birthed in a pantry in the country, not in a stable. Tell us *whose* birth is this stable baby?"

Lucius hesitated and looked Marius in the eye, his own dark eyes becoming steely. "You know very well whose birth it is."

"It is the one you and the Followers call 'the Nazarene,' Jeshua ben Josephus, is it not?"

"Yes," Lucius said.

"Louder, so that his Excellency, the Proconsul can hear you," Marius said.

"It is the birth of the Nazarene in King David's town of Bethlehem," Lucius said. He wished that he had not been so explicit but he knew where Marius was heading with this argument.

"And what is it that you tell us about that birth which is not Caesar's. Let me read your exact words, prisoner,

> '...the angel said to them, 'Do not be afraid...to you is born this day...a Savior who is the Messiah, the Lord...Glory to God in highest heaven and on earth peace among those whom he favors'

"Are these your words, Lucius Maximus?" Marius said, his face contorting and reddening.

"They are the words of the angels, yes," the prisoner responded.

"Don't play tricks with the words here. You are naming the Nazarene, not Caesar, as the chosen one, the Messiah, aren't you?"

"Caesar is emperor in his empire and the Nazarene is king in his," Lucius answered.

"Do we, do you, worship the emperor as god, Prisoner Lucius?" the little man fumed as he limped one step forward.

"When a man becomes a god in his own eyes, he demands worship, but when god becomes man, he receives our worship freely for what he offers us," Lucius argued. The case was beginning to turn.

"And what is that? What does the Nazarene bring that Caesar cannot?"

"Go back before the story of the Nazarene's birth. You have it there," Lucius said.

Marius wrestled with the scroll and rolled it back to nearly the beginning.

Then he read,

"And Mary said,
My soul magnifies Adonai.
He has brought down
the powerful from their thrones,
and lifted up the lowly;
he has filled the hungry with good things,
and sent the rich empty away."

Marius finished and leaned over to the Proconsul, whispering in his ear. The betrayer then drew up his crippled body as straight as he could.

"Are these your words, Lucius Maximus?" Marius said.

"They are the words of Mary, the Nazarene's mother," Lucius said.

"It does not matter. They are treason against Caesar as much as the other words."

"Because the Emperor does not care for everyone in his Empire except to tax them?" Lucius accused.

"So, you do oppose Caesar's taxes?" Marius rebutted.

"I oppose any kingdom which judges, condemns and oppresses everyone ruled by it," the Physician said. "And—"

"And what?" his accuser cut him off.

"*And* you once believed that, did you not, Marius Julius? When you were a Follower? When you brought the same relief to the poor about which Mary sings?"

Marius exploded, "I am not the one on trial here!"

The crowd murmured and chattered among themselves. With Marius' answer the chatter became a roar.

Proconsul Marcus shouted, "Silence! Only the accused and his accuser may speak."

The crowd silenced but Lucius wondered more than ever which side they supported. Were they *for* him or *against* him?

"The Nazarene is king over Caesar. Is that what you mean with all of this pathetic poetry? Tell us," Marius said.

"My words stand. They are the truth which you yourself once believed," Lucius asserted.

The crowd exploded, "Lucius! Lucius! Lucius!"

"Silence!" the Proconsul screamed. The wave of voices outside the colonnade faded.

Marius said to Lucius, "So you are a traitor to Caesar and to Rome?"

Again, the crowd erupted into shouts, "Lucius! Lucius! Lucius!"

"Silence! One more outbreak and I will have the legionaries clear the courtyard," the Governor shouted. The crowd, now becoming more like a mob, rocked back and forth.

The words of the betrayer drew their attention back to the stage.

"You are a traitor and worship the Nazarene above Caesar. He is your chosen one," Marius raged.

The crowd blew up into their own verdict.

"Marius is the traitor!" someone said.

"Traitor Marius!" another shouted.

"Marius, the traitor, lies!" a third yelled.

"Enough!" the Proconsul pronounced.

The crowd quieted as Marius seized the advantage and said, "Lucius Maximus has authored treason. The Nazarene may be king of the poor and sick but does that make him king over all, even over Caesar as Lucius Maximus has written?" He pointed toward Lucius but directed his question elsewhere. "So, what is your verdict, Proconsul?"

The Governor shifted on his seat, perhaps as angry at being forced into a decision by the likes of Marius as he was over the charges against the prisoner. He rose and leveled his words towards the crowd, now pushing hard against the legionaries at the openings in the colonnade.

"Rome finds the prisoner, Lucius Maximus, guilty!" he pronounced. "Henceforth, the prisoner will be retained in the Imperial Prison of Ephesus."

Imperial Prison? Lucius thought. *That is where they brought me.*

"...and," the Proconsul continued, "he will be executed one month from this day. All of his books will be destroyed. Furthermore, the place known as Healing House and with it, the Nazarene's Table will be shuttered *permanently.*"

Lucius' eyes grew wide, not because of the death sentence but because of the references to Healing House as if it were still there—and to a new place, the Nazarene's Table. Someone had realized his dream in his absence.

Tears filled his eyes, not only at this news but also because of what he saw in a gap between the first two columns. As heads bobbed back and forth in the crowd, there was another head between them.

An ivory white veil was covering wisps of blond hair turned to platinum around a pair of large dark eyes. It was *her*. Chloe was staring at him. She was alive.

Her lips formed the words, "I love you, Lucius Maximus."

A wind rippled through the columns and into the theater. It fluttered the robes of the Proconsul, the tunic of Marius and the helmet plumes of the legionaries. There was a silence which did not seem possible but occurred.

Then a voice blew up from the center of the crowd, "Healing House lives! The Nazarene's Table lives!"

"You will not destroy the Nazarene's kingdom!" another voice shouted.

"You will not destroy our well-being! It will not be sacrificed on the altar of Rome's greed!" a third person screamed.

A woman from the righthand side said, "We have the strongest healing center in the Agora! And the only place for feeding the hungry!"

Lucius thought that the last voice sounded like Chloe's, but he was not certain. One thing was certain: this crowd was not with the Governor.

"Enough!" the Proconsul shrieked again.

"You're right about that—enough!" someone shouted from the front of the crowd.

Suddenly Lucius' eyes narrowed. A plan formed in him. His voice went deep as if he were disguising it with a time from his past, from his former centurion days.

He bellowed across the Odeion in Latin, not Greek, so only soldiers' ears would comprehend, "Legionaries, about face! Stand around!"

Every soldier between the columns, apparently thinking that the Proconsul had been attacked, heeded Lucius' order. They pivoted towards the stage and widened their eyes upon the Governor and the prisoner. They also tilted their spears from lateral positions, turning them upright.

The crowd saw no barrier between them and the interior of the theater. They poured through every opening in the colonnade breaching the Odeion like a river overflowing its banks.

A large man with a workman's tunic and dark scraggily beard brushed by Chloe and grabbed for the confused legionary's spear in front of him. Before the soldier could pull his *gladius,* the workman had snatched the handle of his spear and jerked it up striking the legionary's jaw, knocking him unconscious to the floor.

Another slave in a frayed robe reached for the sword of a legionary as the soldier tried to drop his spear and take his *gladius.* The attacker knocked the helmet off the man and took the handle of his sword instead, smashing it against the Roman's forehead. The soldier reeled back and dropped.

Elsewhere along the inside of the colonnade and across the open space in front of the stage, the crowd shoved the remaining guards back and trampled them like a herd of stampeding horses. Some were rushing up the steps on both sides of the dais, moving so fast that the soldiers around the Proconsul seemed confused as to whether they should launch their spears at the mob or protect the crowd's target, the Governor. They chose the Governor nearly dragging him out the far door opposite Lucius.

Members of the throng who had sprinted up the righthand steps overwhelmed two legionaries and descended upon Marius. He had attempted to limp out the same door where the Governor had escaped. He never made it and disappeared beneath the mob's grasping hands.

Lucius reached for the ring of keys on the guard who had them. The legionary jerked back but a large man in a dark robe pulled the soldier's *gladius* and turned it on his throat.

Another smaller man in a well-made flaxen tunic slid the keys from the legionary's belt and said, "Allow me to assist you, Physician Lucius. It is an honor to give you your freedom."

He shoved the key into the lock at Lucius' wrists and snapped them open, doing the same with his ankles. Lucius' other guard tried to retreat to the left side of the stage and out the door where they had brought him in. Six men stomped along the hollow floor and overran him.

A young man with Roman-cropped hair and no beard stepped up to Lucius who was now rubbing his wrists from the cutting by the manacles. He reached a large scroll toward the Physician.

"I believe that you wrote this for all of us, but it is still yours," the rescuer said, handing it to Lucius. The man lowered his head in a brief bow and raising it, continued, "Better come with us now."

"Yes," Lucius said. "The Proconsul has only a few troops in Asia but they are mostly here in Ephesus."

He looked out through the columns. Chloe was gone; but surrounded by Followers, Lucius jumped from the dais and headed into the courtyard of the Imperial Agora and on to the Marble Street losing himself among the crowds of Ephesians.

EPILOGUE

(72 C.E.—REIGN OF VESPASIANUS)

The water droplets falling from the roof to the center pool of my atrium filled the silence as I stopped. My *puellae,* my lovely granddaughters, were all wide-eyed and still gasping at the riot in the Odeion. It had been a long afternoon for them, filled with the heroic adventures of Lucius Maximus.

At last, the oldest, Livia, rolled off her knees and sitting cross-legged, said, "Was Healing House really gone? It is here today, isn't it, *avi?*"

I placed my hand on Livia's blond hair. "Of course," I said. "Long before the Physician returned, Bartholomew and I moved Healing House from that dingy old warehouse at the port to where you see it today, along the Agora. After Bartholomew died of a fever, I took over full direction."

I paused and then added, "Seeing so many coming to Healing House as thin as door posts, the Followers and I also opened the Nazarene's Table to feed the hungry—at no cost."

"And one more piece of news," I said, "Proconsul Marcus never removed either of them; instead, Emperor Vespasianus removed him from Ephesus."

Anoys fidgeted and twisted the dress on a doll made of old rags in her lap. Her blue eyes pierced mine with something which she could not contain.

"That's not what I want to know, *avi*," she complained. "I wondered what happened to the Physician. Did you ever marry him?"

Tears rose in my brown eyes. A tightness constricted my stomach and I said, "No—no, I never married the Physician, not before he traveled with the Apostle and not after he returned two decades later. My letters never reached him, nor did his come to me, much as we tried to communicate."

"But why was this so?" Anoys pleaded. "He sounds so wonderful. And Axsen, his wife, abandoned him for her people."

"Yes," I said. "But after his rescue from the Odeion, I never saw him again. None of us did."

"What happened to him?" she still begged.

"Some say that Governor Marcus re-captured him and be-headed him as you remember wicked Nero had done with the Apostle in Rome," I said.

"Eeww," my girls wrinkled their faces all together.

"I, too, do not believe this," I said.

"Then, what?" Mara pressed.

My servant, Miriam, pattered into the far end of the atrium and broke off my answer. The other slaves in the triclinium were talking and clanking cups and plates for the evening meal.

"These lovelies must prepare for going home, Mistress," she said, scanning all three of them and smiling.

"Let me finish with them first," I protested.

"As you wish," Miriam said and turned towards the dining area.

I knew that dusk was approaching and their mothers would be ending an old grandmother's memories with a walk home and with questions which none of my actual granddaughters could answer.

"Others," I continued, "others said that the Physician was truly free after the crowd, mostly containing Followers, rescued him. They say that he journeyed to the far ends of the Empire, a province northeast of here called Bithynia at the very edge of Asia. They say that he built another 'Healing House,' preached about the full healing of the Nazarene, and then sent his scroll about the Nazarene all over the Empire so that this healing might come to everyone, not just a few."

I paused and drank in the blue eyes of Anoys. Tears filled my eyes again. I said, "But others say that he went way beyond the Empire of Rome, beyond the Euphrates to that other empire—the Parthian one."

Anoys said, "Oh." She saw my eyes watering and then said, "So what does that have to do with us, *avi?*"

"You mean what does Lucius Maximus have to do with *you*, my lovely?"

Her face remained quiet and showed her question already forming without even asking it.

I said, "One day, many years ago, two men came to my door here at the Terrace Houses. They were not workers. They were dark-skinned, muscular and handsome men with faces adorned in well-trimmed beards and bodies dressed in belted robes. They wore no pointed caps but I knew who they were—soldiers, warriors from that other land.

"The taller of the two said, "We are the elite guards of Princess Axsen of Parthia. She has ordered us to deliver a gift to the Physician Lucius Maximus. We have searched the city but we do not know where to find him. We have no one to receive Princess Axsen's gift.'

"The soldier paused and the other now spoke, 'We understand that you know the Physician well, Mistress. We are entrusting Princess Axsen's gift to you.'

"The two parted and a dear dark jewel of five years of age with raven hair and burning blue eyes stepped forward between them. She had the chiseled face of her father.

"The taller soldier said, 'Her name is Anoys. It means 'the Charming One' in our language. She is the child of Princess Axsen and the Physician Lucius Maximus. Though she is the heir to Princess Axsen's throne, her Majesty does not want her daughter raised in our empire, nor in Rome's, but in the Kingdom of the Nazarene—the one spoken of by the Physician.'"

Anoys eyes now grew wide. She was absorbing my every word.

"You mean, *avi*," she said, "her name was mine."

"Yes, little one," I admitted. "The Physician is your great grandfather and Axsen is your *avia*, in truth, your great grandmother."

"Oh, am I a princess then?" Anoys said.

I smiled and said, "We are all princesses and princes in the Nazarene's kingdom through the story which the Physician gave us."

Miriam had come in again and all questions from the girls ceased.

"Pardon me, Mistress. But you have a visitor at your door," she reported.

Then she added, "It is also time for these ladies to gather their belongings for their trips home."

"Aw," Anoys, Livia and Mara chimed in unison.

"Kindly see to the girls, Miriam," I said. "I will receive my guest."

I rose slowly from my chair, pattered across the entry room and ascended the steps towards my front door. Below, the water continued its dripping into the center pool and my servants began to ignite the evening torches one by one, including those lighting the stairs.

My steps became more cautious because of my aching legs. Seeing a robed figure at the door above in the dusky evening, I scrutinized its long robe, drawn in by a belt at the waist.

The form stepped to the edge of a torch's glow and drew back the hood of a cloak. Raven hair streaked with gray tumbled onto a set of square shoulders. But it was the pair of turquoise eyes which were unmistakable.

Before I could greet her, she said, "Is this the house of Mistress Chloe of Corinthia? I am Axsen of Parthia and I have seen the Physician."

Along the threshold of my doorway, a glistening cylinder caught the torch light. A black serpent slithered away behind her.

The Gospel of Luke is the only Gospel in the New Testament which names more rulers of the Roman Empire than any other. Scholars still debate whether this was meant to pacify or to protest the authorities around Luke and his church.

The early Christians established "hospitals" and feeding centers for the sick and the poor in the towns and cities of the Roman Empire where their churches grew up. Unlike the pagan temples, the Christians demanded no charge for their healing and feeding in the name of the one who healed all the sick and fed every person in every crowd—Jesus Christ.

Because of their "hospitals" and feeding centers, the numbers of Christians grew rapidly in the first, second and third centuries C.E. By 311 C.E. the Christian Church overwhelmed the Empire with the kingdom of Christ.

To this day there are Christian churches in Iraq and Iran, possibly dating back to the Book of Acts and the Parthian Empire.

No one knows precisely what became of the one whom the Apostle Paul called "the beloved Physician," the one we now call St. Luke. His ultimate fate is a total mystery, even in the New Testament.

ACKNOWLEDGMENTS

Let me thank my wife, Peg, and my son, Clark, for their patience and understanding when I had to write and edit the text of this novel rather than walk with them or watch Netflix. Also let me thank my own medical professionals who kept me healthy when I ironically experienced my own small crisis with a potentially deadly blood clot at the end of the writing process.

Let me also thank my readers including Victoria Storm, Ray Watters, James Aynes, Christine Kister, Ray Lyles, Katherine Peters, Deborah Johnson, Michael Storm, Jay Johnson, Patricia Aynes, and Leslie Avant.

Finally, let me thank my great editor, Nancy Felt, a third time as she also assisted with Lucius' story as she had with "God's Centurion" and "Prophet of Corinth" previously. Also my appreciation goes a third time to Mikey Brooks, a wonderful book platform expert.

ABOUT THE AUTHOR

Rich Hites is a retired pastor who has made trips to the Holy Land and some of the lands of Paul, including Rome. He loves the background stories of the Bible and its characters, particularly those who remain in the shadows and are given only a very brief cameo like even Lucius (Luke) in the Book of Acts. Because of nearly forty years of parish ministry, Rich also knows the lives and struggles of Christians which remain the same whether ancient or modern. His hobbies include writing, reading, photography and travel with his family. After 32 years of living in southern California with his wife, Peg, and special needs son, Clark, they now reside in Hickory, NC.

www.ingramcontent.com/pod-product-compliance
Lightning Source LLC
Chambersburg PA
CBHW070633180626
46817CB00006B/2111